C000000671

MARSALA MAROON

FRANKI AMATO MYSTERIES BOOK 6

TRACI ANDRIGHETTI

Limoncello
Press

FREE SHORT MYSTERY OFFER

Sign up for my newsletter at traciandrighetti.com to be the first to know about my new releases, deals, and giveaways. And I'll email you a link to download "Fragolino Fuchsia," a Franki-goes-to-Rome short mystery, for FREE!

MARSALA MAROON

by

TRACI ANDRIGHETTI

***

Copyright © 2020 by Traci Andrighetti

Cover design by Lyndsey Lewellyn

Limoncello Press www.limoncellopress.com

All rights reserved. Without limiting the rights under copyright reserved above, no part of this publication may be reproduced, stored in or introduced into a retrieval system, or transmitted, in any form, or by any means (electronic, mechanical, photocopying, recording, or otherwise) without the prior written permission of both the copyright owner and the above publisher of this book.

This is a work of fiction. Names, characters, places, brands, media, and incidents are either the product of the author's imagination or are used fictitiously. The author acknowledges the trademarked status and trademark owners of various products referenced in this work of fiction, which have been used without permission. The publication/use of these trademarks is not authorized, associated with, or sponsored by the trademark owners.

❀ Created with Vellum

To the late Ronald W. Lewis, a peaceful warrior for New Orleans culture

BOOK BACKSTORY

I'm always ecstatic to finish a book, and that's especially true for *Marsala Maroon*. So far I've written nine books and six short stories, and I honestly can't recall much about when I wrote any of them. But I will forever remember that I wrote *Marsala Maroon* in 2020, an incredibly difficult year for all of us. Fortunately, writing provides me with something of an escape from reality, and I hope that reading Franki's latest New Orleans adventure does the same for you.

As with a lot of my Franki Amato mysteries, the plot for *Marsala Maroon* has been in my head for years. The idea for the book started in February of 2017, when I went to New Orleans to be on my first Mardi Gras krewe and to visit St. Roch Cemetery No. 1, the site of Franki's showdown with the killer in *Campari Crimson*. Because Mardi Gras Indians are an important part of the festivities, I decided to learn more about them at the House of Dance and Feathers, a cultural museum which was directed and curated by the late Ronald W. Lewis.

My time with Mr. Lewis, who passed from COVID-19 during the writing of *Marsala Maroon*, was short but memorable. He welcomed me—and looked out for me—like one of his own, and I haven't forgotten it. Although Mr. Lewis was a founder and member of many tribes and social aid and pleasure clubs, I included the Northside Skull and Bone Gang in *Marsala Maroon* in his honor, which is my favorite scene in the book. I also made a donation to the COVID-19 Relief Fund for the 9th Ward Black Hatchet tribe to help preserve the tradition of masking during Mardi Gras.

I would like to thank two readers for their help with *Marsala Maroon*, starting with Antonette Pierce for sharing her hilarious highway story about having to cut into a funeral procession to make her exit, only to have the cars behind her follow her until she finally had to pull over and tell them that she wasn't with the funeral. I told Antonette that I planned to use her story in a book, and now I have. I hope she, and you, like what I did with it. I know Franki didn't, LOL.

Many "grazie" also go to Sal Primeggia, who was kind enough to send me research articles, some of which he co-authored, on Southern Italian comedy and the legendary jazz musician Louis Prima. On a personal note, I'm also grateful to Sal for telling me that I what I do is important. I couldn't even begin to count the number of times I've asked myself why I write books, and 2020 has only exacerbated the self-doubt—for me and for many authors. But the support and stories of readers like Sal and Antonette help get us through it. So, thanks again to them and to all of you for reading.

Speaking of reading, Franki's next adventure takes place during Veronica's wedding in Venice in *Valpolicella Violet*. So stay tuned for a wild gondola ride—and some old Venetian ghosts!

Cin cin (Cheers)!
    Traci

1

"**I**s it me, or is the lemon tradition haunting us?"

My fiancé's question came through my cell phone like a splash of cold water, and I gripped the granite rim of the Jackson Square fountain where I was sitting. The St. Joseph's Day lemon tradition had played a key role in our engagement. *Was he souring on the decision to ask me to marry him?*

I rose and paced the French Quarter park's gravel walkway. "'Haunting' is an interesting choice of words, Bradley. Mind expanding on that?"

"I said it was haunting *us*, Franki, not *me*. And you have to admit that after the pressure to get engaged within the tradition's one-year time limit, things haven't calmed down. Your mom and nonna are pushing us to fast-track the wedding, and weird things have been happening, like my new car breaking down the last three times we've had plans. It's like it's, well, a lemon."

While I understood the pressure part, the car thing was ludicrous. Then again, so was the Sicilian-American custom of stealing a lemon from a church altar for the poor to land oneself a husband. "Surely you don't believe that my taking a piece of citrus fruit is the cause of your car problems?"

"Of course not." He sighed. "I'm sorry. I just want us to be able to enjoy our engagement, which is why I proposed on Mardi Gras. But that party ended as abruptly as the parades."

I sank back onto the fountain. Bradley was frustrated, and I could relate. My mom and nonna had been laying on the wedding pressure as thick as ricotta cheese. I had to do something to bolster his spirits. I glanced behind me at the equestrian statue of General Andrew Jackson in the Battle of New Orleans to summon my combat instincts. "Mom and Nonna are excited, that's all. Give them another couple of weeks, they'll settle down."

"Will they?"

The honest answer was, 'Not a chance in Dante's inferno.' Those women would squeeze us like a garlic press until we produced a bambino, but I couldn't say that to Bradley. He might've gotten cold feet for real and hotfooted it from my life.

I stared at the St. Louis Cathedral overlooking the park and got a divine inspiration. "We have to have faith, that's all."

"I'll try-y."

His two-syllable "try" wasn't convincing, and I couldn't blame him for being skeptical. Because I knew that it would take more than God and a general-turned-president to slow my mom and nonna's march to our wedding altar. "Why don't you go deal with your car, and I'll meet them for lunch? It'll give me a chance to tell them to back off."

"All right, but we've got another problem coming—on Thursday, to be exact—because my mother and grandmother are flying in to talk to me about the wedding."

That statement was foreboding. After two years of dating, I still hadn't met the Hartmann family, so I would have expected him to say that they were arriving from Boston to meet me, their future daughter-in-law. "Is this about the rehearsal dinner?"

"The entire wedding, I'm afraid."

The St. Louis Cathedral bell tolled, and I didn't appreciate its timing. The bell announced the Sunday noon mass, but it could have been a sign that his family was against our marriage.

I licked my lips. "I hope you told them that my parents are super traditional and insist on paying."

"I did, but my mother and grandmother are...particular."

"You mean, about the wedding theme?"

"Among other things."

Do those 'other things' extend to his choice of bride? I gripped the phone a tad tighter. "Well, if they'd like a say in the decorations, I'd be happy to oblige."

"You'd do that?"

The relief in his tone brought a smile to my face because it indicated that the so-called problem coming on Thursday had been solved. "I'd do anything for you and your family. After all, I'm going to be a Hartmann soon."

"I'm so lucky that you agreed to marry me."

The cold-water splash of before turned cozy-warm snuggle. "True. And after I tell my mom and nonna to stand down, I'll send them home to Houston so I can show you just how lucky you are."

"I'd like that." His tone had gone sexy. "Very much."

The creak of the park's iron gate broke the seductive spell. A male in dark jeans, a gray hoodie, and sunglasses entered and headed straight for me. Despite the unusual attire, I recognized the long, lanky figure of my college-student coworker from Private Chicks, Inc.

"Bradley, I've got to run. David Savoie's here to talk to me about a case."

"That's fine." The sexy had turned serious. "Good luck with your mom and nonna."

I stopped myself from saying that I'd need something a lot stronger than luck, like voodoo, and limited my reply to "Love you."

As I closed the call, a flash from the fountain's concrete basin caught my eye. Sunlight had reflected off one of the pennies scattered along the bottom.

Why not? I could use the insurance.

I stood, fished a penny from my hobo bag, and made a wish— more of a plea, really—that my family would give Bradley and me some space during our engagement. I tossed the coin into the fountain and watched it drift down...

And slip through a hole in the drain grate!

I blinked, incredulous.

Then the water stopped flowing.

A tidal wave of shock rolled over me as I realized what had happened.

My penny had clogged the Jackson Square fountain.

What does that mean for my wish? And of all the pennies in the basin, why did mine *get sucked up?*

Anger swelled in me like the pent-up water in the fountain pump. I tied my long brown hair into a knot, knelt on the rim, and plunged both hands into the water.

"Yo, uh, what's goin' on?"

I recognized David's college-speak but didn't look behind me. I was too busy running my hand over the grate, feeling for a knob. "I'll tell you what's going on—this freaking fountain is trying to ruin my wedding."

Silence.

Balancing on both hands, I glanced over my shoulder to ask for his help, but he was opening and closing his mouth like a fish out of water. "What is it, David? Spit it out." I glowered at the fountain. "That goes for you too."

"Um, yeah. So...I don't think you're supposed to take money from a fountain."

I worked my finger into the grate hole and pulled. "After taking a lemon from the poor in a church, this doesn't seem so bad, especially since it was my money to begin with."

"Riiight. Although, I think it's illegal?"

I turned my head and gave him a hard stare. "I'm a private investigator, David, and before that I was a rookie cop, so I'm well aware of the law. But after everything Bradley and I have been through, I'm not going to let a fickle fountain cheat us." I returned my attention to the grate and yanked. "It's going to give me my damn penny *and* my wish for a peaceful engagement."

"Gotcha. But, could you maybe wait and get arrested after our meeting?"

His request hit me with the same cold-water splash as Bradley's lemon tradition question. I'd been arrested once before—on my thirtieth birthday, no less—thanks to a run-in with a woman who'd claimed to be a three-hundred-year-old witch, and I had no desire to return to a Big Easy jail.

I cast a side-eye at the fountain, and then I stood and wiped my hands on my jeans. "While we're on the subject of criminals, why are you dressed like a gang member?"

"I didn't want anyone from the office to see me. I've been thinking about your case offer, but, like, I don't feel right about taking it."

I put my hands on my hips to keep from shaking a finger at him—or shaking him. "You owe me after you investigated why I was still an old maid, or *zitella*, for my nonna. Do you know how humiliating it was to have you running around town looking into why I was an old maid?"

He lowered his head, and the hood obscured his sunglasses.

"Besides, you're a professional PI, so your feelings are irrelevant." I pulled a check from my purse and stuck it under his nose. "But this should make you feel better."

His head popped up, and so did his eyebrows. "This is, like, a month's salary."

"For a job that'll take half that at most."

"I don't get it. Veronica's an awesome boss and your best friend. Why would you want me to investigate who she's interviewing for the PI position?"

"David, you sweet innocent boy." I rested a hand on his shoulder. "Have you forgotten the consultants she hired to help me with my homicide cases? An ex-stripper, a drag queen, and my eighty-year-old grandmother?"

He took the check and crammed it into his pants pocket.

I patted his cheek. "Glad you see things my way, despite those black shades."

My phone rang. *Amato's Deli* appeared on the display. "It's my father. Not a word about your new case to Veronica, you hear?"

"Chill, okay? I don't want to get fired." David tugged his hood low and slunk away.

I tapped Answer. "Hey, Dad. What's up?"

"Your mother isn't answering her cell phone," he boomed in his gruff, I-need-an-antacid voice. "I don't know why she has the blasted thing if she's not going to turn it on. Is she with you?"

It was one of the few times I'd been able to shake her since my engagement two months earlier. "Actually, she and Nonna are at Our Lady of Guadalupe Church for mass, but I'm meeting them at Central Grocery for lunch in an hour."

"I'd imagine they're closed."

"On a Sunday afternoon? That's prime muffuletta-sandwich-selling time."

"There's been a tragedy in the New Orleans grocer community. That's why I'm calling."

I frowned and pressed the phone closer to my ear.

"A customer just came in and told me that our biggest competitor, back when I was still at Central Grocery, has been killed. His funeral is today, and there's no way I can make it from Houston in time, so I'd like for your mother and nonna to pay my respects."

My Sicilian grandma attended funerals like an it-girl attended parties, so that wouldn't have been a problem. Plus, she'd been wearing a mourning dress since my *nonnu* had died twenty-two years before, which meant that she was already dressed for the occasion. "I'll let them know. Did I ever meet this man?"

"No, his name was Angelo LaRocca, of LaRocca's Market on North Rampart Street. He inherited the business from his father back in '85 when he was in his mid-twenties, and like Central Grocery, it's one of the last Italian grocery stores from the old days."

"What did he die of?"

"He was murdered, and I was hoping you could look into it for me."

The St. Louis Cathedral bell tolled, giving me a jolt. I didn't remember it ringing on the quarter-hour.

"I'm not asking you to do any investigating, just keep your ears open. The police aren't releasing any details, but there's a rumor going around that the crime scene was bad—gruesome, in fact."

The bell tolled again, and I glared at the cathedral. I didn't know what was going on, but if the bell pulled that stunt again, I would personally climb the central tower and clock the thing.

"What do you say, Franki? Can you do it?"

"Sure, Dad. I'll get right on it."

"Thanks, honey. I'll let you go. I've got customers at the counter.

He hung up, and I checked the time. My mom and nonna wouldn't get out of church for forty-five minutes, so I had time to kill.

Kill.

I felt sad for Angelo LaRocca and for the community, but also concerned. Because my gut told me that I'd need to do more for my dad and the late grocer than keep my ears open.

A peal of laughter shook me from my apprehension. I glanced across the park at a group of women enjoying the spring day while window-shopping at one of the two block-long Pontalba Buildings that formed either side of Jackson Square.

And I saw my mom and nonna enter the Creole Delicacies Gourmet Shop.

An alarm bell tolled, and it wasn't the one at the top of the St. Louis Cathedral. The odds of my nonna swapping prayer for pralines were about the same as those of the Catholic Church replacing communion wafers with cookies. If she was missing mass, then something big was going down—like meddling.

I rose to go investigate, pausing to scowl at the fiendish fountain. Between my mom and nonna's antics and my dad's somber request, it was obvious that I needed a break in the luck department. Without it, my hopes of a stress-free engagement were in danger of going down the drain like my penny.

THE VANILLA-AND-TOASTED-PECAN odor inside the Creole Delicacies Gourmet Shop filled my nostrils and seduced my sweet tooth. I put my mom-and-nonna investigation on hold and helped myself to some praline samples. A sugar high could only help when confronting Machiavellian meddlers.

As I munched, I spotted my nonna talking to a saleswoman at the rear of the shop, and my mother was at a sale table in the center. Her back was to me, but it wasn't hard to recognize her. Even though she lived in Houston, her dyed-brown salon do had grown to Dallas proportions.

I snuck up behind her. "Uh, Mom?"

She started and went as stiff as her lacquered hair. Then she turned and lowered her readers. "What are you doing here, Francesca?" she asked in her shrill voice. "Aren't you supposed to be at a work meeting?"

Deflection was one of her standard tactics. "It ended early. Why aren't you and Nonna in church?"

"We felt terrible about missing mass, dear, but we had an urgent errand to run."

My brow rose, along with my suspicions. "In a candy and kitchen shop?"

"Well, yes." Her eyes widened to justification-of-a-lie size. "Your nonna and I have some cooking to do for a church function, and you desperately need a new..." She grabbed a gadget from the table. "... garlic press."

I recoiled. I knew she couldn't really squeeze Bradley and me with the thing, but her timing was disturbing nonetheless.

She reached for another item. "While we're here, dear, what do you think of this spaghetti fork?"

I wrested the pronged utensil from her hand and returned it to the shelf. It was well known within the family that my nonna thought spaghetti forks were instruments of the devil. "If Nonna sees you with that," I whisper-hissed, "she'll have Father John call in an exorcist."

"This isn't about Carmela, dear, it's about you and what you like."

My eyelids lowered. There was only one reason I'd need new kitchen accessories. "Are you two picking items for my wedding registry?"

"Now, Francesca, you know we'd never pick your kitchenware. That's a personal decision."

Not only would they *pick* my kitchenware, they'd organize it in my drawers and cabinets and use it to serve Bradley and me a "suitable meal."

"Oh." My mother pressed her hands to her cheeks. "Look how adorable this is." She raised a plump lavender sachet topped with the head of a veiled bride.

"It looks like a severed head on a silk cushion."

"Well, *I* think they'd make darling *bomboniere*."

The Italian term for *wedding favors* exploded in my head like the word's first four letters, and I began to sweat like a pressed garlic clove. As Italian-American traditions went, the bomboniere made the St. Joseph's Day lemons look like harmless citrus fruit. The bride had to choose the bomboniere, and all aspects of the newlyweds' life hinged on that choice—their health, wealth, happiness, fertility, and longevity. That was an awful lot to put on a gal, not to mention on a tchotchke with some Jordan almonds.

"Mom, I know you and Nonna are excited about the wedding, but it's way too early to talk bomboniere—or wedding. I told you that Bradley and I are waiting to set a date until we know when Veronica and Dirk are getting married."

She bit the earpiece of her readers—and bared her teeth. "I don't see why you have to wait just because she got engaged first."

My mother *did* see—but she chose not to. "I want both of our weddings to be special, so I won't even consider getting married for at least six months after she does."

"Then you might want to go with *this* for your bomboniere." She picked up an hourglass kitchen timer and flipped it over. "It's for two minutes, which is about all your biological time clock has left."

I bared *my* teeth—and growled. "I'm thirty-one, not forty-one, so stick a spaghetti fork in it."

She sniffed and resumed browsing. "That's a bad analogy for someone who's reproductive days are almost done."

I squeezed my fists and took a breath. The woman was lucky I'd put the fork back on the shelf.

She gasped and held up a yellow tulle bag. "Little lemon-shaped soaps. They're perfect for your theme."

Yes, the theme of a woman whose relatives kept shoving lemons at her, making her more and more bitter. "Mom, drop the merchandise *and* the meddling. Bradley and I are going to enjoy our engagement for the time being. In the meantime, Dad called and he needs us to go to a funeral this afternoon for a grocer named Angelo LaRocca."

She waved me off with the lemon. "That can wait, Francesca."

"Uh, how do you figure?"

"Because this is about the rest of your life, and that man's already dead."

With logic like that, the only thing to do was go outside. "I'll wait for you and Nonna out front. You don't need me to plan my wedding, anyway."

She huffed like I was the one behaving badly.

I stormed from the store—after grabbing a couple more praline samples—and ran smack into a chubby man wearing a strap-on snare drum.

He leapt backward. "Careful, baby. This instrument is my livelihood."

"I'm sorry." I read the band name written on the drum, *The Tremé Tribe*. "Hey, is Wendell Baptiste still playing with you?"

He ran a hand over his clean-shaven head. "Dat's what me and the rest o' the band wanna know. You seen him today?"

"Oh, we don't hang out. We worked on a steamboat together a couple of months ago." I neglected to add that Wendell had helped me with a homicide case.

"Well, if you do see him, tell him to give his bandmates a shout. We got a gig playing a jazz funeral, and we cain't find him nowhere."

That didn't sound like Wendell. "Is it like him to miss a gig?"

"No, ma'am, especially not one dis high profile. It's for a guy who was murdered, so the whole town'll be watching."

I had a feeling I knew who he was talking about. "You mean, Angelo LaRocca?"

"Dat's him. We linin' up now." He pointed a drumstick toward Decatur Street where a hundred or so people had formed a line behind a horse hitched to a glass carriage, and he shook his head. "It's closed casket 'cause dey said his skull was all jacked up."

I grimaced at the mental image. "'Jacked up' how?"

"Someone, probably an ex-wife or girlfriend, attacked him with somethin' while he was sleeping." He sucked his teeth. "Anyways, I gotta git. You have a blessed day." He set off toward the procession, pounding his drum.

On that note, I turned to go get my mom and nonna and noticed an old woman in a frumpy dress and apron watching me from the doorway of the New Orleans Cajun Store.

She opened her mouth, revealing missing teeth. "A *cauchemar*."

I thought she'd coughed up some phlegm, but based on the way her black eyes drilled into mine, she expected a response. "I'm sorry. Were you talking to me?"

"A cauchemar killed dat man."

It wasn't phlegm she'd coughed up, but rather a French word. "What's that?"

"A nightmare witch, who attack people in der beds at night." Her eyes went horror-story. "She saddle dem up and ride 'em like a horse. And if they don' wake up, dey die."

That sounded like a local folk legend. "I don't believe in that sort of thing."

Her eye twitched, and she rubbed a wart on her chin. "You sleep tight now."

I stared, dumbfounded, as she returned inside the store, because her tone held a threat.

A trumpet sounded. The jazz funeral was underway on Decatur Street. The horse, owing to the weight of the carriage and casket, took halting steps before settling into a reluctant trot.

The image reinforced exactly how I felt—like I too had been hitched to dead weight that I wasn't prepared to carry.

2

My head rested against the backseat window of my mother's Ford Taurus station wagon as it headed down I-10 toward my house. As usual, my mom and nonna were bickering in the front seat, but I wasn't paying attention. My mind was preoccupied with the grotesque image of a cauchemar in action. She sat in a saddle atop a sleeping figure, gripping the reins as she rode her hapless victim to the grave. Even more terrifying, instead of a gnarly old woman, the nightmare witch was my mother.

"Francesca Lucia Amato," my mom shrill-shouted, "are you listening to me?"

I jerked my head in her direction, and for a moment I mistook her big lacquered hair for a witch hat. "Uh, no, I was thinking about some witch—I mean, some*one*."

"I *said*, isn't it nice that so many people came out for Angelo LaRocca's second line?"

"Well, yeah, but it's weird it didn't end with a burial."

Nonna removed the emergency veil she kept in her purse for unexpected funeral opportunities. "Franki's-a right. What's-a the point of a second-a line if they don't-a put-a the body in-a the ground?"

My mom slipped on a pair of oversized sunglasses that made her look like The Fly, which was ironic since she drove at snail speed. "According to the saleswoman at Creole Delicacies, Angelo didn't want a funeral, so the American Italian Cultural Center organized the second line. Sad, isn't it? Buried alone at Metairie Cemetery." Her fly eyes sought mine in the rearview mirror. "All because Angelo was childless."

My non-fly eyes narrowed at that "childless" message.

Nonna gave a resigned sigh. "Angelo was-a strange."

I leaned forward. "Did you know him, Nonna?"

"Not-a well-a. He was a loner, which is-a not-a natural for an *italiano*."

No, they functioned in packs to better gang up on their kids.

She raised a finger. "When I lived-a here with your nonnu, God rest-a his soul, Angelo's father ran-a the market, and-a he was-a real-a people person. And-a funny. *Hoo!*" She slapped her knee. "He had a *marionetta* named-a Ichabod that would-a kick and-a curse at-a the customers."

Its name was unsettling, but I was as impassive as a puppet. Marionettes, mimes, and reruns of *The Three Stooges* had taught me that there was no accounting for old-fashioned entertainment. "Did you and nonnu ever shop at LaRocca's Market?"

"Some-a-times. In-a those days, it was-a too far away. Everything-a after the French-a Quarter, from-a North Rampart Street on, was-a called the Back of-a Town-a. I shopped at-a Central Grocery, which is-a how your *patri* got a job-a there."

My mother removed her fly eyes. "It's tragic, isn't it? A family store that Angelo's grandfather opened in 1919, and there's no one to inherit it." She laid a maudlin look on me. "All because Angelo was childless."

Her message was as transparent as her tactics. "Can you let me get married before you start the kid pressure?"

"Well, it's all part of the same process, Francesca, but I'm glad you brought up the wedding." She flashed a stressed smile. "Your nonna and I disagree about the location, so we'd like your opinion."

"Nice of you to include me in the planning."

"Of course, dear," she said, oblivious to my sarcasm. "Now, *I* think you should get married in Houston, but your nonna wants you to get married here in New Orleans."

I knew what my nonna wanted, and I wanted none of it. "I'm not getting married at Our Lady of Guadalupe, Nonna."

"Why-a not-a? In-a the old-a days, it was-a the Italian church."

"And in the old, old days, it was the Mortuary Chapel for yellow fever victims, which doesn't exactly say 'happily ever after.'"

"But if you get-a married here, you could have-a the reception down-a-town at-a the Piazza d'Italia. They got-a those fancy red and-a green lights out-a-side for special occasions."

I smirked. "That would be great if the Italian flag were my colors."

My mother's eyebrows formed an I-told-you-so arch. "See, Carmela?" She looked at me in the mirror. "I think you should get married at St. Mary's, and then we could have the reception at the deli."

A deli reception sounded as Italian-Americana as my nonna's piazza version. "Oh, sure. And we could give away little salami as bomboniere."

"That's-a not a bad idea," Nonna said, also missing my sarcasm. "My poor sonny would save-a some money on-a the food."

My mother turned to my nonna, her features twisted with years of not-pent-up rage. "We're not going to serve the bomboniere in place of a meal. And your *poor sonny* doesn't earn that money alone, you know. I work at the deli too."

Nonna put on her fake surprised face, which wasn't all that fake. "You do?"

My mom muttered something, and then her taut facial muscles transformed into what I called her "cheerfaux" look. "It's settled. The wedding will be in Houston."

I leaned forward. "Uh, nothing's settled. I told you that Bradley and I aren't planning anything until we have a date."

"You don't need a date to pick the city, Francesca."

"No, but I need to consult my fiancé. And his family."

The Taurus swerved. "His *family*?"

Nonna frowned into the back seat. "They don't-a have nothing to do with-a this."

I breathed deeply before stating the obvious. "Actually, they do since I'm marrying their son. So his mother and grandmother would like a say in the decorations."

The Taurus lurched to a stop like a bull backing out of a bullfight, and my head did a one-eighty to make sure we weren't about to be gored by an oncoming car. "Mom, you can't stop on the freaking highway."

She pressed the gas pedal, and we peeled out. "I can, but you know what can't happen? Those women having a say in our wedding."

"It's *my* wedding, Mom."

Her eyes hit the rearview mirror like bullets. "Your father and I are paying for it, so it's *our* wedding." She returned her gaze to the road. "And we don't even know these people."

Nonna nodded. "Your mamma is-a right. What if they have-a bad-a taste?"

Their taste couldn't be any worse than Italian flag–colored lights and salami bomboniere. "So, the idea is that we'll get to know them since we're all going to be one big, happy family."

My mother sniffed. "Yes, but we're not a family yet. Once we are, maybe they can have a say in how we do things, but we don't have time to get to know them before the wedding."

I hadn't planned on telling her about Bradley's family's travel plans, but she'd left me no choice. "I'll have time, because his mother and grandmother are coming on Thursday."

"*Thursday?*" She shot a frantic look at my nonna. "Carmela, we're going to have to stay to see what kind of demands they're making."

"Damn-a right-a!" Nonna pressed her palms together in outrage. "*Ma che faccia tosta!*"

"I agree with your nonna," my mother huffed. "Those Hartmanns have a lot of nerve."

I wanted to beat my head against the window. *Why? Why had I given these women any information?* "I never said they were making *demands*, Mom. And you guys can't stay until Thursday because Dad said he needs you at the deli."

"What would you have us do, Francesca? Drive home to Houston and come back again?"

If I had my preference, they would drive home to Houston and stay there until the wedding, because if any family had a lot of nerve, it was the Amatos. But that wasn't an option. "Actually, yes."

"Well, we're going to have to stay." She smoothed her lacquered hair. "The five-hour drive is hard on your nonna and me."

Not nearly as hard as another five days with them would be on me. I glanced at a road sign to see where we were—besides hell. "We need to get over, Mom. The exit is coming up."

"I'm trying, but there's a funeral procession in the next lane."

My head jerked toward the window. Another funeral seemed as unlucky as that fountain swallowing my penny.

Nonna smiled. "It's-a good-a day for a funeral."

Yeah. Mine. "Slow down and wait for it to pass."

"In this traffic?" my mother semi-shrieked. "We'll get killed."

I sighed. Apart from the funeral procession, there were all of three cars on the road. "Then I guess we'll miss our exit."

"Oh, no. Your nonna and I have two lasagnas to make. I'm cutting in." She hunkered over the steering wheel, turned on the blinker, and swerved the Taurus into the procession, nearly taking out the front end of a green VW Bug with eyelashes on the headlights and red lips on the bumper.

The woman in the VW laid on the horn and flipped her the bird.

My mother replied with the equivalent Italian gesture and exited the highway shaking her head. "A member of a funeral party behaving like that. I'm sure the deceased would be rolling in their grave—if they were in it."

I rolled my eyes and looked out of the rear window. The VW was following us, sans one of its eyelashes.

And so was the rest of the funeral procession.

"Mom, the cars you cut in front of got off the highway with us."

"*Oddio!*" Nonna crossed herself. "It's-a bad-a luck to lead a funeral procession off-a course."

I hadn't heard that before, but when my nonna emigrated from Sicily, she'd imported a mental catalog of bad luck scenarios so vast that it outnumbered Bible verses.

My mother checked the side-view mirror, and her face set as hard as her hair. "Brace yourselves. I'm going to have to shake them."

She took a hard right and then an even harder right. Each time she turned, my head hit the window, which seemed appropriate.

When the Taurus steadied, I looked back and saw the woman in the VW bug, scowling and hunched forward, determined to stay on our tail. The rest of the procession was also in hot pursuit.

Nonna looked over her shoulder. "They're still-a with us, Brenda."

My mother gripped the wheel with the cool confidence of Danica Patrick in an IndyCar race. "I'm on it."

The Taurus lurched forward, and my mom pulled a U-turn. She watched the procession mimic her move and hung another U-y, tires squealing. The car fishtailed, and she jerked the wheel. Then we careened down a side street.

Breathless from my mom's racecar driving and the guilt of ditching funeralgoers, I looked behind us and didn't see any cars. "I think you lost 'em."

She slid her fly glasses onto her face and gave a sly smile.

I took one last glance out of the rear window and went as still as a dead insect. The funeral procession was back, but that wasn't the issue. The VW bug was gone, and in its place was a neon orange Nissan Cube.

It was a car I hadn't seen since my thirtieth birthday, and one I'd hoped to never cross paths with again.

≈

"WHAT ARE ALL these cars doing on your street?" My mother pulled the Taurus into the driveway of the fourplex where I rented a furnished apartment and shut off the engine. "It's practically a parking lot."

I was as confused as she was. The cars couldn't have come from the funeral procession, and they weren't the FIATs of my nonna's *nonne* friends. I glanced out of the rear window at the tavern facing my house. "Thibodeaux's looks empty, so someone's probably having a party."

My mom and nonna scoot-slid from the car.

I stayed put in the backseat and did a quick check for the neon orange Nissan Cube. I didn't see it, so I thought I'd been wrong about its owner. But part of me doubted I'd gotten that lucky since the Jackson Square fountain had sucked up my penny.

My mother opened my car door. "It's because of the cemetery. There's a funeral service going on."

Anxiety attacked my stomach like a virus. I'd lived across the street from the creepy crypt yard for more than two years, and I'd never seen a soul in it. Plus, an awful lot of dying was happening, and I feared it was spreading.

Nonna smiled and pulled on her emergency veil. "Like I said-a, it's a good-a day for a funeral. I'll drop-a by before we start-a those *lasagne*."

As my nonna shuffled toward mourners gathered at a mausoleum next to Thibodeaux's Tavern, I climbed from the Taurus and cast a worried glance at my mother. "What's going on today? This is the third death we've come into contact with in less than two hours."

A car door slammed. "Someone else is gonna die if one o' yous don't cawgh up the dough for my Bug's eyelashes."

Bewildered by the threat and the not-quite-New-York accent, not to mention a cheap-Spumanti-and-garlic odor, I turned to the female source.

A forty-fiveish faux redhead with a bad perm stood beside the green VW Bug, tarted up like her car and Bad Sandy from *Grease*. And as with Olivia Newton-John when she'd filmed the movie, the woman was no high schooler. Her face was starting to sag, and she didn't have the cheekbones to keep it propped up. Her nose, however, could've supported at least five pairs of sunglasses.

All five-feet-four of my mother rose up. "Did you just threaten my daughter?"

"If she was the driver, then yeh."

My mom gasped and clutched my arm. "She's got more nerve than those Hartmann women."

I sighed. It was becoming increasingly apparent that the meeting between my and Bradley's families wasn't going to go well.

The redhead smacked a piece of gum that had been hidden in her red-glossed mouth. "I hate to tell yous this, lady, but your dawghter's gawt the nerve. She knawcked off my CarLashes and tried to get away wit it."

My mom put a hand on her hip. "*I* was the driver, so don't blame my daughter. She's engaged to be married, and she doesn't need this stress."

Actually, the stress I didn't need was my mother planning my wedding, making enemies of my fiancé's family, and fighting with a woman who put eyelashes and lips on a car. "I'm fine, Mom, so stay calm and settle this in a civilized manner."

"Well, what do you think I'm doing, Francesca?"

The redhead threw up her arm. "See what I mean about her nerve?"

My mother's jaw cocked at me in firing mode. "I'm starting to, yes."

I took a step back. Those women were dangerous, and a blue Prius had pulled up—followed by the rest of the funeral procession.

A distinguished male behind the wheel rolled down the passenger window and leaned across the seat. "Is this the Mullins funeral?"

The redhead jerked her thumb at my mother. "No, this one led us to the wrawng damn cemetery."

My mom turned to the driver. "It's her fault. When I got off the highway, she followed me."

"Because you sheared off my Bug's CarLashes and made a run for it."

"I was merely exiting the highway like a *normal* person, but you wouldn't know about that because you made up your VW like a whore."

The redhead's cheeks flamed like her hair. "I make things beauteeful. I'm an artist."

My mom gave a snort. "You might want to take some refresher classes, because your car is hideous."

A young woman in the street screamed and pointed. "That man is attacking my husband!"

I followed her finger and saw two men from the funeral procession in a fistfight.

Nonna shuffled to the cemetery gate. "Keep it-a down-a. We're-a trying to bury some-a-one over here."

The Prius driver ran from his vehicle to break up the brawl and got laid out by a left hook. Three men exited their cars to come to his defense, and a street fight erupted.

Instinctively, I checked on my mother.

She and the redhead were civilly settling their differences by pulling fistfuls of one another's hair.

"Let go," I shouted, "both of you."

They didn't listen.

I moved in to pull them apart and got gassed by the redhead's perfume. Holding my breath, I tried to wedge myself between them.

The redhead stomped on my foot, and my mom hip-thrust me onto my rear end.

"Ow! Jeez." I rubbed my wrist, which had jammed during the fall. "I was trying to help you guys."

"Then stay out of my way," my mother growled through gritted teeth.

The redhead glared at me from a semi-stooped position. "You can help by getting my fifty dollars from your whack-job mother."

My mom gave her frizzed red curls a yank. "You can deduct it from the sixty you owe me for my hairdo."

I was willing to bet both amounts combined that the scuffle would only improve my mom's look.

Gingerly, I began to pull myself to my feet.

A foghorn sounded, and I fell back onto my backside.

The fighting subsided as everyone looked toward the sound of the blast.

My sixty-something ex-stripper landlady, Glenda O'Brien, stood on the second-floor balcony outside her apartment in an itsy bitsy furkini, cat ears, and a tail. She had the foghorn in one hand and a fur cigarette holder in the other. She surveyed the scene, and her fur-lashed eyes pounced on me. "Can I see you upstairs, Miss Franki?"

I didn't know what she wanted, but I was happy to leave my mother and the redhead. If I stayed any longer, those two were likely to yank out *my* hair.

As members of the funeral procession returned to their cars, I rose and limp-climbed the stairs.

Glenda ushered me into her all-white living room, which was furnished only with a giant champagne glass prop from her performing days. "Sorry if I startled you, sugar, but I needed to clear the street." She closed the door and flipped her platinum Cher hair. "I've got an influential stylist who doubles as a photographer coming over to set up a garden party and a stripper pole for my book cover shoot."

The title of her memoirs was *Like a Polecat at a Garden Party*, so the furkini getup finally made sense—in the roundabout way of all matters involving Glenda. "What did you want to talk to me about?"

"The Visitor Policy." She led me to the adjoining kitchen, where we took our seats at a glass dining table by a window. "As you well know, my single female renters are prohibited from having more than two gentleman callers stay the night at one time."

"Right, because you don't want people thinking you rent to whores. But I've never violated that policy, nor have I ever had two men stay the night."

Disapproval deepened the hard-living lines that creased her face.

"Which is a terrible shame, sugar, and something you might want to rectify before you get married."

I had a feeling I knew why her twelve engagements had failed.

Glenda crossed her skinny, wrinkled legs and bounced a platform shoe that had a stripper-pole heel with a cat straddling it. "Now, I've noticed an uptick in traffic since you got engaged, and if things don't quiet down, I'll be forced to amend my policy to limit your non-sexy visitors too."

"If you're talking about the cars outside, some of them were already here for a funeral, and the others are part of another funeral procession that followed us off the highway."

She blew out a puff of smoke. "I was talking about the Lilliputians, sugar. Although, chaos does seem to follow you."

"To be fair, this time it followed my mother."

"Nevertheless, with my memoirs coming out I can't have your nonna and her little friends tying me up in straitjackets."

I did an inner eye roll. "I thought we'd established that those are bib aprons."

"Tomato, tomahto, sugar."

"*Mmm*, more like tomato, garlic. But what does your book release have to do with the nonne?"

She flapped her fur-lashes as though the answer were obvious. "After my memoirs come out, I'll go from local style icon to global style influencer, so I can't have Lilliputians covering my lady delights."

I took a moment to repress any memory of that last phrase. "A book doesn't make you an influencer. You're thinking of social media."

"Yes, which is why I've opened an account." She opened her arms to highlight her furry mammaries. "I'm going to share my stripping costumes with the world."

I'd have to review my rental contract. With Glenda posting to the world, I was the one who needed to make some policy amendments.

"What I'm getting at, Miss Franki, is that I need to be free to be me without the interference of your family and their friends."

A wistful feeling gripped my chest with the same intensity that my mom had gripped the redhead's curls. "I need that too, Glenda. And you know what else I need? A bed, not a chaise lounge, or a bathtub, or your champagne glass, which is not a great place to sleep. But ever since I got engaged, I can't get my mom and nonna to leave. They're like invading zombies. You can yell at them and lock them out, but they keep coming back to devour you and make you a zombie too."

"Have you thought about staying at your fine fiancé's, sugar? It's bound to be a sextastic time, and if you weren't around, your mom and nonna would likely stay in Houston."

"I can't do that. My family's too old-fashioned, and anyway, they'd just follow me to Bradley's." I glanced at my ruby and diamond engagement ring. I'd lost it during a work trip to Sicily the month before, and I had no plans to lose it again. "And I certainly don't want him to experience that horror until the wedding band is on my finger."

She nodded. "That's savvy, sugar."

I looked at the floor and saw her polecat tail, and the solution sprang to mind. "Your costume closet next door! I could rent it, and we could turn the second-floor into a family-free zone."

"No can do, Miss Franki. You know that every room of that apartment is filled with my costumes and acsexories, and I'll need it to dress for my social media shoots."

"I won't get in your way, I promise. All I need is space for a twin bed. And I made crazy-good money on my last two cases, so I can pay rent."

She chewed the tip of her cigarette holder. Glenda was a businesswoman who never turned down a dollar, as her stripping career indicated.

"Please, Glenda. If I don't get some relief from my family, my life is going to turn into that movie *Four Weddings and a Funeral* in reverse."

"Four funerals and a wedding?" She took a drag. "You only mentioned two funerals. Who are the others for?"

"Mine, if you don't let me rent your costume closet, and a grocer named Angelo LaRocca."

Her fur-lashed eyes widened, and she looked like a mange-infested deer caught in the headlights of a VW Bug with eyelashes and lips. "You're not investigating his murder, are you?"

"Not officially. Why?"

"You remember my Russian waxer, Nadezhda Dmitriyeva?"

I flashed back to a bikini-waxing session that Glenda had forced me to have when I'd performed at Madame Moiselle's strip club to try to catch a killer. The experience had been so bad that I'd nick-named Nadezhda the Wicked Witch of the Wax, and then I'd named her as a suspect in the murder. "The Communist jewel thief I investi-gated a couple of years ago?" I leaned back in my chair and crossed my ankle over my knee. "Yeah, she's fairly memorable."

"She's also the one who found Angelo LaRocca's body."

My foot hit the floor with a thud. *Is the Wicked Witch of the Wax the cauchemar?* "How do you know that?"

Glenda shrugged. "She got out of jail a while back, and I availed myself of her services for this photo shoot."

The irony of getting a bikini wax to wear a furkini wasn't lost on me, but her reasoning for seeing Nadezhda was. "Does your buddy Carnie Vaul know? Because those two despise each other."

"Carnie's still on the road doing her carnival act with *RuPaul's Drag Race*, and what she doesn't know won't hurt her." She pointed her burning cigarette tip at me. "But what she finds out will hurt you."

"Warning received, and now I've got one for you." I leaned over the table. "Be careful around Nadezhda. I wouldn't be surprised if *she* killed Angelo."

"Oh, *pshaw*, sugar. She was a regular at LaRocca's Market. And when Angelo didn't open the store for a few days, she went to his apartment at the back of the building. She knocked on his door, and it opened."

My eyes assumed a skeptical squint. "Or she jimmied the lock to rob the place, but go ahead."

Glenda took a deep drag and let the smoke billow from her lips funeral-pyre style.

An uneasy feeling enveloped me, but I pressed on like the reluctant horse at Angelo's second line. "Well? What did Nadezhda see?"

"Angelo LaRocca in bed," she paused to snuff out her cigarette, "with an ax in his forehead."

Shock prompted me to look out of the window for my mother, and I got another jolt. My mom wasn't outside but a redhead was, and not the one with the VW Bug. The owner of the neon orange Nissan Cube stood immobile in the street as her blood-red caftan rippled in a breeze.

It was Theodora, the self-professed three-hundred-year-old witch. And her green cat-eyes gazed at the window, right at me.

3

Theodora watched from the street as I descended Glenda's stairs, and it was clear she was none too pleased. Her blue-shadowed eyes were half-hooded, and her lips were broom-stick straight. I was at a loss to explain it, but even her teased tangerine hair looked ticked.

I stepped onto the driveway and stopped near my front door—in case I had to go in and get my hair-puller mother. I eyed the salty sorceress, disturbed by how much she resembled Endora from *Bewitched*. "Hi, Theodora. Can I, uh, help you with something?"

She float-footed it up to me, her red caftan fluttering like flames.

I took a side-step toward my apartment. That walk was unhuman. "So, you still doing freelance witchcraft consulting at Erzulie's Authentic Voodoo?"

A green glow flared in her eyes, and her pupils turned to slits.

My head snapped back. I was just trying to make small talk, and no contact lenses could pull off those effects. I lifted a foot to run inside, but her hands shot out and grabbed my hair.

"Ow! Hey!" I bent over horizontal to the driveway to lessen the pressure. "What the hell are you doing?"

"What I should've done last year," she said in a tone as gruff as her manners, "when you moved my Cube without my permission."

"You were blocking my Mustang, and I had a birthday spa appointment, remember?" I tried to pry her fingers open, but, go figure, she had supernatural power. "And besides, I thought we'd settled that when you had me arrested."

"I told you, I have Seasonal Affective Disorder, and I'm in a mood."

"But it's almost summer. You should be glad, not mad."

"Are you daft? We live on a swamp."

She had me there—and by the hair.

Something heavy covered my back, and I got a whiff of leather. Bewildered, I glanced left and right.

Stirrups hung at my sides.

My spine slumped à la old horse, and panic built in my chest like water in a clogged fountain.

Theodora is a cauchemar who's come to ride me to death.

She jerked my long-brown locks as though they were the reins of a saddle. "Penny for your thoughts."

My pent-up panic turned to steam. *Does she know about my wishing penny? And if so, where does she get off bringing that up?* I turned my head upward to speak my mind, and my anger was replaced with shock.

The nightmare witch wasn't Theodora—she was my mother. And she glowed as green as the Wicked Witch of the West.

My mom released me and let out a cackle that made her uvula bounce. "I'm going to plan your wedding however I want, Francesca, starting with deli-meat bomboniere."

She ripped off her witch-hat hair and exposed red curls—made of tiny salami.

I screamed and bolted upright on a lobby couch at Private Chicks.

Veronica screamed and jumped up and down in her pink pantsuit.

I screamed again and flapped my hands.

"Franki, stop!" She put a hand to her white silk blouse.

I exhaled and looked around the exposed brick room. "Sorry. I was having a nightmare about that witch I met last year."

"Theodora? Why would you dream about her?"

I rested my elbows on my thighs and rubbed my face. "She showed up outside our house yesterday, but when I went to talk to her, she was gone."

"That's weird. Any idea what she wanted?"

"None. And I don't want to know after the stunt she pulled in my nightmare." I hit her with a serious stare. "She morphed into my mom as the Wicked Witch, and then the owner of a slutty VW Bug."

"All riiight. I guess that's why you were pulling your hair."

That, and it's genetic, apparently.

Veronica adjusted her ponytail, which was an unfortunate hairstyle given what I'd been through in my dream. "Did you spend the night here?"

"Sort of. I came in at three a.m. after Napoleon knocked me off the chaise lounge for the second time." I chewed my thumbnail. "Sometimes I think that Cairn *terror* is in cahoots with my mom and nonna to deprive me of sleep."

"Why don't you stay with me? I *am* your next-door neighbor."

"You don't need me invading your space with everything you've got going on. Besides, I think Glenda's going to let me put a twin bed in her costume closet."

"Given your propensity for nightmares, I'm not sure that's a good idea." She took a seat on a couch directly across from mine. "She's got some wild stuff in there, so it might be scary to sleep among her props."

"Not any scarier than sleeping in my clawfoot tub among my mom's hand-washed panties and my nonna's enema bag."

Her right eye closed. "I was going to make us coffee, but I think we'll have tea."

"I could use some caffeine." I glanced at the clock. Seven-thirty. "Why are you here so early?"

"I have to call Venice. Dirk and I are hoping to get married at San Zaccaria Church, and I left the number of a priest I need to talk to in my office." She shook her head. "There are so many things to do to plan a wedding that I can barely keep up."

"Don't say that around my mom and nonna. They might try to plan it for you. But instead of a reception at a gorgeous palazzo on the grand canal, you'll end up at a cheesy Italian restaurant with an accordion player and a tarantella troupe."

She smirked and scratched her eyebrow. "Your nonna would never let that happen. The tarantella is Neapolitan."

"Actually, there's a Sicilian version. But instead of a courtship dance, it mimics a days-long hysterical condition brought on by the bite of the wolf spider." I shrugged. "It's basically how I feel with my mom and nonna in town."

Her eyes crinkled. "That bad, huh?"

"Worse. They're cramming this wedding down my throat." The phrase conjured an image of my mom's bouncing uvula. "And of course, they have different ideas about where and how I should get married."

"What do *you* want, Franki?"

I let my head flop on the back of the couch. "That's the thing. I need time to look through some bridal magazines. But now Bradley's mother and grandmother are coming, and they want a say in the wedding too."

"Everyone's going to have an opinion, but don't let them stress you out. It's your day, not theirs."

The bigger stressor was meeting Bradley's family, but it was too early in the morning for that discussion. In my current state, it could bring on hysterical convulsions along the lines of the Sicilian tarantella. "What about you? Have you and Dirk decided on a date?"

She bit her lower lip, but her eyes sparkled. "How does a Christmas Eve wedding sound?"

"Magical." As soon as I uttered the word, I thought of sorcery, and a cauchemar galloped through my mind on humanback. "Make that *marvelous*."

"It wouldn't ruin your Christmas? Your family is invited, of course."

That was less marvelous. The second her wedding weekend got underway, my mom and nonna would follow Bradley and me around Venice, doubling down on the planning pressure. On the flip side, the city was a maze of canals and narrow streets, so we could give them the slip. "Actually, it would improve my Christmas."

She squealed and clapped her hands. "Terrific. I'll get the tea started and call the priest." She rose and straightened her blouse. "Oh, this morning I'm reviewing the applicants for the PI position. With both of us planning weddings, we're going to need extra help."

Veronica headed down a hallway to the kitchenette across from our offices.

I sprawled back on the couch. I'd forgotten about the PI problem.

From my reclining position, I grabbed my phone from the coffee table to text David for an investigation update. I searched for his number in Contacts and spotted "Wendell Baptiste." I paused. If Wendell had shown up for the gig at Angelo LaRocca's second line, he might have some information I could pass on to my dad. Then I'd be free of the obligation to look into Angelo's murder—and the nightmare witches who'd ridden in with it.

I tapped Wendell's number and got a recording that his voicemail was full, which seemed odd. A guy who played gigs for a living would need to check his messages fairly often.

The lobby bell sounded as David entered.

I sat up and waved my arms. "The boss is in," I whispered. "You got anything on the PI applicants?"

His eyes darted to the hallway, and then he rushed to the corner desk of our research assistant, Standish Standifer, aka The Vassal. He pulled a folder from a drawer and approached the couch. "This is all the resumés."

I snatched the folder and rifled through the contents.

David's head turned toward the hallway with the mechanical regularity of a sprinkler. "Um, hurry, okay? Veronica wanted these on her desk first thing this morning."

I looked up at him. "All the applicants are men."

"So?"

"We're Private *Chicks*, not Private *Dicks*."

"Uh, I'm a part-time PI, and I'm not a chick." His brows popped up, and his head retracted. "I mean, a girl. I mean, a woman."

"Right. I hadn't thought about that."

His brows dropped, as did his shoulders.

I lowered my gaze to a resumé to cover the awkward moment. "So, when's The Vassal coming in? I want him to run background checks on these people."

"I already called him and told him to get down here, but he left his lightsaber at home and had to go back."

I didn't ask. The ways of *Star Wars* geeks were alien to me even after their overzealous explanations. "Good thinking. We need him on the PI case."

"Oh, yo, it wasn't because of that. I want him to see a lady sitting outside in a lawn chair. She's, like, straight from a 1960s *Star Trek* episode."

"Nothing weird about that in the French Quarter." I flipped to the next resumé.

"There kinda is." He moved to a window overlooking Decatur Street and peered out. "She's wearing a funky tent dress, and she's all orange. Even her skin."

I dropped the folder.

"Dude!" He bounced backward. "She's totally looking at our window."

I leapt from the couch because I wasn't dreaming. Theodora had come for me.

"I SEE YOU SPYING," Theodora drawled, eyes closed, from her lawn chair.

Surprised, I withdrew inside the stairwell of the three-story brown brick building where Private Chicks was located. *How does she do that?*

"Step on out. I don't have all day."

I exited and kept my distance. I didn't believe she had magical powers, but there was something weird about the witch, besides the fact that she was sunning herself on a French Quarter sidewalk. Case in point—her skin was the same shade as her car. And in light of my nightmare, I couldn't ignore the fact that her maroon caftan was wide enough to hide a saddle.

A couple of middle-aged women in thick skirts came out of Nizza, the Italian restaurant that occupied the first two floors of Veronica's building, and gaped at Theodora.

Her green eyes glared. "You two have never seen a witch before?"

"Witch, *please*," one said and strolled on.

Theodora huffed. "Do you believe that?"

I shrugged. We *were* down the street from Hex, an "old-world witchery" with a flagship store in Salem. "I think it was your lawn chair."

She raised her warted chin. "Private Chicks doesn't open until nine, so I decided to get some sun while I waited. I tried a tanning cream to help with my SAD, but all it did was turn me orange."

I relaxed at the skin explanation but kept my eye on that caftan. "You need sunlight to help with Seasonal Affective Disorder."

"At three-hundred-and-one years of age, you can't blame me for trying to avoid wrinkles."

No, but I could blame her for not trying to avoid me. "Did I, uh, summon you somehow? Like with my subconscious?"

"Your brain communicating with mine?" She erupted into a throaty cackle. "That's the funniest thing I've heard in at least a century."

My lips flattened. I should have expected a crack like that. At her core, Theodora was a basic witch. "Then why are you here?"

"To find out why you were following me in that station wagon yesterday."

"*You* were following *me*. Your Nissan was behind my mom's Ford Taurus."

"I should've known that woman was your mother." She retrieved a jar from the folds of her caftan and opened the lid—and a puff of smoke came out. "The confrontational nut doesn't fall far from the tree."

There was an insult in there, but one I couldn't argue with. And even if I could, I was too busy watching the smoking jar.

Theodora dipped a finger inside and produced a yellow, rotten-egg-scented cream that she dabbed on her ears. "She came barreling off the highway and started tailing my Cube. I turned every which way to shake her, and then she ended up in front of me. That's when I saw you staring out of the rear window."

Her story was believable, but the witch was wily, so I was suspicious. "If you were so anxious to be free of us, why did you come to my house?"

"To ask whether you needed my witchcraft consulting services. But I saw your mother pulling a fellow redhead's hair, so I chose to wait and come to your office."

Okay, that *is plausible.*

She dropped the jar into a black tote bag that said *Payback's A Witch.* "But it wasn't a wasted trip. I took advantage of that funeral across the street to get some fresh grave dirt for a spell—and a spot of indigestion."

My stomach churned like a soil tiller. I'd once seen her eat a weed growing from a crypt, but I'd assumed that was as far as her disgusting dietary habits went. "You should really try antacids."

"Ha! Those'll send you to an early grave." She picked up her tote bag and rose. "Now that we've resolved the confusion, I've got some spell kits to make. If you'd like, I can whip up a little something to help with your mother, free of charge."

I knew it wouldn't work, but after the wishing penny fiasco, I was willing to try anything—even a witchcraft potion. "If there's a spell kit that'll get her and my nonna to go home to Houston, I'll pay you for it. Also, I have a question for you. Have you ever heard of a cauchemar?"

Her eyelids assumed the half-hooded look from my dream. "Have you ever heard of Sherlock Holmes?"

I gave her a half-hooded look of my own. "*Touché*. But he's not real."

"Neither are the cauchemar. The Cajuns believe that when an old witch dies she becomes a nightmare witch who haunts your dreams and, if she's in a mood, rides you like a horse to the netherworld. But it's just a folk legend that predates *Le Grand Dérangement*."

"What's that?"

"An awful time in history, during the French and Indian War in the mid-1700s, when the British forcibly removed the Acadians from Canada. Countless died, but a lot of them came here to Louisiana, where they became known as Cajuns."

There were an awful lot of awful times in history—and even in the present. "So you don't believe in them?"

The corners of her mouth went South. "We witches don't die. How do you think I got to be three centuries old?"

The word *dérangement* came to mind, but in an entirely different sense.

Her blue-shadowed eyelids lowered. "Why are you interested in the cauchemar, anyway?"

"An old Cajun woman said that an acquaintance of my dad's was killed by one."

"You mean the grocer, Angelo LaRocca?"

My head snapped back. "How'd you know that?"

Her pupils narrowed to match her eyes. "I'm a witch. That's what we do."

The crime had been in the news, so I wrote off her witchy intuition as a lucky guess. But I still wasn't sure how to explain those pupils. "Well, maybe the old Cajun woman was just using the term 'cauchemar' generically. Angelo could've been murdered by a, uh, *real* witch like you." *Or a Russian petty criminal named Nadezhda.*

"This isn't a witch crime. If it were, I would've heard about it from some coven or other. So you can forget all of this witch nonsense."

I wanted to, but some "witch nonsense" was sitting outside my office getting a tan. "You're probably right. Angelo's killer is most likely a lunatic or someone who had a grudge against him."

"Franki!" The Vassal ran around the corner in his signature round, coke-bottle glasses, thoroughly buttoned-up shirt, and jeans, carrying a lightsaber. His slicked-down hair didn't move but his backpack bounced. As he approached, he raised his *Star Wars* weapon.

Theodora rose from the chair, raised her caftaned arms like powerful wings, and aimed a finger at The Vassal. "Upendo!"

He fell backward, and his short legs kicked up.

Stunned, I looked from The Vassal to Theodora, not believing what I'd seen, then I ran and knelt at his side. "Are you hurt?"

He went limp and stared at the sky. "That witch blinded me."

"Who's he calling a witch?" Theodora thundered.

I glared at her over my shoulder. "Uh, you?"

"I didn't blind the boy. It was a simple protection spell."

Or the power of suggestion.

The Vassal raised his head. "Your spell is quite similar to 'flipendo,' actually."

"What's that?" I asked.

"The Knockback Jinx from Harry Potter." He pushed up the glasses he was no longer wearing. "It can be used to physically repel an opponent, knock away an object, and blast apart fragile objects and magically charged switches."

My eyes gravitated to Theodora.

Her face went from orange to brown. "Well, where do you think J.K. Rowling got the ideas for her spells? I *am* a freelance witchcraft consultant."

More like a freelance witchcraft con.

I spotted The Vassal's glasses beside his lightsaber and put them in his hand. "These'll take care of that blindness."

He slipped on the lenses, and his eyes grew to their regular lens-magnified size. "I can see again."

Theodora crossed her caftaned arms. "What did I tell you?"

I couldn't believe what I was about to ask her, but the situation warranted the question. "Why did you upend him, exactly?"

"He's a witch hunter, a ruthless breed who mixes deadly weaponry and dark arts to track, hunt, and destroy my kind."

I looked at The Vassal's slack jaw and slicked hair and wondered whether the slit pupils in Theodora's eyes were holes. "Have you even *looked* at this kid?"

"Indeed I have. He's got a martial weapon and an explorer's pack."

My lips pursed. "I don't know what you're talking about, but that's a lightsaber and a *Game of Thrones* shield backpack."

The Vassal pushed up his glasses—successfully, this time. "You'll also note that I'm not carrying a crossbow, and I don't own any studded-leather or scale-mail armor."

She flicked her fingers at him. "You got a copy of *Malleus Maleficarum* in that backpack?"

"Certainly not. But I do have *A Field Guide to Demons, Vampires, Fallen Angels, and Other Subversive Spirits*."

Her lower lip jutted. "That's a good book."

I watched the pair, openmouthed. "Would one of you mind translating this conversation?"

The Vassal rose. "The Witch Hunter is a *Dungeons & Dragons* character, and *Malleus Maleficarum* is a witch hunter's bible that was written by a German cleric in 1487."

My eyes rolled so hard that my brain rolled with them. Nevertheless, I planned to look up that bible in case Theodora returned. "I'm going upstairs to get some work done."

"One moment." The Vassal removed his backpack and pulled out *The Times-Picayune*. "I wanted you to see this." He opened the newspaper to the front page.

And the headline threatened to 'upendo' me like Theodora's so-called protection spell.

"*Local Musician Held in Gruesome Murder of Grocer*."

Beneath it was a picture of my friend Wendell Baptiste.

4

A stooped sixtyish police officer with a flat nose and an apparent fondness for Old Spice led Veronica and me into the attorney visitation room at New Orleans Central Lockup. "Last one on the right." He gestured to a row of stainless steel–encased video screens with phone receivers hanging on the white cinderblock wall. "The inmate will be on camera in a few minutes."

I opened my mouth to thank him, but his hostile glare told me to save it.

He exited with a door slam, and I spun around to Veronica. "Did you see the way that cop looked at me?"

She took a seat on the stool next to the screen. "It's barely eight o'clock. Maybe he hasn't had enough coffee."

I hadn't had enough coffee or enough sleep after a second night on the Private Chicks couch, but I wasn't shooting angry stares at anyone—except for my family when I saw them. "No, he knows me. They all know me here."

"But you were only locked up for one night, and that was over a year ago."

"I'm talking about Sullivan, Veronica." I paced the sterile room. "The whole police force thinks I killed him."

She exhaled, and her jaw took on a grim set. "Aren't you being a little paranoid? The detective hasn't even been declared legally dead."

The mystery of what had happened to Wesley Sullivan onboard the Steamboat Galliano weighed on my chest like an anchor. My instincts told me that he wouldn't die until he'd gotten revenge against me for a series of misperceived wrongdoings, but he'd been missing for more than two months so maybe I *was* paranoid. The only thing I knew for sure about the events on the Galliano was that Wendell Baptiste had my back—or he'd tried to when he hadn't fainted from fright—and it was my turn to have his.

Veronica glanced at a wall clock. "I have to run at eight-thirty. I've got to interview a PI candidate at nine."

The chest anchor plummeted to my stomach. "Who is it?"

"A woman I met at Thibodeaux's Tavern. Ladonna Cuccuzza."

"Uh, she's a no for me."

Her pink-glossed lips parted. "How come?"

I picked up my pacing. "Do you really have to ask when she's got a first name that means *the woman* and a last name that starts with *cuckoo?*"

Veronica sighed. "She can't help her name, Franki."

"No, but research has shown that your name influences your personality."

Her brow rose. "Well, I looked up *cuccuzza*, and it's Sicilian for a type of gourd, so what kind of personality is that?"

I saw her brow raise and raised her my other. "Someone who's 'out of their gourd,' so it's still a *no.*"

She inhaled as though preparing to meditate.

The video screen blinked, and Wendell appeared.

Despite the dire circumstances, his big brown eyes and fleshy trombone-player cheeks brought an affectionate smile to my lips. I slid onto the stool and picked up the phone. "Hey, buddy. How you holding up?"

He slumped at the question. "Awright, considerin'. I appreciate you comin'."

"As soon as I heard you'd been arrested for Angelo LaRocca's murder, I knew it was a mistake."

The lines around his mouth deepened. "It is. I didn't kill nobody."

"That's why I came. And I brought my partner, Veronica Maggio, from Private Chicks because she's also an attorney." She leaned toward me, and I tilted the receiver so she could listen. "Could you tell us what happened?"

"The cops think I killed Angelo so I could steal Louis Prima's trumpet."

I'd heard of Louis Prima, but I couldn't place him. "Who's he again?"

Wendell's eyes popped. "You don't know 'the king o' the swingers?'"

"No, but I'll bet my landlady, Glenda, does."

"What about the song 'Just a Gigolo?'"

My head bounced. "By David Lee Roth from Van Halen."

"Naw, man. That was a Louis Prima cover. Surely you know King Louie from *The Jungle Book*?"

"I thought that was Louis Armstrong."

He ran a hand down his face, dragging his full lips with it. "It was Louis Prima, one of the most famous jazz musicians to come out of N'Awlins. He was Sicilian, so I thought fo' sho you'd know him."

Given the constant meddling of my nonna and her friends, not to mention a cape-wearing marriage broker on Mount Etna, I tried to avoid Sicilians, which was another reason to veto the Ladonna Cuccuzza interview. "So, why would the police think you took his trumpet?"

"Because I went by LaRocca's Market to see it on Thursday night when Angelo was closing. He'd told me about it earlier dat day when I was making groceries," he said, using a local expression for grocery-shopping, "but he wouldn't show it to me till after hours. Anyway, I left the store around half past nine, and not long after dat the murder went down and the trumpet was stolen."

"How did the police know it was missing from the crime scene?"

"The killer left the trumpet case, which is weird because the trumpet didn't have Louis Prima's name on it, but the case did." He lowered his eyes. "It's also got Angelo's and my fingerprints."

Veronica looked at me. "If there are only two sets of prints, Angelo must've cleaned it recently."

Wendell cleared his throat. "All I know is they think I stole it, even though I told 'em I play the 'bone."

"Trombone," I corrected. The video calls were recorded, and it wasn't wise to throw around the word *bone* when charged with a homicide. "Let's go back to Angelo. Did he say why he had a trumpet owned by Louis Prima?"

"Didn't need to. It was the talk of the music community. That trumpet had been missing for decades, then it turned up about a week ago in a storage room that belonged to a liquor store owner named Lucky Mistretta. Lucky passed last month, and his ol' lady gave it to Angelo."

I chewed my lip. Two store-owner deaths might not be coincidental. "How did he die?"

"Angelo said he done choked on a bone from a pig's foot."

That was a far cry from an ax, although no less jarring. "Do you know Lucky's wife's name?"

He rubbed his head. "Uh, it's Russian, like Natasha."

I thought of Glenda's bikini waxer, and the hair on my non-waxed arms rose. "It wasn't Nadezhda, was it?"

"Yeah, dat's it. She runs the liquor store. It's on North Rampart and St. Ann, jus' down the street from LaRocca's."

Veronica and I exchanged a side-eye, but I scrunched my nose and shook my head. It couldn't have been the same Nadezhda because the one I knew would've sold the trumpet—and the pig's bone that had killed her husband, if she thought she could've gotten any money for it. "Why was the trumpet missing in the first place?"

"Now dat's some local history. It was stolen from Prima at Caruso's Market in 1969 when he did an impromptu solo there."

"Wait. He was playing at a grocery store?"

"Not a gig, or nothin'. When he came home, he went 'round visitin' his people, givin' dem a little show. And I think all dem Italian grocers knew each other back den."

My dad had told me that, but there was another person who could verify it—my nonna's elderly friend, Luigi Pescatore, an Italian version of George Burns, who'd gone from selling vegetables from a cart in the French Quarter, like my grandparents, to owning a major produce company. "Is Caruso's Market still around?"

"Naw, it shut down not long after the trumpet was stolen from Prima. It was a huge scandal."

Veronica leaned in. "Have you spoken with an attorney about your case?"

"Yes, ma'am. The court appointed me one, but I turned him down."

My head retracted. "You're not thinking of representing yourself, are you?"

"Oh, hell no. I'm stayin' inside. The killer hacked up Angelo, and I ain't gonna be next."

I knew from working with Wendell on the steamboat, which was rumored to be haunted, that he wasn't the bravest of souls. But wanting to stay in a New Orleans jail was extreme, even for him. "Look, I got big bonuses for my last two cases, so if this is a money thing, don't sweat it. I'm taking your case pro bono."

"That's a generous offer, but my answer is the same. I'm safer here in the joint than out there, so jus' leave me be."

"I can't just leave in you jail when one of Angelo's cauchemars—I mean, customers—probably killed him."

"No, dog, you don't understand. This ain't no nightmare witch." He leaned toward the screen, and his eyes were so wide they practically bulged. "It's the Axeman."

I jerked both because of the name and the hiss in his voice. "The, uh, what?"

"Time's up," an officer barked onscreen.

Wendell rose but held onto the phone. "You listen now, Franki. The Axeman is a demon spirit. He left N'Awlins over a hundred years ago, and now he's come for more blood." He pointed at me. "You git involved, and it'll be yours."

The screen flashed red, as if to underscore his warning, and then as black as death.

My 1965 CHERRY-RED Mustang convertible crawled along St. Ann toward the intersection at North Rampart, two streets I associated with bad memories—the former a disastrous Christmas Eve dinner with my family and the latter disturbing encounters with a mambo at Marie Laveau's House of Voodoo.

A ring sounded from the passenger seat. I reached over and answered my cell phone on speaker. "Franki Amato."

"It's Standish, The Vassal, calling from a public phone outside my Data Structures and Algorithms class."

I didn't know what that meant, but at least it wasn't a course on light-saber jousting. "Thanks for being so confusingly specific."

"Certainly. Veronica said you need me to conduct some research today?"

I parked in front of an abandoned building at the corner. "Yeah, I'm going to take Wendell Baptiste's case."

"What time will you be in the office?"

"Not sure. I have to question someone at Lucky's Liquor."

He chuckled. "You mean Lucky's Liquor and Life Insurance. Their slogan is *Before you get your drink on, get your affairs in order.*"

The liquor-and-insurance concept made more sense than Crescent City Plumbing & Palmistry, a plumbing and psychic services company owned by a couple named Lou and Chandra Toccato who were kookier than the name Cuccuzza. "Hey, before I forget, I need the resumé of Ladonna—."

"I already have a copy. She's the redhead Veronica's currently interviewing."

Another ginger? My fingers curled around the steering wheel. *Just one more reason to block her hiring.* "Okay then, find any articles about a trumpet that belonged to Louis Prima being stolen from Caruso's Market in 1969, and get me the name of the store owner and any descendants."

"Anything else?"

"See if you can find information, probably a local legend or a voodoo thing, on the Axeman."

"O-oh. His character was on the television show *American Horror Story*, the *Coven* season."

I shifted uneasily in my seat. Everything kept coming up *cauchemar*, despite Theodora's protests to the contrary. "Was he a witch?"

"The show doesn't address what he is, beyond a sadistic killer with a penchant for jazz. And in real life, they never found out who he was, but in a letter he wrote to the police, he claimed to be a spirit from hell."

Awesome. "On that note, time to drink some liquid spirits—and look into life insurance." I ended the call and exited the car.

North Rampart marked the end of the French Quarter, or the Back of Town-a, as my nonna had called it. And it showed. The street was undergoing gentrification, but as Lucky's Liquor and Life Insurance indicated, there was still a long road ahead.

The outside of the building was typical of the area—a two-story wooden structure with window shutters and a rickety wrought-iron balcony, the whole of which was notable for its blue peeling paint and hard lean to the right.

I opened the glass door, and a bell rang.

"Velcome to Lucky's." Nadezhda's voice came from behind tall rows of liquor.

Wendell hadn't been wrong to call her Natasha. Because she pronounced her w's like a vampire and growled her l's like a werewolf, she was a soundalike for the Russian vamp from *The Rocky and Bullwinkle Show*—but a lookalike for Boris.

I made my way through the narrow aisles of the cramped store, which reeked of mold and sour milk. She stood at the cashier counter, unpacking a box of liquor bottles shaped like her body.

Matrioshka Vodka, go figure.

My gaze fell to her gray smock. *Lucky's Liquor and Vaxing? And I'd thought the* Vaxing for Vomen *sign at her old business had been the result of someone scraping off part of the w's.*

Nadezhda seemed intent on ignoring me, so I coughed to announce my presence. "Long time no see."

She threw the empty vodka box on the ground and stomped it flat. "Two years, tirty-two days, and four hours."

I stepped back, for obvious reasons. "Glenda told me you were back in the women's waxing biz, but the sign out front mentions life insurance."

"No insurance, only vax. I get new sign soon."

It seemed unlikely that anyone other than my landlady would come to a liquor store to get waxed—then again, waxing was so painful that a stiff drink would help. "You'll have to get a new slogan too."

"Not problem. I change *affairs* to *hairs*."

I had to say it in my head. *Lucky's Liquor and Waxing—er, Vaxing. Before you get your drink on, get your hairs in order.*

"I also vax men." She moved to a wax pot on a burner behind her, hunched over it, and stirred. "You vant I remove mustache and sideburns?"

My hand flew to my cheek. "This is peach fuzz."

She laughed, revealing a hole where an eyetooth should have been. "Who you kidding? You look like bad guy in Spaghetti Vestern movie."

The comment was particularly stinging given that she knew the genre. Years earlier, she'd played a saloon girl in a Borscht Western called *Caviar Cowboy.*

"If you don't vant vax, you vant liquor?"

Not after hearing that she'd been keeping a tally of the days since she'd last seen me. She was likely to sell me a lit Molotov cocktail. "Actually, I came to talk you about Angelo LaRocca's murder."

"Vhy I help you? Last time I vind up in prison."

"Because I'm going to prove that the man in jail for Angelo's murder didn't do it. And since you found the body, I could help you avoid becoming the next suspect, provided that you're innocent too."

She sucked her eyetooth hole. "I handle police myself, darlink."

"Fine. But at least tell me why you gave Louis Prima's trumpet to Angelo."

"I give for lifetime of free pig feet."

Disgust threatened to curl my lips like a pig's tail, but I kept a neutral face. Lucky had choked on a pig-foot bone, and I wouldn't have put it past Nadezhda to arrange it. "What do you do with those?"

"I make *kholodets*, like Russian meat gelatin. Traditional recipe call for sheep head, but I don't vant to brush sheep teeth."

I reached for a bottle of the Matrioshka Vodka, opened it, and took a sizable swig to kill the imagined taste of a bite of meat Jell-O that could bite back.

"Tventy-five dollars."

I paid in cash, and on the off chance that my purchase had softened her, I tried to convince her to help me again. "You know, now that a second man you're connected to has died, the police could go back and take a look at Lucky's death and accuse you of killing him for his store."

"It not my fault he have big tonsils."

Triumph surged through my veins—or maybe it was the vodka. *That odd physical detail was all I needed to win her over.* "Since you knew about his enlarged tonsils, can you *prove* that you didn't put pigs' feet bones in his meat gelatin to choke him?"

She turned off the wax burner. "Ve go to LaRocca's. Vait here."

Nadezhda went into the back room, and I leaned over the counter to look for anything incriminating. I didn't know who the Axeman was or whether he was a witch, but Nadezhda was pretty manly, and she stirred her wax pot like a cauldron.

The only thing that caught my eye was a Russian booklet partially covered in brown wrapping. I lifted the paper and winced.

Putin porn—his annual shirtless calendar.

A door closed, and I jumped from the counter.

Nadezhda strode up the aisle in a blue-sequined shirt and black leather skirt with a huge snakeskin handbag. "Ve must hurry. I have early lunch date with gas station owner."

I exited, hoping gas wasn't her next business merger. Booze, a fresh wax, and a tank full of gas was a problematic combination.

She switched on a neon Closed sign and locked the door.

We headed side-by-side down the cracked sidewalk, but I kept the corner of my eye on her. As we walked the two short blocks, it occurred to me that we were passing Louis Armstrong Park. Jazz was something of a recurring theme in the case, and I wondered whether Angelo's death had anything to do with his store's location.

We crossed an intersection, and I glanced at the street. "Oh! Lucky penny."

Nadezhda stooped and snatched the coin before I could even bend at the waist.

I seethed. *That Communist probably has a hundred grand in savings, and she can't give me one red cent.*

We walked the last block to LaRocca's Market. The place looked more or less like Lucky's except that it was brick red, and the ground floor had an awning in the colors of the Italian flag. The phrase *grocer and deli* was painted on a big glass window, and beside it was a community bulletin board littered with flyers for upcoming jazz and crawfish festivals.

"Ve go to back. Angelo live upstairs."

I followed her down a narrow walkway to a small courtyard with brick paving and a few potted plants. There was no crime scene tape, so it seemed safe to poke around.

Nadezhda rummaged in her snakeskin bag and pulled rubber gloves, shoe covers, and hairnets. "Put on. Ve go inside."

"I'm sure it's locked."

"Not problem." She pulled a lockpick from her bag of crime-committing tricks.

I admired her preparedness, but I worried she had a hatchet—or a hammer and sickle. I was also concerned that what I'd said to Glenda had been correct—Nadezhda had jimmied the lock while Angelo was sleeping and killed him for the trumpet.

While she worked, I put on the gloves and shoe covers. As I stuffed my long locks into the hairnet, I noticed chisel marks around the door. I approached and ran a gloved finger down the frame. "Look at that."

"*Da*," she affirmed in Russian. "Hairnet really show sideburns."

My acidic stare could have stripped the maroon tint from her spikes. *She'd better hope the killer didn't leave his ax, because I might use it.*

Nadezhda opened the door and climbed a weathered stairway.

I told myself that I was only afraid of Nadezhda's waxing, but I made sure to keep a couple of feet between us just in case.

At the top of the stairs, she entered a room to the left.

I peered into the doorway.

Nadezhda stood straight ahead, away from the sparse furnishings.

The unfinished wood walls and musty odor reminded me of an old cabin rather than a bedroom. There was another smell, too —iron.

To my right was a chest of drawers and above it hung an antique picture of a couple, most likely Angelo's parents.

I looked left, and my hand gripped my lips to stifle a gasp. I'd located the source of the metallic smell.

A maroon-colored spatter went from the ceiling and down the wall, where a previously white ceramic crucifix hung, to a dried pool of the same color on the pillow on the bed.

I hadn't expected such a gruesome scene without a body.

Nadezhda gestured toward a night table in front of a window beside the bed. "Look at gramophone."

I wasn't eager to turn my back on her, especially after seeing all that dried blood, but I was compelled to investigate. The horn protruding from the old *Victor-Victrola* reminded me of a jazz instrument. A record on the turntable was called "Ragù Rag" by The Marsala Maroons. I'd never heard of it, but I assumed it was ragtime like the Scott Joplin songs I'd tried to play on the piano as a teen.

"Did you see candle?" Nadezhda asked.

A burned maroon candle with an image of the Virgin Mary sat

next to an unopened bottle of Florio Marsala wine beside the gramophone, but that wasn't what I was looking at.

In the courtyard below stood a man whose gaze seemed to penetrate me through the window. He'd painted red streaks on his cheeks, and he wore an enormous yellow-and-orange-feathered headdress and suit typical of a Mardi Gras Indian.

But it wasn't his colorful costume that held my attention, or his wideset hazel eyes.

It was the tomahawk in his hand.

5

David and the Vassal's lightsabers were raised in combat when I burst into the Private Chicks lobby. "Is Veronica here? She's not answering her phone."

They lowered their weapons, red-cheeked.

And I flashed back to the paint on the face of the Mardi Gras Indian.

David straightened his "Pretty Fly for a Jedi" T-shirt. "Uh, she took a PI candidate named Ladonna to lunch. Based on my investigation, I think she might hire her."

Under normal circumstances, I would have made him refund some of the money I'd paid him for not looping me in on that lunch a little sooner. But since I was running for my life, I didn't have time for a confrontation. I locked the door and leaned against it. "I just saw a guy in a Mardi Gras Indian costume at Angelo LaRocca's, and he had a tomahawk."

The Vassal dashed to his keyboard, his Darth Vader cape flapping behind him.

David's mouth, which had gone O-shaped, stayed that way as he sank onto the back of the couch. "Yo, he could've been the killer returning to the scene of the crime. Was the tribe name on his suit?"

"I didn't see any writing. It had beaded panels of Indian warriors on the chest and down each leg and yellow-and-orange ostrich feathers all over. He ran off before I could get a picture."

The Vassal's coke-bottle-lensed eyes were fixed on his computer. "According to Wikipedia, there are sixty Mardi Gras Indian tribes in New Orleans. Each one belongs to a specific neighborhood, but it's hard to know which one because they're so secretive."

I went to his desk. "Why would they keep their identity under wraps?"

"Because of their origins. In the mid-eighteenth century, escaped slaves hid on the bayous, and the Native American Indian tribes that lived there taught them how to survive. The Creole Wild West was the first African tribe to go public in a Mardi Gras parade in 1885. Now the tribes also perform at Jazz Fest and on Super Sunday, the Sunday before St. Joseph's Day, but we don't know much else about them."

"Which makes me wonder if some of them are dangerous, like gangs."

He pointed to a paragraph onscreen, and I leaned forward, brushing the hair from my face. "This says they used to be violent. But in the 1960s, the Chief of Chiefs, Allison "Tootie" Montana of the Yellow Pocahontas tribe, convinced them to put down their weapons and fight with a needle and thread."

I straightened. "What does that mean?"

He looked at me over his shoulder. "They compete to have the prettiest Mardi Gras suits. They spend the year sewing them, and they're different for the various tribal roles, the Big Chief, the Wild Man, the First Flag, and the Spy Boy. The suits can weigh as much as a hundred pounds."

"Well, the guy I saw at LaRocca's definitely wasn't holding a needle." I paced the walkway from his desk to the entrance. "I thought Wendell was losing it when he said the killer was the Axeman, but it looks like he was on the right track."

David rose. "What're you gonna do? Call the cops?"

I snorted. "And tell them what? That I saw the possible killer from a window in Angelo LaRocca's bedroom?" I shook my head. "Not a chance. With the way the police feel about me after Sullivan's disappearance, I'd be the one to go to jail, not the Mardi Gras Indian."

I put my hands on my hips and glanced at the reception desk. A jar labeled "Dispello" caught my attention, as did a scroll tied to the cork stopper. I didn't need to read the business card beneath the jar to know it was the spell Theodora had concocted to send my mom and nonna home to Houston.

My phone vibrated in my back jeans pocket. I pulled it out.

It was my mother.

She might not be a witch, but she has some kind of power.

"Hang on, guys. I've got to take this." I grabbed the spell jar and headed for my office. Dispello was a load of bullo—like the wishing penny I'd lost to the fountain and the lucky penny I'd lost to Nadezhda—but in desperate times, one needed to believe in something.

I answered the call on speaker. "What's up, Mom?"

"Francesca? It's your mother, dear."

I sat behind my desk, kicked up my feet, and hung my head over the chair back. "Yes, your name shows up on my phone every time you call."

"Isn't that nice? Listen, your nonna invited Luigi for dinner this evening, so be home by six."

"Oh, perfect. I was hoping to ask him about New Orleans in the old days for the LaRocca case."

"I'm sure he'll enjoy that." She paused. "And since your nonna invited a guest," her offhanded tone sounded underhanded, "I invited Bradley."

I sat up and stared at the spell jar. "What's the occasion?"

"I just thought it would be fun for us to get together before his family comes."

A bigger load of bullo than Dispello. I unrolled the scroll and read the instructions.

. . .

TO SEND UNWANTED HOUSEGUESTS PACKING, pour the contents of the jar into a mortar and stir with a pestle in a counter-clockwise motion. Put a pinch in the toes of your guests' shoes and position them to face the outside of the home. Your unwelcome visitors will vanish within seven days.

"SEVEN DAYS!" I dropped the scroll like I'd been scorched.

"Eight days at most, dear."

"Wait." I grabbed the phone and pressed it to my ear. "I was talking about a spell...lling test I have to, uh, take for work. What are you talking about?"

"I *said* that your nonna and I are staying a tad longer. Honestly, Francesca, you're a carbon copy of your father. The two of you wouldn't listen to me if..."

I tuned out the rest of her explanation. "Okay, but I still don't understand why you're staying another eight days, which aren't a *tad*, by the way."

"Because Bradley said his mother and grandmother have extended their trip by a week. Your nonna says they're coming to ask about a dowry, but my bet is that they want control of the guest list."

I picked up the scroll on the off-chance I'd missed an important detail. Bradley and I both were going to need the spell's help, so I had to follow it to the letter. To my relief, I'd missed an optional, but vital, step.

PRO TIP: Add a dash of cayenne pepper to speed up the process.

"WELL?" My mother's shrill pitch struck my eardrum like the Mardi Gras Indian's tomahawk. "Aren't you going to say anything?"

"Yeah. Why do you have to be here the whole time they are?"

"Because they're coming to interfere in the wedding planning, Francesca." Her panicked pitch had escalated with each word.

"They're a wealthy family from Boston, so they probably have hundreds of guests to invite."

"Mom, I told you, Bradley and I aren't planning our wedding right now. So if that's the reason you're staying, you should go."

"Are you saying we're not welcome in your home?"

There was only one way to answer that lethal question. "Hey, could you check to see if I have any cayenne pepper in my spice cabinet?"

The line went dead, like my hope for a peaceful evening.

I put the spell jar in my pocket and returned to The Vassal's desk. "Did you find out who owned Caruso's Market?"

"Joe Caruso. He died in 1970. I'm still looking for his descendants."

A year after the trumpet was stolen from his store. "What have you got on the Axeman?"

David held up a lightsaber. "Dude, it's a gnarly story."

"Not what I wanted to hear after meeting a man with a tomahawk." I pulled up a chair. "But tell me what you've got."

The Vassal pressed his R2-D2 stylus to his tablet and opened the Notes app. "From 1917 to 1919, the Axeman killed six people and injured six others in New Orleans, and there is evidence that he killed four others around Louisiana from 1920 to 1921. He went into his victims' bedrooms while they slept and struck them with an ax." He looked at me over the rim of his glasses. "He always used an ax he found at the scene."

There would've been an easy solution for that—get rid of all the damn axes, especially with an ax murderer running around. "How did he get in their houses? I mean, he would've woken them up if he'd hacked down their doors."

"Right. He removed the back-door panels with a chisel."

I got goosebumps at the thought of the chisel marks around Angelo LaRocca's door frame. "You said he sent a letter to the police. Did he give a motive for the murders?"

"No, the letter was a warning to the people of New Orleans. The police received it on Thursday, March 13, 1919, and it said that he would come to town the following Tuesday and kill anyone who didn't 'jazz it out.'"

"What's that?" I flailed my fingers. "Like jazz hands?"

"No, listening to jazz. Everyone was so scared that they did as he asked, and that night, at least, no one was killed. Someone even wrote a ragtime song about it called 'The Mysterious Axman's Jazz (Don't Scare Me Papa).'"

I thought about the record on the gramophone. *Could it be connected to the crime?* "Do me a favor and google 'Ragù Rag' by The Marsala Maroons."

He did a quick search. "No results."

"Huh. That record was at the crime scene. I'll have to ask around to see if they were a local group." I got up and started to pace again. "How is it possible that the Axeman was never caught?"

"I'm inclined to believe what he said in his letter to the police. He claimed to be a non-human entity from Tartarus."

The Sci-Fi had highjacked The Vassal's head. "Wherever that is, it's made up."

"Actually, in Greek mythology, it's an area within Hades known as the Realm of Punishment."

"You just made my point." *Although, based on that description, Tartarus was a real place, i.e., my house at the moment.*

The Vassal pushed up his glasses. "There is a theory by a crime writer that the Axeman was a Sicilian man named Joseph Manfre. He was shot in California in 1921 by the wife of his last victim, a grocer named Mike Pepitone."

I froze. "A grocer?"

"They were his main targets. Italians, specifically."

Like Angelo LaRocca.

David smacked the lightsaber against his palm. "Dude, sounds like a copycat killer."

In a daze, I flopped onto the couch, and something fell to the floor. Without thinking, I reached for the item—a round container of red makeup. Veronica or the PI candidate must have dropped their blush. I moved to put it on the coffee table, and the words on the lid finally registered.

Body Paint.

Indian Red.

The name of a famous New Orleans song about Mardi Gras Indians ran through my mind—Dr. John's "My Indian Red."

I dropped the container and bolted upright. *Had the Mardi Gras Indian been inside Private Chicks?*

"Is that a stripper pole? In the *front yard*?" I parked in the driveway and squinted through my Mustang's passenger window.

A seventyish male with a camera around his neck moved one of three lights on tripods closer to the pole. The light illuminated a skinny woman in a gold-rhinestone tracksuit who had the long platinum hair of my landlady.

"Has to be a body double," I murmured. Glenda wouldn't wear that much clothing, even if the rhinestones were diamonds, because her skin wasn't accustomed to fabric.

I climbed from the car and slammed the door.

The woman turned. It was Glenda in the flesh—literally. She'd cut holes in the tracksuit to expose her green dollar-sign pasties and matching thong. "Welcome home, Miss Franki."

I crossed the yard. "Thanks. What's with the pole?"

"We left it up after the cover shoot for *Like a Polecat at a Garden Party*. I wish you could've seen it, sugar."

I'd forgotten about the shoot, but I was very grateful I'd spent the past two nights at Private Chicks. I just didn't want to sleep there again after finding the body paint on the lobby couch. "Yeah, I wanted to be here for that," I white-lied, "but I've been crashing at the office."

She pursed gold-glittered lips. "If that's a nudge about my costume closet, you can move in Saturday morning for a grand a month."

Her dollar signs were showing in more ways than one. "To rent space for a lousy twin bed?"

"I'm sorry, Miss Franki, but this stylist-photographer is costing me a pretty penny."

A fountain and a Russian had cost me *two* pretty pennies, but you didn't hear me whining about it—not out loud, anyway. "I could save us both the money," I paused and massaged my jaw to force out the rest of my sentence, "by taking your influencer pictures with my phone."

"But you're not versed in #influencerstyle."

I overlooked the hashtag and eyed the stylist-photographer's journalist vest and khaki pants. "And *he* is?"

She pulled me from the spotlight. "That's Bob Simpson, sugar. He doesn't like to brag about himself, but he went from being a boring old Texas attorney to the Bob Mackie of #strippercouture."

The hashtag didn't faze me, but hearing *stripper* and *couture* together did. "Who's Bob Mackie?"

"The famous designer and costumier, a.k.a. the Sultan of Sequins, the Guru of Glitter, and the Rajah of Rhinestones."

"Never heard of him, or his a.k.a.s."

"Well, my Bob is the Shah of Shards. Think JLo on the #stripperpole in the Superbowl." She elbowed me in the side. "He's the one who suggested the material for that silver Versace catsuit—you know, the one that made her lady parts look like they were covered in mirror shards?"

I didn't know it, but I knew that Glenda's hashtags were slicing my brain like mirror shards.

"Bob created a book-launch campaign that shows me in my #stripperlife #naturalenvironment, starting with a photo of me #poledancing at the fourplex."

I would've scoffed at the concept, but the pole *was* her natural environment—onstage and in her daily stripper life. I'd personally seen her perform on a street light, a lamppost, and even a stop sign.

"He also said it was time for me to upgrade from sequins to these rhinestones, so I've added 'Roi of Rhinestones' to his titles." She raised her right index finger to show me a gold ring with two-inch prongs. "And he introduced me to this little number we're featuring in the photo. It holds your cigarette to free your hand for the pole."

Not that I thought smoking and stripping went hand in pole, so to speak, but even I had to concede that a cigarette-holder ring was perfect for Glenda. "Wow. Bob really knows his #stripperstuff."

The door to my apartment opened, and my mother stepped out in a gingham apron. "We're waiting on you to serve the meal, Francesca."

I sighed. She was punishing me for telling her to go home.

She peered over her shoulder and stepped onto the porch. "Get inside before your nonna figures out that thing isn't a flag pole."

Anxious to avoid a scene, I rushed into my French brothel-style apartment that Glenda had furnished, and I wondered whether Bob could convince her to upgrade it like he had her #stripperwear.

My mom went to the kitchen to help Nonna, and Bradley rose from the zebra-striped chaise lounge, where he and Luigi Pescatore were chatting. "Hey, babe."

I kissed him on the lips. In his textured gray blazer and dark jeans, he looked as delicious as the antipasto plate on the coffee table.

Luigi adjusted his George Burns glasses and rose on old knees to move to the purple-and-gold armchair. "Take my seat, kid." He spoke in a loud rasp despite a car-engine-sized hearing aid. "Can I pour you some Marsala?"

I stared at the bottle on the coffee table—the same brand as the one on Angelo LaRocca's night table. "Please, but I thought Marsala was just for cooking."

"Not in Marsala, Sicily." He reached for an empty glass next to his. "It's a fortified wine, so it's the strong stuff."

The origin of the wine could have been relevant to the case, but a likelier explanation was that The Marsala Maroons had inspired Angelo to have a glass.

Luigi handed me the wine. "How's the PI hunt going?"

I realized I'd forgotten to get Ladonna Cuccuzza's resumé from the Vassal. "Ask Veronica. She's been tight-lipped about the process."

"That's why I invested in the business. She's a smart one."

Except when it comes to hiring PIs.

My mother entered the living room with a garlic press. "Speaking of Veronica, I saw her coming home from work, and she told me that she's getting married on Christmas Eve."

The squeezing of Franki and Bradley is about to begin.

Luigi raised his glass. "*Viva gli sposi.*"

My mom's sigh was less than psyched. "They're not newlyweds yet, Luigi. In fact, I wish Veronica would have the wedding sooner. Her complexion is suited to pastels, and those dark winter colors will wash her out."

The reason for her season protest was as transparent as a bridal veil.

She twisted the end of her apron. "But there's a bigger problem—the cost of us traveling to Italy during Christmas when we're planning a wedding."

Bradley put down his beer. "I'd be happy to contribute, Brenda."

She gasped. "Franki's father and I wouldn't hear of it." She glanced at the garlic press. "But there *is* a way we could do both."

Whatever she was about to propose, I had to cut her off. "Yes, we make Venice everyone's Christmas present."

"No, I meant her wedding and yours, dear." Her eyes sparkled like tinsel. "You could get married in Venice on New Year's Eve."

"To hell-a with-a New Year's Eve-a," Nonna shouted from the kitchen, "we have a double Christmas wedding. That's-a what couples did in the old-a days, right Luigi?"

He nodded. "Those weddings were a hoot."

I grabbed a toothpick and speared an olive. "So are hootenannies, but we're not having one of those either."

"Then-a you have-a the quickie wedding this-a month," Nonna raised her chin, "and we give-a the money we save-a to Bradley's family as-a the dowry." She wiped her hands twice to indicate two problems solved.

Interest flickered across Bradley's brow. "Dowry?"

I stabbed another olive. "I thought dinner was ready?"

My mom's eyes popped. "The garlic bread!" She rushed to the kitchen. "I hope it's not burning."

I didn't know about the bread, but my face was on fire.

Bradley flushed, too.

"Don't worry," I said on the downlow, "I'm going to stop this madness." I entered the kitchen.

While my mom and nonna busied themselves at the table, I went to the spice cabinet next to the stove, where Napoleon lay in wait for dropped food. I gave him a scratch and pulled out the cayenne pepper. The Dispello spell seemed absurd, but I'd poured a love potion into Bradley's drink on our first date, and that had worked out extremely well.

"*Pepe di Caienna?*"

I jumped. Nonna had snuck up behind me like a Ninja.

She held a wooden spoon like a sword. "You're not-a gonna put-a that in-a my ragù."

"Uh, no, it's for...Bradley." I regretted involving him, but it was too late to turn back. "He sprinkles it on his tongue before he eats."

"What-a the hell-a for?"

"To...help with his digestion."

Her mouth took a downturn, and I mentally whacked myself with her spoon. In the Sicilian culture, a weak digestion is seen as emasculating. Then again, Bradley deserved it for telling my mom that his family was staying an extra week.

I returned to the living room under the disapproving gaze of my nonna and almost tripped over the bear skin rug in front of the fireplace. I was distracted—both because I'd undercut my fiancé and because the ragù had reminded me of a question I needed to ask Luigi.

"Here you go, Bradley." I held out the cayenne pepper.

His blue eyes shot up. "What's this for?"

"Don't be shy." I shoved it at him and mouthed *Sprinkle it on your tongue.*

He stared at the spice as though it was cyanide, and his gaze shifted to mine. "You know I was kidding about that dowry."

"Good, because there isn't one. Now take your cayenne."

Still gazing at me intently, he shook the spice into his mouth.

Nonna crossed herself and went back into the kitchen.

I put the container on the coffee table and sat on the chaise lounge. "Luigi, have you ever heard an old ragtime song called 'Ragù Rag' by The Marsala Maroons?"

His lower lip protruded. "Can't say I have. Why?"

"This can't leave my apartment, but that record was on Angelo LaRocca's gramophone."

"Ah. Your mom said you were looking into the case. Terrible the way he died. My produce company never did business with LaRocca's Market, so I didn't know him. But anyway, I wasn't up on the hep music when I was young because I worked all the time. And we didn't have transistor radios like you kids do now."

I smiled, although I didn't know what a transistor radio was.

Luigi brushed wisps of gray hair across his head. "You could try asking at Matassa's Market. They've been competitors of the LaRocca's for three generations, and the original owner's son, Cosimo, started a bigshot record company from his father's appliance store on North Rampart Street. He passed some years ago, but someone there might be able to tell you about the record."

"I'll do that." I leaned forward and speared a slice of prosciutto. "Do you remember hearing about Louis Prima's trumpet being stolen from Caruso's Market?"

"Suuure." He waved his hand as he drew out the word. "That was the talk of the town back in the day, and it ruined Joe Caruso. The police couldn't prove he took it, so they arrested him for running a bookie operation from his store." He shook his head. "Caruso's shut down after that."

"Did he have a family?"

"He was a widower. He had a son, Enrico, like the old opera singer, but he goes by Ric. Last I heard, he was working at Frankie & Johnny's, that seafood joint in Uptown. Johnny Morreale and his brother-in-law Frank Gaudin started that place during World War II.

They were some of the first Italians to transition from grocery stores to restaurants."

The Italian grocer theme kept recurring. "Were there a lot of Italian markets in New Orleans?"

"At one time, they accounted for half the grocery business in the city. I read somewhere that at the peak, there were three hundred and eighty-five Italian-owned stores."

Bradley swallowed a sip of beer. "Wow. That might beat New York City."

"Yessir, and quite a few were in the French Quarter. Central Grocery is still in business, but Muriel's restaurant in Jackson Square used to be Taormina's and Napoleon House was Napoleon House Grocery. There was also Montalbano's—"

"We don't-a talk about-a them," Nonna shouted.

My mother poked her head out of the kitchen. "They're Carmela's mob relatives."

Bradley pulled away from me, no doubt thinking of the cayenne pepper. "You have Mafia in the family?"

"They weren't mafiosi," I whispered, "and Nonna says they're not related. She likes to let my mom think that she has mobster relatives so she'll be scared of her."

He put his arm around my shoulders and chuckled, but I failed to see the joke, especially because my nonna's mob threat didn't work on my mom.

Luigi winked. "Carmela doesn't talk about them because they bought produce from me instead of her and Franki's nonnu. Man, I used to look forward to those deliveries. Montalbano's had a sandwich called the Roma, big as a table. And Biaggio, the owner, had his own St. Joseph's Day Altar with bread and pasta and lemons."

Bradley and I exchanged a look. The guy *had* to be Nonna's relative.

Luigi topped off his wine. "I used to shop at Fortunato's until he left it to Fortunato Jr."

"Why's that?" Bradley asked. "Did it go downhill?"

"Nah, *Fortunato* is Italian for *lucky*, and he turned it into Lucky's Liquor."

Lucky's was a grocery store? I took a swig of Marsala. So Lucky's death could have been linked to Angelo's. But if Nadezhda had killed them, it didn't make sense for a Mardi Gras Indian to show up outside LaRocca's Market with a tomahawk—or in my office with body paint. I speared another piece of prosciutto to take my mind off that.

Luigi laughed and slapped his knee. "You shoulda seen ol' Lucky. He sat on a tiny stool, but he was enormous, big as a bear, just like his dad."

Nadezhda's meat Jell-O came to mind, and the prosciutto I'd swallowed threatened to come up. I grimaced and patted my chest. "Uh, do you know if Lucky and Angelo LaRocca were friends?"

"Not as adults, but as kids. Them and Ric Caruso and a brother and sister I can't remember. But they all had a big falling out."

I sat forward. It was a longshot, but the fight could have been relevant to Angelo's murder. "What was it about?"

"I dunno. Maybe competition among their parents. It was cutthroat among grocers. We weren't popular among non-Italians, and we didn't like each other either. Part of it had to do with regionalism from the old country, but it was also a matter of survival. Italians lived in the same building as their stores, and their social lives revolved around them too. So if you lost your store, you lost everything. And some were willing to kill over it. A perfect example is the Axeman case. You know it?"

I went as stiff as an ax handle. I hadn't mentioned the case to Luigi, so it seemed odd that it would come up. "I've been learning about it, yes."

"It was before my time, but it's the first thing I thought of when I heard Angelo was killed with an ax. We all knew about it growing up because The Axeman was our Jack The Ripper. Police checked out every angle, whether the crimes were ethnically motivated or Mafia hits, but the only people they charged were a father and son who were competitors of one of the Axeman's victims. They were almost hanged, too, then a witness recanted. But to this day, the cops think the Axeman murders were actually killings between competitors."

Bradley rubbed his chin. "Surely relations among the grocers have improved since then."

"Not for the old-school guys like Angelo." He tapped his temple. "That way of thinking was ingrained in us by our parents, and with only a handful of the old markets left, the competition has gotten more fierce."

After seeing the man with the tomahawk, I wasn't sure about the rival-grocer angle, but I couldn't rule anything out. "This might be a weird question, but were the Mardi Gras Indians competitors of Italian grocers?"

"Nah, a lot of them shopped at our markets, especially the ones on North Rampart, like LaRocca's and Fortunato's. Why do you ask?"

"I saw one at LaRocca's Market today. He had a tomahawk."

Bradley put down his beer with a bang. "Franki..."

"Everything's all right." I rubbed his shoulder.

Luigi's eyes darted to Bradley and back to me. "It isn't, kid."

I shrugged off their concern even though it hacked at my indifference. "Any case I investigate is dangerous. This one is no different."

He removed his glasses. "It is. If this is a copycat, you could be a target."

"Why me? Because my dad worked for Central Grocery? Or because of Nonna's presumed connection to Montalbano's?"

"Those things too, but I was thinking about this house."

I glanced around my apartment. "What about it? Does someone want to kill me over the bordello-chic décor?"

Luigi didn't laugh at my joke. He put on his glasses, and the lenses magnified the seriousness of the situation. "I didn't want to say nothing before because I knew you were looking into Angelo's murder, but this building used to be an Italian market."

My head spun, and not from the Marsala. The LaRocca case kept hitting too close to home.

6

A thump awoke me, and my eyelids opened. The fog in my brain was thick, but a question shot through it like a flaming tomahawk. *Was the Mardi Gras Indian Axeman trying to break into my ex-grocery store apartment?*

Stretched out on my back, I stayed as still as a corpse and lowered my eyes from the baroque chandelier hanging from the living-room ceiling to the window overlooking the front yard.

Morning light streamed through a crack in the lavender velour curtains, and I relaxed. *It must've been Glenda and Bob setting up for an influencer shoot.*

Napoleon looked at me with ears erect, still on alert.

I raised my hand and gave him a reassuring pat. "Wait a second." My hand froze in mid-air. "Why am I reaching up?"

I dropped my arm and pulled onto my elbows. I was on the floor beside the bearskin rug because that territorial Cairn terrier had once again knocked me off the chaise lounge. "You're a lot like your namesake, you know that? A short guy with an insatiable need to conquer territory."

Napoleon yawned and licked a paw.

Exhausted, I lay down again. I'd probably caused the thump

when I fell onto the wood floor. My brain was so tired from days of fitful sleep that it might not have registered the body blow.

My head lolled to one side, and my gaze landed on the entryway.

And I scrambled to my knees and took refuge behind the bear's head.

I'd followed Theodora's Dispello instructions to the letter, but against all laws of nature and the universe, my mom and nonna's shoes had changed direction during the night. Instead of facing the outside of the apartment as if to leave, they were turned toward the inside—to stay forever.

Napoleon stared at me with an ear cocked, a sly comment on my half-cocked behavior.

"Go ahead, mock." My whisper was defensive. "But we both know I turned those shoes to the street before I went to bed. Now Mom and Nonna are never going to go home, probably not even when I get married."

His furry brow furrowed in alarm, but mine lowered in anger. As disturbing as it was to think that witchcraft might work, I couldn't help but be mad that the black stuff in Theodora's spell jar had backfired.

The front door opened, and I shot up beside the fireplace.

Nonna shuffled inside in her slippers—black, to match her mourning robe—and closed the door with a thump.

That explains the noise, I thought as I pretended to straighten a candle on the candelabra atop the mantle.

She shook a wad of silky red-and-yellow fabric at me. "I went to hang-a the Sicilian flag-a, but it don't-a work on that-a pole."

No, but Glenda does.

She draped the flag on the coat rack and pointed to the floor. "Did-a you move the shoes-a last-a night?"

My cheeks felt hot both because I'd half-believed they'd moved thanks to Theodora's black magic and because of the white-lie question I was about to ask. "Why would I do that?"

"It musta been-a your mamma." She shook her head. "That-a

woman don't have-a the sense to know that it's-a bad-a luck to point-a shoes at a cemetery."

I shot a glare out of the window. I'd known that harrowing ground was bad luck from the day I'd moved in, but I couldn't have imagined the extent of its beyond-the-grave reach.

Nonna went into the bedroom, and I grabbed my phone from the coffee table. It was eight o'clock, and I'd missed a call from my father. Because I didn't have my robe, I draped the Sicilian flag over my baby-doll nightgown and took Napoleon outside. There was dew on the grass, so I slipped my feet into Glenda's gardening shoes, a pair of green platform Crocs with six-inch heels that said "Garden Ho."

While Napoleon marked the stripper pole, I dialed the deli.

"Amato's. Give me your order."

The bossy voice and command belonged to my mother's best friend, Rosalie Artusi. In keeping with her barrel-shaped body, she had a tendency to barrel over people in conversation. "Hey, it's Franki. Is something wrong?"

"I don't know. Is there?" Her tone held a note of hope.

My lips sealed. Rosalie thrived on crisis and gossip the way normal people thrived on food and water. "I was just wondering why you're answering the phone since you don't work at the deli."

"Oh." Her tone took a nose-dive. "Your mother asked me take over her job while she's in New Orleans trying to get you married, which is a full-time job in itself."

I repressed a sigh. "Can I talk to my dad? He called a while ago."

"He's working on a big order, but I can tell you why he was calling."

I was sure she could.

"He talked to his friends at Central Grocery, and they told him that Angelo LaRocca had a beef with Olive Greco." Her pitch was pregnant with insinuation. "She owns Greco's Grocery on North Rampart Street."

I paced the driveway in the stripper Crocs, albeit like a five-year-old in her mother's heels. North Rampart was where LaRocca's Market and Lucky's Liquor were located, so Greco's Grocery would have been a competitor. And Olive could have been the sister in the brother-and-sister duo that Angelo had a falling out with. "Did they say what the beef was about?"

She harrumphed. "They're men, so they don't have a clue. But I've been to that store, and based on my experience with the woman, I wouldn't be surprised if she killed Angelo."

I stopped short—and almost tumbled. "That's quite an accusation."

"Is it? She shorted me a slice of prosciutto, so she's capable of anything."

I repressed a snort. Rosalie was out to get her over a deli meat vendetta.

"I remember it like it was yesterday. I watched her slice the meat and weigh it, and when I reached into my purse for my wallet, I saw her take a piece from the corner of my eye."

That I believed. Rosalie's eye didn't miss a thing, from the corner or anywhere. "I'll pay her a visit."

"Let me know what you find out. I'll take care of everything else."

The top was down on my Mustang, so I threw my leg over the side and climbed in. I was struggling with the shoes, and I already knew that I had to sit for whatever she was talking about. "What do you mean 'everything else?'"

"Heading up your bomboniere committee."

I repressed a scream. "There's a committee?"

"Yes, your mother, me, and the Bible Study crew from St. Mary's. Now, I know Brenda's got her heart set on baby salami, but I found some bomboniere for half price and perfect for a NOLA bride. It's a pig with lipstick and false eyelashes wearing high heels and a feather boa. You shake her, and Jordan almonds come out of her rear end." She squealed like the animal she described. "Have your mother call me ASAP before someone snatches them up."

I thought of that redhead's gussied up VW Bug and let out the sigh, the snort, and the scream I'd been repressing. "When painted pigs fly, Rosalie. And as of this instant, your committee is disbanded."

"Well! I told Brenda you'd be a Bridezilla." She hung up.

I held my phone in mid-air as a realization struck me—there were probably couples who had to elope because of meddling maniacs in their lives.

It was time to have a word with my mother. I kicked open my car door, pulled myself out, and slammed the door shut. And from the corner of my eye in the cemetery across the street, I saw a flurry of yellow and orange.

I dropped to the driveway and took cover behind the car.

Had the Mardi Gras Indian come to my house after all?

MY BACK WAS flat against the driver-side door of my Mustang, but my legs were in a sprinter position in case I had to run from a scalping. I imagined the Mardi Gras Indian creeping toward my car with his tomahawk raised to eliminate me as a witness. It didn't make sense that someone schooled in the old ways of Native Americans would go on the warpath in such a big, colorful outfit, but all that flash could have been the Mardi Gras influence.

I couldn't stay where I was like a sitting duck, so I waddled to the front of the car. With any luck, the suit would slow him down enough to allow me time to dash to my front door. Then again, I didn't have any luck thanks to a fountain and a Russian.

"What's the matter?" The woman's voice rose from the cemetery like a ghost from a grave. "Did you fall off your shoes and break your ankles?"

A scowl spread across my face. That voice wasn't haunting, it was taunting—and frustratingly familiar. I slammed my hands on the hood and pulled myself up.

The flurry of yellow and orange wasn't the feathers of the Mardi Gras Indian's suit but the fabric of Theodora's caftan, which flapped as the weird witch motioned from behind a mausoleum.

I storm-stumbled across the street in the Garden Hos. Midway, I spotted a lucky penny. Despite the fall hazard, I did a wide-leg squat like I'd seen Glenda do on the stripper stage to collect dollar bills. It wasn't pretty, but the dead wouldn't notice.

Coin in hand, I made it back up and into the cemetery. "Can't we meet at a bar like normal people? Thibodeaux's Tavern is right there, and it's open for breakfast."

Theodora smoothed her tangerine hair as she gave me the once-over. "Not with you dressed like that we can't. And I didn't want your family to see me on their way out of town."

The scowl settled back on my face. "They're not going anywhere. I did the spell last night, but when I woke up, their shoes were pointed inward thanks to my nonna."

Her eyes went feline. "Is she a witch?"

"Sicilian. Their skills are more powerful than spells."

"We'll see about that." Theodora pulled a plastic bag with a razor blade from the folds of her caftan.

Anxiety bubbled in my gut like liquid in a cauldron. "What's that for?"

"Since my charcoal-and-sage ritual salt is no match for a Sicilian grandma, I'm going to whip up a stronger version."

"No, don't," I raised my hand, "uh, go to the trouble. I'll handle my family."

"Nothing doing. This is between your nonna and me."

The last thing I needed was a whacked-out witch in a one-sided war with my Nonna, but I didn't dare stop Theodora. Even though she was standing still, her caftan had begun to ripple, and there was something really wrong with that.

She took off through the tombs. "I'm going to use an old classic to send them on their way—mausoleum moss. The expression 'a rolling stone gathers no moss' comes from this very spell."

A witchcraft history lesson—just what I want as I wander among the dead.

She stopped at a crumbling tomb with a winged angel perched above the family name *Lavigne*. "Èmile has volunteered some of his moss. He's been here since 1810, so he's dying for something to do."

I went rigid. The familiar way she spoke about him made me uneasy.

She knelt at the side of the tomb and cleared dead leaves and debris. "It'll take a day or so to make the new salt, and then I'll put it around your yard. Your mother and nonna will practically run home."

When she put it that way, another spell couldn't hurt.

Napoleon bounded into the cemetery, and I picked him up before he conquered any territory. As Theodora scraped the side of the mausoleum with the razor blade, I had second thoughts. "Are you sure it's okay to mess with a grave?"

"The deceased are bored out of their skulls, so they're happy to help. But you do have to pay Èmile back with an offering."

Napoleon's ears flattened as though she'd said "animal sacrifice," and I hugged him close. "What kind of offering?"

"That penny you found in the street."

I squeezed the coin. "It's your moss, you pay for it."

"It's your spell, so the offering has to be from you."

"But I just found this, and you have no freaking idea how much I need it."

She rose on one knee and rested on her forearm. "Listen, you don't know bad luck until a spirit comes after you for stealing his mausoleum moss."

I was about to call the whole thing off, but I got an image of my wedding guests shaking Jordan almonds from cheap-looking pigs' bottoms. I handed over the lucky penny. "With the Axeman running around New Orleans and maybe my house, my mom and nonna will be safer in Houston, anyway."

Her green eyes glowed. "You mean the serial killer from the early 1900s?"

"Not the actual guy," I said, in case she tried to tell me she used to know him. "I saw a Mardi Gras Indian with a tomahawk behind Angelo LaRocca's market."

"Did you see anything else?"

"It could be irrelevant, but in Angelo's bedroom, there was an old ragtime record, a bottle of Marsala, and a maroon Virgin Mary candle."

She plucked a weed from a grave and stuck the root in her mouth.

I was glad I hadn't eaten breakfast. I'd seen her chew tomb roots before, but it was the sort of thing one couldn't get used to.

"You know what it reminds me of?" She made a sucking sound. "That bottle of amaretto and the candle from that strip club murder you asked me about a couple of years ago."

Sometimes it did seem like the homicides I investigated had a theme—almost as if they were planned. "You said that case sounded like Old New Orleans Traditional Witchcraft, remember?"

She pulled the root from her mouth and pointed it at me. "You keep trying to pin this murder on a witch, and you'll vex the community. They'll put a hex on you."

I felt like they already had. "But this has to be a witch thing. The Axeman was on that show *Coven*."

"Which is fiction. And even if it wasn't, witches associate with all kinds of unusual beings. Look at me here with you."

I resented that comment. There was nothing odd about me— except that I was wearing a Sicilian flag and stripper gardening shoes in a cemetery.

Theodora scraped the base of the mausoleum. "Anyway, if the Axeman is involved, you'll need to consult Odette Malveaux."

Napoleon began to squirm, and I put him down and watched him run back to the house. *Did even* he *know the name of the notorious voodoo mambo?* "I've interacted with her a couple of times at Marie Laveau's House of Voodoo, and she's terrifying."

She cackled. "Mambos aren't as approachable as we witches. It's a cultural thing."

I rolled my eyes. Cat pupils, orange skin, and caftans that flowed on their own weren't what I'd call approachable.

She shook moss from the razor blade into the baggie. "Hey, when you go see Odette, pick me up a jar of her swamp mud. It's good for the complexion."

I noticed she hadn't offered to pay me, because she was literally a penny pincher. But if it would take the orange out, I might be willing to do it. "Does she sell it at Marie Laveau's?"

"No, at her house just beyond the giant bald cypress on Jean Lafitte swamp."

The notorious pirate's lair. "Forget it. Mambo Odette once told me to stay away from the bayou. I didn't listen, and then I found out the hard way that I was allergic to crawdads. I don't want to know what dangers the swamp holds."

She worked the penny into the dirt. "If you want answers about the Axeman, Odette is the one. The LaRocca case sounds more like voodoo than witchcraft, and she knows all about Mardi Gras Indians because she's descended from the maroons."

The word gave me a jolt because of The Marsala Maroons' record on Angelo's gramophone. "Who are the maroons?"

"Most people know them as slaves in Jamaica who escaped the Spanish-ruled plantations in the 17th and 18th centuries and set up free colonies. But people forget that New Orleans was under Spanish rule in the late eighteenth century, so maroons lived here too. Instead of establishing colonies, though, they lived among the Native Americans in the canals and back-country passages from Lake Ponchartrain to the Gulf."

The ancestors of the Mardi Gras Indians that The Vassal mentioned. "I'm starting to think this case involves history somehow."

"History? Speak for yourself." She rose and dusted off her caftan. "I was alive back then."

"Oh, right." My tone was as dry as that grave dirt. "I forgot because you seem so much younger."

She touched her cheek. "That's Mambo Odette's swamp mud."

I knew she wasn't actually three hundred and one, but she was starting to sell me on the product. "But why 'maroons?' Is it from 'marooned?'"

"No, from the Spanish *cimarrón*, which means 'feral,' or 'wild' and 'untamed.'"

I grimaced. "That's horrible, referring to enslaved people that way."

"Yes, and because of that, 'maroon' came to mean 'runaway slave.'"

I wouldn't be able to think of the color in the same way again—or The Marsala Maroons record. I didn't know whether it was connected to the Mardi Gras Indians, but I was certain that the song, the band name, or the musicians, were tied to Angelo LaRocca's murder.

A car pulled into the driveway, and Glenda's stylist-photographer got out. "I'd better get inside before my mom or nonna sees us."

"That's fine. I need to collect some dirt from an interment here yesterday."

"Another one?" I glanced around as though the crypt-keeper might get me. "I really thought this cemetery was abandoned."

Her mouth corners drooped to the tombs. "The interred would disagree with you."

Luckily, they couldn't—at least, I hoped. I stumble-sashayed across the street and saw the stylist-photographer standing on the side of my apartment with a trash bag. *He'd better not be setting up an influencer shoot by my bedroom window.*

He saw me approach and extended his hand. "Bob Simpson."

"Franki." I pulled my flag a little tighter. "What's going on?"

"I'm trying to figure out what to do with Glenda."

"For a #stripperlife #naturalenvironment picture?"

"No, about her #stripperlook." He pulled a business card from his vest pocket. "While we're on the subject, I can take your Sicilian strip-per-gardener vibe to the next level." His blue eyes sparkled as he raised his hands like a director setting a scene. "Think Dolce & Gabbana's citrus fruit line—we could put lemons on you in all the sweet spots." He kissed his fingertips. "Now that's *amore*."

I took the card, and my unkissed fingertips crumpled it behind my back. Oranges maybe, but lemons, no.

Bob sighed and shook his head. "When I think of all the billable hours we've wasted on her new look, it's enough to make me want to raise my rates."

"How are they wasted, exactly?"

"I specifically told Glenda to limit her plumage to peacock, and then I find this on the ground." He reached into the bag and pulled out an ostrich feather. "Yellow and orange to boot, like a low-rent Las Vegas showgirl."

I kicked off the Garden Hos to keep from falling over. That was no Las Vegas feather, it was straight-up New Orleans Mardi Gras Day.

The Indian had come looking for me again—this time outside my ex-grocery-store-apartment bedroom window.

7

"That's random, even for New Orleans," I muttered as I walked up the sidewalk toward Frankie & Johnny's restaurant. The place was more or less what I'd expected, an old yellow two-story with neon beer signs in the windows and white Christmas lights lining the porch. It was what was at one of the tables on the porch that seemed out of place—a big red crawdad smoking a cigarette. Actually, the crawdad was predictable for a Creole-Italian seafood joint, the cigarette was what struck me as odd.

He turned his head and gave me the once-over with two pairs of eyes—his and the big googly ones next to the antennae on his red costume.

Even though I was wearing a mock-neck sweater with corduroys and boots, he made me feel like I was still in my baby doll, flag, and Garden Hos. Annoyed by the crass crawfish, I returned the tactless ogling.

His face was painted red to match the costume, which consisted of a shiny spandex bodysuit, a padded tunic with a long fantail at the back, and two huge claw mitts, one of which was on the table while he held his cigarette. On his feet were another random detail, pointy elf shoes. But the strangest thing of all was that I could have sworn I'd seen the crawdad somewhere.

As I walked up the porch steps, he blew out a puff of smoke like he was telling me to get lost. "We ain't open yet."

I could almost taste the disappointment—and his cigarette. I'd gotten my appetite back after seeing Theodora eat the tomb root, and I had my stomach set on a meatball marinara po' boy for an early lunch. "I didn't just come to eat. I'm looking for Ric Caruso."

His red mouth cocked at a jaunty angle. "And I've been lookin' for you."

So this *Enrico Caruso is a giant mudbug.* I leaned against a porch post. "Great. A wise-cracking crawdad."

"Spicy." He rested his arm on a nearby chair. "I like that in a woman."

"Oh, and fresh too. Aren't you a catch?"

He leaned back and put his pinchers behind his head. "Yeah, so how's about you and me go out tonight?"

I flashed my ring finger. "Engaged."

"So?"

He'd been taking lessons from Bruno Messina, the sleazy son of my nonna's friend, Santina. "So, I'm not looking for a crawfish. I'm looking for a killer."

His real eyes showed no reaction, but his googly eyes rolled.

I took a seat across from him. "I'm investigating Angelo LaRocca's murder, and I came to talk to you about the night Louis Prima's trumpet was stolen from your father's grocery store."

He squinted and pinched the cigarette—between his fingers, not his pinchers—and took a deep drag. "I was ten years old back then." He spat out the smoke. "I've moved on, built a career."

"Doing what?"

"This." He waved a claw. "Being a crawdad is better than being Santa Claus. You don't have to deal with kids, and in The Big Easy, you can work year-round. For instance, I got Crawfish Fest coming up, which is my Christmas season. The only downside is the damn animal-rights activists."

I flashed back to the day I'd met a hippy tour guide named Pam during my vampire case, when she and her far-out friends were protesting crawdad boils. "I realize talking about that night is hard for you, but I'm trying to clear an innocent man."

He snorted. "Good luck with that in this town. It didn't happen for my pops."

His bitterness about his father's situation was understandable, but I had to keep trying for Wendell. "Can I just ask a few questions? Like, were there any Mardi Gras Indians at the store the night of the theft?"

"How would I know? My pops had locked me in my room for egging a neighbor's house. We lived above the store, so I could hear Prima playing, but I didn't get to see anything."

It wasn't the answer I'd hoped for, but I was sure he had other information. "Did any Indians shop at the store?"

"Lots did, but why are you so interested in them? The whole neighborhood was at that show."

I knew better than to give away too much. "I'm just trying to get a picture of your customers. What about your father? Did he ever tell you who he suspected?"

"He never talked to me about that. Like I said, I was a kid, and I wasn't there."

Tires squealed, and we both spun toward the street.

A young guy with a mullet and a bottle of Jack Daniels leaned out of the window of an old Chevy. "Pinch de tail, and suck de head!"

The car sped off.

Ric cocked a red brow, and his antennae wobbled. "Those crawfish-eating instructions were for you."

My stare was as cold as a crawfish cocktail. "I'm allergic."

"Can't blame a guy for tryin'."

I could if he were a crawdad. "Let's get back to the investigation. I assume you know that the trumpet turned up in Lucky Mistretta's storage room?"

He took a drag. "I was number one on the cops' suspect list for

Angelo's murder. My pops died in prison for something he didn't do, so they figured I'd evened the score."

"And had you?"

His eyes narrowed, and his googly eyes shook. "Like I told you, I've moved on with my life."

"Sorry, but I heard you and Angelo and some brother and sister had a falling out as kids, so I had to ask."

He puffed out his Crustacean chest. "I don't know what you're talking about. But even if I did, who chops up a guy with an ax over some childhood spat?"

It did seem unlikely, but sicker things had happened in New Orleans. "Someone told me your father was arrested for running a book-making operation. Do you think the theft of the trumpet was connected?"

"In what way?"

"Louis Prima's trumpet would have been valuable. Maybe someone stole it for gambling money."

"You mean Lucky Sr. He and his son were both greedy gluttons." He rose and went to the porch rail. "It's a shame that Lucky Jr. choked on a pig foot bone, because I would've choked him myself for keeping that trumpet a secret all these years."

His admission was startling, but I'd heard suspects say worse things in anger. "So, you think Lucky Sr. stole it, and Lucky Jr. covered it up?"

"The fact that it was in their storage room proves it."

Anyone could have stashed the instrument above the liquor store to frame Lucky Sr., but I didn't want to argue with him. The crawdad was crabby, and that was putting it politely. "Do you think Angelo LaRocca was killed for the trumpet?"

He snorted out some smoke. "What other reason would there be? The cops said the killer didn't take anything else from the store, not even the cash in the register."

"Maybe whoever killed him went there for some other reason."

"Like what?"

"I don't know, but I heard he had a feud with a woman named Olive Greco."

He laughed, exposing stained piranha teeth. "If you've ever shopped at Greco's Grocery, then you know Olive's a pain in the prosciutto."

Odd he's picked that particular meat after Rosalie complained of the slice-shorting incident.

He flicked his cigarette into the street and put on his pincher. "Nah, Angelo was killed for the trumpet. That thing has some sort of voodoo curse on it."

Wendell shared that sentiment, but I didn't. "Why would you think it was cursed?"

He turned to face me, and his fantail wagged. "Isn't it obvious? That trumpet is death to everyone who touches it—my pops, Lucky, Angelo. Whoever's got it now gets the ax next."

The comment struck me like a blade. "Is that a prediction or a promise?"

"An expression, so relax."

I wanted to, but I couldn't. Because I had a feeling that the Axeman would literally strike again.

Matassa's Market, *Grocery & Deli*. The sign above the white double doors covered all the food-shopping angles, as did the store itself. The entrance of the pale green balconied building faced the corner of two French Quarter streets, Dauphine and St. Philip. And along with deli sandwiches, Matassa's sold liquor and king cake to complete the holy trinity of the New Orleans dining experience.

I stepped inside, but no one was at the register, so I scanned the store. Unlike Central Grocery, which had remained untouched since its 1906 opening, Matassa's had been remodeled but retained the shotgun-style layout typical of the area.

"Are you looking for whatshisname?"

Startled, I turned to a short, round-hipped woman with cropped hair who looked to be around sixty-five. She wore a white T-shirt, Mom jeans, and a Mardi Gras fanny pack complete with a cup holder that had a New Orleans Original Daiquiri in it. "I don't know. What's his name?"

She pressed her temple. "Oh, I'm just terrible with names, but he works here. He's in the back making a huge order of their specialty sandwich."

My stomach rumbled at the word. "Which sandwich is that?"

"I can't remember what they call it, but it's named after the original owner and his hometown in Sicily."

I read the menu on the wall above the deli counter and smirked. The first sandwich I saw was The Rosalie, à la my mom's best friend, made with prosciutto, mozzarella bufala, and arugula. It would have been hilarious if they shorted customers a slice of prosciutto when they made it. I scanned the rest of the menu. "Are you talking about The Johnny Cefalu?"

"That's it. Only his real name was the Italian version of Johnny."

"Giovanni?"

She looked at me like I'd just answered The $64,000 Question. "You're a real trivia whiz."

"Not really. And you are?"

She pulled her go-cup from its holster. "Windy. Windy Spitter."

I could see why she would remember her own name. It was quite something. "Do you work here?"

"No, but I know a little about its history. I'm a tour guide."

Interesting choice for a woman who couldn't remember people and places. "Can you tell me anything about Giovanni's son, the record producer?"

She glanced at the deli menu. "The Cosimo? Oh, I'm sorry. That's his sandwich. I mean, just Cosimo."

I glanced toward the back, wishing the deli guy would come out.

"Cosimo got famous in the 40s and 50s for producing the records of someone who was fat, the 'Tutti Frutti' guy, and a man who was blind and always wore black sunglasses."

I knew a lot about old music from my father's record collection, so

I attempted to fill in the blanks. "Fats Domino, Little Richard, and Ray Charles?"

"Heeey, you should go on that TV show..." She tapped her temple. "*Jeopardy?*"

She gave my bicep a smack. "See? You could win a million."

Not likely, but I'd fare better than her. "Do you happen to know if Cosimo produced a record called "Ragù Rag" by The Marsala Maroons?"

"That Sicilian jazz quartet from the '20s?"

So they were *Sicilian.* "Yeah, do you know them?"

"Oh, they're all dead."

Talking to Windy Spitter was like spitting in the wind. "I mean, anything about them, like a name, or a line from the song."

"The song didn't have any words, which is good. I mean, who remembers lyrics?"

Only pretty much the whole world. "Just to verify, there were no Mardi Gras Indians in the band?"

"No. But they're all related." She waved her go-cup toward the aisles. "Do you like cookies?"

My teeth tensed, both because I was surprised by the subject and because they wanted to bite some biscotti.

"You reminded me that they have macaroons here and some Italian cookies." She headed up a center aisle.

And I followed. I could use some comfort food—any kind of comfort, really.

She shoved a yellow bag at my stomach. "These lemon amaretti are new."

I'd been avoiding lemons for obvious reasons, but the combination was too good to pass up. "So, what did you mean before about jazz Mardi Gras Indians and Sicilians being related?"

"I do a jazz history tour of New Orleans. You wouldn't like to hear it, would you?"

I would, but based on the way the conversation had been going, I might need a slug of her daiquiri to get through it. "Please. The part about Sicilians and Mardi Gras Indians."

She tapped her cup straw against her chin. "Well, jazz was invented in the 1800s just up the street at a square in that park—"

"Congo Square in Louis Armstrong Park?"

"That's it. Slaves would gather there on Sunday, their day off, and play music from Africa and the Caribbean. And some of them were fugitives who lived with Indians—"

"The maroons?"

She pointed her drink at me. "You must be a genius."

If I were, I wouldn't be in a market pumping the likes of her for information.

"Anyway, the maroons brought Native American sounds into the mix, and slaves also borrowed from the brass bands of New Orleans' European immigrants. Presto-change-o, jazz was born."

I knew from my nonna that Sicily had a long-standing brass band tradition, so that explained Sicilians' contribution to the genre.

Windy took a drag off her daiquiri straw and pulled a note pad from her fanny pack. "Over the decades, black and Sicilian musicians continued to borrow from each other." She looked at the pad. "For example, the Sicilians used African blues elements, and the black musicians used the Italian lyric trumpet sound."

The trumpet got my attention.

"And then the problem happened."

A trumpet blew in my head, signaling a warning. "What problem?"

"Well, black musicians had already been performing jazz at funerals when a local Sicilian group went to New York and made the first jazz record. When it became successful, one of the band members took credit for inventing jazz, and that started a controversy in the community that rages to this day."

It wasn't likely, but I had to ask. "Was this group The Marsala Maroons?"

She stuffed the notes into her pack. "No, but I know who it was, because my mother's name is involved. The Original Dixieland Jass Band."

"Jass?"

Her face fell like her sagging fanny pack. "No, her name is Dixie."

I'd gathered that, but even if I hadn't, she was one to point the finger for getting a name wrong. "I meant, why 'jass' and not 'jazz'?"

"Oooh." She nodded and slurped some daiquiri. "It's the original name for 'jazz.' It comes from a NOLA slang term for something, like 'excite' or 'pep up,' maybe. Anyway, the name was changed to Original Dixieland Jazz Band."

"Which band member took the credit?"

"Uh, Dominic or maybe Nick..." She chewed her straw. "What's the name of that grocery store owner who was just killed?"

I didn't say *LaRocca* because my mind had already moved on. *Was Angelo related to Domenic LaRocca? And if so, was he murdered to settle a score about the origins of jazz?*

MY RING TONE blared from my purse as I carried two huge bags of groceries from Matassa's to my Mustang, but I ignored it. After I'd finally told Windy that Angelo's last name was LaRocca, she'd changed the subject to Ferrero Rocher and led me to the Italian chocolate aisle. Besides golf-ball-sized truffles, they had ten kinds of chocolate-hazelnut spreads, including the almighty father of them all, gianduia. At that point, I did the only thing I could.

Shopping spree.

I deposited the groceries in the passenger seat, and my phone resumed its blaring. I thought it might be Bradley calling to tell me that his mother and grandmother had arrived, so I pulled out my phone.

An unlisted number. "Hello?"

"It's Wendell. I'm glad I caught you. I only got four minutes o' phone time left."

I went to the driver's side and climbed in. Inmates' calls were not only recorded but available to prosecutors for screening, so I had to be careful about what I said. "You ready to get out of that jail yet?"

"Not with the Axeman out dere, I ain't. But I got assigned a public defender anyways, and unlike most of 'em, this little dude knows his stuff. He even knew you came to see me."

Wendell's tone was casual, but I wondered whether his words held a warning. His attorney could have known about my visit because the police were watching me, and not just because of the LaRocca case, but because of Detective Sullivan's disappearance too. "There's nothing wrong with visiting a friend in jail."

"True dat, and I could use a friend in this place. A guard told me there's a brother in here I should meet. He plays the trumpet like Louis Armstrong. Not only dat, we both like Italian food."

That wasn't casual, that was code. Wendell had never mentioned Italian food, so he must've been referring to Italian grocery stores. Someone in the jail had information about Angelo's murder, and Wendell planned to talk to him. "You should talk jazz with him during rec time," I said, assuming Wendell's same tone. "By the way, I've been taking your advice about brushing up on music history, and I learned that a local Sicilian musician took credit for inventing jazz. Is that still a sore spot in the community?"

"For some o' the older brothers, it is. Why you askin'?"

I couldn't tell him about the Mardi Gras Indian outside Angelo LaRocca's window because the police would ambush me with an obstruction of justice charge. "Well, a guy paid me a visit, indirectly, in a feathered costume—"

"Oh, Lawd." The casual and conspiratorial tones had been replaced by coward. "It coulda been a *bokor* or a *caplata*. Man or woman?"

"A man but—"

"A bokor. Sweet Jesus." He made a humming sound, as though even his vocal cords were trembling.

Despite my better judgment, I tensed and glanced in the rearview mirror. "What's a bokor?"

"A voodoo witch. If anyone offers you a drink, and especially a white one, don't take it. Dat's how dey turn you into a zombie."

I relaxed against the headrest. A cauchemar riding people in their sleep was one thing, but a bokor turning humans into zombies was too far out there. It begged an important question, however—why *did* Louisiana have so many witch legends?

"Listen to me, Franki. You got ta go to a voodoo houngan or mambo for help because the Axeman coulda had a root doctor put a root on you."

I wasn't sure what he meant, but if anyone had put a root on me, it was that weed-eating witch, Theodora. "I don't want to offend you, but I don't believe in," I hesitated before saying *voodoo* because that was his religion, "zombies."

"Well, believe dis—de police jus' got a letter from the Axeman after a hundred years. So you got ta jazz it out, girl, 'cause he's back to pick up where he left off."

I went as stiff as my lemon amaretti cookies. I wasn't worried about Wendell breaking the code and outing my involvement in the Angelo LaRocca case to the police. But I was worried about the yellow-and-orange feather Bob Simpson had found outside my bedroom window.

Was I next on the copycat Axeman's hit list?

8

The two grocery bags of food I'd binge-bought at Matassa's Market weighed as heavily on me as Wendell's words as I climbed the three flights of stairs to Private Chicks. Actually heavier. My arms and thighs were about to give out. But on the plus side, the calories I was burning would offset my cookie-and-chocolate-hazelnut binge.

I pushed open the door with my shoulder and deposited one of the bags on the reception desk.

David glanced over his shoulder from a lobby couch with a cell phone pressed to his ear, and I remembered that I needed to find out Ladonna Cuccuzza's PI credentials. If an ax murderer was hunting me, then I needed Veronica to interview quality investigators.

I went to The Vassal at his corner desk. "Hey," I whispered, "do you still have that resumé for me?"

He glanced around for Veronica and pulled it from a drawer.

I shifted the grocery bag to my hip and stuffed the paper into my purse. "Also, forget tracking down Joe Caruso's son, Ric, because I found him."

"Did you get any good information?"

"Not really. He's a crawdad by profession, so he's got a hard shell."

The Vassal pushed up his glasses. "Makes sense."

It did in New Orleans. "Do me a favor and look into whether Angelo LaRocca was related to a local jazz musician named Domenic, or Nick, LaRocca."

He nodded, and his lens-magnified eyes landed on the lemon amaretti protruding from the grocery bag.

I gave him one cookie. "You'll get more of these if you and maybe David help me move a twin bed into Glenda's costume closet on Satur—"

"We'll be there." He was so eager to accept that he'd semi-hopped from his chair, and it had nothing to do with my cookies. Glenda's costumes were the closest he and David got to any female action.

David hung up the phone. "Yo, Franki, Veronica wants to see you."

I glanced at the hallway. When my boss and BFF called me in, it wasn't usually good news. I popped a cookie into my mouth to sweeten whatever was coming and headed to her office.

Veronica was at her desk, staring at her computer. Although she'd gone for a soft look—a frilly peach blouse and wavy hair—her face looked hard.

I decided to try to derail any bad news with an offering. I pulled a sandwich from the bag. "Want a gavillacio from Matassa's Market? It's Genoa salami, smoked bufala mozzarella, arugula, artichokes, and sweet roasted peppers on ciabatta bread."

She leaned back in her fuchsia leather chair. "I'm going to lunch with Dirk in an hour. You go ahead."

"I'm still working on breakfast." I raised the bag of lemon amaretti.

"Yum. I'll take some of those."

Nice going, Franki. Veronica was notorious for eating more than her share of sweets, and I was notorious for not sharing them. I flopped into the armchair in front of her and shook two lemon amaretti onto her desk.

"Speaking of lunch," she bit into a cookie, "when is yours with Bradley's family?"

"The Last Supper? It's tomorrow."

"It's going to be fine, Franki."

My brow couldn't help but hike halfway up my forehead.

She exhaled a laugh. "Okay, there might be a few little bumps."

"You mean a lot of giant potholes and gaping sinkholes."

"Everyone's going to be on their best behavior for this first meeting, at least, so I wouldn't worry too much." She swallowed the last of her cookie and dusted crumbs from her fingers. "Anyway, I called you in because David and Standish told me about your encounter with the Mardi Gras Indian, and I didn't like the part about the tomahawk."

I relaxed against the chairback, relieved that she wasn't going to drop any work bombshells. "You're not going to like hearing that the supposed Axeman sent the police another letter."

Her head tipped forward. "What?"

I gave a slow nod. "Wendell called from jail this morning. Apparently, the Axeman's back on the hunt for skulls to whack, which looks bad for the Mardi Gras Indian. But, we both know his tomahawk could've been a costume prop rather than a murder weapon."

"You don't think this is an open-and-shut case?"

"It's tempting, but I want to look into a feud that Angelo had with another grocery store owner, Olive Greco. Also, I'm not ready to rule out Nadezhda. She's probably just your common Communist criminal, but I wouldn't put a homicide past her."

"So what's your next move?"

I kicked my legs over the side of the chair and positioned the cookie bag on my stomach, where it belonged. "I'm going to have a chat with Ms. Greco, and I also need to locate the Mardi Gras Indian. Odette Malveaux can tell me which tribe he belongs to, but she lives in Jean Lafitte swamp, and there ain't no way I'm going to see a voodoo priestess in an old pirate's den. That's a bad combination."

"I think you should." Veronica paused and put on her bright face. "You could take our new PI."

I jerked, rocked by the work bomb she'd just dropped on me.

She held up a hand. "Stay calm, Franki. It's just a trial period."

"For how long?"

"As long as it takes to solve the case and free Wendell from jail."

I tossed my cookies—literally, not figuratively—and put my feet on the ground to stop the reeling. "She's working with *me*?"

Veronica sighed. "You shadowed me on your first homicide case, so this is a great training opportunity for her."

That was frustrating, but fair. "What's her experience?"

"She doesn't have much, which is why we're doing the trial period."

"You hired the cuckoo woman, didn't you?"

Veronica folded her hands on her desk. "Ladonna Cuccuzza is not a cuckoo, and it's not okay to call her one based on her last name."

I threw my head back. "You're right. I'm just stressed because there are so many minefields in my life right now."

"I know, but having another PI around could take some of the stress off you." She leaned back in her chair. "And I think you'll like Ladonna. You have some things in common. For instance, she's Sicilian."

My lips puckered, and not from the lemon in the amaretti. "Given my nonna, that's not a stress reliever, Veronica."

The lobby bell sounded.

Veronica looked at the clock. "That's her now." She rose. "Why don't you take a minute to collect yourself and meet us in the lobby?"

I gave a military salute. "You're the boss."

She left, and I tipped the bag into my mouth. There were no more cookies. I crumpled the bag, full of regret. I shouldn't have given away those three lemon amaretti, and I shouldn't have doubted Veronica's judgment. Besides being a smart best friend, she was a smart businesswoman. When she'd hired Glenda, Carnie, and my nonna, it was for temporary assignments. For a full-time gig, she would have picked someone suitable. After all, she'd hired me.

Feeling more confident about the new hire, I went into the hallway and got a whiff of a familiar Spumanti-garlic odor.

No. It has to be coming from Nizza downstairs.

I entered the lobby, and that confidence took a swift hit—like a missile to a submarine. Because the first thing I saw was the back of a fuzzy lavender-and-gold sweater and a zebra skirt that matched the chaise lounge Napoleon had conquered. Dressing like my bordello-chic living room was a tactical error for any day on the job, but on the first day it was a major blunder.

The woman signed what I feared was a contract on the reception desk and turned.

I saw red—as in curls—and a torpedo struck what was left of my confidence. As the missile emergency siren blared, I spit out one word. "YOU."

"Oh, Gawd." Ladonna threw up her bangle-braceleted arms and looked at Veronica. "It's the hair-puller's daughter. Her mom is the one who wrecked my VW Bug and refused to cawgh up the fifty bucks for a new CarLash."

Veronica's face fell. "Oh, Franki. That was your mother?"

I dressed down Ladonna first. "You don't have to be a mechanic to know that losing an eyelash does not constitute a wrecked car." Then I addressed Veronica. "*Now* do you see why the lunch with Bradley's family could go really, really wrong?"

She looked at the floor, and David and The Vassal tiptoed out of the door.

Ladonna crossed her arms against her chest and rubbed her biceps. "My poor Carmela looked like she'd been kicked in the face, remember, Veronica?"

My confidence began to take on seawater. "Is that the name of your car?"

"Yeh, *Carmela*." Her face went as soft as her fuzzy sweater. "Adorable, isn't it?"

Not if my nonna finds out she shares a name with the hussy VW Bug. I looked at Veronica. "And what's with the 'remember'? You weren't there when the hair-pulling happened."

"I told you, I met Ladonna at Thibodeaux's Tavern."

Ladonna pushed up her sleeves, her bangles jangling. "I was so upset that I had to have a drink before I could drive home. Veronica and I got to tawkin' at the bar, and I told her about you and your mother."

Her tawkin' sounded more like squawkin', and I was sure she'd squawked to the whole tavern.

Veronica frowned at me. "Why didn't your mom just pay her for the damage?"

"Because Ladonna, who is also a hair-puller, ruined her sixty-dollar hairdo."

Ladonna gave her curls a bump. "If anything, I improved it. Her hair looked like a jaggerbush before I got my hands on it."

My lips wrinkled. "A what?"

"Yous know. A bush with thorns."

I didn't, but I got the picture—and it was accurate. "Here." I pulled cash from my front pocket. "Get your car's eyelash fixed."

She took the money. "I already did, but this'll get her some crystal eyeliner."

The last of my confidence sank down, down, toward the seafloor.

Ladonna rose and grabbed her purse from the reception desk. As she put the money inside, I noticed that it had red lips and false eyelashes like her VW Bug. My confidence hit sea bottom, and I cast Veronica a final, silent plea for help.

She avoided my gaze and gestured to the two opposing couches in the middle of the room. "Let's start over, shall we?"

I took a seat, but I didn't make any promises. Ladonna had spoiled my binge-eaten breakfast, not only because of the shock of learning that she was our new PI but also because her tight red curls had brought back the nightmare of the baby salami bomboniere.

Veronica sat across from me. "Franki, I've told Ladonna a lot about you. What would you like to know about her?"

I wanted to ask why she had a deep-seated need to put overly made-up human faces on inanimate objects, but for Veronica's sake, I opted for the standard "Where are you from?"

"Whaaat? Yous think I have an *ack*cent or something?"

Lacks self-awareness—strike one. "Just a bit."

"It's because I'm from Scranton, in Lackawanna County, but I'm from Philly originally. My husband, Rocco, and I moved here with the twins, Gino and Gina, after Hurricane Katrina. He's in construction."

Veronica shot me a triumphal brow arch. "See that, Franki? She's been here longer than you."

I wished I had a cookie to crunch.

Veronica turned to Ladonna. "I told Franki that you'll be shadowing her on the Angelo LaRocca case."

"That reminds me," Ladonna patted the couch, "I've been thinking about the band name, The Marsala Maroons. Do you think the Marsala part is a reference to the Marsalis family? They are New Orleans jazz royalty."

This is the best a Sicilian PI can do? I cleared my throat to clear out the criticism. "The Marsala Maroons came before the Marsalis family. The name could refer to the wine since there was a bottle on Angelo's night table."

"Ooooh." She tapped her chin. "Veronica said there was also a maroon Virgin Mary candle. That's my middle name."

Gives extraneous information about self—strike two. "There are lots of Marys."

"But not Virgin Marys. Well, the Italian version, Maria Vergine." Her smile was beatific. "Ladonna Maria Vergine Cuccuzza."

There goes praying to the Virgin for a new PI.

"Also, yesterday, Rocco and I took Haunted Herstory's tour on the Axeman."

I nestled against the couch cushions. "You mean, Haunted *History*?"

"No, this company focuses on women in history."

I hadn't heard of them, but it sounded like a good fit for hippy Pam. "Why would they do an Axeman tour? Even his name has 'man' in it."

"Because there's a theory that he was a sadist, whose real target was the ladies of those grocery stores and that he only killed men when they tried to stop him from killing their wives and daughters."

I shifted to an upright position. The ex-grocery store fourplex I lived in had nothing but ladies—well, *women*, anyway—Glenda, Veronica, me, and, unfortunately, my mom and nonna. "Whose theory is that?"

"Our tour guide, such a sweet woman, couldn't remember who said it."

That "sweet" ruled out Pam, but the "couldn't remember" sounded like another guide I knew. "Was her name Windy Spitter, by chance?"

Ladonna snapped her fingers and pointed. "Have you taken one of her tours?"

"No, I met her at Matassa's Market this morning."

"Well, she's real patient with questions."

Probably because of those early-morning daiquiris. "Did she take you to any of the old grocery stores?"

"A couple, but she couldn't remember all their addresses, so we wound up at Fat Tuesday on Bourbon Street."

I smirked. Fat Tuesday served nothing but frozen drinks, like daiquiris.

Veronica smiled, satisfied. "Well, I'm impressed by your initiative, Ladonna."

I rolled my eyes right as Veronica laid hers on me. "Franki, I'm surprised you didn't think to ask Windy about the Axeman."

I couldn't admit that I'd gotten distracted by ten kinds of choco-late-hazelnut spread. "I got sidetracked by her jazz history tour."

Ladonna's eyes widened with know-it-all excitement. "Oh, but the Axeman is all about jazz, and so is Angelo's murder, evidently."

Shows me up in front of the boss—strike three. Definitely out.

"In fact," Ladonna continued her know-it-all roll, "Windy said there's another theory that the Axeman was getting revenge against Italian-Americans because black jazz musicians weren't getting their due credit for inventing jazz."

I cleared my throat. "She mentioned that to me too, and I asked Wendell about it earlier, but I'm not convinced that was a factor in Angelo's murder. Almost no one knows that Italians were involved in the creation of jazz, so the idea of a revenge killing feels a century too late."

Veronica looked at Ladonna. "Do you have any guesses about the motive?"

"When a crime like this happens, I think you need to know about the victim's extended families and their connections in the community before you form any opinions."

As reluctant as I was to admit it, she had a point. Angelo was only ten years old when the trumpet was stolen, so the theft would have affected his father more than him.

"What are you suggesting?" Veronica asked. "A rivalry of some sort?"

Ladonna shrugged. "Or bad blood, a vendetta, even an oath. All I know is that when I lived on the West Side in Scranton, we Italians knew everything about each other, good and bad. If one of our kids was hiding something, which my sweet babies would never do, we could find out what was going on at the deli or the nail salon or the drycleaner..."

Or at a rival grocery store.

∾

LADONNA STROLLED the length of Greco's Grocery, taking in the floor-to-ceiling goods, and she fit right in with her Spumanti-and-garlic perfume. "What a charming mini-mart."

I eyed the dimly lit room. Greco's was more chilling than charming, and it had nothing to do with the cold storage shelves. Instead of a food market, it looked like a creepy antique shop where something terrifying would pop out, like a marionette named Ichabod who kicked and cursed, but without the help of his puppeteer. Even the smell was disturbing—a mix of mildew, rancid flour, and rotting meat. If it hadn't been for familiar food brands on the shelves, I would have sworn the place was much as it had been during the Axeman's rampage.

I scanned the store for an employee. It was a two-story building, and there was a door marked Gifts next to a staircase on the back wall, but my gut told me to stay by the entrance with the hanging cured meats. Despite the threat of salami bomboniere, Italian cold cuts made me feel safe, kind of like a father—one of many issues I might want to discuss with a psychiatrist.

"Did you need some help?"

I almost jumped out of my salami casing. The brash female voice had emerged from the shadows around a cash register directly across from me. I squinted and spotted a woman in her late fifties with dyed-black 50s-style hair, a startlingly thick face and neck, and a mole above her mustached lip that was too plump to be a beauty mark. I'd heard of wallflowers, but blending in to grocery shelves was extreme.

Ladonna approached the counter. "Oooh, you're craftin'." She waved a bangled arm. "Franki, come see."

I ignored her request. She acted like the woman was spinning gold, and I'd just gotten an idea at a shelf that was as momentous as Reese's marriage of peanut butter and chocolate—*I could dip hazelnut Quadratini wafers in Nutella.*

Ladonna held up what looked like a blue ceramic hamburger stuffed with green olives. "Is this a round hoagie?"

"Hoagie?" I practically hacked up the word. "How long did you say you've been in New Orleans?"

The cashier put on a pair of green cat-eye readers and picked up a tube of glue. "They're mini muffulettas. It's a sesame seed bread from Sicily, but the sandwich is a New Orleans invention—ham, salami, mortadella, Swiss, provolone, and olive salad."

"Sounds like a Schlotzky's."

My head snapped back, and the cashier's did the same. Veronica was wrong about Ladonna—she wasn't Sicilian-American; she was Space Alien.

The woman glued wiggle eyes and orange lips on the top of the bun. "Back when the French Quarter had an Italian section, they used a smaller version of the muffuletta bread, about the size of this plaster version, to make a spleen sandwich called the *vastedda*."

I stuck out my tongue. "I can see why those didn't catch on. Eating spleen is disgusting."

Her puffy face shot forward. "It's tradition, which is important.

And who are you, anyway? A New York City food critic?"

Ladonna's pink lips thinned. "You are kind of finicky, Franki."

I wanted to point out that she'd known me for all of an hour, but I didn't want Olive to ask questions about who we were and why we were together. Instead, I held up the Quadratini. "Would a finicky restaurant critic buy this?"

Olive's face receded into her neck, and she turned to her crafting.

She was confrontational—the type who could easily have a feud with a rival grocer, like Angelo LaRocca. I did a quick check of the package expiration date and headed to the register. Her nametag confirmed what I'd suspected.

Olive studied me over the rim of her readers as she screwed the cap on the glue. "Ask me why I know so much about muffulettas."

"Uh, because you own an Italian market."

She looked at Ladonna. "Did I say *tell* me why I know so much about muffulettas?"

"She definitely said *ask*."

I laid a look on Ladonna not unlike the crazy-eyed one on the muffuletta. "Thanks for clarifying."

"Well?" Olive pressed. "Are you going to ask me?"

One thing I was sure of—this Olive was a nut. "Why do you know so much about the sandwiches?"

"Because I'm a distant relative of Frank Di Nicola, the Muffuletta Man. He sold them door-to-door in the early 1900s."

I saw a chance to turn the conversation to the investigation. "I wonder if he knew a Sicilian jazz quartet called The Marsala Maroons."

She looked at the counter. "Never heard of them."

For someone who was so precise about questions, I found her denial intriguing since I'd asked whether her ancestor had known of the band, not her.

Ladonna stared at the blue muffuletta. "How much are you chargin' for this one?"

I wanted to cram the thing in her mouth for diverting the conversation back to the sandwiches.

Olive removed her readers. "They're not for sale. They're throws for a women's Mardi Gras dance troupe I belong to called the Muff-a-lottas."

"Shoot. I really love their little eyes and lips."

I snorted. *She would.*

Ladonna held up a muffuletta. "These would make great bomboniere."

My blood cooled to cured-meat temperature. *Surely she hasn't been talking to my hair-puller mother or Rosalie's disbanded committee?*

Olive pointed to the back room. "I have some bomboniere in the gift shop, but I couldn't sell these without the Muff-a-lottas' permission. Oh, you should see our costumes." She stepped from behind the counter, and she was as squat and round as a muffuletta. "We dress like 50s diner waitresses. We carry food trays and wear red sparkly hats, cat-eye glasses, and saddle oxfords. And instead of poodle skirts, ours have a little muffuletta on them."

I tried to look interested. "Yeah, I saw you guys during Halloween in the Krewe of BOO! parade."

"We used makeup to look like we were moldy." Her features contorted, and she clenched her chubby fists. "Ugh. I wish I had more time to do the charity events. We're serving food to the homeless this weekend, but I can't go."

Ladonna leaned an arm on the counter. "I hear ya. I'm so busy with Rocco and the twins, I couldn't work it in."

"Oh, this muffuletta never found her po' boy," Olive said, sticking with the sandwich theme. "I just have a deadbeat big brother, Tony. He's sixty but still acts sixteen."

The same age as Angelo, Lucky, and Ric. Were the Grecos the brother and sister Luigi had mentioned who were part of the big falling out?

Ladonna examined her manicure. "All men are children, I don't care how old they are. Does he help you out here in the store?"

"He's supposed to, but he's been MIA for two weeks, probably on a bender. But that's only one of the reasons I can't go. I need to come up with a fun stage name for my diner waitress nametag, like Peggy Sue or Bunny."

I thought of the obvious. "Olive?"

She sniffed. "Did I say I needed a *name* or a *stage name*?"

I held up my hand before Ladonna could answer. "I know, I know, you definitely said *stage name*, but olives are in muffulettas, so your name works. You could also translate your last name and go by Greek Olive."

Olive's mouth opened in horror. "A *Greek* olive in an *Italian* muffuletta? That's sandwich sacrilege."

Ladonna scratched her head. "Yeh, with a name like that, the Muff-a-lottas would probably kick her out."

I gave up. They were a tough crowd, and I had a case to investigate. "Since we're talking about Mardi Gras groups, do any Indians shop here?"

Olive's head sank into her neck. "Are you a police officer?"

I was startled—and suspicious. *How had I gone from restaurant critic to cop? Is it because she has a reason to fear the authorities?* "We're PIs, investigating the murder of Angelo LaRocca."

She took a step back. "Why would you come here?"

Ladonna put her hand on the counter. "Honestly, hon, it's because we heard the two of you were feuding."

"We argued because he kept a shipment of Marsala that was supposed to be delivered to me, but that doesn't make me a murderer."

Was it one of the bottles on his night table? If so, did it matter? "No one is calling you a murderer. I just want to know if you have any thoughts on why someone killed Angelo and stole Louis Prima's trumpet."

She put on her readers. "Everyone in the neighborhood knows what happened. Some crook heard that Angelo had the trumpet and killed him for it. I'm sure it's already for sale on the black market."

"I'm assuming your father knew Angelo's since they would've been competitors. Did your father ever mention him? Or Joe Caruso, since the trumpet was stolen from his store?"

"My father, Vito, was a drunk, and I spent most of my life trying not to talk to him."

"What about Ric Caruso? I spoke to him this morning, and he seems to know you."

She stopped so suddenly that the mole above her lip wobbled.

I waited for her to speak, but she didn't, so I pressed on. "Ric is about your age, so I'm sure you and your brother, Tony, must've known him."

"Yeah, him and about sixty other kids from elementary school. Now if you're done shopping, why don't you pay for your Quadratini and go? I've got muffulettas to finish."

She hadn't answered my questions. Nevertheless, I handed her a five. "You really like those sandwiches, don't you?"

"Can't stand 'em. I'm a vegetarian."

And she gave me lip about eating spleen.

She jerked open the register. "You got a penny?"

I didn't because of that damn fountain and Nadezhda and Theodora. "I don't."

She sighed and counted the change. "Anyone who eats meat should be slaughtered, just like the animals they're consuming."

Is she violent? Or just advocating it? "Then why do you sell them?"

"Family tradition. It's in my DNA." She slapped the change into my hand and picked up a muffuletta throw. Her face softened. "And who can resist these little mugs?"

Ladonna touched her tight curls. "I'm with you, Olive. I mean, about those darling faces, not the meat. Once a week, I have to have my sausage and peppers with a nice glass of Chianti. And Rocco and the twins would kill me if I refused to make that dish."

Olive slammed the cash drawer. "The next time you eat sausage, you should think of the darling face of the pig." She bagged my food and thrust it at me. "People who slaughter them should get the pigs' feet shoved down their throats."

The Quadratini wafers crunched between my fingers.

Lucky Mistretta had choked on a bone from a pig's foot. *Is it coincidence that she mentioned shoving them down people's throats? Or was it a telling slip of the tongue?*

9

"A grocery store?" Glenda wobbled on her pink Marabou stripper slippers and grabbed her front door jamb for support. "With food?"

My landlady was infamous for not eating, but this was ridiculous. "That's what grocery stores sell, digestible items with nutrients." As admittedly questionable evidence, I held up my breakfast of the hazelnut Quadratini I'd bought at Greco's Grocery the day before.

She narrowed pink-Marabou-lashed eyes at the package. "I'm aware of what they sell, Miss Franki. But when I bought this fourplex, the realtor told me that it used to be a brothel, hence the décor. Now what am I supposed to do?"

"Redecorate." I said it as a command to avoid any question. "I'll ask Bob if he can upgrade it like your #stripperwear."

"Mm-*mmmm*, sugar. Bob Simpson cannot know about this grocery store business. It's so unsexy that he's likely to call off the photoshoots, and we've got one scheduled in my boudoir at ten-thirty this morning. I'm going to do a stripper everyday make-up tutorial."

She looked down, and in violation of my policy to never look at Glenda's midsection while I was eating, my gaze followed. Instead of her fully sheer robe, this one had a smattering of rhinestones in place of pasties and, in place of panties, a lone tuft of pink Marabou.

"Bob picked out this robe for the shoot. What do you think?"

I wanted to say that I wished he'd picked out something to go underneath, but there was no point. "It's sparkly and sheer."

"You don't think it's too much?"

"Too much *what*?"

"Rhinestones. I feel so covered up."

"You're so not. But while we're talking about your costumes, did you happen to throw out any yellow-and-orange ostrich feathers?"

She gave a flip of her platinum hair. "I did not, and don't mention it again, or Bob's likely to have another hissy fit and quit. Now let me get a cigarette for my ring holder, then I'll let you in to your new digs."

I nodded and stayed on the balcony outside her apartment, munching a fistful of Quadratini sans Nutella. I'd slathered the last of my jar on the first half of the bag, and I should have stopped then. But I needed to stress-eat something before my lunch with Bradley and his family.

Glenda exited the apartment and strutted the length of the balcony.

I kept my eyes on the back of her head to avoid finding out what was covering her behind and whether it stayed put while she walked.

She stopped at the door of the costume closet and eyed my hazelnut wafers. "You be careful with those around my costumes. This isn't Hotella Nutella."

Emotion welled in my throat and slid to my belly as smooth as the chocolate-hazelnut spread. "Is that a real place?"

"It was a pop-up in Napa Valley, but it's gone now. I'm surprised you didn't hear about it."

It was a good thing I hadn't. The place sounded like the Eagles' song "Hotel California" incarnate, because I would have checked in and been unable to leave.

Glenda opened the door, and I entered behind her. The apartment-turned-costume-closet had the same layout as my apartment below, but so crammed with props, clothes, and "acsexories" that it was hard to tell.

When we entered the bedroom, my jaw went slack à la The Vassal. In the middle of floor-to-ceiling clothing racks stood a five-foot-tall go-cup, not too much bigger than the size they sold to tourists—and Windy Spitter—on Bourbon Street.

Glenda gave a low chuckle. "I know what you're thinking, sugar— what's a sophisticated stripper like *moi* doing with a plain old go-cup prop?"

Actually, I was wondering whether she expected me to sleep in the thing like I had the champagne glass in her living room.

"It was my first prop when I started out in the business, just little old Glenda O'Brien in a common cup. I used it as motivation to work my way up to the stage name Lorraine Lamour and a champagne flute."

"Everyone needs a source of inspiration," I said, although I thought it was odd that hers was glassware.

"Anyhow, I'll clear some space after my boudoir shoot. Now that Bob has me wearing rhinestones and peacock feathers, I intend to box up the sequins and goose-feathers. But if he says one thing about my vinyl or metal, I'm putting my six-inch-heeled foot down. After all, a woman's got to pamper herself."

I couldn't argue with the pampering part, just the materials. I popped a couple of Quadratini and glanced at a toolbox on the floor. "You're doing some repairs too?"

"That's another one of my early props. It was for my Handy Woman routine. Open at your own risk."

Uh-uh. Too risky.

"I tell you, looking around this room brings back so many memories."

I stayed silent, hoping she wouldn't share any.

"Would you just look at this?" She used the tone of someone who was about to show their baby blanket, but instead, she held up a string of paperclips.

"What is it?"

"My first thong."

I looked at the toolbox and wondered whether there was anything in it that would get her to stop sharing.

Glenda hung the paperclips on a hanger. "Everyone was wearing them in the 1970s because of the punk rock scene. In the 1980s, we had big hair and leg warmers."

"I guess you couldn't wear shoulder pads with pasties."

"Sure we did. The strap-on kind. Fringe, spikes, beads, you name it. Then in the Nineties we all got our wings thanks to the Victoria's Secret Fashion Show." She gestured to a black pair in a corner that I'd seen her wear before. "That was after the grunge look, of course, when we were wearing thrift-store thongs."

I closed the Quadratini bag.

She ran her hand over three small Slippery-When-Wet signs linked by chains. "Bob has been looking for creative dress ideas like this one to make me the influencer of the decade. He suggested we look at a hardware store or a junkyard."

Maybe I don't want Bob redecorating my apartment. "Awesome. So, I have to get ready to meet Bradley's mother and grandmother. What do I need to do to finalize the rental?"

"Sign the agreement and pay me fifteen hundred and fifty dollars."

"You said the rent was a grand."

She struck a Mae West pose with her unlit ring-finger cigarette. "There's been a complication, Miss Franki. When I told Nadezhda you wanted to rent it, she offered to go as high as fifteen hundred."

I smashed the Quadratini bag, imagining the crunch was Nadezhda's greedy fingers, and shoved it in my purse. Not only had she stolen my penny from the street, she'd caused me to lose fifty-five thousand more. "What's wrong with the house she inherited from Lucky?"

"It's above the liquor store, where his family has lived for generations, and it's a real pigsty."

That's probably why Nadezhda fed him the pigs' feet bones—unless that mad Muff-a-lotta, Olive Greco, killed him. I signed the contract and pulled a check from my pocket.

"While you're at it, sugar, tack on the three hundred and fifty you owe me for having an extra tenant in your apartment. Your rental agreement only allows for one."

Shock rendered me rigid. "My mom and nonna are guests—uninvited, but guests nevertheless."

"Not if you're living in my costume closet. They're renters now, so they'll need to sign a separate agreement acknowledging The Visitor Policy."

I stared at her. She couldn't possibly think that my mom and nonna would have gentleman callers, much less more than two per person at one time.

Actually, she could.

I sighed and filled out the check. The wedding my parents were paying for was going to cost me a fortune.

Nadezhda entered the bedroom wearing a sparkly red dress, purple snakeskin slingbacks, and resting Russian face.

I matched her expression. "Come to jack up my rent some more?"

Glenda plucked the check from my hand. "Miss Nadezhda called to tell me the gory details of Angelo LaRocca's crime scene, and I mentioned that you were signing the rental agreement this morning."

"And I vant to show you sometink." Nadezhda pulled a record from a snakeskin tote that matched her heels. "I find 'Ragù Rag' in closet at home. Like one from gramophone."

That record was too old and obscure for both Lucky and Angelo to have it by coincidence. "The Marsala Maroons are connected to the case, but I can't figure out how. Maybe the Jazz Museum would give me some insight."

Glenda blew out just-lit cigarette smoke. "My mother might know."

My head spun like I'd chugged from the giant go-cup. "*You* have a *mother*?"

Nadezhda opened her mouth and made a sound like a Kalashnikov firing bullets. "And she tink she can solve murder."

Apparently, that shooting sound was her cackle.

Glenda pulled an ashtray from a windowsill. "My mother's been alive for ninety-three years and kicking for seventy-seven."

Nadezhda nodded. "She dance like ashtray voman."

Confused, I stared at the vintage ashtray in Glenda's hand. A woman in a bustier, on her back, with stockinged legs in the air. "Your mother's a stripper too?"

"Lord, no, child." Glenda rolled pink Marabou-ed eyes. "She's a prude of the highest order."

My next guess was unlikely, but she *had* said *order*. "She's not a nun, is she?"

"Worse, sugar. A burlesque dancer."

Nadezhda's resting Russian face went rigid. "And mother-in-law."

Glenda nodded. "That's right, Miss Franki. My mother introduced us."

I jerked like I'd been kicked by Dita Von Teese. The issue wasn't with Glenda's burlesque-dancer mother being a Mistretta, it was that both Glenda and Nadezhda were involved in the case, and with Ladonna Cuccuzza in tow, the investigation threatened to turn into a vaudeville act as exaggerated as Glenda's go-cup.

"I'll call her, sugar. Now that I know this fourplex was an Italian grocery store, I'm a little distressed about this Axeman character, not to mention the fact that I don't own an ex-brothel, so I'll set up a meeting and go with you."

My cauchemar nightmares were coming true. "You've got to do your influencer shoots. I can handle the case on my own."

Nadezhda fired a round of laugh bullets. "How? You don't even know Glenda have mother."

I spun on her like a Russian squat dancer. "I wouldn't laugh, if I were you. I haven't ruled you out as a suspect in either of the murders."

Her eyebrows shot up to her maroon spikes. "You tink I kill husband?"

Glenda ashed her cigarette in the tray formed by the dancer's skirt. "Really, Miss Franki. She loved Lucky, right Miss Nadezhda?"

"*Da.* That piece of idiot."

Her comment didn't seem loving, but she was Russian, so it could have been a term of endearment. "Did you do the Heimlich maneuver on Lucky when he was choking?"

"Who get arms around big galute?" She jerked down her shirt. "Anyvay, I vork downstairs in store vhen he choke."

I sat on the toolbox to process the revelation. "You weren't with him when he died?"

"Vy you shocked?"

"Because I went to Greco's Grocery, and the owner, Olive Greco, made a comment about shoving pig bones down people's throats."

Nadezhda didn't have to move a facial muscle to scowl. "That voman is ass dandruff."

I tilted my head. "What?"

"You heard. Dandruff from ass big insult in Russia." She looked at Glenda. "It not insult here?"

"No, but it should be, Miss Nadezhda."

It *was* pretty good. "Did you and Lucky have a run-in with Olive too? I heard she had a feud with Angelo LaRocca over Marsala."

"She fight vit Lucky about Marsala."

Glenda stubbed out her cigarette. "That's right, Miss Franki. Olive didn't get a Marsala shipment and threatened Lucky when he refused to sell her any of his stock."

I would have paced, but the room was too crowded. The bottle of Marsala on Angelo's night table definitely had something to do with his murder. *The question is, did Olive?*

"Keep it together, Franki," I said to my reflection in the bathroom mirror at Emeril's Delmonico restaurant. "This is just a getting-acquainted lunch, and the introductions went well. Plus, the jazz trio in the bar will drown out a lot of the conversation."

But no matter what I told myself, I didn't feel better. We'd just been served the appetizers, which meant that I still had to get through the entrees and dessert without my nonna insulting anyone or my mom pulling anyone's hair. And it didn't help that I was pale, my hands trembled, and I had a raging headache. Something was wrong, and it was more than nerves and Amato family damage.

I leaned forward to examine my eyes and grimaced in horror.

A freakish vein had erupted on my forehead.

The greenish-blue line, together with my humidity-frizzed hair, led me to an inescapable conclusion. "I don't look like Bradley's future bride, I look like The Bride of Frankenstein."

I opened my purse to get my concealer and saw the crumpled Quadratini bag. I pulled it out to throw it away and noticed a detail I'd missed earlier—a small cup with coffee beans.

"Dear God, I got espresso, not hazelnut."

Frantic, I checked the ingredients. The wafers contained caffeine and based on the comically small serving size, I'd eaten enough to fuel a Mardi Gras krewe—and the tractors that pulled their floats.

My eyes darted to the mirror.

The vein had started to pulsate.

I gasped and pointed. "You stop that."

But the vein didn't listen. It picked up the tempo as if to keep pace with the song the jazz trio was playing—Louis Armstrong's "Where the Blues were Born in New Orleans."

"Yep," my tone hit a bitter note, "my blues were born right here in Emeril's Delmonico, the day Bradley's mother and grandmother discovered that he was going to marry Frankenstein's woman."

I pulled my hair over my forehead and exited the bathroom into a hallway that overlooked the French-Creole dining room and adjoining bar. I stopped in the shadow of a staircase to spy on the table.

No one was talking, and the seating arrangements only accentuated what looked like a Hatfield-McCoy standoff. The Hartmanns were on one side of the table, and the Amatos were on the other. And in terms of attire, my family was clearly the bad guys. Bradley's mother, Lillian, and his grandmother, Cordelia, wore white-and-cream silk dresses that blended with the understated décor. But my mom's frilly navy number and fascinator made her look like a regular at the Kentucky Derby, and my nonna's veiled hat and baroque cross necklace were what a Mafia don's widow would wear to his funeral.

Clenching my fists to hide the tremors, I entered the dining room.

Bradley rose and, under the watchful eyes of his mother and grandmother, pulled out my chair. When I was seated, he gave me a peck on the temple.

"Francesca," Lillian drawled in an accent as posh as her ice-blonde side lob, "I had our server bring you a brandy alexander."

The white drink brought back Wendell's voodoo warning. But even if Bradley's mother was a caplata trying to turn me into a zombie, I was so desperate for something to calm me that I'd drink anything but an espresso martini. I took a sizable swallow.

Lillian touched her son's shoulder. "I was just saying to Bradley that when you went to the powder room, you looked positively green around the gills."

My hand went to my forehead. *Was that a crack about my Bride-of-Frankenstein vein? Or my olive skin?*

Bradley cleared his throat. "While you were gone, the waiter told us something that you'll find interesting. Before Emeril Lagasse bought the restaurant, it was owned by a Sicilian immigrant named Anthony LaFranca, who lived upstairs with his family."

I was glad Delmonico's hadn't been an Italian grocery store because, thanks to the Quadratini, I was already jacked up enough. "Well, it's a beautiful place, perfect for events like showers and rehearsal dinners."

My mother's eyes lit up like the chandeliers, and the feathers on her fascinator shook. "I thought you said we couldn't talk about wedding stuff."

I froze à la my brandy alexander. I'd made a terrible error, like when a parent tells a child no and goes back on their word.

She gripped her wineglass stem, preparing to give me and Bradley the squeeze. "I'm hoping these two lovebirds will get married in the bride's hometown," she shot a look at Lillian and Cordelia, "since that *is* tradition."

Lillian gave a laugh as cold as a Massachusetts winter. "Yes, well, Hartmann family tradition dictates that Bradley wed in Boston, preferably in the Dome Room at the Lenox Hotel."

That took me aback. Bradley hadn't mentioned any wedding traditions. But because he'd been married once before, and to a society woman like his mother, I couldn't help but wonder if that's where they'd tied the knot.

He glanced from me to his mother. "Franki and I haven't decided where we're getting married."

"When you do, make sure it's in Boston."

I took a slug of zombie-maker. My mom's style might be garlic press, but Bradley's mom's was crab-leg cracker.

Cordelia's gray eyes glinted like her sterling-silver hair. "An equally important choice is the registry. Which will it be, Francesca, Bergdorf or Saks?"

Those stores were too pricey for my family and friends. "I'm not sure I'll register anywhere, especially since my side of the wedding party will mostly give us envelopes of money at the reception."

Lillian coughed and gulped some martini, and Cordelia, who was shaking like my mother's fascinator, patted her back.

I glanced at the band. The way the conversation was going, I half-expected the trio to break into a hair-raising rendition of "The Mysterious Axman's Jazz."

Nonna raised a finger. "In-a Sicilia, the most-a important thing is-a the bomboniere, even-a more than-a the groom."

Seeing the Hartmanns' shock, I forced a chuckle. "She's kidding."

"No, I'm-a not."

Cordelia mustered a smile as cool as her pearls. "I suppose bonbons would be a nice touch, provided there's a palate cleanser before the cake is served. I suggest deLafée of Switzerland's gold chocolates, unless you know a suitable chocolatier in Italy?"

Nonna looked at me. "Is-a she speaking-a English?"

I glanced at Cordelia. "Um, *bomboniere* is the Italian word for wedding favors."

Lillian touched her diamond necklace. "In that case, the only choice is Tiffany's. They have a selection of gifts for two hundred and fifty dollars and under."

The Amato heads retracted as though hit by a hurricane gust.

"Actually," I slid lower into my seat, "my mom was thinking mini salami from our deli."

The Hartmann heads recoiled as though blown by a blistering nor'easter.

Lillian's face turned the color of her Royal Red Shrimp Cocktail. "This is starting to sound like *Tony n' Tina's Wedding.*"

I went rigid at the reference. *Tony n' Tina's Wedding* was immersive theater with the audience serving as guests at a dysfunctional Italian-American reception.

Nonna pinched her fingers together. "Who are-a Tony and-a Tina? They sound-a like a nice-a couple."

"It's a play, Nonna, about an Italian couple getting married."

"They get-a paid for that?"

"Yes, quite a bit."

"*Madonna!* I'll-a pretend to get-a married if they give-a me some cash."

Bradley laughed and reached for the Stuffed Boudin Balls.

Nonna pointed at him. "Don't-a forget your cayenne-a pepper, eh?" She shot an accusatory stare at Cordelia. "Your grand-a-son's got-a the weak-a digestion."

"I do not." Bradley shouted as though he'd been called impotent.

Cordelia looked down her nose. "My grandson has refined taste. He's not used to heavy Italian cooking."

Nonna's face went as black as her mourning-lunch dress. "I'll-a show-a you heavy."

Instinctively, I kicked her handbag under the table before she could wave it at Cordelia, and my big toe connected with what I'd always assumed was a portable statuette of the Virgin Mary. I let out a scream that sounded like The Bride of Frankenstein's when she first met her monster groom.

Lillian's hands rose in surrender. "Please, let's not quarrel in public. I can solve this." She reached into her purse and pulled out a checkbook. "Bradley's father and I will pay for the wedding."

The chill that fell over the Amato side of the table was colder than the Steak Tartare, and it didn't help that my shriek had silenced not only the entire dining room, but also the jazz trio.

The musicians rose to take a break, and I decided that it was past time for Bradley and me to do the same. "Can I speak to you in private?"

He placed his napkin on the table. "Of course."

Because of my injured toe, I limped like Igor to the hallway, where I spun on my fiancé. "Could you please reign in your mother and grandmother?"

He let out a breath and massaged his forehead.

I gasped. "Are you making fun of my vein?"

"What? No, look, I'm sorry about the check incident, but they're trying to help."

"Help?" I flailed my arms. "They want to buy the rights to our wedding."

His lips went flat. "What about your mom and nonna?"

I wobbled backward as if Hurricane Hartmann had struck again. "What about them?"

"Come on, Franki. We both know that they've overstepped their bounds in the wedding planning."

Not only had they overstepped them, they'd stomped on them like grapes in a vat. "Yes, but they're paying for it—"

"And my mother wants to contribute," he interrupted. "We *are* going to be a family."

I decided to try my mother's line on him. "Yes, but we're not a family yet."

His brow shot up as his chin went down.

I should know better than to quote a hair puller. "What I mean is, until we're married, I'm their daughter. It's a point of pride for them to pay for my wedding."

"And I respect that, but you *did* agree to let my family have some input."

"About the planning, not the paying."

He sighed and shoved his hands into his pockets. "You're right. I'll tell my mother to keep her checkbook in her purse, but be forewarned that she'll go for broke with the rehearsal dinner."

My eye joined my forehead vein in a riotous round of pulsating. With the Hartmann's wealth, going for broke on the rehearsal dinner could reduce my wedding to the equivalent of a hobo cookout at the railroad tracks.

Bradley glanced at a group of customers coming in the door. "I'd better go back to the table. But do me a favor." He gave me a pointed look. "Tone down the My-Big-Fat-Italian wedding stuff."

I pulled back as though I'd been slapped. "We're Italian-American, Bradley. Is there a problem with that?"

"Babe," he took me by the shoulders and stared into my eyes, "you know that's one of the things I love about you and your family. But salami bomboniere?" He snort-laughed. "Seriously?"

He returned to the dining room, and I flounced onto a bench beside the bathrooms. If he thought I'd been exaggerating about my mom and the mini salami, we were in bigger trouble than I'd thought. And contrary to what he believed about his mother and grandmother, they weren't going to help in that department. If anything, the checkbook gesture would send my mom and nonna into wedding-planning overdrive—actually, over-overdrive.

My back went rigid as a terrifying realization struck me. *My mom and nonna could decide to stay even longer.*

No, no, no. I shook my head. If Theodora's mausoleum moss spell didn't send them packing, I would have to do it myself. Otherwise, I wasn't sure if there would *be* a wedding.

A member of the jazz trio exited the men's room, and an older band member in a fedora came to meet him. "Hey Lenny, do you remember that old Marsala Maroons number, 'Ragù Rag'?"

I gripped the bench.

Lenny took a glass from a passing waitress. "It's been a while, but I think I got it. Give me a minute to finish my water, and I'll be ready to go again."

The older man left, and I rose, pressed my twitching eyelid, and dragged my injured foot toward him. "Excuse me, sir. I heard you mention The Marsala Maroons, and I was wondering whether you could tell me anything about them."

His friendly eyes crinkled. "They were way before my time. But the American Italian Cultural Center has an exhibit on Italian jazz musicians, so you could check with them."

The same organization that arranged the second line for Angelo La Rocca. "Thank you, I will. But is there any special reason you're playing 'Ragù Rag'?"

"Yeah, to honor the passing of Angelo LaRocca. His father was in the band."

My heart began a ragtime beat.

"Come to think of it, I know the name of one of the other members, a trumpet player." He swallowed some water. "Vito Greco."

Olive and Tony's father?

10

"Did I, or did I not tell you that the Hartmann women had nerve?" My mother, galled and fists balled, paced the empty lobby of the American Italian Cultural Center.

I glanced around to see whether the ticket seller was coming. "Many times, so could you wait until we get home to tell me again?"

"No, I cannot, Francesca. Bradley's mother tried to buy us off just like she bought the lunch."

Nonna raised her chin and a finger, both indicators that she was about to shout. "What about-a Cordelia? *Quella ha la puzza sotto il naso.*"

My mom put her hands on her hips. "If anyone has the stink under her nose, Carmela, it's Lillian. Did you see the way she frowned at my fascinator?"

I eyed the blue goose feathers sprouting from her hat, and in all fairness to Lillian, Glenda's stylist-photographer, Bob Simpson, wouldn't have approved of it either.

A matronly woman with white hair and a dress similar to my nonna's approached the desk and clasped her hands. "Did you ladies come for the museum or our Italian language classes?"

"Definitely the museum." I angled a glare at my family. "I already get too much exposure to Italian."

The woman chuckled. "I heard. Ten dollars, please."

I handed her the cash. "Would it be possible to speak with the person who organized the second line for Angelo LaRocca?"

"That was Marcella, one of our volunteers." She handed me a ticket. "You'll find her in our gift shop."

My mother took my nonna by the arm. "Let's go see if they sell amaro, Carmela. That lunch gave me indigestion."

I was glad to see them go. Those two were wound tighter than spaghetti around a fork, which clashed with my Quadratini jitters.

I limped inside the museum. It was small, only a few rooms. I passed an exhibit on Italian immigration and spotted a wall labeled "Famous American Italians in Jazz." Louis Prima, Nick LaRocca, and the Original Dixieland Jazz Band were featured prominently, as was Sam Butera, but there was no mention of Angelo LaRocca's father, Roberto, or The Marsala Maroons.

Disappointed, I rounded the corner for the exit and bumped into a table—a permanent exhibit on Saint Joseph's Altar.

Go figure.

A lone lemon rolled from the top to the bottom tier and fell to the floor.

My eyes rose to the statue of Saint Joseph that towered over the display of bread, wine, and citrus fruits. *is he mocking me in light of the lunch fiasco? Or is he offering me a steal-a-lemon-land-a-proposal do-over?*

Whatever his intent, I didn't pick up the fallen fruit for fear of getting caught up in another cockamamie tradition.

I went to the gift shop.

My mom and nonna were huddled over a table with a forty-something female who had a blanket of black hair. She was as big as a New Orleans Saints linebacker and even wore the team colors—a gold shirt and black skirt with gold eyeshadow and heavy black eyeliner to match.

My mother's fascinator popped up. "Come here, Francesca. Marcella is showing us their bomboniere."

As I'd predicted, they were back on the planning wagon. I considered shutting them down, but I didn't want to hash out my personal business in front of a stranger. "I thought you wanted baby salami."

"After the way Lillian reacted? Oh, no. I'm going to show her that the Amatos can do high class too."

My eyes strained to look at her fascinator, but I wouldn't let them.

She moved to browse another table, and Nonna approached. "Franki, I know-a how to fix-a this mess. We bring-a in Maurizio Bonsignore, that-a marriage broker from-a Sicily. He find a back-a-up *fidanzato* to give-a Bradley a run for his-a Boston money."

Marcella pursed maroon-lined lips plastered with beige matte lipstick. "That's not a bad idea given his weak digestion."

My unlined lips went flat. Not surprisingly, I was the only one who hadn't wanted to discuss my personal business with a stranger. "We're not bringing in Maurizio, or any of the nonne's grandsons, for that matter. Bradley and I will be fine if our families just leave the wedding planning to us."

Marcella's gold eyelids pulled up in panic. "But you can't survive on lean meat and veggies. You're genetically wired for pasta and garlic bread."

I almost added Nutella, but I didn't want to encourage her. "I appreciate your concern, but this is none of your business."

Nonna pressed her hands in prayer and shook them at me. "Sure it-a is. I told-a her all about it."

"And your nonna's right about the location." Marcella pressed on as though I hadn't told her and my family to butt out. "You and Bradley need to compromise and get married in our Piazza d'Italia out back." She pointed to a poster of the postmodern piazza, which was neon red and green and gold with disembodied faces spitting water onto cobblestones. "They don't have anything like this beauty in Italy."

No, they didn't, but Disney's Epcot Center probably did.

"Now, if you want to show Bradley's uppity Boston family, here's what you do." She slid a pad of paper and a pen toward me, assuming I'd want to take notes. "For the meal, Martini & Rossi Spumante with veal scaloppini and angel hair pasta—because *angels*. The wedding cake is tiramisu—because *lady fingers*. And the entertainment is the Ragusa brothers doing their dueling accordion version of 'Funiculì, Funiculà'— because '*Funiculì, Funiculà*.'" She gave my arm a whack. "You tell me, what's classier than that?"

Too many things to list.

Nonna's nostrils flared with satisfaction. "And-a the ceremony is-a at Our-a Lady of-a Guadalupe Church."

"Because Father John." Marcella gave a lovesick sigh. "Now there's the kind of man you want to marry."

I scratched my neck. "Except that he's a priest."

"But so *bello*, no?" She batted her gold-shadowed lids. "Why are the good ones always taken?"

"Uh, you'll have to take that up with God."

"Oh, I do." Her tone had turned as sour as the lemons on the Saint Joseph's Altar exhibit. "Every. Single. Night."

I decided to shift the conversation to the investigation before someone got hurt. "So, the woman at the front desk told us you organized Angelo LaRocca's second line. Did you know him well?"

"Not really. He was such a private person. Plus, I split my grocery shopping between several other stores to support them. And I only shop Italian."

Nonna lifted a ceramic seashell with the holy family painted on it. "Marcella, how-a much is-a this?"

"That's for baptisms."

Thank God.

Marcella pulled back her hair blanket. "But a statuette of the Virgin Mary would be nice for a Catholic wedding."

I thought of the one in my nonna's purse that had cracked my toe —and of Ladonna Cuccuzza. "I'd rather throw Mardi Gras beads."

My mother shook her fascinator. "That's tacky, Francesca."

"Tackier than a pig with lipstick and a boa that poops Jordan almonds?"

She scurried to another table.

Judging from her guilty reaction, that busybody Rosalie hadn't disbanded the committee. I turned to Marcella, who was attaching refrigerator magnets to a display. "Do you ever shop at Greco's Grocery?"

"Sometimes. But Olive Greco's attitude makes it hard to shop in there, although a lot of that is her brother, Tony's, fault."

"Because he doesn't help out?"

Her black-and-gold eyes narrowed. "That and he pays her next to nothing."

"He pays her? Don't they both own Greco's?"

She picked up a magnet that said "*Vaffanculo* is Italian for have a nice day" and snorted. "Their father, Vito, left the store to Tony, since he's the favored son. And their mother died when they were toddlers, so she wasn't alive to stop him." Her lined lips formed a hard line. "That man always mistreated Olive. Prime example—Vito sent her to a Catholic boarding school after the incident, but Tony got to stay at home."

"Francesca," my mother held up a ceramic angel, "Gabriel with his trumpet would be perfect. It's religious, and he's mentioned in 'The Eyes of Texas.'"

Nonna waved off her suggestion. "He won't-a work. We don't-a wanna wait for him-a to blow that-a thing before Franki and-a Bradley get-a married."

I started to say something, but a magnet that said "I'm not yelling, I'm Italian" shamed me into swallowing my anger.

Marcella's smile was exaggerated, like her lip liner. "The Angel Gabriel is best for funerals, anyhow. Louis Prima has one on his mausoleum."

"You've been?"

"Of course. He did so much for Italians. He continued playing Italian songs during that awful Mussolini business and made Italy fashionable. And he started the whole Las Vegas entertainment industry."

I appreciated Prima's cultural efforts, but I wasn't so sure about the Vegas part. "Where is his grave?"

"At the Metairie Cemetery, where Angelo LaRocca is going to be buried."

My brow shot up, as did my interest. "Angelo hasn't been buried yet?"

"No, and I'm not sure why."

Was there a delay with the autopsy? Or is something else going on?

"Metairie is the perfect resting place for Angelo. Lots of important people are buried there, and I visit their graves to support them. But I only visit Italian."

She picked up a magnet that said "Whats'a matta wit you," which captured how I felt about her statement. "So, what was the 'incident' you mentioned a minute ago?"

"The theft of Louis Prima's trumpet from Caruso's Market."

She had my full attention. "Why would Vito Greco send Olive to a boarding school after the trumpet was stolen?"

"I always thought it was because he didn't care about her, but maybe she was too much for him to handle. Her mother died when she was young, and he and the other band members were in and out of the police station for a while."

"What band members? Louis Prima's?"

"No, The Marsala Maroons. They were playing with him at Caruso's Market when the trumpet was stolen."

The Quadratini caffeine was wearing off, so my heart ditched its earlier ragtime rhythm in favor of a cool jazz beat. "Can you tell me their names?"

"I can do you one better." She pointed to a wall of the gift shop labeled the Luke Fontana Gallery of Jazz Photography. "We have a picture of them outside LaRocca's Market that night."

I followed her to a photo of Louis Prima in the middle of four men, smiling and holding their instruments, including the twice-stolen trumpet.

What stories could that thing tell?

Marcella knelt and pulled back her veil of hair in preparation to unveil one of the many mysteries of Angelo LaRocca's murder. "This is Roberto LaRocca, then we have Lucky Mistretta Sr., and on the right, Joe Caruso and Vito Greco."

I didn't have any more questions for Marcella. However, I had quite a few for Ric Caruso and Olive Greco, starting with why neither of them had told me that their fathers were in a band together. But first, I had to drop off my mom and nonna and make another stop—one that was sure to blow my mind harder than Louis Prima blew his infamous horn.

THE QUADRATINI CAFFEINE had worn off, but the sight in front of my eyes provoked a new round of twitching. My mother—long before she'd turned hair-puller—had taught me to be polite to strangers, but the totality of Glenda's mother in her boudoir was so explosive that I couldn't hide my feelings. "Mamma. Freaking. Mia."

"That's right, sugar." Glenda's proud tone told me she'd mistaken my shock for awe. "You're looking at a living legend of burlesque."

Her mother was living, all right. But barely. Beneath her short red silk dressing gown, she looked like a stooped skeleton trying to slough its skin. Even more disturbing, she had drawn-on lips and eyebrows and a wig that screamed "Someone Scalped Little Orphan Annie." And thanks to black sunglasses and hearing aids bigger than Luigi Pescatore's car motors, I wasn't sure she could see or hear me.

Her mother's fingers wrapped around a floor lamp tawdrier than the one from *A Christmas Story*, and her skinny, skin-sloughy leg lifted millimeter by millimeter.

If *Roget's Thesaurus* needed an antonym for "greased lightning," then "Glenda's mother" was it. "What's she doing?"

Glenda puffed from her cigarette-holder ring. "Limbering up for her ten o'clock show at Fleur de Tease."

It was six p.m., and even if she stretched all four hours, it wouldn't be enough. Instead of limber, her joints cracked like dry timber, and I was afraid she might break or combust. "Should I start asking her questions?"

"I'll tell you when the time is right, Miss Franki. For now, have a seat on the bed and take it all in."

I wasn't sure I could. The "overwhelm" factor wasn't the issue, it was that her mother slept in a giant clamshell. But my toe was aching, so I perched on the edge.

And fell in.

The water mattress undulated so violently that I slid across the pink satin bedspread and conked the back of my skull on a ceramic pearl the size of a soccer ball. I turned my head to rub the knot and came eye to eye with an old doll that had a cracked face, a cigarette between her lips, and a clamshell on each of her lady parts. "Get it away from me."

"That's Claribel, sugar." Glenda pulled me across the bed by the ankles with her #poledancingmuscles. "She's a vintage Cubeb Smoker boudoir doll and my bestie when I was a kid."

That doll explained a lot of things about my landlady, including the rhinestone rose on each of her lady parts—but not the random leopard spots.

Having arrived at the edge of the shell, I climbed out and surveyed the pink room. Next to the bed was an old TV with rabbit ears, and everywhere I looked was a clamshell tchotchke of some sort and Pearl beer cans. By comparison, my French brothel décor was elegant enough to host a tea for Bradley's mother and grandmother and their Boston society friends. "I guess your mom likes mollusks?"

Glenda took a seat at an antique pink vanity. "She wanted to go by the stage name 'Pearl the Clamshell Girl,' but Kitty West had already taken 'Evangeline the Oyster Girl,' and she went after anyone whose act was even close. In the forties, a dancer named Divena had a mermaid act at the Casino Royale, and Kitty took an ax to her tank while she was in it."

What's up with axes in this town?

"I wasn't scared of Kitty or her ax." Glenda's mother's comment rocketed across the room much like I had on her bedspread. Her voice was dry like her skin but as spry as a spring clam. "I just came up with a better act."

She inched a foot into a shoe which made me doubt that—it was covered in newspaper, lined with red glitter, and had a corncob heel and a plastic crawfish on the toe.

"Mama," Glenda said, "this is my tenant I told you about."

"Delilah Dare. The pleasure is all yours, I'm sure."

She was definitely Glenda's mother.

Glenda batted red-crystal lashes. "That's her offstage name, Miss Franki."

I hadn't realized there was such a thing. "What's your stage name?"

Delilah dropped her dressing gown to reveal a bikini with pinchers protruding from the cups and a fantail on the bottoms similar to the one on Ric Caruso's costume. "Caressa the Crawdad Queen."

Two crawdads in one investigation? I guess crawdads do get a lot of work in New Orleans. "So, what does a crawdad queen do, exactly?"

Glenda crossed leopard-spotted legs. "She rolls in bayou mud, sugar. The men love it."

Delilah gestured to her elephant flesh. "And it's good for the skin."

Not as good as Mambo Odette's swamp mud, from the look of things. "If you don't mind my asking, what's your real name?"

"I'm ninety-three, child. Who remembers?"

I was sure Windy Spitter didn't.

She inched her foot into the other shoe. "I've been married twenty-four times, so my real name got lost in the shuffle."

And I can't get married once.

Glenda rolled her eyes. "She keeps getting hitched because she says sex outside of marriage is a sin."

Delilah grunted. "And so is whatever you're wearing."

"I told you, Mama, this outfit is #strippercouture. My stylist-photographer says it's a re-envisioning of Dolce & Gabbana's leopard and roses line."

"Well, you tell Bob Simpson that he needs to re-envision the fabric around those spots and roses. You look like you've got a bad case of syphilis."

Glenda's face turned as red as her roses, and she got up and tossed herself into the clamshell. I thought for sure it would expel her, but she rode that mollusk like a seasoned sailor.

Delilah gripped the vanity and slow-lowered her fantail into the chair. "Glenda filled me in on your investigation, and I'm just sick about it. Finding out that fourplex was a grocery store came as a real blow."

Apparently, the preference for questionable property ran in the family.

Glenda huffed a puff of smoke. "Mama thinks I should've bought a place on Iberville Street like her because my granddaddy owned a saloon here back when it was part of Storyville."

I should have guessed that Glenda had a personal connection to the old Red-Light District. "What happened to it?

"It went out of business after the Navy shut down Storyville at the end of 1917."

I glanced at Delilah's reflection in the mirror. "That's the year the Axeman began murdering Italian grocery store owners."

"Yes, child. And I remember my daddy saying that the Axeman was reacting to the closure of Storyville because he thought it was the 'birthplace of jazz.'"

"I thought jazz was created in Congo Square."

Delilah fluffed her wig. "It was, but Storyville liked to claim jazz because the greats played there, Louis Armstrong, Jelly Roll Morton, Charles Buddy Bolden."

"Who is Charles Buddy Bolden?"

"New Orleans' first trumpeter and the man who paved the way for guys like Louis Prima. Jelly Roll Morton called Bolden 'the blowingest man since Gabriel.'"

To hear my Nonna tell it, Gabriel wasn't going to blow his horn again if my and Bradley's wedding depended on it. "But why would the Axeman blame the closure of Storyville on Italian grocery store owners?"

"Because it shut down after four soldiers on leave were shot and killed, and some people thought the Mafia was behind it. The Italian store owners were Catholic, and they didn't like drunks and prostitutes around their establishments. In fact, Storyville is what prompted Italians to leave the old Mortuary Chapel and move to St. Mary's Church in the old Ursuline Convent Chapel."

I'd never heard that.

Delilah reached for a tube of cream. "By the way, Glenda said you're having trouble keeping a man, so put a little of this behind your ears and you'll trap one like a clam does a grain of sand."

I appreciated the advice—and the analogy—but not the gossip from Glenda. "What is it?"

"Liquid Mayhem, a bass attractant for fishermen. It's made from real crawfish, so it drives menfolk into a feeding frenzy."

My lips grossed out, but if I hadn't been allergic, I might have tried it on Bradley.

Glenda sat up and stubbed out her cigarette. "She married Lucky Sr. four times, sugar, and all because of that crawdad cream."

By all accounts, the Mistretta men *did* enjoy their food. "Did Lucky Sr. ever talk to you about being in The Marsala Maroons?"

Delilah swigged from a can of Pearl. "The band was local history by the time I met him, but he told me how they came up with the name. Marsala was their hometown in Sicily, and they all drank the wine like it was water. They chose maroon as a show of solidarity with the Black jazz community and because it meant 'wild.'"

Now that I knew the context, the name made sense. But I still didn't know whether the bottle of Marsala on Angelo's night table was his to drink or a sign from his killer. "Did Lucky tell you what happened when the trumpet was stolen?"

"Just that the band broke up, and then Joe Caruso was murdered in prison."

Ric said he'd died, but he hadn't mentioned a murder. It must've been too painful for him to talk about. "Who killed him?"

"Some thug in the prison yard. I don't know why." She picked up a pot of rouge. "But I always knew Joe was innocent because he ran a bookie operation on the side and didn't need to steal a trumpet for money. If you ask me, Lucky stole it and decided not to sell it after the heat was turned up."

"Why would he take it?"

With her sunglasses still on, she painted a streak of red across her cheek that reminded me of the Mardi Gras Indian. "He needed money. In those days, customers at Italian grocery stores paid on credit, so the owners were always broke. To make ends meet, Lucky and Vito Greco placed bets with Joe and played some Italian version of poker at his place above Caruso's Market."

Probably a card game called Scopa. "What makes you think Lucky took the trumpet and not Vito?"

"Because Tony Greco came to the house looking for it once, and they got into a fight that sent Lucky Sr. to the hospital."

Delilah's revelation made Tony's MIA status all the more suspect. "Do you remember anything they said?"

"We were between marriages, so I missed the boxing match. But Tony went to jail for assault."

The news hit me like a right hook. Olive Greco hadn't mentioned her brother's criminal charge, just like she hadn't mentioned her father, Vito's, membership in The Marsala Maroons. *Did Tony Greco kill Angelo LaRocca for the trumpet, and maybe Lucky Jr., too? If so, was Olive in on it?*

As I FOLLOWED Glenda down the steps of her mother's shotgun-style house, I realized the heels of her strippers shoes were leopards with roses in their mouths. I wasn't a fan of Bob Simpson's taste, but I had to give him credit for his attention to detail. "You need a ride home?"

"Nadezhda's here, sugar. We've got a double date."

I followed her gaze to a silver Jaguar gleaming under a street lamp. So that's what that Communist did with her pennies.

Nadezhda rolled down the window. "Vat you find out?"

Glenda sashayed to the passenger side. "Those Grecos are the main suspects, Miss Nadezhda. Olive and her brother, Tony."

Now that I knew more about The Marsala Maroons, I didn't think Nadezhda was behind the deaths of Lucky Jr. or Angelo LaRocca.

Nadezhda squeezed the steering wheel. "If Olive kill Lucky, I shove whole sheep head down throat and chase with Molotov cocktail."

On the other hand, I might've been too hasty in ruling her out.

She shot me a look as pointed as her maroon spikes. "Ve talk about investigation in office tomorrow."

"Uh, no ve *von't*," I shouted.

Nadezhda rolled up the window as she sped off, and I marched to my Mustang and shoved the key in the door.

It was unlocked.

"That's weird." I thought I remembered locking it, so I stepped back and looked through the window. I didn't see anyone, but it was too dark to be sure. I turned on my phone light and shone it into the back seat.

Empty.

It had been a long, hard day, so maybe I *had* forgotten to lock it. I yanked open the door, and my breath was cut short.

An ax lay on the driver seat.

And the blade glinted in the lamplight like Nadezhda's silver Jag.

11

"Penny for your thoughts," Veronica said from the doorway of my office.

I looked up from my laptop. "Could you say 'nickel' or 'dime'? I haven't had much luck with pennies lately."

She eyed the Nutella jar and biscotti bag on my desk and smoothed her square-necked navy dress before pulling up an armchair. "Judging from your breakfast, I'm guessing yesterday's meeting of the families didn't go well?"

I swallowed the last of my third cookie, wishing I still had some espresso Quadratini. I hadn't slept after finding the ax in my front seat, so I could have used the extra caffeine. "Picture Blanche and Sophia from *The Golden Girls* meeting Cinderella's stepmother and Maleficent."

She scrunched her face. "I can't."

"Exactly." I got up and faced a window overlooking Decatur Street. "Bradley and I will probably have to elope, because our families don't agree on anything, down to who's paying for the wedding."

"I'm sorry, Franki, but don't give up hope. Sometimes it takes a while for families to blend."

I spun and flailed my arms. "Oh, there will be no blending. Lillian and Cordelia made it clear that we do things the Hartmann way—period. And only a Boston society wedding will do for their Bradley."

Her lips formed a determined line. "He's his own man. He'll put a stop to any domineering behavior."

I wasn't so sure after his big-fat-Italian-wedding comment. I chewed my thumbnail and wondered what Marcella from the American Italian Cultural Center would have to say about Bradley's remark.

"Is something else bothering you?"

Too many things to count, but since we were talking about marriage, I stayed with the theme. "Yes. What if it's not the wedding the Hartmanns are dissatisfied with, but me?"

She shook her head. "Don't even let yourself go there."

I cocked my head.

"But since you already have, you should call Bradley and invite him to lunch so you can talk about what happened and regroup."

I sank into my chair. "I have a more pressing issue to work out first."

"What's more pressing than your relationship?"

"The ax I found in my front seat last night."

Veronica went still.

I leaned back and ran my fingers through my hair. "Someone put it there while I was at Glenda's mother's house."

Her eyes widened. "What were you doing at Delilah's?"

"Asking her about her marriage to Lucky Sr."

"I didn't know they were married."

"And I didn't know Glenda had a mother. I mean, the woman doesn't eat food or drink anything but champagne, so I never thought of her as entirely human. I can't imagine her as a kid." When I tried, I saw a child-sized version of the Cubeb Smoker doll with deep wrinkles and platinum hair.

"Forget Glenda. We've got to find out who put that ax in your car, and the obvious place to start is the man with the tomahawk. Have you figured out which Mardi Gras Indian tribe he belongs to?"

I gestured at my laptop screen. "I'm trying, but there's no online guide to their costume colors, and even if there was, it's not like the tribes are listed in the phone book."

She stood and pulled me by the hand. "Come on."

I rose but resisted. I wanted to stay with my Nutella and biscotti. "Where are we going?"

"I'm calling an emergency meeting."

I sighed but gave in. We often used the conference room as a neutral place for strategizing, and I needed a plan.

We went through the lobby and out of the main door to the room across from the stairwell. I followed Veronica inside and almost ducked. The all-white conference space had been marked like the territory of a dog—in heat.

Red satin drapes, a pink faux fur rug, and glittering gold bookshelves hit me like fireworks explosions. Once my eyes became accustomed to the glare, I took in the furniture. In the middle of the room sat a red-and-gold couch and armchairs in plastic wrap with white pillows featuring Andy Warhol's blue Marilyn Monroe. And in the back, a pink desk and a Venetian screen with gondolas navigating the canals.

Given Veronica's upcoming wedding in Venice, I might've thought she was the redecorator were it not for a print of the Mona Lisa, who'd been tarted up with false eyelashes, red lips—and enhanced cleavage.

"Ladonna," I breathed.

"Right behind yous girls." She entered in a getup that matched the room and dropped a box to the floor with a boom that echoed the impact of her décor.

Chicken Soup for the Soul for Grandmas fell from the box. I had no idea what kind of stories were inspirational for regular grandmothers, but the Sicilian nonna version would have held tales of granddaughters getting married, having babies, and cooking big pasta meals—all of which made me wonder when Theodora was going to sprinkle the Dispello spell in my yard.

Ladonna's eyes glittered like her bookshelves. "What do you think of my new office?"

My gaze went sideways to my employer, who hadn't informed me of the change. "It's certainly colorful, and that's an interesting painting."

"I did it myself." She fluffed her red curls. "The Mona Lisa needed a makeover."

The Louvre would disagree with her.

Ladonna unloaded *Chicken Soup for the Soul* books onto the shelves. "Rocco made these bookcases, and he and my son, Gino, moved in the furniture after work yesterday. It's wonderful being married to a contractor. If you ladies weren't happily engaged, I'd fix you up with his colleagues."

I flopped onto the couch, and the angry crackling of its plastic cover reflected how I felt about the "happily engaged" comment.

Veronica shot me a nervous look. "That's sweet of you, Ladonna, but we need to talk about a development in the case. The killer left an ax in Franki's car."

She gasped and pressed fingers to her temples. "Oh, gawd, honey, no."

"I'm all right." My tone was stoic, but I picked up a blue Marilyn and cradled her to my chest.

"I've gawt just the thing to make you feel better." She rummaged through the box and handed me a book that made my mouth pucker.

Chicken Soup for the Soul: Lemons to Lemonade.

Veronica snatched the book from my hands and put it on the shelf. "Ladonna, I need you to clear your schedule for the rest of the day. You and Franki are going to Jean Lafitte swamp to see a voodoo priestess named Odette Malveaux."

I tossed Marilyn aside like John F. Kennedy after the "Happy Birthday" incident. "I told you, I'm not going to the swamp." *And if I were, it wouldn't be with Ladonna after that lemon book recommendation.*

Veronica put her hands on her hips. "It's the only way to find out who the man with the tomahawk is."

Ladonna's curls bobbed up and down. "She's right, because masking for Mardi Gras is like mumming."

Masking referred to wearing a costume, but I didn't know what mumming meant. One thing I did know—I wasn't lucky enough for it to entail Ladonna going mum.

Veronica pulled some books from the box. "What does 'mumming' mean?"

"It refers to the Mummers Parade in Philly. It's one of America's oldest folk festivals, and it's a lot like Mardi Gras, only it's on New Year's Day. And instead of krewes who put on parades, you have divisions, like the Fancies and the Comics, who do street satire and barge into random houses to demand soup or alcohol."

I stared at Ladonna open-mouthed. Philadelphia sounded like a strange and terrifying land. "What do bad plays and breaking and entering have to do with the Mardi Gras Indians?"

"The Indians and the Mummers both change costumes and colors every year, so there's no way to figure out what tribe the tomahawk guy belongs to without knowing which one wore yellow and orange this season."

"Fair point. But Jean Lafitte swamp is dangerous."

She gave a proud smile. "My Rocco is a fisherman, so we can take his motorboat and steer clear of the wildlife."

I wasn't convinced. I'd once driven into a swamp near a plantation and run into a couple of angry gators. "It's not just that."

Veronica took a seat in the armchair. "Don't tell me you think pirates are still out there?"

"Thanks to the annual Shore Leave festival in the French Quarter, we both know that swashbucklers are alive and well in New Orleans. Granted, they're the partying kind and not the plundering ones, but still." I sat forward. "The problem is that Mambo Odette isn't known for giving detailed explanations, so I'm not sure it's worth the risk to go see her. I think we should focus on finding Olive Greco's brother, Tony. Not only is he suspiciously MIA, he went to jail years ago for assaulting Lucky Sr. over the trumpet, so he could be the one who left the ax in my car."

Ladonna's eyes narrowed. "Olive didn't mention him being arrested."

"She didn't tell us her father was in The Marsala Maroons, either."

She clenched her hair-pullers. "Why that double-crossing Muff-a-lotta."

Veronica looked from Ladonna to me. "Did I hear that right?"

I nodded. "Olive Greco is obsessed with the muffuletta, down to the dance krewe she's in. There's something seriously wrong with the woman."

Ladonna frowned. "That's not fair. If there was a Nutella krewe, you'd join it."

"No, I'd be a paradegoer so I could catch all the throws."

Veronica laughed. "You would too, so you could stock up on Nutella for the year." She gestured to the Venetian screen. "Ladonna put a vanity back there. Have a seat, and she'll do your makeup."

I touched my cheek. "To go to the swamp?"

"You're being hunted by an ax murderer, so you'll need to go undercover."

"Fine, but why would *she* do my makeup?"

Ladonna stiffened. "Because I'm a body painter. It's on my resumé."

I really should've read that thing, because it explained a lot about her, including the VW Bug and the Mona Lisa. "Okay, but just so we're clear, I want camouflage, as in regular green and brown, and only on my face."

"So finicky."

I rolled my eyes and went around the screen. I climbed into a cheetah-print salon chair and stared at the round makeup containers on the vanity counter—and I watched in the mirror as my face turned the shade of the one I'd found in the lobby couch. "Are you missing a pot of 'Indian Red'?"

She whacked my bicep. "That fell out of my purse. Where is it?"

"In my office. I'll give it to you later."

Ladonna spun the chair to have me face her and picked out some makeup.

If I'd read her resumé, or gotten a heads-up from David, I

would've put two and two together sooner, and I wouldn't have suspected the Mardi Gras Indian of breaking into the office. But since he'd been to my house and my car, I wasn't sure it mattered—unless he wasn't responsible for any of it.

My phone rang. Hoping it was Bradley, I yanked it from my pocket. *The jail.* I tapped *Answer.* "Wendell?"

"I got news." He sounded exhausted. "There were a couple o' break-ins last night. Wanna guess where?"

"Lucky's storage room and LaRocca's Market?"

"Dat's right."

The killer was looking for something, but what? "How do you know this?"

"I been up all night for another round o' questioning. The cops think it was Tony Greco."

So Tony was a police suspect. "That's good for you, right? It proves you're innocent."

"The cops don' see it dat way. They think I'm working wit de guy even though I swore I never met him."

I groaned and gripped the phone tighter. "If it was Tony, what do you think he was after?"

"No idea, but I need you to know sumpthin'." He paused. "It looks like the Axeman struck again."

I swallowed. "What do you mean 'it looks like'?"

"When the cops went to Lucky's, the whole room was covered in blood."

The phone dropped to my lap. *Nadezhda?*

THE BROWN, brackish water of Jean Lafitte swamp loomed close in the VW passenger window, as did a bald cypress tree stump. I gripped the arm rest and shot Ladonna a frown. "I wish you'd let me drive. You're hugging the shoulder."

The whites of her eyes popped from her camouflage face paint, which she'd accessorized with a faux-fur camouflage jumpsuit. "I told you, the motorboat is Rocco's baby, and he won't let anyone but me tow it. Besides, your cherry-red Mustang would stick out like a smashed thumb."

"And your car's lips and eyelashes don't?"

"Carmela is green, like nature." She gave the dashboard a loving caress, and I eyed a tarted-up Virgin Mary statuette in the center. Nothing about the car or its owner was like any nature I'd witnessed.

She stared at a roadside parking lot and flipped on her blinker. "That must be Nadezhda and Glenda."

The sight of the silver Jaguar gave me a pang of regret the size of a punch. When I'd called Nadezhda to make sure the blood in Lucky's storage room wasn't hers, she'd insisted on coming to see Mambo Odette—and on bringing Glenda. The two of them in tow would be like a motorboat on my back.

Ladonna pulled into the lot and turned the car around to back the boat trailer into the water. Meanwhile, Nadezhda exited the Jag in pink tights and a neon green faux snakeskin frock with matching boots. Glenda sashayed out in a sexy alligator outfit—gold gator-eye pasties, a faux gator thong, and stripper shoes with resin mouths built into the platforms, displaying giant teeth.

I snorted in disbelief. "*That's* their idea of camouflage?"

Ladonna shut off the engine. "I know. Your landlady should've worn alligator instead of crocodile, but what can you do?"

My mouth opened like the ones in Glenda's shoes. When the investigation was over, Veronica and I were going to have a frank talk about her hiring practices.

We got out of the car, and Nadezhda sprayed me with machine gun laughs. "You look like big circus bear."

Granted, the brown rubber fishing pants that Ladonna had lent me did nothing for my waist, but given Nadezhda's matryoshka middle, she would've been wise not to comment.

Glenda loaded a cigarette into her ring holder. "Miss Nadezhda's right, sugar. What's up with the Yogi look?"

Clearly, she wasn't referring to a yoga practitioner, so I peered into the VW's sideview mirror—and drew back like Yogi Bear himself had come to chat. Instead of camouflage, Ladonna had given me a brown-and-tan face with a huge black nose and whisker stubble. I spun on the prankster body painter. "This is funny to you?"

"Whaaat?" Her palms turned skyward. "You're a nutria, and this is their territory. And don't bother trying to wipe it off. It's waterproof." She bent to release the winch to slide the boat into the water, and just before her face went out of view, a crocodile smile spread across it.

If anyone should be in crocodile, it's Ladonna, not Glenda.

I turned to my landlady and winced. The sun was reflecting off crystals on her skin. "Since we're asking about looks, what's the deal with the body jewels?"

"It's #strippercouturecamouflage, sugar. Bob was a consultant on Kim Kardashian's Met Gala wet look, so when I told him I was coming to the swamp, he added crystals to make me glisten like I've just slithered from the water."

Camouflage wasn't supposed to look wet, and neither was a Met Gala dress.

Nadezhda pulled an ax from the trunk, and I gaped at her, stunned. "Is that really a good idea with the crime I'm investigating?"

"Da. I give Axeman vack." Her Russian-man brows furrowed. "Tanks to him, I pay cleaning fee for storage room."

Considering that someone had lost a lot of blood and maybe their life, she might want to rethink her priorities.

Glenda took an awkward drag from her ring-finger cigarette. "Personally, I think we need the ax for protection, which reminds me, I've hired David and his vassal friend to install security devices around the fourplex."

That wasn't a bad idea under the circumstances.

She blew out smoke. "They're also putting a bed in the costume closet. You'll sleep tight tonight, sugar."

Not with a copycat Axeman prowling around our ex-grocery-store house.

Ladonna opened her car door. "I need to pull the trailer from the water. All yous all can start boarding while I park."

And to think people made fun of Texans for saying y'all. I walked to the water and took in the scenery. To my surprise, the swamp was actually kind of nice. The bald cypress were green with trumpet vines and Spanish moss. At their trunks, flowers grew among the saw grass, alligator weed, and lizard's tail. Insects chirped and birds sang, creating a rather pleasant atmosphere.

I climbed into the boat. My phone rang, and Bradley's name was on the display. My pulse picked up as I answered. "Hello?"

"Hey, babe. My mother and grandmother went to visit a family friend. I thought I'd call you to discuss the wedding while they're out."

I sank onto the bench-style seat. "What did you want to say?"

"It's about the Boston tradition my mother mentioned. She and I talked, and I—"

The phone flew from my hand like a gull taking flight and plunged into the water. I turned and death-stared at the source— Nadezhda. She'd clambered aboard and bumped my arm with the ax, causing me to miss the critical part of the conversation and costing me another six-hundred-thousand pennies by ruining the device.

For a split second, my fingers tensed, and I eyed her maroon spikes. But, for fear of showing my hair-puller roots, I got a hold of myself and fished my phone from the shallow water.

Ladonna stepped into the back of the boat. "If you put your phone in a bag of rice, it'll absorb the moisture."

My tongue moved to my molars. "Too bad this is a swamp and not a rice paddy."

Glenda boarded and handed me her cell. "Call your man back, sugar."

I dialed Bradley's number, but he didn't pick up. "He probably thinks I'm a telemarketer." I ended the call. "I just hope he doesn't think I hung up on him. If his mother gets wind of that, she'll convince him to call off the wedding."

Ladonna switched on the motor and guided the boat from the slip. "Do you have future-mother-in-law issues?"

I gave a bitter laugh. "She might be a bigger foe than the copycat

Axeman. She's trying to buy me off by offering to pay for a huge wedding."

"Lucky for you, she's not Italian. Italy's lawyer league says the mother-in-law is the number one reason for divorce in Italy, and I don't doubt it. No one is ever good enough for their sons. The first time I met Rocco's mother, she looked me over and said, and I'm translating because she doesn't speak English, 'this one isn't even worthy of being my son's mistress.'"

Nadezhda squeezed her ax. "And you still marry?"

Ladonna shrugged. "She lived in Italy, so I figured we wouldn't see her that often. But after we got married, she insisted on living with us. So I had Rocco build a mother-in-law cottage in our back yard. Then I moved in."

My head tilted forward. "*You* moved in?"

"Yeh, his mother lives in the main house."

Glenda sucked in a drag. "And that doesn't bother you, Miss Ladonna?"

She glanced at the pristine manicure on her free hand. "Why should it? She does the cooking, cleaning, and washing the way she sees fit, and I get quality time with Rocco and the kids."

I studied her camouflaged face. Beneath that makeup and Shirley Temple mop, she might have a decent head on her shoulders.

Glenda blew out a cloud. "I avoid monsters-in-law by not getting married."

Nadezhda sucked her eyetooth hole. "I marry only if monster-in-law is dead."

I cocked a brow. "Glenda's mother is very much alive." *Okay, somewhat alive.*

"Delilah is stepmother-in-law. Lucky's mama, Anna, die vhen he vas eighteen."

Ladonna's lips pursed to pout. "Aww. At least she was there for his childhood."

Nadezhda shook her spikes. "She leave Lucky Sr. for Vito Greco vhen Lucky vas child."

That was a shocker. Anna was probably part of the reason Lucky

Sr. and Tony had such a violent fight over Louis Prima's trumpet. "Did they get married?"

"*Nyet*. She leave Vito vhen he gamble everyting and lose. Even grocery store."

I looked at Ladonna. "How can that be? Olive and Tony still own Greco's Grocery."

Glenda put out her cigarette in the swamp. "I guess Vito got a loan, Miss Franki."

It was possible, but I would need to verify that.

"Ooh." Ladonna pointed. "A big lizard just slipped into the water. I guess yous don't have any hellbenders in this part of the country."

Glenda crossed her legs and bounced an open-mouthed shoe. "Sounds like a night of hard drinking on Bourbon Street."

"Actually, it's a giant salamander. Pennsylvania's crawling wit 'em."

My skin began to prickle. "Could we drop the reptile talk?"

Ladonna rolled her eyes. "Fine. We'll talk about the plants." She gazed at a bush on the bank. "The pigment in those Cardinal flowers would make a gorgeous body paint."

The blood-red color reminded me of the streaks on the Mardi Gras Indian's face. I shuddered and scanned the saw grass along the shore. The Mardi Gras tribes passed down the swamp survival techniques their maroon ancestors had learned from Native Americans. *Is the one with the tomahawk lying in wait?*

Nadezhda pointed, and I followed her finger—to two eyes like Glenda's pasties protruding from the algae-covered water.

She crouched and raised her ax.

The boat wobbled and dipped low, and I tumbled into rotten egg-scented water. I surfaced and paddled like a nutria on espresso Quadratini. I grasped the side of the boat and tried to hoist myself on board, but my fishing pants had taken on a few gallons of the swamp. "Quick! Pull me up."

She extended her ax. "You get gator head for kholodets."

"We're not here to hunt ingredients for Russian meat Jell-O," I shouted. Then I glanced over my shoulder to look for the gator, who probably thought I was a whale-sized nutria. "But I'm going to be meat Jell-O if you don't hurry."

Nadezhda pulled me onto the boat with a hand from Glenda—only one because she held her cigarette-holder ring away from the water.

I knelt on the bench, emptied some of my pant water over the side, and returned to my seat. A pain pierced my behind. I shot up, the boat listed, and I went overboard again. When I surfaced, a crawdad floated out of my fishing pants with his pinchers splayed wide, and I hoped he hadn't broken the skin. The last thing I needed was for my crawfish allergy to flare in my rear end.

Ladonna scowled. "You need to get your swamp legs, Franki, or you're going to sink Rocco's baby and the investigation."

I mentally retracted my earlier thought about her decent head. The woman was as imbalanced as her husband's motorboat.

As Glenda and Nadezhda pulled me to safety, I cursed Theodora for not giving me a protection spell like Upendo or Dispello for the trip. It was the least she could have done when I was braving aggressive mudbugs to get her Mambo Odette's swamp mud.

Gingerly, I sat my smarting behind on the bench, and we motored in silence. Even though it was early afternoon, sunlight waned as though night was falling. I looked up expecting storm clouds, but the darkness was due to the dense trumpet vines and Spanish moss strangling the trees. Oddly, the branches and the vegetation were gray, not green, and the water had turned black, like roux. Most disturbing, there were no insect noises.

We'd entered the heart of the swamp.

And it was dead.

We passed a large animal carcass on the bank. And another. They hadn't been picked clean by predators. They'd been skinned.

And decapitated.

Ladonna rubbed her forearm. "What's Mambo Odette's address?"

I cleared a frightened frog from my throat. "All I know is that it's just past a huge cypress in the middle of the water."

Glenda wiped a smudge from one of the teeth on her shoe. "I

came out here years ago, but it's been too long for me to remember. I consulted Mambo Odette about a man and a voodoo dance striptease I did at Madame Moiselle's. I think I told you about that, sugar."

The frog in my throat now trembled at the thought of her reminiscing about the snake that had covered her lady parts. "You did, so no need to do that again."

Seconds passed that seemed like hours. We came upon a bald cypress so big that it partially blocked our passage. Just beyond it was a rundown shack with a porch and a dock.

I chewed my lip. "This must be her place."

Ladonna maneuvered around the tree, and my stomach rocked like the boat. I heard a *whoosh* of air—the sound of the breath fleeing all of our lungs.

A terrifying figure stood on the bank with an enormous boa constrictor writhing at his neck. Bald as the cypress trees, his face was made up like a skull. White paint, cowrie shells, and bits of moss adorned his near-naked body. And most horrifying of all, there were bones where his arms should have been.

He gazed at me and spread his lips, revealing a black void. And his arm bones raised a staff with a skull threaded through it—and an ax head on the end.

I gripped the bench, no longer concerned about swirling gators. The only thing I could worry about was whether the half-skeleton, half-human was a bokor or a voodoo Axeman.

12

T he skeleton man ran along the bank with the boa coiled at his neck, shaking the staff and shouting in what I guessed was Haitian French. My brain screamed "Gas the motor," but the words wouldn't come out, partly because I wanted to know whether he was Angelo's killer and because I was scared arm-bone stiff.

The door to the shack opened, and a phrase finally escaped my lips, "Holy Mambo."

Odette Malveaux stood in the doorway, a ghastly, ghostly figure. She wore a muslin dress that matched her headwrap, her cheeks had sunk deep into her skull, and her cappuccino skin was a chalky color —as though she'd drunk the white drink of a bokor and turned into a zombie.

As I tried to make sense of the scene, the voodoo priestess raised her arm as slow as the undead and gestured to me. "Come, chile."

Ladonna elbowed my ribs. "She sounds like Tia Dalma, that mystic from the *Pirates of the Caribbean* movies."

"*Shhht*," I hissed, stunned from my stupor. "Do you really want to offend these people?"

"Whaaat? It's a compliment." She gave her curls a defensive

bump. "The actress who played Tia has a sexy voice, and I read that her Jamaican mother was her accent coach."

I took a breath and turned my back on her. But in a way, Ladonna was right. Mambo Odette epitomized the common local sentiment that New Orleans wasn't the deep south, but rather the northernmost point of the Caribbean.

"Good ting I bring ax," Nadezhda said.

I turned to make sure she wasn't wielding the thing and came eye level with Glenda's phone.

"Could you move, sugar? I need a picture of this for Bob. This all-white look would make a fabulous influencer shot."

I pressed the phone down. "This isn't a swamp tour, all right? I think we've interrupted some sort of voodoo ritual, and we don't dare disrespect it." I motioned to Ladonna. "Pull up to the dock, so I can get out."

She guided the boat toward the rickety platform, and I tried to find my courage. I had no reason to believe that Mambo Odette would hurt me, but I wasn't sure about her creepy companion.

We reached the dock, and Ladonna's jaw tightened. "You can do this, Franki. In *Chicken Soup for the Soul: Tough Times, Tough People*, they say that tough times don't last, but tough people do. Remember that, no matter what happens in the shack."

Easy for her to say from the safety of a motorboat. "Just don't leave."

"I wouldn't think of it, hon."

Given her maternal nature, I felt somewhat certain she wouldn't. But Ladonna was unpredictable, much like Mambo Odette.

I rose and stepped onto the dock, and my legs wobbled like I was still on the water. As I walked up the creaky wood, I kept a side-eye on the semi-skeleton man. When I reached land, I realized he did, in fact, have flesh arms and teeth that he'd painted pitch black. But the discovery wasn't the least bit comforting. The guy was still terrifying, and so was his slithering snake.

I arrived at the porch and made another discovery. Mambo

Odette was covered in a powdery white paste, which convinced me that she and the skeleton had been performing a voodoo ceremony.

She went inside without a word and sat slumped over at a table set with a plate of herbs, Haitian rum, and a bottle marked Florida Water. I wouldn't have minded a shot of the former to calm my nerves, but there was no way I'd drink the latter. Based on the #FloridaMan stories I'd read on social media, there was definitely something in that state's water.

From the threshold, I checked on the skeleton man, who hadn't left his position at the bank, and then I took what I hoped wasn't my last look at the boat.

Glenda and Ladonna raised their thumbs, and Nadezhda raised the ax and an iron fist.

I held my breath and entered the shack. There was only one window and no electricity or running water. An oil lamp hung from the ceiling and ten or so candles sat atop scrap wood that had been nailed to the walls. A cot was on one side of the room, and a washstand was on the other with an open cupboard that contained bottles and jars of unknown—and unnerving—substances. In the back of the room was an altar similar to the one at Marie Laveau's House of Voodoo on Bourbon Street, where I'd first met Mambo Odette, except that it was authentic.

Chillingly so.

The altar's centerpiece was a skull that I had no doubt was human. On its cranium was a top hat in the style of Baron Samedi, the voodoo loa who dug the graves of departed souls and led them to the underworld. To the right of the skull was a severed alligator head, a gris-gris bag, and a primitive voodoo doll with pins. To its left, an antique doll torso in green sequins with a pipe and a mummified creature in a cape. Decorative touches included Mardi Gras beads, chicken feet, and candles. Pall Mall cigarettes, a bottle of Tabasco, and coins littered the altar, offerings to the god of the dead.

I wiped clammy palms on my fishing pants and, careful not to make any sudden moves, eased into the chair across from the slumped voodoo priestess.

She raised her head slowly, as though drunk or in a trance. "Why do ya come ta Mambo Odette lookin' like a half-drown' rat?"

I froze for a second. She wasn't usually so direct, but it was probably the Florida Water talking. "Uh, a coworker pranked me with face paint, and I fell out of the boat."

Her white lids lowered. "Someone put a root on ya."

Although I was skeptical of the root business, my mind again went to Theodora. "How did they do it, exactly?"

"Goofer dust."

The name was too ridiculous to be scary. "That wouldn't be made with grave dirt or black salt, would it?'"

Her amber eyes probed mine. "Powdered snake."

In that case, Nadezhda was the likelier culprit. "My friend Wendell Baptiste said the same thing about the root. He thinks someone impersonating the Axeman of New Orleans had one put on me. Have you heard of him? He was a serial killer over a century ago."

Her white-powdered lips formed a half-smile. She pulled a lighter from a pocket in her dress and lit the herbs. A bluish smoke rose that smelled like burning weeds. "Ya need a mojo ta undo it—a dime in a bag around your ankle."

It was a good thing she hadn't prescribed a penny, because I didn't have one, and I sure as heck wasn't going to take one from her Baron Samedi altar. "I'll take care of that as soon as I get home, but right now, I need your help with something else. Wendell's in jail for murdering a grocery store owner named Angelo LaRocca, but he didn't do it. We think the real killer might've been a Mardi Gras Indian with a tomahawk. He was wearing yellow-and-orange ostrich feathers. Do you know which tribe that is?"

Her eyes narrowed, and her wide nostrils flared. "When ya point fingers wit'out reason, ya risk da wrath of Erzulie D'en Tort."

She was another voodoo loa it wasn't wise to mess with, as I'd learned on a couple of prior investigations. "I don't want to accuse anyone unjustly, especially after what happened to my friend, but someone is stalking me—with an ax."

"Y'are in danger, chile. It's as plain as da paint on your face. Keep da cayenne pepper wit' ya ta keep 'im away."

I flashed back to sprinkling the spice into Bradley's mouth. *Had I driven a wedge between us and sabotaged our wedding?* "What if I gave cayenne pepper to someone I love?"

"Das bad, chile."

A stab pierced my gut, like one of the voodoo doll's pins. "How can I undo it?"

"Ya got ta figure dat out fo' yaself."

I couldn't—unless it involved sprinkling it on our families, which I was more than happy to do. "What about the Mardi Gras Indian? Can you help me find him?"

"Seek da counsel of da Big Chief at Jazz Fest."

The festival started at the Fair Grounds Race Course yesterday, so that would be easy. "How will I know who he is?"

She raised her head high. "Da king wear da biggest crown."

It wasn't the answer I wanted, but Mambo Odette wasn't known for specifics. "I have one more question about the murder."

"Baron Samedi come at midnight," she announced as she retrieved the voodoo doll from the altar.

I stared at the thing, hoping she wasn't about to get revenge on me for asking so many questions. "What does Baron Samedi have to do with this?" No sooner had I asked than I thought of the new blood that had been found in Lucky Mistretta's storage room. "Someone else died, didn't they?"

"His work ain' never done."

I wasn't sure whether she was referring to a second murder or deaths in general, but there was no point in pressing her on the subject. "Listen, the killer stole a trumpet, and yet he still seems to be looking for something. I need to know what that is, maybe to prevent more murders."

"Ya got ta go ta Metairie Cemetery and take an offering ta da grave. Dere ya will find da answers ya seek." She pulled a pin from the doll.

I eyed its sharp point, wondering whether it was my cue to leave.

"Okay, but whose grave do I need to visit?"

"I can tell ya only dis." She stabbed the pin into the doll with a thwack.

And I jerked back.

Mambo Odette's torso serpentined toward me, and her eyes rolled back in her head. "Don' look to da flame. Look to da spirits."

THE FULL MOON cast an eerie glow on the crypts of Metairie Cemetery. I should have been grateful for the light, but it reminded me of werewolves, vampires, and that lunatic psychic Chandra Toccato. And lifelike statues and hulking trees weren't doing anything to improve the ghoulish atmosphere.

I stopped to check for a surname on a tomb, and someone bumped into me. I spun faster than a figure skater.

It was Nadezhda. With her weapon.

I clenched my jaw and gave her a warning glare. The cemetery was already evoking all kinds of slasher-movie scenarios, so the last thing I needed was an ax-wielder sneaking up behind me, especially one whose moonlit spikes and snakeskin frock were scarier than a hockey-masked Jason.

Ladonna shined a flashlight in my face.

I squinted and shaded my eyes. "Could you please point that to the ground?"

She huffed as though I was being finicky and lowered the light. "I was trying to read the name on the crypt behind you." She hugged her camouflage faux fur and looked around. "I wish that voodoo mambo had told you whose grave we're supposed to visit. This is spookier than Holler's Eve."

I assumed she was referring to Halloween, but after learning about the alarming antics of the Mummers Parade, Holler's Eve could have been a late-night home-invasion screaming festival. "It could be Angelo LaRocca. Marcella at the American Italian Cultural Center said he was going to be buried here."

Glenda slithered up with her gator-eye pasties and stripper-shoe teeth all aglow. "We would've heard if that had happened, Miss Franki."

"Yeah, probably. The only other option is Louis Prima. Marcella said he's buried here too, and I did ask Mambo Odette about his trumpet."

"Then I say we start there, sugar. How do we find it?"

I pulled out my cell and tapped the power button, but the device was as dead as the cemetery residents. "I'd google it, but someone knocked my phone in the swamp."

Nadezhda huffed à la Ladonna. "And somevone vhiny baby."

I loomed over her like a graveyard tree. "Maybe so, but you're going to pay for a new one."

She flashed her eyetooth hole at me.

Glenda stared at her phone. "Prima's tomb is up ahead, ladies."

We set off along the path, and my foot caught on something. I went flying and slid to the snarling mouths in Glenda's platform shoes.

She pulled her platinum hair to one side and frowned down. "Honestly, sugar, you're going to hurt somebody if you're not more careful."

'This bites,' came to mind. I checked to see what had tripped me.

A tree root erupting from a tomb.

I grimaced. I was starting to believe in the root business—and in the nefarious skills of three-hundred-and-one-year-old witches.

Following a rigorous grave-dirt-dusting of my clothes, we set off again and came upon a mausoleum that could have been a house.

Ladonna jumped. "Oh my Gawd."

I went rigid. "What is it?"

She pointed to a life-sized statue of a woman with an armful of flowers reaching for one of the mausoleum's double doors. "I thought she was a real person."

Glenda stuck out a leg that went surprisingly well with her gator outfit and gazed at the mausoleum. "That was Josie Arlington's tomb until her heirs sold it out from under her dead body to make some cash."

At the mention of money, Nadezhda's eyes lit up like the moon. "Who is her?"

"Only the most infamous madame in Storyville history, Miss Nadezhda. Some say the statue comes to life on the anniversary of Josie's death and wanders the grounds."

I checked the date on the tomb, relieved to read that she'd passed on Valentine's Day, a solid ten months in the future.

Glenda put a hand on her crocodile-thonged hip. "And that's not all. Cemetery caretakers have seen those granite flames on top of her tomb start to burn."

I shivered, and Mambo Odette's parting advice echoed in my head. *Don' look to da flame. Look to da spirits.* I doubted she'd been alluding to the Storyville madame's mausoleum. But if experience was any indication, deciphering her words would be key to my investigation.

Wings flapped in a nearby magnolia tree.

"*Oof!*" Ladonna threw up her hands and started speed-walking. "Let's get moving before a murder of ravens flies out."

I got goosebumps on my goosebumps and hurried behind her. "You *had* to use that phrase in a cemetery, didn't you?"

"Whaaat? It's correct."

"So is a 'flock of birds,' and it's not terrifying."

"Unless you've seen the Alfred Hitchcock movie."

My lips pursed. She'd better hope there wasn't an empty crypt in the vicinity, because I might lock her in it while I finished investigating.

We passed graves adorned with animals, gargoyles, and crosses, but they weren't half as creepy as the porcelain tombstone pictures of the deceased. I would've sworn their eyes followed us as we walked past their final resting places.

Ladonna pointed to an Italianate mausoleum with four columns on the façade and an artificial grass yard. "Hey, I wonder if that's Tony and Olive's family."

"Greco" was etched in block letters above the arched entrance. "I don't see any first names, so there's no way to tell."

Nadezhda came up beside me and tipped her head back as she took in the size. "You could live in zat ting."

"Forget it." I started walking. "You're not getting the costume closet."

We continued along the path. After what seemed like eternity, we came upon a simple gray tomb marked "Prima," where the "Just a Gigolo," as described in the inscription, was buried with his mother and father. As Marcella had mentioned, perched on the top was a statue of the Angel Gabriel with his trumpet.

As I gazed up at the instrument, I remembered what my nonna had said about Gabriel's trumpet and my wedding—and what Mambo Odette had told me about the cayenne pepper. *Have I sabotaged my shot at wedded bliss with Bradley?*

No, I'm being silly.

I turned and stumbled across a tomb root.

Then again, this is New Orleans, and the town is clearly crawling with wily witches.

"Money!" Nadezhda dropped to her knees and scooped pennies into her purse.

There were hundreds of them around the base of the tomb.

Ladonna smacked a coin from her hand. "You stop that, ya hear?"

"Vhy? Him can't take to grave."

Ladonna's eyes blazed like her fiery red hair. "Soldiers leave pennies to pay their respects to fallen servicemen and women. Besides, it's not like they're dower bills."

I blinked. "You say *dower* bills?"

"What's wrong wit it?"

"The missing l's, for one thing. And it sounds like dowager."

Glenda flipped her hair. "Watch out, both of you. I made my living from dollar bills, so let's see that they get the respect they deserve. Now, I read somewhere that people leave those pennies because of Prima's hit song 'Pennies from Heaven.'"

I pondered the coins. *Do they hold the answers I'm seeking?* Pennies had certainly been a theme in my life lately, but I couldn't imagine how they related to Angelo LaRocca's murder.

Ladonna reached into her bag. "We should all leave a penny for our offering."

Nadezhda returned one of the pennies she'd stolen.

My eyelids lowered. That was probably all I'd get of the six hundred thousand pennies she owed me for the phone. "I don't have any change."

Glenda spread her arms, and her gator-eyes shimmered. "This is Louisiana, sugar. Thanks to the voodoo tradition, you can leave anything you think would be meaningful to the deceased. If I'd known about this visit in advance, I would've brought him a pair of my pasties."

That would have been awkward with his parents in the same tomb. I rummaged in my bag and discovered a refrigerator magnet that said "Italians don't live in the present... They live in the pasta!" It must have fallen into my purse when Marcella was arranging them on the display. The message was a little off-color given the circumstances, but then again, Prima was an advocate for his ethnicity, and who didn't love noodles? I placed it with the pennies.

Nadezhda pulled out a flask. "Ve drink to Lucky and Angelo." Her lips spread in her best approximation of a smile. "And vhat the hell? Louis too."

I figured a sip would take the edge off our excursion. "What are we drinking?"

"Special vodka from Russia." She elbowed my side. "It put hair back on chest."

She handed me the flask, and I took it, wondering about that "back." I swallowed a slug and exhaled fumes, fairly confident that I'd just consumed leftover rocket fuel from the failed Russian space program.

Glenda fired up her lighter, and I snapped my mouth shut for fear of igniting. But I couldn't take my eyes off the fire.

Don' look to da flame. Look to da spirits.

Instinctively, I shifted my gaze to the Prima tomb, and the pennies from heaven gave me a spark of divine intuition.

Angelo's murder has to do with money.

I looked up at Gabriel's instrument. And it wasn't the money that would've been made from the sale of Louis Prima's trumpet. If it were, the original thief would have sold it on the black market long ago. There was only one other link to money in the case—Joe Caruso's book-making operation. *But how is that related to Angelo LaRocca's savage killing?*

Gravel crunched in the night, and we ducked behind the tomb.

"Did you guys see anyone?" I whispered.

Three heads shook.

The crunching grew louder.

And insistent.

Is it one of the caretakers Glenda had mentioned? Or is the Mardi Gras Indian coming for me?

I motioned for everyone to stay down, and I slowly rose.

Crrrawww!

I stepped behind the Angel Gabriel. *Is that a raven?*

I moved my head to take a look, and a penny fell from the horn of the trumpet. I peered under an angel wing and scanned the graveyard for the source.

And what I saw convinced me that Nadezhda's rocket fuel had blasted my brain into orbit.

Skeletons with skulls the size of enormous jack 'o lanterns marched through the cemetery like unearthly soldiers with butchers' aprons at their waists. Some of the skulls had antelope horns, and one of the skeletons carried a bone as big as a tibia—with bits of flesh still attached.

They had to be people dressed as skeletons. *But why? Are they the so-called spirits I'm supposed to look to for information? Or voodoo bokors hunting humans to turn into zombies?*

A second *crrrawww* pierced the night, and a shiver snaked down my skin-covered spine. Because the raven-like caw had come from one of the skeletons.

A drum began a tribal beat, and something clinked in time with the rhythm. I squinted and realized that the noise came from a skeleton beating a jar with a bone.

Ladonna, Glenda, and Nadezhda rose and huddled around me with eyes as round as the full moon.

The procession stopped, and the skeletons made like cemetery statues.

Or corpses.

The four of us exchanged fearful looks and turned back to the morbid scene.

And from behind a tall mausoleum, a nine-foot skeleton emerged with a cane. He wore tails and a top hat decorated with cowrie shells, and an awful grin on his skull face.

The breath escaped my lungs as though my soul was departing for the grave. Because based on his attire, the giant skeleton was none other than Baron Samedi, the voodoo loa of the dead.

I swallowed, but my throat was as thick as a tomb root. Mambo Odette had said the Baron would come at midnight, but of course I'd assumed she was speaking figuratively. "Stilts." I whispered it aloud to reassure myself. "He's just a man wearing stilts."

The music resumed, and so did the macabre procession. The nine-foot skeleton began cane-walking with a bone-rattling gait.

And then he danced.

"If you don't live right, the Bone Man is comin' for ya," a voice shouted.

"The end is near," another yelled.

"You next," a third cried.

Are they talking to us?

The nine-foot skeleton flailed his arms, and the beat ceased. His head rotated as smooth as an owl's in our direction. Then he lifted his leering skull face.

And beneath it was a skull.

I pried Nadezhda from my leg, and the breath left my lungs again —this time with a command. "Run for your lives!"

13

A scream pierced my brain.

I shot up and found myself on the floor of Glenda's costume closet. After the horrific night at the cemetery, I figured I'd screamed in my sleep. *Speaking of which, why aren't I in the bed David and The Vassal had set up?*

I turned and locked eyes with Napoleon. "You couldn't give me one night, could you?"

He nestled into the covers, which I took as a no.

I picked up my phone to see whether it had revived. The display lit up and showed ten after six, but the bottom half of the screen was scrambled. "I agree," I said to the device. "It's too early to think."

I dropped the phone, pushed Napoleon over, and crawled onto the mattress. It was Saturday, and another hour or five of sleep was in order.

A cry rang out that could've been a raven being murdered.

Napoleon and I bolted up.

Is that a skeleton man?

Or the Mardi Gras Indian?

With my blood pumping as hard as my lungs, I glanced at the toolbox from Glenda's Handy Woman striptease. I still didn't know what was in it, and even though danger seemed imminent, I still didn't want to find out. But I could use it to knock the killer out—after I'd made sure the lid was locked up tight.

"Come outside and face me, you half-rate Sicilian sorceress!"

That's Theodora, talking to my nonna!

"If you're not out here in the next sixty seconds, I'll curse you and your descendants for eternity!"

And that's proof she had a root put on me.

I rushed out to the balcony in a long sleep shirt as Glenda exited her apartment in nothing but her sparkly, sheer robe. We stood at the railing, taking in the eye-level sight.

Theodora dangled by a stockinged ankle from the top of the stripper pole. And as she struggled to keep her orange thighs covered, I remembered that I hadn't gotten her the jar of Mambo Odette's swamp mud.

"Stop staring, fools," she flapped a black caftan sleeve like a wing, "and free me from this blasted snare."

Glenda's brow went saucy. "Sounds like David and The Vassal trapped us an uppity intruder, Miss Franki."

I'd completely forgotten that she'd hired my coworkers to install security devices, and when she'd told me, I'd assumed she meant alarms. But a stripper-pole trap was exactly what I should have expected from a couple of undersexed college geeks. "She's not an intruder. She's a witch I hired to do a banishing spell in our yard, and you met her a couple of years ago when I was working the homicide at Madame Moiselle's."

"I remember her, sugar." Glenda's lip corners curled. "But she looks like a cross-dressing ax murderer."

Theodora's black caftan swirled like an ominous cloud as she pulled herself upright and hugged the pole. "Careful, you faded Blaze Starr. She just reminded you that I'm a witch."

Glenda's body tensed—the parts that could—as though she planned to pounce. "As if I needed a reminder. You're riding that pole like an old hag on a broom."

I held up my arms before a witch-bitch war broke out. "Both of you stop it. My mom or nonna could come out."

At the threat of my family, the orange hag and the polecat went silent.

"Now let me see if I can figure out how the trap works." I jogged down the stairs in my bare feet and looked up. And I shuddered. From the ground-level, Theodora looked like a tangerine-haired raven on a perch.

She scowled down at me. "Forget the banishing spell. Your nonna and I need to handle this witch to witch."

"This trap isn't Sicilian sorcery. It's stripper."

Her green eyes flashed red at Glenda, who had a phone pressed to her ear. "I ought to upend her right over that railing."

I gripped the pole. "Trust me, you don't want to see that."

Glenda hung up and leaned over the balcony. "Bob's on his way for our influencer costume fitting, and he's bringing a ladder."

Theodora growled low in her throat. "Who the hell is Bob?"

"The Sorcerer of Sparkles. You should ask him to add some dazzle to that hideous tent you're wearing."

"This is a caftan," she whisper-shouted. "And you'd do well to wear one over that failed invisibility cloak."

I smirked at the Harry Potter reference, assuming Theodora was taking credit for that too, and rolled my eyes—just as Glenda spread her arms and legs.

"Why would I hide all of this?"

"Ack!" Theodora covered her face with a sleeve. "Get me off of this thing before your landlady blinds me."

With what was left of my own scarred vision, I studied the pole. David and The Vassal had attached a chain pulley to the top, which was at least three feet over my head. "I can't reach you. And even if I could, I should leave you up there until you undo the root you had put on me."

"I beg your pardon. I don't do voodoo, and I have no use for bokors. I'm a witch, remember?"

It was hard to forget with her Endora hair and matching skin.

I looked around the yard for something I could use to free her ankle, and the tarted up VW Bug pulled up in front of the fourplex. The day was going to drive me to a hellbender—as in the Bourbon Street booze binge, not the Pennsylvanian salamander.

Ladonna exited Carmela with a foil-covered platter and a Humble Bagel bag. Based on her pink satin jacket and black unitard, I figured she was channeling a Pink Lady Sandy.

She walked up the driveway, gaping at Theodora. "What in the world is that woman doing on that john?"

My head snapped back. "It's a stripper pole, not a toilet."

"Who said anything about a toilet?"

"You. *A john?*"

Her brow tensed and relaxed. "Ohhh, I meant j-a-w-n. It's a word for 'thing' in Philly."

Apparently, they drank Florida Water in Pennsylvania too. "What are you doing here, anyway?"

She licked pink-glossed lips. "I wanted to make sure I didn't miss you before you went to Jazz Fest. I've never been, and I want to meet this Big Chief guy. I called and left a voicemail, but then I remembered that your phone might be ruined. So I decided to come over with beggles and my homemade scrapple."

My eye dropped to the foil. "Is that like an apple cobbler?"

"Hello!" Theodora rattled the chain pulley. "Are you really going to discuss recipes while I'm hanging from this thing? Call the fire department!"

I put a hand on my hip. "And take them away from an emergency? Just hang on with one hand and try to free your ankle with the other."

"You think I haven't tried? The chain is tight."

I sighed, tired of her whining. "You're a witch. Figure something out."

She snorted, and I thought I saw a tiny puff of smoke come from her nostrils. Nevertheless, I wanted to leave her hanging a little longer. Even if she hadn't put a root on me, she'd had me arrested on my birthday.

"*Una strega?*" Nonna's voice hissed behind me.

Dread filled my veins. Now that she'd found a witch on the premises, she'd notify her nonna friends, who'd summon an exorcist and turn the stripper pole into a cross. I turned, and Nonna shook pinched fingers at Theodora. "Is that how she got-a that flag-a pole to work-a?"

For the first time in days, a smile threatened to cross my lips. Instead, I turned and made a zip-it motion at Theodora in case she decided to out me for the stripper pole or the banishing spell. Because a lifetime of experience with my nonna had taught me that Sicilian sorcery was not only real, it was more potent than any witch Louisiana could produce.

Ladonna turned to my nonna. "*Buongiorno, signora. Piacere conoscerLa.*"

Nonna nodded at the greeting and looked at me. "She speak-a the high Italian."

You'd never know that from her English. "And she brought us breakfast."

Ladonna handed Nonna the platter. "It's a Pennsylvania Dutch dish made from a mush of pork scraps and fat, cornmeal, wheat flour, and spices. You form it into a congealed loaf, slice it, and panfry it."

"Grazie." Nonna eyed the platter as though it held Nadezhda's Russian meat Jell-O, and I took the bag from Ladonna's hand. Beggars *could* be choosers, and this beggar chose the beggles.

"Ahem." Theodora motioned to the bag. "Toss me one, will ya?"

I threw her the onion flavor.

Nonna shuffled to my apartment. "I take-a the food inside and-a call-a Father John. We're gonna need a lotta holy water."

Something told me she planned to use it both to cleanse the yard of sorcery and the platter of that scrapple.

Ladonna reached for my hair, and I ducked, thinking she was going to pull it. "Stand up, Franki. You've got a tangle." Her fingers worked a knot. "That's weird. It's a penny, and it's sticky." She stuck out her tongue and dropped the coin into my hand.

My stomach churned because I knew where it was from. "It was stuck to the trumpet on Louis Prima's tomb." I finally got a penny but from a dead man's grave, which was anti-lucky. "Thank God my nonna didn't see this." I forced a light-hearted tone. "She would've told me some crazy superstition about grave robbing leading to my untimely death."

Theodora puffed. "That's the *best*-case scenario."

I gave her a stare that rivaled her feline pupils. "Another word, and I'll shimmy up that pole and stick a broom in your bagel hole."

Ladonna's nose wrinkled. "I think the penny *is* a bad omen. You should take it back to the cemetery."

"*Pff!*" I slipped the coin into my shirt pocket and tried to act nonchalant. "I'm not *that* superstitious."

Tires squealed, and we looked toward the street.

Bradley's black Mercedes rounded the corner—with Lillian at the wheel and Cordelia in the passenger seat.

"I've got to get rid of that damned penny."

Ladonna chewed her cheek. "Your future mother-in-law?"

"And her mother."

The Hartmanns exited the car dressed for a Paris fashion show. Cordelia pointed to the stripper pole, and to my surprise, her lips spread, delighted. "A maypole. How lovely."

Evidently, stripper poles weren't part of grandmothers' mental knowledge base.

Lillian removed oversized Chanel sunglasses the exact shade of ochre as her pantsuit, and her eyes widened at the sight of me in a sleep shirt with a witch, a stripper, and a Pink Lady Sandy. She shoved them back on as though she too feared blindness and stalked across the yard. "Francesca, I'm glad we caught you at home."

At the word 'caught,' I took a step back. I sensed a trap along the lines of the one that had snared Theodora. "Where's Bradley?"

"At home, of course. We told him we were going to pick up *pan chocolat* at a *patisserie* to lift his spirits." She gave me a flinty look over the rim of her sunglasses. "He's not happy that you hung up on him yesterday."

"I didn't hang up on him. I dropped my phone into the sss...sink."

It was a lie, but I couldn't tell her that I'd dropped it in the swamp while visiting a voodoo ceremony.

"He'll be relieved. Now, I was hoping we could have a quick tête-à-tête."

Glenda snickered. "I know that's French for 'head to head,' but at Madame Moiselle's it means a whole nother thing."

Lillian shot her a look that could have lit the balcony on fire.

And I was with Lillian on that. "If this is about the wedding—"

Cordelia squeezed my wrist. "It is. Bradley said the ceremony will be wherever you decide."

"Aww." Ladonna made a mushy face, which matched my insides. My Bradley was a wonderful, selfless man.

Lillian attempted a smile that came out a sneer. "Yes, my Bradley is a selfless man. Sometimes too much so, which is where I come in."

I was right to take that step back—the woman could read minds. "Why are you so set on a Boston wedding? Is it because you want to make sure it's up to your society standards?"

"This isn't just about decorations, Francesca. It's also about connections. Bradley gave up a prestigious position as bank president for you, and before you get married, he'll need to find another one. A better one."

Cordelia touched a diamond *H* on her lapel. "Yes, how would it look if he married you unemployed?"

I wouldn't have minded, but my father would have. "I understand your point, but what does getting married in Boston have to do with Bradley finding a job?"

"A wedding brings people together, and between his father, Cordelia, and me, we know quite a few CEOs and CFOs."

Theodora squawk-laughed. "And UFOs too, I'd imagine."

Glenda cackled and slapped the railing. "Good one."

I dug in my heels, literally. "I'm sure you know important people, but Bradley can find a job on his own, here in New Orleans."

Cordelia exchanged a side-eye with her daughter-in-law. "These are tough times, and he's been out of work for almost a year."

I couldn't argue with that.

Lillian raised her nose. "And I think we can all agree that he needs to think bigger than New Orleans. So tell him you want a Boston wedding and leave the rest to Cordelia and me. It's in your best interests too." She pulled a check from her purse and stuffed it into my shirt pocket with the damned penny. "If you need more, let me know."

Theodora slid down the pole, emitting the rotten-egg odor of the yellow cream I'd seen her use while sunning outside Private Chicks, and marched up to the Hartmanns. "Women like you give us witches a bad name."

Lillian's icy expression thawed enough to allow her to open her mouth to reply, but Theodora flashed her cat eyes and pointed like she intended to shoot a spell.

Lillian and Cordelia blanched and ran to the Mercedes, which sped away faster than a Formula One car.

Theodora cracked her knuckles. "I'll factor in those two to the Dispello ingredients."

Ladonna's curls tilted. "Whatever that is, can I get some?"

Theodora pulled a card from the folds of her caftan. "Here's my contact information." She set off across the lawn. "I'll be back after I make the adjustments to the formula."

Glenda leaned over the rail. "Are you all right, sugar?"

"Yeah," I said, although I was worried. I'd taken it for granted that Bradley would find another job in New Orleans, but in light of my conversation with his family, I realized that nothing was certain. I turned to Ladonna. "I'll go change for Jazz Fest."

"I'll come with you." She followed me toward the stairs. "The killer could be there, so I'll need to do your makeup."

"Not after that nutria stunt you pulled." I kicked Veronica's newspaper and stooped to pick it up. "I'd stick out less going as myself."

"Oh, come on. I was just having a little fun."

I was about to throw the paper onto Veronica's porch when a phrase caught my eye—*Tomb of Late Grocer*. I pulled the paper from the plastic casing and saw another word from the article title that chilled my bones.

"You look like Rocco when he's eaten too much scrapple," Ladonna said.

"Angelo LaRocca was laid to rest at Metairie Cemetery yesterday morning, and that's not all."

She looked over my shoulder, and I tapped the title.

Tomb of Late Grocer Desecrated.

She covered her mouth. "Do you think it was those skeleton men?"

"No one intending to tamper with a grave would announce their presence at the cemetery like those guys did last night."

Ladonna chewed a leopard-print fingernail. "It might've been the Mardi Gras Indian."

"Don't forget Tony Greco." I closed the paper, frustrated, and left it at Veronica's door. "I just wish we knew what he was looking for, because he sure as hell didn't think Angelo was buried with the stolen trumpet."

I headed up the stairs, and the penny weighed heavily in my pocket. The tomb desecration was a jarring reminder that we still didn't know whose blood was shed in Lucky's storage room. It was also a sign that the killer was growing more desperate, and I had personal reasons to fear his next move.

"Two passes and schedules with a map of Fair Grounds Race Course." The goateed ticket seller slid the items through the window slot. He smiled behind Ray Charles sunglasses. "Jazz it out, ladies."

I froze. *That was the Axeman's threat in his letter to police—anyone who wasn't jazzing it out when he returned to New Orleans risked the ax. Is this guy trying to tell me something?*

Since I couldn't see his eyes, I checked his body language. He was quivering, but not from fear. It was from repressed laughter, and I knew the reason. I grabbed the passes and scowled at my reflection in the ticket window. Because thanks to Ladonna's handiwork, I looked like I was ready for a Jazzercise workout—in the 1980s. I had teal eyeshadow from my brow to lower lashes, glossy neon-pink lipstick, and a purple jazz hand on each cheek.

I turned to the so-called artist, who'd added teased hair and a headband to her pink-satin jacket and unitard, and handed her a pass and a map. "Here you go, Jane Fonda."

"Oh Gawd. Finicky Franki's at it again. I told you I'd never been to Jazz Fest."

"Judging from my look, you haven't been to the twenty-first century either."

She adjusted her headband. "If you'd stayed awake while I did your makeup, you could've told me to change it."

"I was tired. I got woken up by a nightmare witch, remember?" I yanked down my vintage Jazz Fest shirt of an alligator playing a saxophone. "And you left your body paint remover at home on purpose."

"I wouldn't do thaaat."

My steely teal stare said I knew better.

She lowered her head to the map, and I thought I caught the corners of a crocodile smile.

"All right, boss, where should we start?"

I scanned the schedule. "Let me check the line-up for any mention of the Big Chief and tribe names."

"There's a Native American Village not far from here."

"The Mardi Gras Indians won't be there. They'll be at the Congo Square African Marketplace or the Congo Square stage."

"I didn't know Jazz Fest was so multicultural."

"Yeah, the whole point is to celebrate the indigenous music and culture of New Orleans and Louisiana."

"Well something smells scrumptious." She looked around. "Ooh, I see the Food Heritage Stage. Let's go over there."

"Uh, we've got work to do." Although, if that scrapple was any indication, she could've used one of their live cooking demonstrations.

I returned my gaze to the schedule. "None of the tribe names jump out at me, but we're closest to the Congo Square stage, so let's start there."

We headed across the grassy field. The 145-acre horseracing track was packed with people and tents and stages, and the ground vibrated from the music. The sounds of jazz, Zydeco, and a Cuban rumba came at us from three different directions, as did the smells— sausage, Creole seasoning, and grease frying. A Food Area sign with a plate of red beans and rice got my attention.

Ladonna stuck out her tongue at a row of portable toilets. "That's cucky."

I assumed from context that the term was Philly slang for 'yucky.' "Every festival has porta-potties."

"Sure, but did you read the company name and slogan?"

"PoohDat. 'You make it, we take it.'" The play on *who dat* was kind of funny, and the slogan wasn't as bad as Lucky's Liquor and Vaxing's *Before you get your drink on, get your hairs in order.* Nevertheless, I decided against the red beans and rice.

"Hey," Ladonna said, "they have a crawfish Monica stand. Want some?"

I shuddered at the mention of the mudbug mac n cheese. "I'm allergic to crawfish, but you go ahead."

She got in a long line, and I studied my map. The race track was so big that I was afraid we'd never find the Big Chief. But Mambo Odette had said to seek his counsel about the Mardi Gras Indian, and after the awful events at the cemetery, it was vital that I find him. I just had to look for the Indian with the biggest crown.

Pain shot through my bottom—a pinch in the same spot as the swamp crawdad. I spun and came face to face with another mudbug, Ric Caruso.

He eyed me, but the googly eyes of his crawfish costume didn't. "You're made up for the wrong festival. Southern Decadence is in September."

"You're really going to take a shot at a gay and lesbian event when you're dressed like a giant crustacean in elf shoes?"

He opened his claw arms. "Yeah."

The crawdad had zero class. "If you put your pinchers on me again, I'll crack you like a lobster."

His antennae jiggled. "My native habitat is the mud. Wanna wrestle?"

I ought to introduce him to Glenda's mother. "You're disgusting, not to mention dishonest. Why didn't you tell me your father was in The Marsala Maroons with Angelo LaRocca?"

"I already had the cops on my neck, and I didn't want a PI on me too. And yet here you are, while I'm trying to do my job."

I glanced at the crawfish Monica stand where Ladonna stood in line. "Looks to me like the servers are doing all the work while you stand around pinching bottoms."

He grinned and puffed out his red chest shield. "I told you being a crawfish was a good gig."

I pursed my lips. I needed to keep my distance from the fresh shellfish. "Olive and Tony Greco are the brother and sister you had a falling out with, aren't they?"

"I had a falling out with the world after my pops' arrest."

My frustration ebbed. The arrest must have been terribly traumatic for a ten-year-old. "I'm sorry to ask you this, but I heard your father was killed in prison. Do you know who did it, and why?"

"There was a big fight in the prison yard, so they never figured out who did it."

"I also heard that Vito Greco gambled and lost the store to your dad. What do you know about that?"

His googly eyes went ballistic. "Like I told you, I was a kid when all that happened. And my pops didn't talk business with me."

"Fair enough. But from the sound of things, he was making money. Is it possible that he hid some somewhere?"

"If he did, I'd like to know where it is. I got nothing after he died. The grocery store had to be sold to cover his legal expenses."

I paused. I might not like Ric, but he'd been through a lot. "I'm sure you've been questioned by police about the break-ins at LaRocca's Market and Lucky's storage room."

"They called me in, but I told them I was working at Frankie & Johnny's."

His alibi must have checked out since the police had released him. "Did they say whose blood was in the storage room?"

"Nah, but they asked me a bunch of questions about the Grecos."

"Like where Tony is?"

"And about Olive."

I was a little surprised, but then again, that muffuletta was a nut sandwich. "What about her?"

He shrugged. "She fought with Angelo, and her brother's missing. I'm guessing they want to know whether she offed him."

Olive had wished death to meat eaters, but that was a far cry from killing her brother. "A likelier scenario is that she's keeping his whereabouts under wraps, because Tony is a more viable suspect."

Ric's red face tightened. "You think he killed Angelo?"

"Pretty Spyyyyy Boy!"

I looked around. "What was that?"

"A Mardi Gras Indian announcing himself."

"Do you see where he is?"

Ric pointed a pincher. "By the Fais Do Do stage, but his colors are all wrong."

The Spy Boy stomped and swayed in a black-feathered suit with accents that matched my Jazzercise makeup while holding a fake rifle. "I'm a Spy Boy from way downtown." He semi-sang his words. "The 9th Ward Black Hatchets. *Coochiema*."

Coochiema meant nothing to me, but his tribe name was a chop to the gut. *Could the chief of the Black Hatchets be the Big Chief?*

I walked toward the Spy Boy and locked eyes with a young man in the crowd.

I knew him, even though we'd never met. His wideset hazel eyes were unmistakable.

He bolted.

And I gave chase.

He weaved in and out through throngs of festivalgoers headed toward the Congo Square stage, where a Mardi Gras Indian tribe was performing "Iko Iko."

Shoving, apologizing, gasping for breath, I stayed on him as best I could. But he was fast, and my legs and lungs were on fire. I was about to give up, and he ducked into a tent.

I've got him.

Without slowing my pace, I dashed through the tent curtains and slammed into a mass of feathers and beads.

Arms wrapped around me, and I struggled. But I didn't scream. There must have been twenty-thousand people outside, and most of them were chanting with the tribe onstage.

Someone whooped, and I was freed.

I backed away and took in my surroundings.

I was surrounded by Indians, but not the Black Hatchets.

This tribe wore yellow-and-orange ostrich feathers.

14

Drums pounded outside the tent that had nothing on my pulse. I tried to read the faces of the Mardi Gras Indians surrounding me, but they were hidden by elaborate crowns and beaded masks.

I considered yelling, "I come in peace," but it sounded like a line from an old Western, so I kept my mouth shut. And I had another reason to stay silent. Mixed with the scent of earth and leather, I thought I smelled fear. *Have I misunderstood their intentions?*

The only thing I knew for sure—I was glad Ladonna wasn't with me in that ridiculous headband.

Two Indians broke the circle, and before me were two men at a card table. One was half-dressed in beaded suede pants, sewing the chest panel of his suit. The other was an elderly man in a massive yellow-and-orange-feathered crown adorned with crystals and intricate beadwork.

The Big Chief.

He raised his arm, and a couple of children I hadn't noticed scurried from the tent. He gestured to a chair, and I sat. I fidgeted as he pondered me in silence. His dark eyes were serious but lined with kindness.

The drums outside the tent ceased.

His crown lowered in a faint bow. "Welcome, Ms. Amato."

Either Mambo Odette had told him I was coming, or the man I'd chased into the tent had told him who I was.

"I'm Big Chief Alphonse Bayonne." His voice was deep and vibrant despite his advanced age. "This is my tribe, the Golden Flames."

Flames. They were the flame the voodoo priestess had referred to. What I didn't know was why she would send me to see the Big Chief when she'd told me not to look to the flame. "Mambo Odette Malveaux said I should seek your counsel about my investigation into Angelo LaRocca's murder."

He massaged calloused fingers. "As a PI, you know New Orleans isn't the French Quarter. It's a port city, a tough city. And it's poor. Those things, and others, have made it hard for my people." He paused and studied my face. "So when I heard about Mr. LaRocca, I had to look into the situation for the sake of my tribe."

I stole a glance at the young man I'd chased into the tent. Mambo Odette had told me not to look to the flame because he wasn't Angelo's killer, he was the Big Chief's eyes, his Spy Boy. But I wasn't clear on what he was supposed to be scouting for—or why he thought it was a good idea to bring a tomahawk to the scene of an ax murder. I mean, if anything, a peace pipe. "How does Angelo's death concern the Indians?"

"Because of who he was and the way he died."

"You mean, an Italian grocery store owner killed with an ax, like one of the Axeman's victims?"

His eyelids lowered in place of a nod. "Our people, yours and mine, had a special relationship back in the day. Our bond was so tight, the late Big Chief Tootie Montana declared that Indians would mask on Super Sunday, the Sunday before St. Joseph's Day, as a show of respect for our Sicilian brothers."

I was reminded of how The Marsala Maroons had chosen "maroon" as a show of solidarity with Black jazz musicians.

"We continue to honor that tradition and to look out for them.

And in this case, the similarities to the Axeman are strong, so we also have to look out for ourselves."

"Why is that, exactly?"

"In 1918, a woman who survived an ax attack claimed the Axeman was a mulatto, but then she retracted her statement and accused her lover. A year later, the nieces of another victim said they saw a dark-skinned man running out of the house. Two Black men, Lewis Oubicon and James Gleason, were arrested without evidence. Here we are more than a century later, and it's still happening."

The "still" told me he was referring to more than Wendell Baptiste's arrest.

The Big Chief looked at a tambourine on the table and slowly spun it. "Masking is an African tradition, and it honors the Native Americans who helped our ancestors survive."

"The maroons who lived in the swamps."

He gave another faint nod. "It also reminds our children that the struggle of our people continues. And in the face of that struggle, we must remain united."

His gaze moved to the panel the man was sewing. It was clasped hands—a symbol of solidarity and brotherhood.

What is he trying to tell me?

The man beside me snipped the thread from his needle and stood. A member of his tribe helped him into his suit. Below the clasped hands was a black-and-white skull.

And I thought of the skeleton men. I cleared my throat. "I was at Metairie Cemetery last night, and I saw men dressed like skeletons shouting threats."

The Big Chief's lined face drew into a frown. "I can't speak for them."

But he knew them. "Can you tell me who they are?"

A man in a Rasta hat stuck his head in the tent. "The Flames are on in fifteen minutes."

The Big Chief smiled. "We're ready." Then the corners of his mouth relaxed as he returned his attention to me. "We've spoken of tribes, brotherhood, and traditions and the lessons they seek to teach. These things aren't unique to Indians."

Little did he know how aware I was of tradition, like the St. Joseph's Day lemon, the bomboniere, the wedding, and the joys but also the burdens and sacrifice they often entailed. "I understand, but what does that have to do with this case?"

"There was a band."

"You mean, musicians. The Marsala Maroons?"

"Of brothers, like my tribe. But the pressures of poverty were too great. They were divided. What lessons did they learn, and what did they teach?"

I rubbed my thighs, bewildered. I'd come to seek his counsel. I needed answers, not another question. But I knew that the Mardi Gras Indians were secretive, and I understood the reason.

The drumming resumed on the Congo Square stage, and I recognized the song—"Shoo-Fly (Don't Bother Me)," a favorite of Mardi Gras Indians. It was as though the ancestors had intervened and were telling me it was time to leave.

I rose.

The Big Chief stood with difficulty beneath the weight of his suit. "We're counting on you to free our brother Wendell."

"I will. I promise you that."

I took one last look at the Spy Boy, who was putting on his suit. His hazel eyes were guarded, as though there was something he wanted to tell me but couldn't. I wished I could stay and talk to him, but I had to respect the Mardi Gras Indian traditions and find my own answers.

I left the tent to look for Ladonna.

And to look to the spirits.

"*Oof!*" Ladonna squirmed in my passenger seat and rubbed her throat. "Something I ate at Jazz Fest gave me agita."

As I eased the Mustang to a stop in front of Greco's Grocery, I had a bad flashback to the digestive issues of my old police partner, Stan. Then I thought of Bradley and the damage I'd done with that cayenne pepper.

She burped and covered her mouth. "I think it was the crawfish Monica."

I pulled the keys from the ignition. "Yeah, crawdads seem innocent enough, but they're dangerous." I frowned at the souvenir in her hand. "And that trumpet-playing crawdad you bought is giving *me* agita."

"Whaaat? It'll remind me of my first Jazz Fest and our first case together."

She *would* buy a memento that I was allergic to. "It reminds me of hives and those poor stuffed frogs playing instruments that tourists used to buy in Mexico. So I wouldn't bring that inside to show Olive. If she thinks they killed a crawfish to make it, she might kill you."

Ladonna climbed from the car. "You're the one she's got a beef with. So don't say anything finicky, or she won't cooperate."

I didn't make any promises given the age of Greco's Grocery's inventory. Plus, Olive wouldn't cooperate regardless of what I said. I slid from the car and followed Ladonna into the store.

Olive was behind the register in a 50s-inspired skirt and sweater, batting her eyelashes at a sixty-something male with thinning greased hair in a pair of gray coveralls with a "Metairie Meats" logo.

The meat man sidled up to the counter. "Got another one for you. Why did the pepperoni want to be a salami?"

"Why?" Olive asked in a breathy whisper.

"Because it was tired of being treated like a pizza meat." He did a combo teeth-smack and wink. "Get it? *Pizza meat* sounds like *piece o' meat*?"

Olive threw back her thick neck and let out a laugh that could have doubled for a dolphin mating call, and the plump mole above her mustache vibrated with every chitter.

The guy flashed a smile as greasy as his hair. "Always loved a woman who enjoyed a good joke."

"Oh, I do, Jerry." Olive pursed her lips and flipped her black 50s hair.

And my stomach flipped with it.

He picked up a box and spotted Ladonna and me. "Good timing, ladies. You just got yourselves some SalaMini on the house." He hit us with his teeth-smack and wink and threw in a finger-point. "It's a takeoff on the Italian word for mini salami, *salamini*. Get it? The capitalized M emphasizes the *mini*."

I got it—too much of it. But despite his mansplaining, I was psyched about the free baby salami, just not enough for it to be my bomboniere.

Ladonna dropped the package into her purse. "What's the occasion?"

Olive beamed at her meat man. "We're celebrating a business deal. I'm converting the gift shop into a muffuletta café, and he's supplying the cold cuts at a discount."

Now I knew what they saw in each other—money and cheap meat. "So you're not selling gifts anymore?"

"I'm moving the gift shop to the storage room, after some renovations." She pointed to the staircase next to the door marked Gifts on the back wall. "No one's been in it for years."

I wondered where she'd gotten the capital. "That won't be cheap."

She forged a smile. "No, but we can swing it."

"How does your brother, Tony, feel about another loan?"

Her smile faltered. "We've never taken a loan, not that it's any of your business."

"Your father did, right? I heard he lost the store to Joe Caruso, so he must've taken out a loan to buy it back."

Her lips did a downturn, and her mole went with them. "The Grecos have never borrowed money, all right? Now I think you need to leave."

She hadn't denied that Vito had lost the store. There was a story in there that I had to get out of her non-muffuletta-eating mouth.

"Now, ladies." Jerry held up the box of SalaMini like a shield.

"Let's take the temperature down about ten degrees, like I do with my meats."

"I'm with Jer." Ladonna stuck out her lower lip. "This was supposed to be a happy occasion for us too. We came to pick out bomboniere for Franki's big fancy society wedding."

I clenched my teeth. We hadn't discussed using my personal life as a cover.

Olive tilted forward like a bowling pin about to fall. "How many guests we talkin'?"

"Yeah." I side-eyed my partner. "How many, Ladonna?"

"Four," she twisted a curl, "maybe five hundred."

Olive bounced in her bobby socks. "That's a lot of bomboniere!"

"It is." I wanted to shove my SalaMini into Ladonna's loose lips. Thanks to the extra rent I was paying Glenda for my mom and nonna and the costume closet, not to mention Nadezhda jacking up the amount, the wedding that my parents were paying for—and Bradley's mother and grandmother were trying to pay for—was costing me a lot of money. So any bomboniere expenses were on Ladonna, who, now that I'd thought about it, hadn't offered to repay me for her Jazz Fest ticket.

Olive used her Muff-a-lotta might to strong-arm me to the Gifts door. "Let's get you shopping, Bride-To-Be."

Jerry rushed me with his card. "I gotta run, but if you need any deli meat for the reception, I'm your guy. I can get you the SalaMini wholesale."

My mouth dropped. It was like the universe wanted me to have baby salami at my wedding.

Ladonna stopped to look at old photographs on the wall. "Is this your family?"

"The top two are my *nonni* and my parents."

I could see where the thick neck and facial hair had come from— her mother.

Olive pointed to a more recent photo. "That's Tony and me about ten years ago."

If Tony had longer hair and a thinner mustache, he could've been

Olive's twin. "Could I get his number? We'd like to talk to him about the investigation."

"I can't give it to you without his permission, and I haven't heard from him in over two weeks."

Ladonna blinked. "Have you tried to call him? It seems odd that he wouldn't answer his phone for that long."

Olive huffed. "He does this all the time." She grabbed my wrist. "Now let's pick out some bomboniere."

Against my will, I let her drag me to the gift shop.

And I latched onto the doorjamb with my free hand to steady myself.

Besides the bomboniere, the room was full of dolls—babies and toddlers—and they were creepier than a marionette named Ichabod and Glenda's Cubeb Smoker. They were eating, sleeping, even bathing. Others held various objects, a xylophone, a stuffed animal, a trumpet. And they were so lifelike they could have been paralyzed— or embalmed.

Olive grinned like a proud mother. "They're reborns. Ask me why they're called that."

I breathed deep and looked at the ceiling. "*Why* are they called that?"

"Because they're silicone dolls made to look and feel like live babies."

Ladonna snuggled an infant. "Reminds me of when my Gino and Gina were eensy."

It figured she would like reborns. Even though they looked natural, their lips and eyes had technically been tarted.

I moved through the shop, looking for anything that could help me solve the case, but the room had surprisingly poor lighting. There was a small transom window with the curtains closed, which was just as well. I didn't want a good look at the merchandise.

Olive nudged me toward a doll. "Touch one."

"Uh-uh. I don't have any experience with babies—skin or silicone."

"If you're getting married, you'd better get some."

I didn't need any. With my mom and nonna in the picture, I'd be lucky to hold my child before it started school.

Ladonna rubbed the head of a girl in a high chair with spaghetti dangling from her lips, and I gagged. "How come so many of them are eating?"

Olive adjusted the boy's bib. "We want to push the baby food and diapers. Also, our clientele is still mainly Italian, and you know how they are about feeding children."

I did, and I had a lifelong weight problem to prove it.

"I wish my mother could see the reborns." Olive gave a sad shake of her head. "She sold dolls in the store, so I keep up the tradition in her memory."

She used the word tradition a lot. I thought about my conversation with the Big Chief about the challenges of poverty and the importance of tradition and staying united. Tony and Olive's parents had been poor, and they'd divorced after Vito gambled away the store. *What lessons did Tony and Olive learn from that, and did those lessons have anything to do with Angelo's death?*

Olive rubbed her hands together. "You ladies keep shopping. I'm going to go get a little something your guests will adore."

She exited the room, and I stared at the selection—a child bride and groom salt-and-pepper shaker, a Cinderella pumpkin carriage oil diffuser, a butter knife with the inscription "spread love." *All disturbing.*

Ladonna browsed at a table next to mine. She picked up a crystal pig in a veil that my mother's best friend Rosalie Artusi and the bomboniere committee would have been thrilled to see at my wedding.

I raised the butter knife. "You even *think* of ordering 500 of those, and I'll carve on you with this love-spreader until I've sliced you like a prosciutto."

She shook her curls. "If I were you, I'd put that down. Knives are bad luck at a wedding because they signify a broken relationship. If you receive one, you're supposed to give a penny to the gift giver as payment to undo the damage."

I dropped the knife like a hot jar of cayenne pepper. I'd already done enough damage to my relationship, and the only penny I had was the one I'd accidentally stolen from a dead man's tomb.

Olive returned holding a plate depicting an illustrated 50s diner waitress. "This is Mary Muff, the Muff-a-lottas' mascot, and she's perfect for serving muffulettas."

"Oh." I feigned a bummed-out face. "Most of my guests are from Boston, so they wouldn't use them."

She rolled her eyes. "Freakin' chowder eaters."

"Hey, Olive." Ladonna pointed to a wine bottle on a display shelf. "How come that Marsala is up there?"

I strained my ears to listen. Angelo and Olive had feuded over a Marsala shipment, and I still believed the bottle on his nightstand had a significance I'd yet to grasp.

"I keep it in here because I don't want grocery customers to think it's for sale. It was my grandfather's. After he died, my father refused to open it, even though he and his friends from Marsala, Sicily, drank the wine every Sunday as a tradition."

There's that word again. I was sure she was referring to his band-mates in The Marsala Maroons.

"Like one of those Italian men's clubs?" Ladonna asked.

"Well, no women were allowed." Olive's tone held a sneer, and I couldn't blame her for being resentful. As much as she celebrated tradition, she also suffered its burdens, specifically the custom of fathers favoring their sons by dismissing their daughters and disin-heriting them from the family business.

Olive exhaled. "But they called it a brotherhood."

The Big Chief had used that same term. *He chose the word on purpose, but what was he trying to tell me?*

Still pretending to browse so as not to interrupt their conversa-tion, I picked up a Corno, the red Sicilian horn talisman that protected against the evil eye. *Finally, something practical.*

"Wow, this is an old vintage."

Ladonna was holding the bottle, so I stole a glimpse. The label was torn and yellowing, and it was bottled by Florio, the same brand as the Marsala on Angelo's night table.

Olive took the bottle. "My grandfather bought this with his first profit the year he opened the store." Her eyes were alight with pride. "My dad said he was a ruthless competitor who stopped at nothing to drive other Italian grocers out of business." She patted the bottle lovingly. "That's why Greco's Grocery is here today."

I remembered my nonna's friend Luigi Pescatore telling me that the New Orleans PD still believed the Axeman murders had been killings between competitors. I glanced at the Marsala label.

And I dropped the Sicilian horn.

1917. The year the Axeman killed his first victims.

THE SECOND-FLOOR PORCH light was on when I pulled into my driveway at nine-thirty, and I was glad to see it. I was still creeped out about the 1917 bottle of Florio Marsala. I didn't really believe that Olive's grandfather was the original Axeman, but then again, they did claim to be related to the Muffuletta Man, so it was possible.

I turned off the engine and leaned over to grab my purse from the passenger floorboard. When I sat upright, I noticed a silhouette perched on the stairs.

The copycat Axeman?

I hunkered down. *Could he be Tony Greco?*

Slowly, I peered over the dashboard.

The silhouette waved.

Unless he was a friendly serial killer, it wasn't him. I leaned forward and squinted.

Bradley.

I gripped the door handle and hesitated, thinking about the check from his mother that I'd left upstairs. Bradley didn't have a key to the costume closet, but Glenda could have let him in. And if he'd found the check, it would have done more damage to our relationship than a whole jar of cayenne pepper, the "spread love" butter knife, and the Sicilian horn talisman I'd broken.

He approached the car, his eyes apprehensive.

Reluctantly, I opened the door and got out.

He gave a cautious smile, and that's all it took. I jumped into his arms, clinging to him as he nuzzled his face in my hair and my neck. I wanted the crises with us, with our families, with Wendell to all be over so that we could just be engaged.

Bradley's lips met mine, and I forgot about all the problems. After a long, sexy kiss, he pulled back and looked into my eyes. "That's quite a welcome from a woman who hung up on me yesterday and hasn't returned my calls since."

Lillian hadn't told him about my phone. But then, she wouldn't have wanted him to know she'd come over to bribe me for the sake of his career. "I dropped my phone in some water, and I still don't know whether it works."

"Want me to take a look?"

I tensed. I'd left it upstairs, and I couldn't take a chance on him going up and finding that check. "That's all right. I'm due for a new model." *That Nadezhda was going to pay for.* "Have you been waiting outside for long?"

"Only a few minutes. Your Nonna saw me pull up and made me go inside to have a *digestivo*." He flashed me an under-the-lash look. "For my weak digestion."

I bit my lower lip. "I'm sorry about that. I didn't want my nonna to know why I really needed the spice."

He gave me a questioning look.

I tugged at his shirt button, embarrassed. "Don't judge me, but this self-professed witch I know told me that if I sprinkled cayenne pepper in her and my mom's shoes, they'd go home to Houston."

He chuckled. "That's funny, because the digestive your nonna gave me was Strega."

My head jerked toward the house. Theodora might've been more right about her than I'd thought.

"I guess your witch friend is the reason Father John came over with holy water?"

"You saw him?"

He nodded. "He was finishing up in the yard when I arrived."

I wished I'd been home to talk to him. As a priest at the old Mortuary Chapel, Father John knew a lot about the way Catholicism and voodoo comingled in New Orleans both because the chapel housed the statue of a controversial saint named Expedite, who was venerated by Catholics and voodoo practitioners alike for his heavenly assistance with court cases, and because its cemetery held the remains of Marie Laveau, the most notorious voodoo priestess of all time. If anyone could help me decipher Mambo Odette's cryptic advice about looking to the spirits, it was him.

Bradley kissed my head. "By the way, your nonna tried to get him to convince me to have the wedding at his church."

I stiffened and pressed the side of my face to his chest. *Should I do what Lillian asked and tell Bradley I want to get married in Boston?* "And did he?"

"He gently told her it was best to respect the couple's wishes and traditions, and she not-so-gently told him..."

I didn't hear what Bradley said. The word "tradition" was trying to tell me something, and I knew what it was—a Boston wedding that my parents couldn't afford. I refused to take Lillian's money, so I'd have to cover the difference, which would probably take my life savings. But sometimes tradition called for sacrifice, and Bradley was worth anything I had to give up. "I've decided to have the wedding in Boston."

His head tilted, and he didn't smile. "Why would you want to do that?"

I didn't have a ready answer that didn't involve his mother. "I think it's because Veronica is having a destination wedding."

"You *think*?" He leaned back and scrutinized my face. "Franki, what's going on? Is there something you're not telling me?"

I didn't want to lie because I'd been there and done that with Bradley, and it had caused all kinds of trouble. But I didn't want to out his mother, either, because that was also a lose-lose situation. "It's just...I'm tired. Can we not discuss this right now?"

He stepped back. "I'll let you sleep."

"Bradley, don't be mad." I followed him down the driveway. "It's a weird time."

He crossed the street to his Mercedes. "The only thing weird about it is you." He opened the door. "Call me when you have a new phone and want to have an honest conversation about getting married."

I watched helplessly as he sped away. I was starting to think that I actually needed an antidote for the cayenne pepper I'd sprinkled on his tongue. With a sigh, I turned toward the house.

And a glint drew my gaze upstairs.

My hands went to my mouth.

Embedded in my new front door was an ax.

15

Father John stood outside the three white arches of Our Lady of Guadalupe Catholic Church, greeting parishioners arriving for the nine-thirty a.m. jazz mass.

I sat in my Mustang, scratching my arm. The itching was a psychosomatic reaction to the Catholic guilt of being a less-than-model parishioner and the heebie-jeebie-inducing experience of visiting the priest. The old Mortuary Chapel, as the church was originally known, was built in the back of the French Quarter in 1827 to spare citizens from the miasma and the "exhalations of the dead" thought to be responsible for the yellow fever epidemic, which, for me, cast a pall over the place in perpetuity—and its creepy cemetery across the street. And the other issue, as Marcella at the American Italian Cultural Center had awkwardly implied, was that Father John was sexy enough to be a men's underwear model, and that was just wrong for a man of the cloth.

The bell in the clocktower tolled at nine-fifteen, and I was reminded of the ominous tolling of the one at the St. Louis Cathedral a week before. I was also reminded that I was being stalked by a killer, so I had to quit stalling. Because the copycat Axeman's ax gifts had moved from my front seat to my front door, which was a sign that he was closing in on ending my life.

I got out of my car and approached Father John, who was deep in conversation with a young man. I stood to the side, awaiting my turn, and glanced inside the church.

My mom and nonna sat in a back pew.

I side-stepped behind an arch. I hadn't told them or anyone about the ax in my door, not even the police, so I didn't want them nosing around while I talked to the priest.

"Francesca?" My mother's tone was shrill with shock.

I wanted to beat my head on the back of the column. *Why? Why did I look inside?*

"What are you doing in church, dear?"

She had *to ask that in front of a priest.* "Never mind me," I said, trying to deflect from the reason for my visit. "What are you and Nonna doing here?"

"We're going to mass." Her eyelids dropped. "You should try it sometime."

Now she's blatantly outing me to Father John. I scratched my neck and stole a glance in his direction. He was still talking to the parish-ioner. *Thank God.*

My mom's eyes twinkled. "Are you here about the wedding?"

"The Angelo LaRocca case."

"Oh. Well, I suppose you saw Bradley last night?"

I didn't want to tell her about that either. "Uh-huh."

She angled toward me like the Leaning Tower of Pisa. "Any word from his mother and grandmother?"

There was no way I would tell her about Lillian and Cordelia's latest argument for having the wedding in Boston. For Brenda Amato, them was hair-pullin' words. "Speaking of mothers and grandmoth-ers, why isn't nonna out here trying to get me to commit to having Father John officiate my wedding?"

Her eyes grew serious. "She said she's got 'big-a business' to discuss with the heavenly father."

I looked inside. Nonna knelt in her mourning dress, hands

clasped tight. She was either praying for the miracle of a double wedding with Veronica or asking forgiveness for whatever she'd not-so-gently said to Father John when he'd told her to let Bradley and me decide where to get married.

"Francesca," Father John boomed, "come to hear some jazz?"

That was the last thing I wanted to listen to. Although, jazzing it out allegedly kept the Axeman away. "I'm looking into the murder of Angelo LaRocca, and I was hoping to get your opinion on something."

"I'm happy to help, if I can. But the service starts in less than fifteen minutes."

"It won't take long." I turned to my mother. "Do you mind?"

"Not at all, dear."

That was easy—too easy. I turned to the father. "I got some advice that I need your help interpreting, from a, uh, mambo."

His eyes showed no surprise. Lapsed Catholics asking for voodoo interpretations must've been a fairly routine experience for priests in The Big Easy.

"She told me to 'look to da spirits' to solve the case. I think she's referring to something that happened with Angelo's father's band, The Marsala Maroons."

He looked down and rubbed his square model jaw. "That's pretty general."

"You're preaching to the choir, Father. All I really know is that the murder involves a stolen trumpet that belonged to Louis Prima, and the descendants of the band aren't talking." I hesitated and looked at the street. "And this is going to sound crazy, but I wonder whether her advice has anything to do with some men I saw at Metairie Cemetery, who were dressed as skeletons."

"That sounds like the Northside Skull and Bone Gang."

"They're a gang?"

He waved at a parishioner. "Not a criminal gang. They're like Mardi Gras Indians but with a unique costume."

"I'll say. One of them had a bone with meat on it."

"They call it 'masking skeleton,' and they've been doing it for over two hundred years, since 1819, I believe."

"Not the same skeletons, I hope."

He flashed a Calvin Klein smile. "They can be a little frightening, but that's the point. They see themselves as death spirits who awaken young people to the dangers of drugs and violence through songs and shouted warnings."

That explained what I'd interpreted as threats. "How does their message relate to Mardi Gras?"

"It teaches kids, adults too, that the carnal pleasures celebrated at carnival are fleeting and even dangerous. They start at the Backstreet Cultural Museum at four-thirty a.m. on Mardi Gras Day and end at Congo Square. The whole way they're knocking on doors, telling people to live right or the bone men will come back for them."

I didn't know what would be more terrifying—seeing a skeleton at my door at five a.m. or having one of the Fancies from the Mummers Parade burst into my house to demand soup and booze. Probably the latter. "Why would the Northside Skull and Bone gang creep around in a cemetery?"

He raised perfectly arched brows. "Well, the creeping stems from Blacks' exclusion from Mardi Gras. Since they were banned from participating, they came up with their own secret celebrations. That's why the Indians creep around unannounced in neighborhood streets on Mardi Gras morning."

I knew about that custom. In New Orleans, it was considered good luck to see an Indian on Mardi Gras Day, or on any other day, really.

"As to why they were in the cemetery, it's not unusual for them to send off a spirit for safe passage."

I suspected that the Northside Skull and Bone Gang, like the Mardi Gras Indians, had taken an interest in Angelo's death because of the nature of the case, which meant that I'd been off base about both groups. But again, tomahawks and fleshy bones weren't things one should carry around town.

A saxophone played inside the church.

I looked back, and my mom ducked behind a column. *Great. Now I'm being stalked by a madman* and *a madwoman.*

Father John shot me a grin straight out of a photoshoot. "I've got a few more minutes. Let's look to the spirits, shall we?"

I wasn't sure what he meant, but I was ready to escape my hair-puller stalker mother. "Yes." I scratched my shoulder. "Let's."

I followed him around the side of the chapel and knew instantly where we were going—to New Orleans' most infamous graveyard, Saint Louis Cemetery Number One.

We crossed Basin Street and entered the tall iron gate. The grave-yard was enclosed in white plaster walls that also served as tombs for stacked rows of bodies in what looked like openings to pizza ovens. Unlike Metairie Cemetery, St. Louis had no grass and no open spaces, just narrow concrete pathways lined with tombs so old and decrepit that at least one had collapsed into a pile of rubble. All of them looked like miniature houses, some with black iron fences like private yards, which was the origin of the nickname 'city of the dead.'

I assumed Father John would take me to Marie Laveau's unmarked tomb. Instead, he stopped at a huge white mausoleum that towered above the others.

"The New Orleans Musicians Tomb." He walked around to the side so that I could see the openings to the three crypts it held. "It belongs to the Barbarin family, a jazz dynasty who definitely knew Louis Prima, and they've generously set aside space in the tomb to serve as a final resting place for impoverished musicians. Originally, though, it belonged to the Sacred Union Society."

Old society tombs were common in New Orleans, and I'd never really understood their historical significance. "Were the societies ever referred to as 'brotherhoods'?"

"Not that I know of. People often called them benevolent or burial societies. Incidentally, they led to the creation of jazz and the custom of paying to see musicians perform."

"The societies for *funerals*?"

"Yep. During the yellow fever epidemic, we had the highest death rate in America. Societies arose to help cover the costs of above-ground burials. To join one, you signed three contracts—one for the society, one for a doctor, and one for a brass band to play at your funeral, because that was fashionable in Europe. So, the society movement spun off a brass band movement, which is where all jazz musicians, including Louis Armstrong, got their start." He patted the first crypt. "By the way, Armstrong called Isidore Barbarin, here, 'Pops.'"

"And those musicians had been influenced by the slaves and maroons at Congo Square."

"That's right." He crouched and brushed debris from the base of the tomb. "They followed the body as it was taken to the cemetery, which is how second lines came about. Competition arose among brass bands, so they looked for what was known as a 'getoff man,' a guy who played in a way that got people excited. The best getoff men started attracting fans, which led to performances in dance halls and brothels in Storyville and beyond."

I stared at him, impressed. Like Theodora, the man knew his history. And given his voodoo knowledge, I was tempted to ask him whether he knew anything that would undo the adverse effects of sprinkling cayenne pepper in a fiancé's mouth. But if I was going to push my luck with anyone, I figured it shouldn't be a priest.

I looked down at a black rosary with four silver skulls that had been left at the base of the tomb. It was a Memento Mori, Latin for "Remember Your Death," and the four skulls served to remind the faithful to live virtuously with the time they had left on earth, the same message as that of the Northside Skull and Bone Gang.

But for me, the four skulls represented The Marsala Maroons, Roberto LaRocca, Lucky Mistretta Sr., Joe Caruso, and Vito Greco.

Look to da spirits.

I walked to the remaining two crypts but didn't see anything that shed light on the cryptic phrase. "Did you ever hear of any groups that described themselves as 'brotherhoods'?"

"You mean, in relation to jazz?"

"That or in the Italian community."

"Can't say that I have, but the Italians don't come to Our Lady of Guadalupe anymore."

It was probably because of the plague pall hanging over the chapel, but I didn't say that.

I crouched and looked at the tokens visitors had left on a shelf below the inscription. A plastic daisy, a ceramic angel, a cigarette. On the ground below were some Mardi Gras doubloons and a miniature toy trumpet. On closer inspection, I spotted a scroll that had been inserted into the horn. "Is that voodoo?"

Father John crouched beside me. "It's probably just a note from a fan. Both Isidore and Charles Barbarin, his grandson, were trumpeters."

I flashed back to Gabriel's horn on Louis Prima's crypt and the penny taped to it—the damned one that had ended up in my hair.

I couldn't see the spirits, but I thought I heard them whispering to me.

A PHONE RANG SOMEWHERE in St. Louis cemetery. Father John had gone to deliver mass, and as far as I could tell, I was alone—except for the dead.

The ringing stopped.

I knelt before Marie Laveau's tomb and stared at the X marks left by followers who sought her favors from beyond the grave. I'd stopped by on the off chance that the notorious voodoo priestess would give me clarity on Mambo Odette's look-to-da-spirits advice. Not surprisingly, she hadn't.

The ringing resumed, muffled, but close.

I scrambled from the tomb. *Is Marie Laveau calling me from beyond?*

Then I remembered. I'd put my cell in my purse to take it to a repair store. I really had to get a grip.

I pulled out my phone, but the ringing still sounded muffled. It had to be swamp-water damage, but at least it was working. Despite the unknown number, I answered. "Franki Amato."

"This is Louis Armstrong."

He sounded like a kid pinching his nose, so I suspected a prank. "The jazz performer?"

"I'm afraid he's dead. And I'm no relation."

With a voice like his, the last point was obvious.

"I need to talk to you about an urgent personal matter. Could you meet me at the statue of Louis Armstrong?"

My prank-call radar blared like a trumpet. "You're Louis Armstrong, and you want me to meet you at the statue of Louis Armstrong?"

"Yes, the one in Louis Armstrong Park."

I hung up.

My phone rang again. Same number. "Listen, Louis—"

"Please don't hang up. This is my first case, and I need to win it."

"You're an attorney?"

"Yes, and this is a matter of life and death. Come right away." He hung up.

The only person I knew who would have an attorney was Wendell. On the other hand, the caller could've been the copycat Axeman—with a super unfortunate voice for a killer.

Or the Spy Boy. He'd seemed like he wanted to tell me something.

"Hey, Mambo Marie," I said to the tomb. "I'm not stealing from your grave. I just need to borrow this for a second." I picked up a quarter and flipped it. Tails, so I had to meet the guy. I returned the quarter, but I blamed my bad luck on the damned penny from Prima's tomb. I had to return that thing, and soon.

Louis Armstrong Park was just up the street from the cemetery. I decided to walk so that I could pass through Congo Square on the way. As soon as I entered the historical gathering place, I saw a statue of a Mardi Gras Indian, masking in a massive feather suit and crown. I stopped to read the plaque. *Allison "Big Chief Tootie" Montana.*

Ancestors, traditions, brotherhood.

My text tone beeped. It was a message from Louis Armstrong.

The statue is the one with the trumpet.

The reference to the instrument seemed suspiciously timely. I looked at the Chief of Chiefs. *Are the ancestral spirits whispering to me too?*

Deep in thought, I headed for the designated meeting place. Louis Armstrong—the twelve-foot bronze statue, not the mystery caller—held a handkerchief in his right hand and a trumpet in his left. I eyed the instrument, but nothing seemed out of the ordinary. I wondered whether I'd read too much into the penny and the scroll at Prima's and Barbarin's tombs in my desperation to solve the case.

I took a seat on the circular steps at the statue's base.

A young guy in an N95 mask and a suit too big for his slight body crossed the grass. I didn't know whether he was sick or trying to hide his identity, but either way, he'd unintentionally provided me with a viable alternative to Ladonna's makeup.

The masked man made an abrupt turn toward me, and my gut knotted.

The caller.

The killer?

I trained my eyes on his hands—and that briefcase.

"Franki Amato?"

I nodded.

"Louis Armstrong." His voice was muffled like my phone.

I almost laughed. In a homicide case involving masked identity and masking Indians, I was meeting with a guy in an actual mask.

He took a seat on the steps, and I scooted around the circle. Until I knew the reason for the N95, I wanted to keep at least six feet between us. "What's this about?"

Louis pulled down the mask, and except for the fact that he wasn't wearing glasses, he could've been The Vassal's kid brother, which was saying a lot since my colleague was only twenty. He was even mouth-breathing. He pulled a box of Puffs from his briefcase and blew his nose. "Sorry. I don't know whether this is allergies or the flu."

It was considerate of him to wear a mask. Nevertheless, I moved to a higher step.

He dropped the tissue on the step beside him. "I have a video on my phone from my client, Wendell Baptiste."

"*You're* the public defender who knew I'd visited him in jail?"

"I do my homework."

He looked like he did—in high school. "Who for? Yourself or the police?"

"Excuse me, but I'm an honest professional." He huffed and jerked his suit coat.

And I covered my nose and mouth. "You know, that mask isn't effective if you lower it to blow your nose and talk."

"OK, boomer."

If I wasn't still half-suspicious about the contents of his briefcase and oversized suit, I would have risen up like the twelve-foot statue of Satchmo. "I'm *Gen Y*," I growled through my teeth, "which is two generations *after* the baby boomers. And good hygiene isn't an out-of-touch idea."

He pulled up the mask.

"Now what's with all the secrecy around this video?"

Louis looked behind him and then scanned the trees in front of us. "What Mr. Baptiste has to say is explosive, and I can't risk it getting out, for all of our sakes. His safety would be compromised, and he says you could be in serious danger. And like I told you on the phone, this is my first case, so it's really important to me. And my mom."

I knew why he wore that N95—because his mother made him. "When was the video recorded?"

"Last night in an attorney-client meeting room."

I made sure his mask was on properly, and then I moved closer. "Let's see it."

He did one more scan of the park and tapped the play icon.

"Oh, Franki." Wendell rocked in his chair, clearly self-soothing. "I talked to that brother, de one de guard gave me a tip about, and I was right to stay in here. Yes I was."

My stomach tightened. *Not an auspicious start to the video.*

Wendell used his jumpsuit sleeve to wipe the sheen from his brow. "Ric Caruso's dad was beaten to death in prison, and da cops didn't never solve his murder."

That confirmed what Ric had told me at Jazz Fest.

"But my source said it was common knowledge dat his killer was a guy named Jack Marino, and get dis," he widened his eyes, "da dude was a friend o' Vito Greco's."

My body tensed like my gut. That was how Vito had been able to keep Greco's Grocery after he'd lost it. He'd canceled his gambling debt by having a thug cancel Joe Caruso.

Wendell tugged at the collar of his jail jumpsuit as though it was choking him, but it wasn't touching his neck.

Feeling stifled myself, I unzipped my jacket.

"Turns out dis Marino guy was in jail for extortion and assault, and everyone knew who he worked for at da time. And girl, it's someone we both know."

My eyes darted to Louis.

He stopped the video. "Me? I'm only twenty-two."

"I didn't think it was you. But now that I know your age, is it even legal for you to be a public defender?"

"I'm an adult, aren't I?"

That was debatable. I flicked my wrist at his phone. "Turn it back on."

He tapped the screen. Wendell looked green, and it had nothing to do with the video quality. "And he didn't like Joe Caruso neither, because his bookie business cut into his profits."

"Wait. *Who* didn't like Joe Caruso?"

"Sorry, sometimes the video skips ahead." He rewound it.

"...And girl, it's someone we both know." Wendell paused.

My heart paused with him. *Is he talking about Detective Sullivan?* No. He was most likely dead. And like Public Defender Louis Armstrong, the detective hadn't been born when Joe Caruso was killed.

I looked at the screen. "Who is it?"

"Franki, Lawdy be," he replied as though the conversation were live, "it was da G-Man."

I leaned forward. "Come again?"

"You heard me," Wendell said, anticipating my reaction during the videotaping. "Vito Greco's killer worked for Gigi Scalino."

I collapsed backward on the steps like I'd been Tommy-gunned. Luigi "Gigi" Scalino was the mob boss Wendell and I had helped send to prison. *Is the brotherhood I'm trying to track down the Mafia?*

I STARED at the Mississippi River from the safety of my car. Given my well-established tendency to fall into bodies of water and the possible involvement of the Mafia in the case, I didn't want to wind up like one of the fish floating near the bank.

I crunched a Zapp's Voodoo potato chip and concentrated on the river. After the Mortuary Chapel and the cemetery, the Mississippi was the only other place I could think of to look to the spirits. Native Americans viewed it as sacred and had buried their dead in mounds on its banks, and the Spanish Explorer Hernando De Soto had even named it the "River of the Holy Spirit." But despite the river's spiritual associations, my thoughts were still much like its water—murky and dark.

It didn't seem likely that Gigi Scalino had ordered the hit on Joe Caruso. Since Caruso was in prison when he was murdered, his bookie operation was already out of business and no longer a threat to Gigi Scalino's profits. The likelier scenario was that Vito Greco's mob friend, Jack Marino, had acted on his own when he'd killed Caruso.

One thing I knew for sure was that if the truth about Joe Caruso's murder was common knowledge, as Wendell had said, then Ric Caruso had lied when he told me that he didn't know who killed his father. *But why?* The murder of a family member could be a motive to kill, but I wouldn't have suspected Ric of killing Angelo LaRocca for a crime that Olive and Tony's father had ordered. The only explanation

I could come up with was that Ric feared for his own life if he talked. But that didn't make sense either because all of that was past history. *Unless...*

...the brotherhood extended to subsequent generations.

I threw the chip bag to the passenger seat and grabbed my phone. My dad had grown up in New Orleans and worked in the grocer community. He might've heard about a brotherhood.

I dialed the deli, hoping my mother's friend Rosalie didn't answer.

"Amato's Deli. This is Joe."

For once, a lucky break. "Hey, Dad. You got a minute?"

"Just one. The church crowd is here."

"I'll be quick."

"Are you okay, honey? You sound stressed."

"I'm all right," I fibbed. "It's the LaRocca case."

"I didn't mean to put any pressure on you when I asked you to look into it. Why don't you leave it to the police?"

"I can't, Dad. Believe it or not, the suspect is a friend. He was the last person to see Angelo alive, so they arrested him without any evidence."

"The case is really hitting close to home, isn't it?"

I thought of the axes in my car and front door. "You could say that, yeah."

"Well, I wish I could be there to help out. I've gotten a few calls from old friends and colleagues since Angelo died, but we mainly talked about old times."

"Dad, this is important. Did any of them mention a brotherhood?"

"Not that I remember. Why?"

"I think The Marsala Maroons had some sort of brotherhood that could be a factor in Angelo's death."

"Honestly, 'brotherhood' sounds like a term the immigrants from the old country would've used. You might ask your nonna's friend Luigi Pescatore. He'd know more about that generation than I would."

He had a point. It might be a good time to sound out Luigi on some of the emerging particulars of the case.

"Hang on a sec, honey. I've gotta ring up a customer."

The phone banged onto the counter.

And then someone picked it up.

"Franki?" Rosalie's brash voice battered my ear. "Did Olive Greco confess to shorting me that prosciutto slice?"

The question was so outrageous that I did a double eye roll. "I didn't ask her about your meat, Rosalie, because I'm investigating a murder."

"Oh, so I'm busting my hump heading up your bomboniere committee, and you can't be bothered to get justice for me?"

I pressed my forehead to the steering wheel. "A stolen prosciutto slice isn't even something the police would take seriously, and I told you that I disbanded your committee."

"When all I'm trying to do is help you out. So, while we're on the subject, I'll give you one more crack at the confetti pigs."

She was cracked if she thought I would ever agree to have those pigs at my reception. "Rosalie, for the last time, this is my wedding, so please stay out of it."

"Whoa! Bridezilla returns."

I had sounded kind of demanding—but not unreasonable.

"Just hear me out, okay?"

My head hit the headrest. I might as well since I'd told my dad I'd wait for him to ring up that customer. "Fine."

"Your mother said the pigs aren't classy enough for the Hartmanns, so I called the company, and they said they can add rose gold to their lips. *Rose. Freaking. Gold.* What's classier than that?"

Apparently, Rosalie wasn't familiar with the expression *putting lipstick on a pig*, but it did seem like she knew Marcella from the American Italian Cultural Center. "No amount of rose gold, or any other precious metal, will make those pigs acceptable."

"I know what will—after they poop the almonds, they can be used as piggy banks. The kids'll love 'em."

I envisioned parents watching their children shake pennies from the pigs' bottoms and wondered how she could think that was a selling point.

Then I thought of the penny taped to the Angel Gabriel's trumpet.

And the note inside the toy trumpet at the New Orleans Musicians Tomb.

"Holy crap." I hung up and gaped at the Mississippi River. Because the spirits had spoken to me loud and clear.

Something is hidden inside the stolen trumpet, and that's what the copycat Axeman is after.

16

Someone was climbing the Private Chicks' stairwell.

And I was alone.

I grabbed my Ruger and rose from the plastic-covered couch in Ladonna's office, where I'd spent the night among the blue Marilyn Monroe pillows. It was seven a.m., so Veronica could have been early to work. But the copycat Axeman was due for a visit to my place of business, if he hadn't already come.

The footsteps got louder, like the beat of my heart.

I'd left my Mustang in the office parking lot to lure the killer away from the fourplex and keep my family and friends safe. I figured that he'd think I was sleeping in Private Chicks because no one, not even a psychotic ax murderer, would be daft enough to think I'd spend the night in Ladonna's office—unless they knew that one of my apartments resembled an old French brothel and the other was a stripper costume closet.

The footsteps reached the landing and stopped.

Between my heartbeat and my breath, I had to strain to hear. I expected the sound of Veronica's keys or someone tampering with the Private Chicks door.

But I heard the footsteps come toward Ladonna's office.

I raised my gun and took aim. An ax was no match for a bullet.

"I'm armed, and I've called the police," I fib-shouted.

"Franki, it's Veronica."

I dropped the Ruger, relieved. "Sorry for the confusion. You're clear to come in."

Veronica entered in a black pantsuit that matched her glower. "I've been frantic trying to reach you, and your gun confirms what I feared—the damage to the costume closet door came from an ax."

My phone didn't show any missed calls, but evidently the swamp had struck again. "Has Glenda seen it too?"

"She's the one who showed it to me. She's got a big photoshoot today, and she needed something from the costume closet for her outfit. She called me, worried sick, when she couldn't find you, and you didn't answer her calls."

I was touched by Glenda's concern. That was a side of her I didn't often see.

"She also says you're going to pay her for a new door."

And that was a side of her I saw often.

Veronica ran a hand through her hair. "I don't suppose you've called the police."

I sat on the couch, and the groan of the plastic reflected my sentiment. "They'll tell me that I brought this on myself for interfering in the investigation, and it's not like they'll give me protection."

"No, but they'll be aware of the situation."

"Uh-huh, and they'll tell me to call 9-1-1 when I need them. But I don't." I leaned forward to slip on my shoes. "Because I'm closing in on him."

"The chunk he took out of your door shows he's closing in on you." Veronica flounced in a red-and-gold armchair. "Who do you think it is?"

Footsteps prevented my reply.

We tensed and shared a look, and then Veronica eyed the door. "I'm sure it's just someone coming to work."

Ladonna waltzed in with a grin. "I thought I heard you two in here."

Veronica relaxed, but I didn't. For one thing, Ladonna wore a silver holographic dress that brought back the lunar lunatic vibes of The Crescent City Medium, Chandra Toccato. And for another, Chandra had been in my head a lot lately, which might've been a psychic sign that she was about to show up.

Ladonna deposited her things on the gold desk. "Are we having a meeting?"

I looked over my shoulder. "I was about to catch Veronica up on the particulars of the case, and I have updates for you too."

She sat in an armchair with a bottle of orange nail polish. "I'm all ears. Just gotta fix a chipped nail."

"As of right now, Tony Greco is the obvious suspect, but his sister, Olive, hasn't seen him since before Angelo was killed, and the police can't find him. So either he's in hiding or something has happened to him."

"Yeh." Ladonna shook the polish. "And there's a wrinkle in the Tony-is-guilty assumption because Olive says their dad belonged to some kind of brotherhood."

Veronica's lips protruded. "Which could mean that someone else in this brotherhood could have wanted to kill Angelo and sell the trumpet on the black market."

I raised my index finger. "I don't think the killer plans to sell it. I think he wants something hidden inside."

Ladonna paused in mid-shake. "Where'd you get that idea?"

I thought it best to skip the cemetery-and-bomboniere origins of my theory. "I was thinking about this last night. Wendell told Veronica and me that the trumpet case, not the trumpet, had Louis Prima's name on it. By leaving the case behind, the killer made it clear that the famous origins of the trumpet were irrelevant—he wanted the trumpet for some other reason, most likely for something inside it. And, he could've been sending some sort of message to the brotherhood."

Veronica nodded. "Sounds plausible. Any ideas about what the brotherhood is or who might be in it?"

"That's another wrinkle. Wendell found out that Tony and Olive's father was killed by a guy who worked for Gigi Scalino."

Ladonna looked up from her polish. "The Mafia boss?"

Veronica gripped the chair arm. "Who is *hardly* a wrinkle."

"Right?" Ladonna pressed her breast. "He's a big gaping hole, like a chest wound."

I hugged a blue Marilyn to my chest, which suddenly felt vulnerable. "I seriously doubt the Mafia is involved. Gigi was responsible for at least half of New Orleans' crime back then, so it's probably a coincidence that the guy who killed Vito Greco was one of his men. And if Gigi was behind Angelo's murder, he wouldn't send an Axeman to whack me. It would be a hitman with a gun or garrote."

Ladonna painted her thumbnail. "Not necessarily. Mafiosi use all kinds of methods to kill their victims, and some of them have the nicknames to prove it, like Anthony 'Gaspipe' Casso and Vincent 'Vinnie Aspirins' Congiusti."

Veronica's brow formed a V. "He killed people with aspirin?"

"No, a power drill." She tapped her temple. "Got rid of their headaches."

My arms tightened around the blue Marilyn. "Excuse me, but I'm trying to reassure myself here."

Ladonna gestured to the bookshelf. "Then read some of my *Chicken Soup for the Soul* books. They really are soup for the soul."

I wondered whether her obsession with the series had to do with the Mummers Parade and the home-invasion soup tradition.

Footsteps pounded the stairs, and Veronica looked at the door. "That sounds like David and Standish."

"Be careful, Mother." Lillian's voice boomed in the stairwell. "These old stairs are as thin as matchsticks."

"It's the Hartmanns," I whisper-hissed. "Bradley probably told them that I agreed to have the wedding in Boston."

Veronica's mouth was as round as her eyes. "You did?"

"They pressured me into it, and he doesn't know."

"In that case," she pushed herself from the chair, "I'll tell them you're out."

Ladonna screwed the lid on her polish. "Yeh, you shouldn't talk to those two without Bradley present."

That was a policy I planned to follow moving forward.

Ladonna and I sat in silence, trying to eavesdrop on Veronica's conversation with the women.

"That's odd," Cordelia drawled. "Francesca's car is in the parking lot."

Veronica cleared her throat. "Yes, but she's not in her office."

"Well, this is urgent." Lilian's tone was as taut as the skin on her face. "We must speak to her at once."

"I understand," Veronica said, "and I'll give her that message."

"That won't do. We need her cell phone number."

"I'm sorry, but I can't give out her personal information. Company policy."

"That's absurd." Lillian huffed. "I'm her future mother-in-law."

"I can't make exceptions."

The exchange was so awkward that I squirmed on the couch, and the plastic protested, ratting me out.

A silence fell over the stairwell.

"Miss Maggio." The suspicion in Lillian's voice was palpable. "I don't want to seem neb—er, nosy, but who is in that room?"

"Our new detective, and I need to get back to our meeting." Veronica spoke in a clipped tone that bordered on cutting. "I'll let Franki know you stopped by."

"I would appreciate that," Lillian said, but she didn't sound grateful.

Footsteps resumed on the stairs, thankfully descending.

Veronica returned and smoothed her blazer as though there'd been a tussle. "I can see how you'd feel pressured by them."

"I'm surprised they didn't try to bribe you with a check like they did me."

"They tried to *pay* you?" She flopped into the armchair. "What are you going to do?"

"I don't know. Bradley's mad at me because he suspects that something's up. He wants me to call him to have an 'honest discussion'

about the wedding, but I can't tattle on his mother and grandmother."
I laid back on the couch. "How is he so oblivious to their tactics? I
certainly see the stuff my mom and nonna pull."

Ladonna touched her hair where my mother had pulled it.
"Because they're painfully obvious."

I'd set my family up for that.

Veronica sighed. "Mother-son relationships are complex."

Ladonna pulled a book from the shelf. "I've got a book for you,
Chicken Soup for the Soul: Moms and Sons."

"Is there one for harassed daughters and daughters-in-law?"

Ladonna's lips tightened, and she rearranged books on her shelf.
"Families can be a pain, but I miss living near mine, and I would even
miss my mother-in-law if she went back to Italy."

I started to say, "Even after she invaded your house?" But then I
remembered that was accepted parade behavior in Philly.

Ladonna took her seat. "I always remember that the meddling
comes from a good place, like love or concern or tradition. So you
can't take it personally—except when your mother-in-law grabs your
boobs in a bridal shop and says you'll never be able to fill out a dress."
She stuck out her chest. "Then it's personal."

I clung to blue Marilyn with all my might.

Footsteps pounded the stairs, and Veronica held up her hand.
"Those are definitely the feet of David and Standish. I need to give
them their work assignments."

She left the office, and Ladonna turned to me. "Hey, what's
Bradley's mother's maiden name?"

I had to think for a moment. "Linde. Why?"

"I was just wonderin' whether she came from a society family like
her husband."

I sighed. "It would seem so."

"Well, I've got just the thing to cheer you up." Ladonna hopped
up and went to her desk.

"Let me guess. Actual chicken soup."

"Nope. Shoo-fly cake."

I'd never heard of it, but if it was anything like scrapple, it might've been a better option than Theodora's tweaked Dispello spell. "Any chance it has the magical power to shoo away unwanted guests?"

"No, but it'll chase your blues away."

Or turn me as blue as blue Marilyn.

Ladonna put a slice on a napkin in front of me. "I started craving this after I heard some Mardi Gras Indians sing a shoo-fly song at Jazz Fest."

The Spy Boy crept into my head. *What had he wanted to tell me in the tent?*

The door opened, and David entered followed by The Vassal and Veronica. He shot me a somber look as he handed me an unmarked envelope. "Yo, uh, someone left this for you."

"How do you know it's for me? You caught Theodora in that stripper pole trap you made, so it could be for you."

The Vassal closed his slack jaw to swallow.

David shook his head. "That would be singularly terrifying, but, like, we found it on your windshield."

All eyes were on me.

"Chill out, guys," I said, although there *was* something ominous about the discovery. "I'm sure it's just Bradley's mother telling me to call her."

Their eyes lowered to the envelope.

I breathed deep and pulled out a folded piece of paper.

A piece of ostrich feather—part yellow, part orange—fluttered to my lap.

Ladonna hmphed. "That didn't come from the Hartmanns' brunch outfits."

No, it's from a Golden Flames suit—the Spy Boy's. The bite of cake in my gut weighed on me like a boulder as I opened the note.

After Wendell Baptiste left LaRocca's Market, Tony Greco went into Angelo's apartment.

～

EVEN THOUGH IT wasn't quite dusk when I left Veronica's apartment, stage lights illuminated the fourplex, casting a glow on the stripper pole in the yard and Luigi Pescatore's green Lamborghini in the driveway. Glenda and her stylist-photographer, Bob, were nowhere to be seen, and as far as I could tell, neither was an ax murderer. Nevertheless, I had a gun strapped to my calf beneath my jeans as I headed next door to my apartment.

I entered to a blast of garlic, tomato, and basil, and Luigi pushed himself from the purple armchair. "Nice to see ya, Franki." He pointed a knobby finger at the door. "Hey, did I take your parking spot?"

"No, my car's at the office." I didn't tell him that I'd ridden home with Veronica because I was trying to hide from the copycat Axeman —or that I'd been sleeping on her couch for the past five hours because I'd stayed up all night afraid that he would hunt me down and hack me to death. "Thanks for meeting me."

"Always a pleasure, kid." He inched back into the chair. "And it doesn't hurt that I get to eat your nonna and mother's cooking."

My mother stepped from the kitchen with a gleam in her eye that matched the one on the dish she was drying. "Oh, it's all Carmela, really. I tell you, she could own her own restaurant, and such a good housekeeper too."

I gave her a go-back-to-the-kitchen glare. She'd never given up on marrying her mother-in-law off to Luigi, and I wanted to get rid of her before she proposed a triple wedding for Veronica, me, and Nonna.

Luigi poured me a glass of Barolo. "How's the case coming?"

I took the wine, grateful it wasn't Marsala, and sat on the chaise lounge. "I got an anonymous letter today."

His watery eyes widened behind his George Burns glasses. "Those are a big thing in the Sicilian culture."

This wasn't Sicilian. It was Spy Boy. "It implies that Tony Greco is the killer."

Luigi's hearing aid almost popped from his ear. "From Greco's Grocery? You think he killed Angelo?"

"It looks that way, but no one's seen him since the murder, which seems odd. Did you or your produce company ever do business with the Grecos?"

"With his father, Vito, but not for long. He was an angry, suspicious character, didn't trust a lot of people, so he changed distributors a lot, and we weren't sorry to say sayonara to his business."

"Did he ever mention belonging to a brotherhood?"

"Not that I remember, but a lot of Italians formed groups like that, brotherhoods, fraternities, orders. It reminds me of that book by... Oh, what the heck was his name?" He snapped his fingers. "John Fante. *Brotherhood of the Grape*."

The grape made me think of the Marsala bottle on Angelo's night table and the one in the Grecos' gift shop. "Did you read it?"

"Years ago. It's about a guy who tries to play peacemaker when his elderly parents decide to divorce. But he has a lot of friction with them too, because his dad's a drunk and because they're disappointed that he didn't become a stonemason like his dad or a devout Catholic like his mother." He paused and looked down at his lap. "It's about family obligations and traditions. And this might surprise you, but those can do damage to kids."

Visions of St. Joseph's Day lemons, pig bomboniere, and double weddings danced the tarantella in my head. I took a swig of wine to drown them out.

My mother returned to the living room, but the gleam in her eye had turned glower. "I don't know who this John Fante is, but traditions are wonderful."

She didn't think so when Lillian had announced that it was traditional for Hartmann weddings to take place in Boston, and she definitely wouldn't think that if I told her about the Fancies of Philadelphia bursting into homes and demanding soup and booze.

Nonna appeared waving a wooden spoon. "Brenda is-a right. Traditions keep-a the family together. Look at-a us."

We were together, all right. Too often. I held up my nose and made a show of sniffing the air. "I think the sauce is burning."

As I'd intended, they scurried to the kitchen.

Luigi leaned forward. "Don't tell them I said this, but some traditions don't make sense for the younger generation."

That could've been what had happened with Angelo, Tony, Olive, and Lucky Jr. They might've been told by their fathers to respect the terms of a brotherhood that didn't make sense to them, except for maybe Olive, who was a vocal proponent of tradition. On the other hand, allegiance to a brotherhood might explain why Ric was reluctant to talk about the death of his father. Whatever the situation, I couldn't imagine what the brotherhood would have that could be inside the trumpet.

"What's on your mind, kid?"

"Louis Prima's missing trumpet. I think there's something hidden in it that the killer wants."

He brushed a wisp of hair from his lens. "You know who you could ask? My old friend Manny Vitale."

"Who's that?"

"A jazz trumpeter who played with Prima a few times. Before you came in, I was telling your mom and nonna that he's playing at Crawfish Fest over at Central City BBQ tomorrow. It's a long shot, but he might know something that could help." He shifted in the chair and reached into the pocket of his high-waisted pants. "I'll write his number on my card."

A boom sounded that shook the fourplex, and my mother screamed.

"It sound-a like a bomb-a!" Nonna yelled.

That was no bomb, but it wasn't an ax, either. I looked around the room. Everyone appeared shocked, but fine.

I pulled the gun from the holster beneath my jeans.

"Francesca Lucia Amato, what are you doing with a weapon in my house?"

I wanted to say, "Staging a coup to take back my house," but I went with, "Everyone stay indoors until I tell you it's clear."

They nodded, but I didn't have much hope that my mom and nonna would listen. "Luigi, help me out with that."

"You got it, Franki."

With my gun drawn, I slipped from the apartment and found the source of the noise.

The stripper pole had crashed into the balcony.

I rolled my eyes and crouched to slip my Ruger into the holster.

"Don't put that gun away, Miss Franki," Glenda shouted from above. "I need to shoot me a witch."

I looked up as Nadezhda descended the stairs in a short snakeskin trench coat followed by Glenda, who wore what looked like a circular shower rod with a curtain of rhinestone fringe—that was slowly opening.

"Child, don't look at me like that." Glenda's face was as frosty as her crystal lips. "Theodora tried to kill me by tampering with my #stripperpole and ruined my biggest #influencershoot."

It looked like she'd ruined her #dress. "I'm not looking at you. It's your outfit."

Glenda relaxed and flipped her hair. "Bob designed it after our trip to the junkyard, sugar. The fringe is remote-control operated, but when I climbed on the pole and it fell, it hit the control unit on the way down. So now the damn fringe keeps opening and closing."

That was unfortunate because of what she wasn't wearing underneath. "Why do you think Theodora did this?"

Nadezhda sneered. "She vant even score for Axeman trap."

Glenda waved her arm at the stage. "The proof is in the pole, Miss Franki. The bolts aren't stripped—they were unscrewed."

I looked for signs that Theodora had been there, i.e., a black-salt mixture that would send my apartment-squatters packing, but I didn't see any. I shrugged. "What can I say? Payback's a witch."

Glenda huffed and lit a cigarette, and Bob stormed down the stairs and began loading the lighting into his car.

"What's with him?"

She blew out a drag. "He's so mad about the shoot being ruined that he can't speak. I kept trying to talk to him, but the words wouldn't come out."

I stared at him, fascinated. As an Italian-American, I couldn't wrap my mind around the concept of silent anger.

"If he quits my #influencercampaign because of Theodora, that witch will never mount another broom."

Nadezhda nodded her spikes. "Da. Ve show her vhere crawfish hibernate."

"Huh?"

"It Russian expression."

"Yes, sugar. Miss Nadezhda says it means to teach someone a lesson."

That made absolutely no sense, which was perfect for Louisiana. "Well, based on what you're paying him, he'll be back tomorrow."

Glenda batted crystal eyelashes. "Oh, Bob doesn't do this for the money, sugar. He's a generous man who just wants to share his #stripperccoutureart with the world."

That was my cue to go in—and also, her fringe was opening again. "I'd better get back inside and let everyone know what happened."

"And we'd best try to get through to Bob." Glenda sashayed across the yard, her shower curtain rod swaying, with Nadezhda in tow.

I turned to enter my apartment and saw a flickering light in the cemetery. Someone must have left an electric candle at a loved one's grave. I opened the front door, and Napoleon bolted across the yard to the cemetery.

"You *would* do that after the sun has set."

Begrudgingly, I crossed the street, cursing whoever had left the graveyard gate open. "Napoleon! Come on, buddy."

I heard leaves rustle. I hoped it was Napoleon rooting around, but I had my doubts.

"Let's go, boy. Time to eat."

Dead silence.

My stomach churning, I set off through the tombs. A gargoyle bared his teeth from atop a mausoleum, probably mocking me for walking through a creepy cemetery after dark when I was being stalked by an ax murderer.

"Fair enough," I said to lighten the somber mood, "but I could do without the attitude." I crouched, dismayed by the earthy odor of decay, and pulled my gun from its holster. As I rose, I saw the source of the flickering light.

A maroon Virgin Mary candle, like the one by Angelo's death bed.

The back of my neck tingled, and the hair on my arms stood at attention.

That candle is no coincidence. Is the killer in the cemetery?

Ruger raised, I walked toward the flame, fearing a trap along the lines of Glenda's stripper pole. As I got closer, I saw that the candle had been positioned in front of a large hole.

In the shape of a grave.

Don' look to da flame, look to da spirits.

I pivoted to check behind me and jumped at a horrifying statue of a figure in a shroud. With my lifeblood furiously pumping, I turned and peered inside the burial plot.

And a scream erupted from my lungs.

The lifeless-lifelike body of the spaghetti-eating reborn doll lay at the bottom with the 1917 bottle of Florio Marsala.

17

The odor of diesel mixed with Central City BBQ filled my lungs as I leaned against Manny Vitale's tour bus outside Crawfish Fest. "Something doesn't smell right."

Ladonna took a step backward on the sidewalk and once-overed the wet-umbrella bags I'd pulled onto my calves. "Yeh, that plastic wrap you're wearing. It's a sunny day. You can't go in Crawfish Fest looking like that."

I tightened the hood of my disposable rain poncho. "I'm allergic to this entire festival, so I can't take any chances, and it's no worse than when you made me up as a nutria and an 80s Jazzercise freak."

"I made you look cute, not homeless in a storm."

I did look like a bag lady, but I had to protect myself. Crawfish were every bit as dangerous as the copycat Axeman. "Anyway, I was talking about the case. After finding that grave in the cemetery last night, I feel like something's off."

"Like what?"

"If I knew that, I'd tell you."

"Well, I think you're exhausted from staying up two nights in a row. Why don't you spend the night at my house tonight?"

Not with her controlling Italian mother-in-law in the vicinity. I already had mother-in-law problems, and I didn't even have one yet. "Thanks, but I'll barricade myself in the costume closet for a nap this afternoon."

"That shouldn't be hard with all that junk in there. Now that you're renting it, Glenda needs to red up the place."

"Red up? You mean, paint it?"

"No, it means tidy up. Clutter isn't good for the psyche."

Neither were all the redheads I'd been dealing with. Speaking of which, I glanced at my new phone—that Nadezhda had better reimburse me for, or I'd show *her* where the crawfish hibernate. "No word from the witch on whether she unscrewed that stripper pole."

"The Axeman could've done it to give you a scare."

"I think it was Theodora. What I'm more concerned about is how the Axeman knew we'd been in the Grecos' gift shop—and what we looked at."

"Maybe he was watching from that transom window."

The curtains were closed, but there could have been a small opening between them. "Assuming the killer is Tony, it could mean that Olive has talked to him after all. For all we know, they're in this together."

The door to the tour bus opened, and a middle-aged male who'd already introduced himself as Manny Vitale's manager stepped out. "He can see you in fifteen minutes."

We watched him head toward the festival entrance.

Ladonna shoved her hands into the pockets of her fuzzy blue tracksuit. "I can't wait any longer. I need to visit the powder room."

I pointed at blue porta potties across the street. "You make it, they take it."

"I'll make it inside Central City BBQ, thank you."

She set off toward the restaurant in her fuzzy pink UGGs, and I looked at my phone. I needed to call Bradley, but it wasn't the right time. I knew it was silly, but I'd lived in New Orleans long enough to semi-believe in curses wrought by cayenne pepper. And I had no thoughts on a possible antidote, except for maybe some of Central City BBQ's brisket bombs. But I wasn't in the right frame of mind to talk to Bradley, anyway. Because that spaghetti-eating reborn doll and 1917 bottle of Florio Marsala had reminded me that I might not live to see my wedding.

The bus door opened, and a seventyish man leaned out who was literally all white—his suit, his glasses, even his close-cropped hair and beard. And he had diamond studs in his ears. "Come in, Franki."

"But your manager said—"

"Ignore him." He waved. "He's a cool cat, but a little controlling. I'm a diabetic, so he wants me to eat before I go on. Is it all right if I have a bite while we talk?"

"Absolutely." I boarded the bus, and the first thing I saw was a double rack of trumpets. I halfway wondered whether the one the Axeman was after was among them.

"I made it my goal to own a trumpet that belonged to every one of my idols."

"Do you have one of Prima's?"

"Not yet, but I have two by other New Orleans Sicilian jazz legends." He pointed to a trumpet in front of me. "That belonged to Wingy Manone, and the one next to it was given to me by Sharkey Bonano."

Their nicknames reminded me of animals, wild and untamed like The Marsala Maroons.

He gestured to a tiny kitchen table, and I slid onto the cushioned bench behind it as he leaned in to the refrigerator. "Luigi said you wanted to know about the missing trumpet. It was a balanced Selmer, but Prima normally played a custom King with his name etched on it."

"What does that mean in non-jazz-musician speak?"

He chuckled as he pulled out a Tupperware container. "Just that it wasn't one of his favorites." He slammed the refrigerator door. "Hey, would you like some tofu and bean sprouts?"

I would almost rather eat a crawdad. "I'm good. So, Luigi said you played with Prima. Did he ever tell you what happened the night the trumpet was stolen at Caruso's Market?"

Manny grabbed a fork and joined me at the table "I didn't know him well enough to ask. I was just lucky enough to sit in on a few sessions. But for what it's worth, I heard about it secondhand from his drummer."

"What did he say?"

"Keep in mind that this happened over a half-century ago, so I'll tell you what I remember." He popped open the container, and the block of tofu reminded me of the reborn doll in the grave. "Apparently, he left the trumpet behind the counter when he went upstairs to have a glass of Marsala with the owner of Caruso's and his band."

Marsala. "You remember the kind of wine they drank?"

He swallowed a bite. "Only because my father came from Marsala, Sicily, and the Maroons had this group they called the Brotherhood of the Marsala."

Finally, I had a name, one that might've explained Olive and Angelo's feud over the case of the wine. "Was this group just for the band members?"

"I think so, because they supposedly made a big deal out of making Prima an honorary member, even though his dad was from Salaparuta, Sicily, not Marsala."

"So all four members of the band went upstairs with him?"

He shrugged. "That's what I heard."

A band began playing at Crawfish Fest, and Manny looked out of the window. "After the trumpet, the accordion and the *frottoir* are the sounds of New Orleans."

"The *frah*-what?"

He laughed and covered his mouth. "It's French for 'rubboard,' or 'washboard,' the instrument Cajun and Zydeco musicians wear on their chests to make that scratching sound."

"Speaking of sounds, did that drummer happen to say whether Prima put anything inside the trumpet?"

His chin retracted. "Not a chance. He wouldn't have been able to play it."

"Right. It's just that I have a feeling that Angelo LaRocca's killer is after something hidden inside the trumpet."

"Maybe someone stashed money in it."

I got a vision of pennies falling from the boaed pig's bottom—and then I got irritated. *Why couldn't I think of the penny taped to Prima's trumpet, like a normal person?*

He pointed his fork. "Whatever's inside that thing, it's related to *vendetta*."

That's what Ladonna had said when we'd first theorized about the motive for Angelo's murder. "Why do you think that?"

"My father always said that when Sicilians came over, they brought two things with them—clannishness and a distrust of authority. So they settled their differences with vendetta, and they passed that custom down to their children."

A perfect example of a tradition that isn't good for anyone.

Manny glanced at his watch, and I slid from the bench. "I'll let you get ready for your performance. But one last thing, did the drummer happen to tell you anything about the man or woman who might've taken the trumpet?"

"Oh, it wasn't an adult. It was a group of kids."

And I was willing to bet they were all ten years old.

"Where are you?" I pressed the phone to my ear, straining to hear over the blaring zydeco accordion.

"Inside the festival," Ladonna said. "I came in to get a wooder ice."

"It's too loud for Philly-speak."

"Sorry, Miss Finicky, it's a wah-ter ice."

"That's what ice is. Water."

"Oof. It's an Italian ice, okay? They're selling them at the American Italian Cultural Center tent, near the back. By the way, the Muff-a-lottas are here, and I met one who knows you. Her name is Marcella."

It figured Marcella was a Muff-a-lotta. As a cheerleader for all things Italian, she wouldn't want to miss an opportunity to promote the Sicilian sandwich. "I'll see you both there in a few minutes."

I hung up and crossed the street to the entrance.

"*Boo! Hiss!*"

I recognized that heckling. I ducked behind a rotating hat display stand near the ticket booth and peered through the merchandise. As Ric had predicted, animal rights activists were at Crawfish Fest. And sure enough, it was a gaggle of aging hippies with Pam at the helm alongside her "old man" and her dachshund, Benny, in a tie-dye T-shirt and tiny Jesus boots. They were staging a sit-in against the practice of boiling live crawdads, and harassing attendees as they entered the festival.

I bought a cap that said "Who's Your Crawdaddy?" and pulled it low on my forehead. Already on edge because of the case, too much caffeine, and the incessant rubboard scratching, I was in no mood to be hated on by hippies.

I handed my ticket to a young girl at the gate and waited while she scanned it.

Pam waved her paisley-bell-sleeved arms to get the attention of her flower-children-turned-flower-fogy friends. "Get this chick in the rain poncho. Her cap says 'Who's your crawdaddy?'"

Her old man was so aghast that the fringe on his vest shook. "Crawdad killer!"

"Like," a shade-wearing burnout said, "would you boil your own daddy, man?"

I stared straight ahead. I probably should have bought the cap with the crawdad that said "Say No to Pot," but I wasn't sure the humorless hippies would've gotten the joke, and the marijuana double entendre could have provoked a Make War, Not Love declaration.

The girl returned my ticket, and I hurried inside the grounds around Central City BBQ. Before I went to meet Ladonna and Marcella, I wanted to find Ric Caruso and get his take on Manny Vitale's revelation. Part of me wondered whether he already suspected his childhood friends of taking the trumpet and sending his father to the pen—and the grave.

The spaghetti-eating reborn doll popped in my head, and so did the 1917 bottle of Marsala. They were muddy thanks to New Orleans' high water table, which was the reason the deceased were buried above ground. So, after taking some photos for evidence, I'd bagged them and put them in the trunk of my car.

And I hadn't opened it since.

I shuddered and looked for a man dressed as a crawdad. It was four o'clock, and the festival had been underway for an hour. I weaved through crowds and inhaled barbecue smoke and the paprika-scented steam from boiling crawfish pots. Finally, I spotted a long fantail by a stand selling crawfish bread. "Hey, Ric. You got a minute?"

He turned around. But it wasn't Ric—it was a guy who came at me with his pincher pointed. "You a friend of Ric Caruso's?"

I held up my hands. "I barely know him."

He shook his head in disbelief, and his googly eyes went ballistic. "He didn't show up for his shift, which goes against the Crawdad Code of Conduct."

I'd like to get a hold of that document. It would make for some side-splitting reading. "Like I said, I hardly know the guy."

"Uh-huh. If you talk to him, tell him Big Chuck is missing his baby brother's jail-release party, and he's ready to kick some crustacean tail."

I was pretty sure that violated the Crawdad Code of Conduct, but far be it from me to tell that to Big Chuck. "You got it."

My gut fluttered like crawfish were crawling in it as I went to find Ladonna. Ric had mentioned that the three-day festival was the equivalent of his Christmas season in terms of earnings, so it didn't make sense that he would miss it. And not only didn't I have his number, I wasn't sure that I would recognize him out of his costume. I'd never even seen his hair under that googly-eyed head, and what was exposed of his face had been painted red.

"Over here!" Ladonna waved from the green, white, and red American Italian Cultural Center tent.

Marcella was in costume beside her, and thanks to her height and linebacker shoulders, she was a lotta Muffa-a-lotta. She wore the same maroon lipliner with beige lipstick, but she'd switched to a blue smoky eye to go with her satin Muff-a-lotta skirt.

As I walked over, Marcella checked the position of her sparkly red pillbox hat. "Hey, Franki. What a coincidence that I would meet your partner, and what's even crazier is that I've visited both of her hometowns, Scranton and South Philly. Gotta support those Italian cities."

The only thing crazy about that was the reason she'd visited them. Everyone knew that Italian cities were only in Italy.

Ladonna zipped up the jacket of her fuzzy tracksuit. "What took you so long?"

"I was looking for Ric Caruso. He didn't show up for his shift today."

Marcella pulled back her curtain of hair. "Really? He was here yesterday."

"You know him?"

"Not well. He's a crabby crawdad."

Not as bad as Big Chuck.

"But I can kind of understand it. I mean, he was orphaned as a young boy when his father went to prison." She slipped on her Muff-a-lotta cat-eyed sunglasses. "Anyway, I overheard him saying that he was having car trouble. I'm sure he'll be here soon."

I imagined a giant crawdad motoring around, possibly in an old convertible, his long claw-arm resting on the seat back.

Marcella pulled a serving tray from a card table. "Would you like a crawfish muffuletta? Proceeds benefit the American Italian Cultural Center."

Ladonna pulled out her billfold. "She's allergic, but I'll take one."

I eyed the sandwich and pulled the poncho plastic over my mouth. "Olive Greco would have a heart attack if she saw a muffuletta with crawfish."

Marcella puckered her lined lips. "She needs to try some new products. Her store won't make it to the end of the year if she doesn't."

I could understand why—groceries and reborns didn't go

together, even if the dolls *were* eating and excreting. "She's opening a muffuletta café in the store, so that might help."

"Well, I hope the sandwiches are fresher than the ones I saw at Greco's the last time I was there. They reminded me of the moldy-looking costumes we Muff-a-lottas wore for the Krewe of BOO! parade."

Ladonna grimaced at her sandwich. "You ladies should encourage her to expand her inventory."

Marcella lowered her cat-eyes. "Why would we do that?"

I shrugged. "You're a women's organization, and she *is* one of your members."

"Olive's not a Muff-a-lotta."

Ladonna choked on a bite.

And the lead singer of a band named Zydeco Force that had just taken the stage stared straight at me as he scratched his rubboard and repeated a single word.

"*Kush-mal.*"

I wasn't sure how I knew this, maybe it was his plaintive wail, but the word wasn't Philly or even Russian.

It was corrupted Cajun for *cauchemar.*

And a sure sign that what I'd feared for days was becoming a reality.

The nightmare witch was coming.

THE DOOR to Greco's Grocery was locked, which was strange. According to the sign, the store closed at ten p.m., and it was nine-fifteen. A cold, brisk wind blew down North Rampart Street as if to underscore the uneasy chill I'd felt since Crawfish Fest. I pulled up the collar of my peacoat and stared at the empty street.

No Ric.

No Olive.

Tony missing since Angelo LaRocca's murder.

I turned and scanned the storefront. Salami and prosciutto hung like ghosts of the past in a window with the word *muffulettas*, another phantom that hung over Olive and presumably Tony. But for me, the most haunting aspect of Greco's Grocery was the scalloped awning between the two floors, because it should have been the green, white, and red of the Italian flag—instead, the red was maroon.

The color of the wine, the candle beside Angelo's death bed, and the one at the grave meant for me. And the name of the band, the fugitive slaves fighting to survive in the harsh swamp terrain, and their descendants.

But also, the state of being marooned, left to one's fate with no hope of a ready escape. *Was that, ultimately, what led to Angelo's murder?*

"What are you doing here?"

The female voice almost shocked my hair from my scalp, and I spun around to Windy Spitter.

True to form, she pulled a New Orleans Original Daiquiri go-cup from a holder attached to a yellow fanny pack with *Tour Guide* written in black. "If you came for my tour, you missed the first half. As soon as the others come back from the bar break, I'll start the second part."

Is it possible that Greco's Grocery was on the tour Ladonna and Rocco had taken, and she hadn't told me? "Is this a stop on the Axeman tour you do for Haunted Herstory?"

Windy took a sip of her daiquiri and spat it out. "Eww, this is a margarita."

I took a step back. I'd just watched Windy Spitter literally spit in the wind. "So, is it a stop, or not?"

"No, this is a new tour I'm debuting tonight. I call this one," she peeked at some writing on her palm, "'Axeman or Copycat Assassin?'"

If I'd had a sip of her margarita, I would have spat it in the wind, too. "Can you elaborate on that?"

"Sure. After my break." She rummaged in her fanny pack. "Do you like pralines?"

I swallowed a surge of frustration. "I do, but could we focus on the tour name for a minute? I need to know what you meant by 'copycat assassin.'"

She sighed. "Honestly, the Axeman killed so many people that it's too much for one tour. So I thought it would be easier to do one on similar crimes from that era and let my clients decide whether they were the work of the Axeman or a copycat."

I wondered whether Glenda's fourplex would be a future stop on a contemporary version of the tour.

"Here come my clients." Windy gazed at a group of six adults walking toward us. "I'm over here," she called, pointing to the *Tour Guide* written on her fanny pack.

I stood back, thinking she really should get a flag like others in her profession. "Mind if I stay and listen?"

"The tour's half over, so it'll cost you a... Who's on the ten-dollar bill?"

That was one name I didn't know either. I pulled a ten from my wallet. "Alexander Hamilton."

"Yeah, one of him." She took the money and shoved it into her fanny pack along with an unopened Aunt Sally's praline.

The group assembled on the sidewalk, facing Greco's Grocery.

Windy pulled out a sheet of paper. "It was January 2, 1917, the year the Axeman began his bloody killings."

And the year Olive and Tony's grandfather, Ruggero, opened Greco's Grocery and bought the bottle of Florio Marsala to mark the occasion.

"A married couple who ran a grocery store in this building," she looked at her notes, "Tomaso and Elena Fasula, were asleep in their bed on the second floor. Elena heard a noise and opened her eyes just as the ax came down." Windy smacked her pack. "*Whack!*"

The fanny pack sound effect was another reason to root for the tour-guide flag.

"The next time Elena woke up, she was in the hospital with head and neck wounds, and police told her that her husband had died from the same kind of injuries. She swore their attacker was a man they'd refused to sell their store to the week before, but she couldn't remember his name." Windy lowered the paper. "Names are hard to remember even without a head injury, don't you think?"

Non-injured heads nodded.

Windy resumed reading, bouncing from one Naturalizer to the other. "Elena died an hour later, and the case remains unsolved."

I had a feeling I knew who'd done it. But whether Ruggero Greco was the Axeman or quite literally the cutthroat competitor that his granddaughter Olive had described, I didn't know.

"The brutal hack attacks happened right up there." Windy shone a flashlight on the second-floor window. "What do you all think? Real Axeman or copycat assassin?"

I didn't answer. I was studying a long, thin piece of wood in the storage-room window. It leaned at a forty-five-degree angle, which was odd because it didn't appear to be resting against the glass. *Is it a lever to a trap door? Or something even more foreboding?*

While the group debated who killed the Fasula family, I slipped into the narrow walkway between the store and the building next to it. There was a stack of cinder blocks below the transom window. I stepped on them. "Don't look down at the reborns," I urged myself for the sake of my heart health, "just at the wine display."

I checked, and as I'd suspected, I could see through a crack in the curtains. The shelf that had held the 1917 bottle of Florio Marsala was empty, as was the high chair where the spaghetti-eating reborn had sat. The killer hadn't bothered to replace them. *Is that because it was Tony, and this was his store?*

I jumped down and went around to the back of the store. I pulled a credit card from my wallet and worked it between the door and the strike plate. After a few seconds of maneuvering, the lock opened. I switched on my phone light, took a breath, and entered.

"Charming," I whispered. I was in a windowless office littered with junk and trash, as though a hoarder lived there. The walls were lined with old appliances, newspaper bundles, and milk crates, some of which contained rotten vegetables. On one end of the room was an old wooden desk buried beneath an avalanche of paper, and on the concrete floor beside it lay a rat in the advanced stages of decomposition.

"*Bluuuh.*" My torso and legs made like jelly as I gave in to a round of grossing out. Then I switched off my phone light and went into the store.

A street lamp provided a weak light in the gloomy room, and from what I could see, Windy and her clients had gone. My unease escalated to anxiety. I'd wanted them to be outside when I searched the room where Tomaso and Elena Fasula had been murdered.

And maybe someone else.

I went to the stairwell in the back of the store, careful not to look in the gift shop.

The steps creaked beneath my feet. "That does nothing for the atmosphere."

I arrived at the top of the stairs and slowly turned the handle of the only door. Then I checked behind me and pushed it open.

A wave of humid air that reeked of mildew—and the distinct smell of death—greeted me. I coughed and gagged and covered my nose and mouth with the lapel of my peacoat. Olive said that no one had been in the room for years, but I smelled a rat—or maybe an actual rat like the one downstairs.

The street lamp emitted a faint light, but the storage room was so packed with stuff that I couldn't see the window. I made my way through a maze of stacked boxes, crates of mechanical parts, even a cigarette vending machine, all while trying to ignore the hair-raising feeling that the copycat Axeman was stalking me.

I rounded a wall of boxes and came to the window, and my heart dropped to my gut. Gasping for breath, I backed up and knocked over a box.

Pots and pans clattered on the floor, and I screamed and pulled out my gun. But it wasn't the noise that had shaken me. It was the piece of wood that I'd seen from the street below.

Because it wasn't a lever.

It was an ax handle.

And its blade was planted in the top of a decomposing head.

There was no blood spatter, as there had been in Angelo's bedroom. A "Ragu Rag" record leaned against the wall below the window, flanked by a bottle of Florio Marsala and a maroon Virgin Mary candle.

But I didn't look to the flame.

I looked to the spirit.

Even though, technically, I'd never actually set eyes on his face, I would have known him anywhere—what was left of him, at least.

It was Tony Greco.

And he looked as moldy as the Muff-a-lottas' costumes on Halloween.

18

As soon as I pulled into my driveway behind my mother's Ford Taurus, I knew I couldn't stay. The night was young, and I was being hunted, so my presence was a danger to everyone at the fourplex. What I didn't understand was why the killer hadn't attacked me at Greco's Grocery, because it was clear from the freshly lit candle beside Tony's body that he'd been expecting me.

Or she.

Veronica must have been at Dirk's because her car was gone. I was tempted to call her to tell her about Tony and talk through how I'd been so wrong about his role in the case. But as an attorney and the owner of Private Chicks, she would have called the police to report Tony's murder, and I wasn't ready for that yet. I'd broken in to the store, and I couldn't risk getting arrested, even though, like Wendell, I would have been safer in jail. I needed a little time to figure out the best course of action.

I scanned the yard. The stripper pole had been moved from the balcony to the ground, but other than that, everything seemed normal. I moved my gun from the calf holster to my waistband for easier access and got out of the car.

Something crunched beneath my feet. It was some kind of dirt, sprinkled around the Taurus.

The black salt of Theodora's Dispello spell. "Let's hope it works on ax murderers too."

I took the stairs two at a time. Glenda's lights were off, and it was only ten-thirty, so I assumed she was out.

Which wasn't good for me.

I pulled out my gun, entered the costume closet, and switched on the light. There were so many outfits and props that I feared the killer would erupt from them.

Like a stripper zombie from a grave.

"Stop it, Franki," I said as I inched my way through the room with my gun aimed. "You're not helping the situation."

My ears picked up a noise in the bedroom.

"Freeze, or I'll shoot."

The sound continued, vibrating.

Is it me, trembling?

I checked my legs, but they were still.

I entered the bedroom and lowered my weapon.

The vibrating was coming from Glenda's Handy Woman toolbox. I gave it a kick, and it stopped.

After clearing the bathroom, I sat on my bed and considered crawling inside Glenda's giant go-cup prop. I wanted to lose myself in a glass without losing control of my senses, which I desperately needed at the moment.

Another option was to jazz it out until morning like the citizens of New Orleans had done over one hundred years before to ward off the Axeman, but I didn't want to drown out the sound of his copycat arriving to take me out—to a date at the cemetery.

The best thing to do would be to return to the French Quarter and make an anonymous tip at a public phone. In case someone else was in danger like me, I owed it to them to report Tony Greco's murder, and soon.

But what else did I want to tell the police? Since I'd been so off base about Tony, I was hesitant to add that his sister, Olive, was the killer. *What if I'm mistaken about her too?*

Olive and Tony didn't have a good relationship, and yet she was about to renovate the store he owned. *Did he give his permission? Or had he refused, and she'd killed him in a rage? And where did she get the money, since it allegedly wasn't a loan?* Maybe Tony had a life insurance policy. Like her, he didn't have a spouse or family, so she would've been the likely beneficiary.

But why kill Angelo La Rocca? The only motive I could think of was that he'd found whatever was inside the trumpet and made some sort of demand.

It was all plausible, and Olive had advocated violence against meat eaters, going so far as to say that they should be slaughtered.

But there were two things that bothered me. For starters, the lack of blood around Tony suggested that he'd been killed somewhere else, and the likely location was Lucky Mistretta's blood-spattered storage room. And if Olive had killed him there, I couldn't understand why she'd bring him to Greco's Grocery, a place that would cast suspicion on her. Another issue, albeit a small one, was that Olive had left the store before closing time without putting a note on the door for customers, and that didn't seem like something a woman obsessed with tradition would do. *Had she rushed out for some reason? And did it have to do with Ric Caruso?*

Ric had been a no-show at Crawfish Fest, and my gut had told me that it wasn't because of the car trouble that Marcella had mentioned. *Had Olive gone after him too? If so, why?* He was the one who'd been hurt the most by the original theft of the trumpet and the death of his father in prison. So, if anyone had a motive to kill, it was Ric—especially if he suspected that the group of kids who'd stolen the trumpet was comprised of Lucky, Angelo, Tony, and Olive. *Is he murdering them one by one, like the killer in Agatha Christie's* And Then There Were None?

And what do the Brotherhood of the Marsala have to do with any of this?

I flopped backwards on the bed. For once I had it all to myself, since Napoleon was downstairs, and yet I couldn't sleep in it.

I reached under my head and pulled out my wadded-up sleep

shirt. The check from Bradley's mother, Lillian, fell from the pocket, along with the doomed coin from Louis Prima's tomb, which had landed tails-up on my pillow. "Now I know the origin of the phrase 'keeps coming back like a bad penny.'"

I put the coin in the front pocket of my jeans. I was going to take that thing back to Metairie Cemetery at daybreak. With my bad luck, it would counteract the effects of Theodora's Dispello spell, and my dad and two brothers would join my mom and nonna for an extended extended-visit.

The penny brought up another nagging question. *What is hidden inside the missing trumpet? Is there money inside, like Luigi's friend Manny Vitale had guessed?* It didn't seem likely that the instrument could hold many bills, and I doubted that it held a check from the Sixties.

I picked up the crumpled check from Lillian. The amount had been left blank.

Of course, I had never intended to keep it. I gazed at my engagement ring and thought of Bradley's shock and disappointment when I'd announced that the wedding would be in his hometown. I'd been surprised to see that he didn't seem to want to get married there. And relieved. There was hope that we would work out our differences after our families left. Before that happened, I had to give the check back to his mother without him knowing. *But had I implicitly promised Lillian and Cordelia to have the wedding in Boston when I'd accepted it?*

Surely not. I hadn't signed a binding agreement, like a contract or a promissory note.

I shot up.

A promissory note.

Was that the motive for the murders?

"It makes sense, right?" I looked at my Mustang's passenger seat as though Ladonna were in it instead of on speaker phone. "Vito Greco used his grocery store as collateral for a bet he placed with Joe

Caruso, and he lost. Since Joe was a bookie, there would've been some sort of paper trail."

"I agree. No self-respecting bookie would operate on a verbal agreement," she paused to chew something crunchy, "not even for a friend."

I turned into the French Quarter and slowed for pedestrian traffic. "What I don't know is whether a promissory note would be legally binding for subsequent generations."

"Maybe that's where the brotherhood comes in. There could've been a code of honor they had to follow. Like, if something happened to Vito and Joe, then Olive and Tony still had to honor their father's debt and give the store to Ric."

"That's what I'm thinking." I scanned the street for a parking spot. "Assuming there is a promissory note, did Vito steal it back from Joe and stash it in the trumpet? Or was it their kids?"

"You'd have to ask them, but my vote is the kids. No child wants chaos and anger in their life. They want happy, healthy families, and peace."

That's all Bradley and I want between our families. Will we get that?

Ladonna made another crunching sound into the receiver. "Where are you going to make the anonymous tip?"

"The Tropical Isle Bar on Bourbon Street. It has one of the few remaining pay phones in the city."

"Isn't that the place that has a mascot for its signature drink?"

My jaw clenched as I waited while a crowd crossed at the intersection. "The Dancing Hand Grenade."

"You sound like he's your enemy."

"Let's just say that we have an explosive history."

She gave a growl. "Sounds sexy."

I envisioned the dopey, green, Humpty-Dumpty-shaped mascot wearing a pair of briefs with his brown clown shoes. "It's totally not. It involves the steamboat case I worked with Wendell."

"Bo-ring," she sing-songed. "What's the plan after you call the police?"

The crowd had passed, so I hit the gas. "I'm going to try to find

Olive."

"Want me to come with?"

"Fugghedaboutit, or however 'all yous all' say that in Pennsylvania. I've got this. Besides, I might need you to take over while I'm catching up on sleep tomorrow afternoon."

"But it's dark out, and an ax-wielding maniac is hunting you."

I opened my mouth to thank her for the striking reminder, but she screamed, splitting my ears and shattering my nerves.

I screeched to a stop, and a couple who'd just stepped onto the street leapt onto the sidewalk. "What is it? Is he or she there?"

"No, Gino and Gina are here watching a gawdawful horror movie."

I lowered my head onto the steering wheel, my heart racing like the Mustang's engine. "Could you maybe move to another room, since I'm on edge, and all?"

"Oh, sure. Let me go to my bedroom."

A car honked behind me, and I sped off, wondering why I'd called.

"All right." Her voice oozed contentment. "I'm all comfy in my bed now."

Glad to know she's all cozy while I'm tracking a killer.

"Hey, do you want me to send Rocco to help you? He's rushing the growler, but he'll be home soon."

I almost screeched to another stop. "Please tell me that's not a Philly expression for tackling a dog."

"Honestly." Her tone was miffed. "Where would you get such an idea?"

"Your odd use of English, maybe?"

She sniffed. "We're closer to the Queen's English than all yous all down heyuh in the South."

I exchanged a look with myself in the rearview mirror. *Case in point.*

"And it means 'getting booze,' for heaven's sake."

It was more bizarre than I'd thought. "Listen, I found a parking spot, so I'll let you go."

"Okay, but call with updates. I'll be awake thanks to the gory movie."

I didn't make any promises before I hung up.

I parked, put my gun in my waistband, and got out. The wind had picked up, and because of the crowds I was five blocks away from the pay phone. But after the call with Ladonna, I welcomed the brisk walk—even though, as she'd so graphically pointed out, I was being stalked.

Bourbon Street was packed with partiers, as per usual. I blended in with the crowd, looking over my shoulder every few seconds.

A sidewalk sign advertised a jazz show inside Musical Legends Park, a small square surrounded by restaurants, known for its life-sized bronze statues of some of New Orleans' most famous performers. At the bottom of the sign, it said "all-you-can-eat crawdad boil."

Ric. He could be working.

I had to have a look. I passed the statues of Fats Domino, Jumbo Hirt, and Pete Fountain at the entrance, and, as though in a trance, I walked straight to a statue of Louis Prima. It was in front of steps leading down to Café Beignet, and he had his head thrown back while playing his trumpet.

Where is the stolen trumpet?

I'd assumed the missing instrument was with whoever had killed Angelo, but with Tony dead, that wasn't necessarily true. The Spy Boy had seen Tony enter Angelo's apartment the night of the murder, so Tony could have killed Angelo for the trumpet and then gotten killed for it himself. That would explain why someone had desecrated Angelo's tomb—they were looking for where Tony had hidden the trumpet, just like me.

But did the killer find the instrument when he or she murdered Tony? Or is it still out there somewhere?

I racked my brain to figure out where Tony would have put it. Either the trumpet was someplace I'd never think to search, or it was somewhere obvious, maybe even out in the open like the bronze version on the statue before me. But the only trumpets I'd seen were the ones on Manny Vitale's tour bus and the one at—

I sank into a chair as a realization blasted me like a note from The King of the Swing's missing horn.

I had to go back to Greco's Grocery.

My text tone beeped. It was Bradley, asking if we could talk.

I fired off a text. Then I got up and ran from the park, vowing not to turn into a hapless female victim from a sicko slasher flick before my fiancé and I got to have that conversation.

I jog-ran north on Bienville, the crowd thinning with each of the three short blocks. When I got to North Rampart at the end of the Quarter, no one was around. I turned right and went to Greco's Grocery.

The old two-story building loomed like an enormous mausoleum, and it was. There were two dead bodies inside, Tony's and the rat's.

I took deep breaths, trying to exhale the anxiety that vice-gripped my chest at the thought of having to go back in. But it was immediately apparent that there were no breathing patterns that would relieve the stress of being hunted by an ax murderer.

I glanced behind me and checked my phone. No messages. And it was midnight.

The nightmare-witching hour.

I pulled my Ruger from my waistband, rushed down the side of the building, and turned the corner around the back.

And I came face to blade with an ax.

"COULD YOU SMILE, OR SOMETHING?" I huffed as I stomped past Nadezhda and her weapon to the back door of the grocery store. I already had an ax to grind with her over the ax causing my swamp spill, and yet here she was with it again. "You look like an ax murderer, which is some pretty lousy planning on your part."

She spat through her eyetooth hole. "You interrupt date."

I gave her the once-over. She had on more protective gear than I'd worn to Crawfish Fest. In addition to the hairnet, shoe covers, and gloves she'd worn when we broke into Angelo LaRocca's apartment, she wore a blue plastic medical gown. "Who with? A PPE supplier?"

"Nyet. Just penis from mountain."

"Uh, I'm not sure what that means, but I think it's too much information."

"It expression for 'random man.'"

I scrunched my face. Pairing a penis with a mountain was certainly random, but other than that, the phrase didn't add up. "Like, an 'average Joe?'"

"English so weird."

I gave a half head-shake and pulled a credit card from my pocket. I was willing to bet that the people of Philly would say that *average Joe* was closer to the Queen's English than *penis from the mountain*. "I thought you'd be down the street at Lucky's Liquor when I called. How'd you get here so fast?"

"I *vas* at Lucky's." She smile-sneered. "Average Joe buy me my own booze."

Only Nadezhda would turn a date into a money-making venture. "Well, you could've texted me back. I thought you weren't coming." I worked my credit card between the strike plate and the lock. "But now that you're here and flush with extra booze profits, you can pay me the six hundred dollars you owe me for the new phone."

At the mention of debt, she made like a wrecking ball with her matryoshka body and blew through the door.

She was a penny-pinching Communist, but she was also a no-fear and no-nonsense accomplice, which was why I'd texted her over Ladonna.

I entered the store and found her browsing the meat aisle, probably looking for free ingredients for her kholodets. "I wouldn't touch that, if I were you. There's a dead body here, remember?"

She shrugged. "He upstairs."

I swallowed my disgust. "Well, we're not taking anything but the trumpet."

"I deserve sometink for my help."

"You should be helping me for free since your late husband had the missing trumpet, but consider this repayment of one of those six C-notes the phone cost me."

I saw her heavily lined eyes shift to the cash register. She'd be lucky to find the five bucks I'd paid for the espresso Quadratini in that drawer, never mind the five hundred she owed me, but I didn't say a word. If Nadezhda thought there was a single cent to be had, she'd take it, as I knew from experience. "Let's go to the gift shop."

I entered first with my gun aimed, and I almost dropped it from shock.

The reborn spaghetti-eater was back in her high chair, and the 1917 bottle of Florio Marsala was on its shelf, which meant that someone had broken into my trunk and stolen the items. *But when? And was it Olive? Had she put everything back to erase her attempt to frighten me off the case?* "The killer has been here."

"No vorries. I handle Olive—and zese dolls." Nadezhda unrolled a black felt bag of cat burglar tools—a slim jim, a lockpick, a screwdriver, an angle grinder, a flashlight, and a hammer.

Everything but a sickle, I thought. Then I studied her medical gown for semi-circular protrusions, just in case.

"Vhere ve search?"

I approached the toddler holding the trumpet. "If I'm right, there's a promissory note inside the instrument."

Before I could even extend my arm, Nadezhda had ripped the horn from the doll's hands. I would have been annoyed, but Ric Caruso had said the trumpet had a voodoo curse on it, and with the damned penny still on my person, I couldn't take any chances.

She removed the mouthpiece, but it was too small to hold a document. One by one, she pushed each of the trumpet's three valves and removed the corresponding tuning slides.

While she worked, I kept an eye on the door and an ear on the upstairs, listening for sounds from the storage room where Tony's body lay. Somewhere the killer was lying in wait.

She put the instrument to her lips and blew, but nothing came from the open tubes.

I was disappointed, even though my theory had been a longshot. "I guess I was wrong about the trumpet too."

"Vait. I not finished." She unscrewed one of the valve-bottom caps.

"You know a lot about trumpets. Did you play one?"

She stuck out her lower lip and shook her head. "I study safe-cracking in prison. Everyting else piece of cake."

Nice to know that inmates learn useful skills for when they get out.

Nadezhda unscrewed the last cap, and a yellow, rolled-up piece of paper fell from the valve.

I stared, unable to believe what I was seeing.

Nadezhda unrolled the paper, and I looked over her shoulder. As I'd guessed, it was a promissory note using Greco's Grocery as collateral signed by Vito Greco in 1969. "I don't get it. Why would the copycat Axeman leave this in the store?"

Her hard eyes went steely. "Olive is killer. Maybe she check trumpet and don't find nusink."

If Olive was the murderer, there was another possibility. "Or, the doll always had a trumpet, and she didn't know that Tony switched it with Prima's."

Nadezhda rolled up the promissory note and moved to stuff it down the collar of her medical gown.

"Give me that." I snatched the note with the tips of my fingernails before it disappeared to a place as dark and scary as a cemetery.

"I know good forger. He change 'Joe Caruso' to 'Lucky Mistretta,' zen ve get store and open detective agency vit vaxing salon. Tink about it. Ve make killing."

I didn't want to "tink about it," but I was tempted to ask her thoughts on the company slogan. "Like I said, we're not stealing anything." I put the note in the pocket of my peacoat. "I'm taking it to the police right now."

Nadezhda picked up her tool bag and hoisted the ax over her head.

The hair on my arms rose like her maroon spikes. The woman had an edge as sharp as the blade, and even though I didn't think she was the killer, I still didn't trust her with that thing. "Walk ahead of me. I'll cover you with my gun."

She went ahead, and I followed her through the store and the back room, monitoring the area as we advanced. We walked around to the front of the building without incident, but I couldn't shake the tightness in my chest.

The search had gone well.

Too well.

The killer had been inside Greco's Grocery within the past hour. And yet he—or she—had done nothing to stop me from going back inside to look for evidence. I smelled a trap, a rat trap, and it stunk even worse than Greco's Grocery.

My text tone beeped, and I remembered that I'd texted Nadezhda before leaving Musical Legends Park, but not Bradley. *Is he upset?*

I pulled out my phone and gaped at the message.

Nadezhda's Russian-man brow furrowed. "Who it is?"

"Olive."

"Vhat she vant?"

I leaned against the building. "She confessed to killing Angelo and Tony, and she says she's on her way to make peace with her ancestors...and then end her life."

"Vat did I tell you? Olive is ax assassin."

I grimaced. "Looks like you were right. Nevertheless, we can't let her harm herself. It's not right, and my friend Wendell needs her to tell the police what she knows and take responsibility for her part in the crimes."

"Nyet." Nadezhda set off down the street for Lucky's Liquor. "I vash hands."

Apparently, that body-part phrase translated. I rubbed my lower lip as I pondered the text. There was only one place I could think of to make peace with one's ancestors, and Olive's specifically.

The Greco family mausoleum at Metairie Cemetery.

And I had a sense that what awaited me there would make the encounter with the Northside Skull and Bone Gang skeletons seem like a cute kids' party.

The silver Jaguar's engine raced in the parking lot as though the car itself wanted to speed from Metairie Cemetery. And I sympathized. Gray, decaying tombs stood like hundreds of haunted houses—with zombie bodies and skeletons.

Nadezhda stared through the windshield at the eerie scene. "Zis trip vorth five hundred."

I glared at her from the passenger seat. "We agreed on three hundred, and you should be ashamed of yourself for trying to rene-gotiate the amount of money you owe me when we're here to save Olive's life."

She smacked her eyetooth hole. "Take or leave."

I should have known better than to barter with a tight-fisted, Communist criminal. "Fine. Forget the damn phone."

Nadezhda's lip curled in a Chechen-cat smile.

"Now let's go find Olive." I pulled out my gun and climbed from the car.

We'd parked at a funeral home at the cemetery's north entrance on Pontchartrain Road. Since Bradley had resigned from a bank of the same name to spend a year with me, I worried it was a sign that I might have played a role in killing his career and our future together.

At the same time, the cemetery was a foreboding reminder that a Boston society wedding neither of us wanted wouldn't breathe life into our relationship, but send it to an early grave.

And I would tell that to him and his family—if I survived the night.

Nadezhda slammed the car door, shaking me from my grim thoughts. She stripped off the blue medical gown and shoe covers to reveal her date outfit—a purple-and-black sequined number with studded combat boots that accentuated her maroon spikes. Then she slipped on a mink coat that looked like it predated the 1917 Russian Revolution and went to the trunk to get her cat burglar bag and ax.

For once I didn't complain about her weapon. A frigid wind howled in our ears, and thick clouds obscured the moon. We were in the cold, dead black, and we needed every object at our disposal to confront a killer who might have been lying about being repentant.

I buttoned my peacoat and walked to the gate. Then I texted an update to Ladonna. "Hurry up, okay?"

"I have short legs. I am voman, remember?"

She'd said that like I wasn't. I thought of her offer to wax my mustache and sideburns and the drink that would put hair "back on" my chest, and like her liquor store my head did a hard lean to the right. *Does she think...? No, that's ridiculous.*

Nadezhda pulled the lockpick from the black felt bag and opened the gate in under ten seconds.

I set off along the gravel path at a brisk pace.

She jogged behind me. "Slow down."

"We have to get to Olive before it's too late." I continued walking.

After about a minute, I stopped to get my bearings, and a pain shot up my backside. "Ow. What the—"

Nadezhda was holding the lockpick.

I ripped it from her hand. "Why didn't you put that away?"

"It for lock on mausoleum door."

No, it wasn't.

She reached for the tool, and I stuck it in my bra—very carefully. "I'll give it to you when we get to the Greco mausoleum."

She muttered something in Russian, probably an insult involving an unflattering body part in a random location.

We walked in silence, the wind blowing in powerful gusts. We rounded a corner and saw a light in the distance.

It was coming from the Greco mausoleum, and it was flickering.

Anxiety churned in my abdomen like a casket-lowering device. "Olive must be inside with a candle."

But is it a maroon Virgin Mary?

I swallowed a lump the size of a tree knot. "This could be a trap. Keep your wits about you."

"Vhat mean 'vits?'"

"Your perception, as in stay alert."

"You tink I sleep right now?"

The cemetery was so spooky that I didn't even "tink" the dead were resting. "Just watch out. Something doesn't feel right."

We passed the tomb of Josie Arlington, the infamous Storyville madame. Like Ladonna, I was startled by the statue of the woman at the mausoleum's double doors, but not because she was lifelike. Someone had wrapped a cheap feather boa—that Glenda's influencer guru, Bob Simpson, would have strongly disapproved of—around the statue's shoulders. It was yellow and orange, the Golden Flames' colors.

I thought about the Spy Boy and the Big Chief and wished they were with us. I would have even welcomed the Northside Skull and Bone Gang—and Glenda and Ladonna.

I stopped dead in my tracks. I didn't hear Nadezhda's footsteps behind me.

My blood turned smoothie temperature.

I spun with the Ruger raised.

Nadezhda was removing the boa from the statue.

I lowered my gun and threw my head back. "Leave that alone."

"Vhy?" She wrapped it around her neck. "She don't need."

"That's stealing from a grave. And trust me," I patted the damned penny in my pocket, "you don't want to do that."

"But it go vit outfit."

"Yellow and orange with purple?" I held up my hands in a what-the-hell-are-you-thinking gesture. "Those colors are all wrong together."

The last sentence jogged something in my mind. Someone had said the same thing to me recently. It was Ric Caruso at Jazz Fest, when he'd told me that the 9th Ward Black Hatchet Spy Boy's colors were all wrong. I'd written off the remark as a crack about the Indian's multi-colored feathers matching my tacky Jazzercise face paint, but there was another interpretation—one that was much more telling.

And terrifying.

Ric meant that the Black Hatchet Spy Boy wasn't the one I'd seen standing outside Angelo LaRocca's apartment the day after his murder because his feathers weren't yellow and orange. But he couldn't have known that I was looking for a Mardi Gras Indian, much less one wearing specific colors, unless he'd been stalking me from the start of my investigation.

Nadezhda walked past me in the boa, but I stayed where I was and leaned against a tomb, dizzy from the memory of another comment Ric had made.

The first time I questioned him, he said that the missing trumpet spelled death to everyone who touched it—and that whoever had it was going to get the ax next.

The wind screamed like the scream in my head.

Ric Caruso basically told me that he's the copycat Axeman.

My legs pumped double time toward the Greco mausoleum.

Nadezhda was approaching the arched entrance.

"Stop," I shouted. "Ric is the murderer, and he's going to kill—"

She disappeared below ground, as though Baron Samedi had dug her grave and snatched her to the underworld.

I blinked, trying to process what I'd seen.

Pain blasted my brain.

But I couldn't understand why. After all, the lockpick was still in my bra.

I dropped to my knees and faceplanted in the gravel.

And I didn't feel or see anything else.

MY EYELIDS OPENED to two pairs of eyes hovering over me—Ric Caruso's and the googly ones on his crawdad costume.

I tried to move, but I couldn't. I was on my back with my hands bound beneath me, and tape covered my mouth. And I was freezing, because Ric had taken my peacoat along with the promissory note.

I groaned, in part because I wanted to speak, but also because the sight of a crawfish in a cemetery was somehow more terrifying than the nine-foot skeleton.

Ric crouched at my feet and tied rope around my ankles. His pointy elf shoes were encased in plastic bags, and instead of claw mitts, he wore surgical gloves. "I tried to scare you off with the axes, but you wouldn't take the hint."

Angry, but muffled Russian erupted near me.

Nadezhda. The hole beneath the artificial grass. I turned my head to look for her, and my brain lurched as though it had been knocked loose in my skull.

Ric looked at the Greco mausoleum. "Hey, Little Moscow, I forgot to thank you for the ax. I had to rush here from a gig, so I didn't have one with me."

Heated Russian ensued, and I had some choice Italian for myself. *I knew I should've thrown her ax into the swamp when I had the chance.*

Four eyes returned to me—two, actually, because the others were all over the place. "I saw you find the promissory note."

I tensed. He must have planted cameras in Greco's Grocery and monitored them with his phone, which meant he'd heard me tell Nadezhda that I was going to the police.

"You found the note a little earlier than I'd planned, but it worked out. Olive was already in my trunk, so it was a quick fix to send you that text from her phone."

My body went as cold as a corpse. Now I knew why Olive had left

Greco's Grocery before closing time without leaving a note for customers—he'd abducted her.

But is she dead?

If not, how long was she alive in the back of his car? I feared it was at least since three p.m., when Ric didn't show up for Crawfish Fest, and at least ten hours had passed since then.

I groaned again, hoping Ric would remove the tape. I had to try to reason with him, talk him out of making another mistake.

He knotted the rope. "To answer the question on your taped lips, the gift shop camera was in the doll with the trumpet. Tony told me where the trumpet was before I knocked him off, and check this out —he didn't think to search the valves for the promissory note." He tapped his temple. "Brain rot from alcohol. So he thought Angelo had hidden it in a pocket watch he was buried with, and when he didn't find it in his tomb, he went back to Lucky's storage room, where I caught up with him."

And where you killed him before taking his body to Greco's Grocery to frame Olive.

"I found the note in the valve in two minutes, but I left it in the trumpet in the doll's hands to lure you to your murder." He glanced at the artificial grass. "That hole was for you, but whatever. One thing being orphaned taught me was adaptability."

Awesome that he intends to put that life skill to use to kill Nadezhda and me. Slowly, I tried to free my wrists, but they were half numb from the binding and the weight of my body.

Ric rose and crossed his arms across his padded Crustacean tunic. "But even though Little Moscow ruined my plan, I'm grateful to her. If she hadn't given Angelo the trumpet, I never would've known that my old friends had cost me my pops and Caruso's Market."

So, the kids *had* stolen the trumpet.

"And here's the rub. They pulled that stunt after I stole the promissory note from my own father to save Tony and Olive's pop from losing Greco's Grocery." He laughed and shifted his hands to his hips. "That's what I get for believing in the brotherhood bull our fathers taught us."

The Brotherhood of the Marsala.

"We hid the note in the trumpet while all of our pops were drinking with Prima. He would've found it the next time he played the thing, but we were dumb kids, so we thought it was a genius hiding place." He snort-laughed. "When he got ready to leave, the trumpet was gone. After my pops was arrested, I asked them one by one—Lucky, Angelo, Tony, and Olive—if they knew what had happened to it, and they lied."

Ric began to pace, and I worked my wrists harder.

He ran his hand through his antennae. "And do you know what Tony told me in Lucky's storage room before I killed him?"

I shook my head and saw stars—but there weren't any.

"While I was risking my behind to get the promissory note from my pops' lockbox, unbeknownst to me Lucky convinced Angelo, Tony, and Olive that they should all keep the trumpet to sell it for candy. So my pops died, and I was orphaned and left penniless for crap that they could've stolen from our store that night."

If my mouth hadn't been taped, I would have told him that the story was tragic. Because it was.

He stared at me, but his eyes were as unseeing as the ones on his costume. "It's one thing to keep quiet about the trumpet as kids, but as adults, they should've come clean. Instead, Angelo sold the trumpet and the note to Tony. Can you believe that crap?"

"Mm-mm," I replied through the tape.

"I knew something was up when Tony came by a bar I was working at for a drink, first time I'd seen the guy in decades. He seemed guilty or something, so I followed him to Angelo's and saw him leave with the trumpet." The corner of his lip curled. "Of course, I let Angelo know what I thought about that, and since this whole mess started with jazz and Italian store owners, I used his ax because it just felt right."

The confession was a chilling reminder that the same fate awaited me.

Within minutes.

I tugged at my wrists.

"Then I mailed an Axeman letter to the cops to throw them off my trail." He bit his lip. "As for Lucky Mistretta, he was 'lucky,' all right, because if he hadn't choked on that pig bone, I would have roasted him alive on a spit."

Another round of Russian insults emerged from the hole. And if "random guy" translated to "penis from the mountain," I couldn't imagine what Nadezhda was calling Ric for threatening her late husband.

He marched to the mausoleum. "I would shut it if I were you, Little Moscow. Otherwise, I'll fill in your grave right now."

She went silent.

And I pulled hard on my wrists.

Ric returned to me with a goofy grin on his face. "You gotta admit, seeing her drop into that hole was funnier than a Wile E. Coyote cartoon."

Given the contentious nature of my relationship with Nadezhda, it might have been the tiniest bit funny in other circumstances, as long as she didn't get hurt. But I didn't have to admit that because my mouth was taped.

He chuckled, and his googly eyes bounced. "I still can't believe she fell for that old trick. Get it? *Fell*? Because she *fell* in the hole?"

Great. Mansplaining like Jerry, the meat man. Apparently, I've already died and gone to hell.

"Well, enough gabbing." He rubbed gloved hands together. "I left my phone at work so I've gotta git."

My heart dropped to my spine. Without his cell phone, there would be no way for police to trace him to the cemetery without a witness.

"It's a shame it came to this. You and I go way back, you know that?"

I didn't shake my head. Instead, I focused on my wrists.

"I saw you a few years ago looking all hot in your Mustang convertible, pulling into the parking garage at the Hotel Monteleone."

I hadn't been there since I confronted a murderer who'd strangled a woman with a yellow scarf. But for some reason, maybe the head injury, I remembered seeing a crawfish smoking outside the hotel's Carousel Bar. I knew the crazed crawdad had looked familiar.

"When you showed up that day at Frankie & Johnny's, I thought destiny had gone my way, like maybe you and I were gonna hook up." His human eyes turned hard. "Then you started with the questions about Angelo LaRocca's murder and the trumpet, and I knew destiny had come to cheat me of what was owed to me once again."

And his solution was to murder and steal instead of taking the Grecos to court.

"You'll rest for eternity in the mausoleum with Olive. Like your Russian friend, she's already in her grave."

The wind howled, reflecting the scream in my head. Panic rising like the New Orleans water table, I twisted my wrists.

He stood and wiped grave dirt from his fantail.

Proof that he'd been at the cemetery.

He saw me watching. "I know your evidence meter is going crazy, but no one will suspect a guy dressed as a crawdad of committing murders."

I wanted to laugh in his painted red face. Far crazier things had happened in New Orleans, and I could think of quite a few people who would disagree with him, starting with Pam, her old man, and their hippy friends.

He rose and pushed a board across the hole to the doorway of the mausoleum.

Nadezhda growled. "You von't get avay vit zis."

Ric put pincherless hands on his hips. "You're funny, Little Moscow. And thanks for being so short. Saved me a lot of extra digging."

I wondered whether she still had her cat burglar tools. But even if she did, they couldn't help her after the hole was filled in.

He lifted me by my biceps and dragged me toward the mausoleum. My gun and phone lay in the artificial grass. Ric had scattered them to make it look like there had been a struggle between Olive and me. Given the stereotype about Sicilians and vendetta, the police would probably assume that she'd killed me to get even for investigating her and driving her to taking her own life. And there would be no way to tie Ric to any of it.

I had to do something, fight back somehow. I thrashed and twisted.

"Ain't no use in fighting. You're going inside. Forever."

Ric was right about one thing—it was pointless to struggle because I needed to free myself from the rope. I wrenched my wrists, and something jabbed my armpit.

The lockpick.

I still had it.

But how could I get to it before he axed me?

He dragged me across the plank, and Nadezhda spat at him, which I didn't appreciate since I was in her direct line of fire.

"Franki, you fight. You strong guy."

Her words made me thrash harder—not because she'd urged me to react, but because the woman who'd once given me a bikini wax thought I was a man. And I didn't want to go to my grave without telling her what I thought about that.

Ric pulled me across the threshold. The interior was marble and concrete with gold sconces on either side of the door. Because it was open, I couldn't tell whether there was a keyhole on the inside—not that it would matter since he planned to kill me before he left.

I dropped to the floor and hit the back of my head. Dazed from pain, I blinked and looked to my left.

And I saw a flickering maroon Virgin Mary candle.

Don' look to da flame. Look to da spirit.

I looked to my right.

Olive Greco lay next to me, unbound.

Is she now a spirit?

Ric gazed at the coffin niches in the mausoleum walls. "My only regret is that Olive wouldn't have been able to lift you, so I can't put you in one of these slots."

Even though it looked like I was at the end of my life rope, I did feel some relief. I'd been locked in a coffin before, and I didn't want to go back into one, not even when I was dead.

He walked back across the plank.

I contorted and yanked my wrists as hard as I could.

But the rope was too tight.

The killer crawdad returned with the ax.

I'm about to become a spirit.

Fear as hard and cold as the marble floor surged through every cell in my body. I thrashed and shouted *no* through the tape.

He raised the blade. "*Buonanotte, bella.*"

20

Over my screams and the howling wind, I heard wailing.
Police sirens.
Ric lowered the ax and looked out of the mausoleum door, antennae on alert.

Had Ladonna called the police? Or someone reporting suspicious activity at the cemetery? Or are they just passing by on their way to another crime?

"My car." He rubbed his neck.

Hope flickered in my body—weak like the candle flame, but it burned nevertheless. *Is Ric going to leave? Sure, this is New Orleans, but a giant crawdad in a cemetery might stand out.*

The sirens came closer.

"I'll be back." Ric closed the door with such force that the candle went out.

The Greco mausoleum went as dark as death.

And I came to life.

Because I was going home to my meddling family and my bed-stealing dog. And then I was getting married to my love, Bradley Hartmann. Just not in Boston.

I thrashed from side to side, fingers tingling, head throbbing, trying to free my hands.

And I bumped into Olive.

She was warm, and breathing. But barely.

I had to escape and get help for her, and for Nadezhda and me. Because if the police weren't at Metairie Cemetery, we were all as good as dead.

Nadezhda. I didn't hear her.

Or the sirens.

Has she escaped?

Or is Ric already back?

A blast of adrenaline coursed through me that was so strong I pulled my right foot from my boot. Stunned, I sat still for a split second. Then I got a grip. "Move it, Franki."

I rocked forward and stood, but I lost my balance and fell on my behind.

A jolt went from my spine to my brain.

I already had a head injury, I couldn't afford to break my tailbone.

Carefully, I rose to my feet, used them to brace myself, and pulled my right arm with all of my strength. The sensation was searing. I was sure that I'd dislocate my wrist or my elbow or both, but I kept pulling.

And freed my hand.

I threw off the rope, pulled the lockpick from my bra, and ran my palms over the wall in front of me. I located a sconce and lowered my hand. Something clattered on the marble floor.

The ax. Ric had left it inside the mausoleum to reinforce the fiction of Olive as the killer if he didn't make it back.

I felt the surface of the door until I located the keyhole.

Even though I shivered from fear and cold, sweat broke out on my face as I twisted the lockpick. Precious seconds ticked by that I didn't have to spare.

Something clicked.

The lock?

Or Ric cocking my gun outside the mausoleum?

Shaking, I picked up the ax and pushed open the door. And I saw the faint flashing of red-and-blue lights.

The police were at the cemetery.

Who called them?

I peered out and looked down at the hole. Nadezhda, still wearing the feather boa, was trying futilely to dig footholds and handholds with her screwdriver. But there was no way I could pull her out without potentially falling in myself. "Hey."

She looked up, her lined eyes wide with shock. "I knew you break out."

"The police are at the funeral home. I'm going to make a run for it, so take this." I lowered the ax. "I'll get you my phone."

She nodded.

I crossed the plank like a sprinter from the starting blocks and searched for my gun.

Gone.

I picked up my phone, and—after a quick glance around—I unlocked it and lowered it into the hole. "Call 9-1-1 and tell them we need an ambulance."

She punched the numbers.

Holding the lockpick like a switchblade, I dashed through the maze of tombs. I went ten yards and tripped, hitting the ground with a grunt.

Another tomb root?

No, the rope's still on my lone boot.

My head ached, but I kicked off the rope and took off again. The faces of statues and gargoyles and porcelain tombstone photos seemed to stare at me as I ran. But I was no longer afraid of them— just a giant crawdad holding my gun. My body was electric, expecting him to jump out from behind a tomb or shoot me in the back or head.

The red-and-blue flashing lights grew brighter with each step.

Will I make it?

Or will Ric cut me down in the final stretch?

Only a handful of tombs loomed between me and safety. I clenched my teeth and summoned the last bit of life in me.

Three.

Two.

One.

I exploded into the parking lot, on the verge of collapse.

But the police weren't at the funeral home. They were a hundred or so yards down Pontchartrain Road.

And they had Ric in handcuffs.

Instead of relief, dizziness and nausea swept over me. I put my hands on the hood of Nadezhda's silver Jag to wait for it to pass, and my gaze fell on a piece of paper under the windshield wiper.

A flyer? In the middle of the night at a funeral home?

But it was old and yellowed.

The promissory note.

I stared at Ric as he waited beside the squad car with his googly-eyed head lowered. His padded tunic and red bodysuit were torn as though he'd resisted arrest and the officers had struggled to subdue him. If he'd wanted to unload incriminating evidence, he wouldn't have left the promissory note for me to turn in to the police. And I was sure he knew that the Jag belonged to Nadezhda. *So who put it on the windshield?*

An ambulance siren headed for the cemetery.

I set off across the parking lot to tell the officers what had happened and lead the paramedics to Olive, and I found the answers to my questions.

A smattering of yellow-and-orange ostrich feathers.

The Golden Flames.

The tribe had been watching over me. They'd called the police, and they'd fought Ric for the promissory note.

When Wendell Baptiste had been released from jail, I would do my best to find the Big Chief and the Spy Boy to thank them for their brotherhood. I thought about the local saying that spotting a Mardi Gras Indian was a sign of good luck and half-smiled to myself.

Who needs lucky pennies in a city with Mardi Gras Indians?

I slipped my hand into my pocket. After I got help for Olive and Nadezhda, there was one last thing I had to do.

VERONICA CROSSED Ladonna's office carrying a tray with a tea service. "After this cup, why don't you let me take you home?"

I sat up on the plastic-covered couch. It was seven-thirty in the morning, and I *had* been up all night battling an ax murderer and answering police questions at the station. "I drove here from Bienville Street after Nadezhda took me to my car. I'll be fine to drive to the fourplex."

Ladonna adjusted the neckline of her pink-and-orange tiger-striped dress, sending off a waft of cheap-Spumanti-and-garlic odor, and leaned forward from her armchair to pour herself a cup. "The one thing I don't understand is why Ric didn't whack you with the ax before he left. It would've only taken a second."

I cocked my jaw like a gun and set my sights on her face. For someone who claimed to speak the Queen's English, Ladonna needed a royal lesson in diplomacy. "Because he would've had blood on him, which isn't a good look for meeting up with police."

Veronica took a seat between us, no doubt to prevent a scuffle. "What do you know about Olive Greco's condition?"

I picked up my tea and swallowed a sip. "When she was loaded into the ambulance, her lips were as blue as the muffuletta throw she was painting the day Ladonna and I met her. An officer at the scene told paramedics that Ric had confessed to tying a chloroform-soaked rag around her face before loading her in his trunk, and then he gave her an overdose of liquid diazepam at the cemetery."

Veronica shuddered. "Isn't diazepam the same thing as Valium?"

I nodded. "I looked it up, and I think Ric picked it because suicidal thoughts are one of the possible side effects. The police would've thought she'd taken too much and decided to take her life and mine in the process."

Ladonna drizzled honey into her tea. "I wonder if she'll survive."

"She's going to be fine. When Nadezhda and I were at the police station, the investigating officer said he'd already received word from the hospital that she was stable enough for them to question her." I paused. "What I want to know is whether she knew Tony stole the trumpet. I'm inclined to think she did, because the sale of that instrument is the most likely source of the money she needed for the muffuletta café and gift shop renovations."

Veronica clenched her fists and pounded her lap. "It's just so frustrating. Ric should've taken Tony and Olive to court instead of killing them."

"Said the attorney," Ladonna quipped. "I'm not defending the guy, but lawsuits cost a lot of money that us regular folks just don't have."

I nestled into a blue Marilyn pillow. "And after what happened to his dad, Ric lost faith in the justice system. Since neither Tony nor Olive had any kids, I suppose he figured that no one would contest his claim to Greco's Grocery when he produced the promissory note."

Veronica picked up a teapot and topped off her cup.

I stared at the steaming liquid. "I think it boils down to the betrayal of his friends and the symbolism of The Marsala Maroons."

Ladonna scratched her head. "What do you mean?"

"The record at the scene was a taunt for violating the brotherhood, which was important to their fathers and reflected both in the word 'Marsala' and in 'maroon,' which they chose as a show of solidarity with Black jazz musicians. And the maroon Virgin Mary candle was a message that Ric's religion was himself."

"Could you put that last part in plain English?"

I resisted the urge to say, *You mean in Phillyese?* "After the betrayal, Ric went rogue, 'wild and untamed' like the negative definition of 'maroon,' because he was orphaned, marooned, an island unto himself." I paused and thought of the Big Chief's words about ancestors and tradition. "And he learned the worst possible lesson from his hardships—that he was justified in taking what he thought was his by any means necessary, including violence." I lay my head on the blue Marilyn. "And look at the results."

We went silent, lost in our thoughts.

"Well." Veronica smoothed her skirt. "I'm going to the jail to see what I can do to speed up Wendell's release."

I was certain that Public Defender Louis Armstrong was working feverishly on that—at the insistence of his mother—but I wanted to be there when Wendell got out. "I'm coming with you." I stood and got a massive head rush. "Maybe not yet."

Ladonna rose and helped me back on the couch. "You should go home to rest."

"She's right, Franki," Veronica said. "It's going to take time for his release, and if Wendell's up to it, I'll bring him by the apartment to see you."

I sighed. "I could use some sleep, and I really need to call Bradley."

Footsteps pounded the stairs.

Veronica headed for the door. "I'll be right back."

Ladonna stirred honey into her teacup. "Speaking of Bradley, when his mother was here the other day, she started to say a word we use in Scranton, 'nebby' for 'nosy,' but then she caught herself."

I wrinkled my lips. "You're mistaken. If anyone speaks the Queen's English, it's Lillian Hartmann and her mother, Cordelia."

"That's what I thought too, but I did some investigating in the *Boston Herald* society pages and tracked down Cordelia's wedding announcement. She married a Linde, but her maiden name was Italian."

No, Bradley would have mentioned that. "Why wouldn't she tell that to me and my obviously Italian family?"

Ladonna's brow lowered. "Italians were discriminated against back then, so she probably hid it after marrying Bradley's grandfather."

I shook my head, which had begun to spin like I was back at Metairie Cemetery. "It's got to be one of those names that looks Italian."

"I don't think so. It's an Italian word for 'crazy.'"

I smirked. "You mean, Cuccuzza?"

"Very funny. It's Toccato."

My mouth went dry. *The same surname as Lou and Chandra, the plumber and the Crescent City Medium? Is that why Chandra had been on my mind lately?*

Couldn't be. I'm not psychic—like Chandra, for that matter—and what were the odds? Still, I checked my pocket for the damned penny. I hadn't hallucinated returning it to Louis Prima's tomb before leaving the cemetery. "This head injury is messing with me. Could you repeat that?"

"Toccato. I looked it up, and there aren't even five families with that name in Boston."

Lou and Chandra's hometown.

The plastic groaned as I spread out like a patient on a therapy couch and pressed a blue Marilyn to my face. Not only would my mother-in-law be Italian, I would be related by marriage to Lou, which meant that Chandra might be a guest at my wedding.

And at family gatherings.

Veronica entered the office with a large envelope. "One of your maid-of-honor gifts was just delivered. I'm going to give it to you now, because you could use it."

She has no idea. None.

I grabbed the package, hoping it was a sedative, and ripped it open. As I unrolled the bubble wrap, I could tell that it was a utensil. I hoped it wasn't the butter knife with the "spread love" inscription from the Greco's Grocery gift shop, and luckily it wasn't. It was a silver spoon with the engraving *Nutella is amore.*"

"Aww." Ladonna pressed tiger-striped fingertips to her cheeks. "What a great gift."

It was better than great, it was perfect because it was me. I looked at my best friend. "Would you be okay with me making this my bomboniere?"

Her eyes crinkled. "Really? I would be flattered."

Ladonna sighed. "I'm sorry I'll miss that wedding."

"Of course you'll be invited."

"I'm not sure I can make it. Now that the case is solved, it's time to give you the news—Rocco and I are moving back to Scranton with his mother and the kids. All the mother-in-law talk made me realize that I miss living near my family."

I didn't have the luxury of missing mine, but Ladonna had reminded me how important they were. And compared to her mother-in-law, Lillian Hartmann was doable.

"We'll be sorry to see you go, right Franki?"

"We will," I said, and I meant it. Ladonna got on my nerves, but she was well-meaning and had solid instincts, and with more experience she would've made a good PI. And I was going to miss her Italian-mother-in-law advice.

"Before I start bawlin'," she went to the bookshelf, "I've got two advance wedding gifts for both of you. Veronica, since you're getting married first, you get *Chicken Soup for the Soul: Here Comes the Bride*. And Franki, yours is *Chicken Soup for the Soul: Happily Ever After*."

I forced a grateful smile and took the book, knocking my maid-of-honor gift to the floor. There couldn't be a happily ever after if I didn't make things right with Bradley, and I seriously doubted the chicken soup authors had included a chapter on warring families, a blank check, and the antidote for cayenne pepper sprinkled in a fiancé's mouth.

I picked up the Nutella spoon. The solution was written all over it.

21

I 'd never been happier to see the rundown, ex-Italian-grocery-store fourplex than when I turned onto Maple Street at eight-thirty. I wouldn't even have minded if the stripper pole had been re-erected and Glenda had hung her old Mardi Gras boob decorations from the balcony. I parked in the driveway behind my mother's Ford Taurus and smiled. Evidently, Theodora's new-and-improved Dispello spell hadn't worked, and that was fine with me. After the ordeal of the past twelve hours, I was thrilled to spend the day with family.

But just one. If my mom and nonna didn't leave after that, I would load them in the car and drive them to Houston myself.

I climbed from the Mustang and slammed the door.

"*Psst.*"

I looked for the source of the sound. No one was outside Thibodeaux's Tavern, so I reluctantly scanned the cemetery. From behind her usual mausoleum, Theodora flagged me down with purple caftan bell sleeves that hippy Pam would have envied.

I sighed and crossed the street. Theodora was the real nightmare witch, because it wasn't right that I had to go to a graveyard so soon after my close encounter at Metairie Cemetery. "What's up?"

She folded her arms on top of the tomb. "Glad to see you survived your ordeal with the Axeman last night."

I wasn't going to make the mistake I'd made the last time we'd had this conversation. "Let me guess—you knew about that because you're a witch."

Her red-shadowed eyelids lowered. "No. It's all over the news this morning."

I just can't win with this witch.

Theodora rested her chin on her hands and grinned. "I told you the killer wasn't one of my people."

"Is that why you called me over—for an I-told-you-so moment?"

She stood as erect as a cauldron stick. "For your information, I came to tell you that your mom and nonna are packed and ready to leave, thanks to me."

Skeptical, I scrutinized the Taurus. It did look like there might be baggage in the back of the wagon, but I wasn't convinced her black salt mixture had done the trick. On the off-chance it had, I wanted the recipe. "What did you put in it?"

"The same stuff I put in the last one."

I looked at her, surprised. "I thought you were going to tweak it with some special ingredient."

"I did. I knocked on your door and told your mom and nonna that it was time to leave you and your fiancé alone and go home." She fluffed her Endora hair. "Worked like a charm."

Open-mouthed, I stared at my apartment. Theodora might have had magical powers after all, because I'd been telling my mom and nonna to leave for years, and it had never worked. "I don't know how to repay you."

"That's why I asked you for that jar of Mambo Odette's swamp mud."

I shoved my hands into my jeans pockets. "I'm sorry, but things got a little crazy when I went out to her place, so I forgot all about it."

Her cat pupils flashed like she planned to pounce. "I see how it is. I help you out, and in return, I get the shaft."

"Look, I would've gone back to Mambo Odette's, but you know

how hard it is to get to her house. And to be fair, you did say that the banishing spell was free of charge."

Theodora huffed and pointed at me, and I braced myself for Upendo, hoping I wouldn't hit my injured head.

"I got strung up by my heels for you—"

"Hey, that reminds me. Did you unscrew the bolts on Glenda's stripper pole?"

"Of course I did. Payback's a witch."

That's exactly what I said.

"Now you owe me, lady. And I *will* come to collect." Theodora spun, her caftan swirling like purple smoke around her, and fled deep into the cemetery.

I left the graveyard with a bigger sense of dread than when I'd gone in. *Why can't I find a way to ditch that witch for good?*

"Miss Franki," Glenda sashayed across the yard wearing nothing but a garden hose and the "Garden Ho" Crocs. "Child, I just heard the news, and you've got to stop going to cemeteries."

I eyed the green coils around her body, surprised she hadn't used the hose's metal ends as pasties. "I will, if you stop going to hardware stores."

She dragged off her cigarette-holder ring. "What's wrong with my dress? Bob Simpson said I should think out of the box with my #influenceroutfits."

"Well, I think you need to run this one by him."

"I can't, sugar." She blew out a sad smoke ring. "He announced his retirement yesterday."

"That came out of nowhere."

"I thought so too. In fact, I worried that he'd retired because he couldn't hope to top me as a client."

After advising the likes of JLo and Kim Kardashian, I really didn't think that was the reason. "Did you ask him about it?"

"I did. He said, and I quote, 'It's the darnedest thing, but my wife, Linda, doesn't support my new profession.'"

"That's a shocker," I said, although it totally wasn't.

"I hear ya, sugar. I don't understand people sometimes. But on the bright side, I posted some of the pictures Bob took, and I've already got over five hundred thousand #followers."

Half a million? I don't understand people sometimes, either. "That's awesome. Listen, I hate to run, but I need to get inside before my mom and nonna see the news."

"You should do that, Miss Franki. But real quick, I researched land records for Orleans Parish, and I found out some wonderful information about the fourplex. The lower floor was a grocery store, but the costume closet was a speakeasy. I've got half a mind to turn it into one after you move out."

I imagined a bunch of drunks parading up and down the stairs, stomping around on the floor above my apartment, and maybe even pole dancing in the yard. "You know, Thibodeaux's Tavern has been good to us, and I don't think they'd appreciate the competition."

"True. And Nadezhda wants to rent the place as soon as you move out."

My throat tightened as though she'd wrapped her garden hose around my neck. I never imagined that she would rent the costume closet after I was done with it, much less to Nadezhda. And even though I would be eternally grateful to her for helping me bring Ric Caruso to justice, I didn't want to live in the same building as a cheap criminal who thought I was a man—even after waxing me. "I'm going to hang on to the costume closet a little longer."

"Suit yourself, sugar."

With my stomach now aching like my head, I went inside my apartment.

My mother rose from the armchair and pressed a hand to her heart. "Oh, thank goodness. We heard about what happened at Metairie Cemetery, and we've been terrified."

"I'm all right, Mom."

Nonna came from the kitchen, holding a rosary and crossing herself.

I hugged her and my mom. Tight.

The relief on Nonna's face turned to reproach. "Your mamma called-a you at least-a twenty times. Why you not answer?"

"I never heard my phone ring." I pulled my cell from my purse, and the envelope with the maid-of-honor gift fell out. I'd shown Ric's text to an officer at the police station, and she must have turned it off. I pressed the power button, and a barrage of missed calls and texts appeared, including a panicked message from Bradley saying that he was on his way over.

My mom picked up the envelope. "What's this, dear?"

"A gift from Veronica—and my bomboniere."

She ripped into the bubble wrap and gasped. "I've seen Nutella knives but never a spoon."

Nonna jutted out her lip. "It's-a good. You give-a the guests something they can-a eat with."

A typical Italian nonna response. I turned to my mother. "What do you think?"

"I love it. It's your personality, and it's perfect for the Hartmanns."

I took the utensil. "How do you figure?"

"Silver spoons say 'money,' Francesca." She practically hummed with excitement. "Now I'd better call your father and let him know you're all right."

There was a knock at the door, and Bradley burst in followed by Lillian and Cordelia and wrapped me in his arms. I snuggled in the warmth of his chest and his love. I raised my head, and we kissed.

Then the whole Hartmann family surrounded me.

Lillian slid her arm around my shoulders and gave me a squeeze. "You gave us such a fright, Francesca."

Cordelia took my hand. "You're a heroine. A Hartmann heroine."

I teared up at their reactions because they cared about me more than I'd realized. Then I remembered that Cordelia was actually a Toccato, and the tear went a little cold.

Lillian removed her arm, and I spotted a charm bracelet, not unlike the one that jangled on Chandra's wrist when she allegedly channeled a spirit that brought me bad news.

The room tilted, and I pressed my palm to my forehead, still holding the Nutella spoon.

"Come on." Bradley led me to the chaise lounge. "You need to lay down."

"I think I just need to eat."

Cordelia recoiled. "Let's get this girl some food."

Spoken like a true Italian.

Cordelia, Nonna, my mom, and Lillian rushed into the kitchen.

Bradley sat beside me and kissed my cheek. "I'm sorry about the way I left the other night, but when you announced that you wanted to get married in Boston, I knew my mother and grandmother had gotten to you. I went home and confronted them, and my mother confessed about the check."

"I'm sorry that I—"

"You don't need to apologize. They want to apologize to you, and they went to Private Chicks a couple of days ago to do just that, but you weren't there."

So that's why they came when I was hiding in Ladonna's office.

"They're going to apologize today, when the time is right."

And while we were having that conversation, I planned to ask them about their family genealogy.

My mother put a tray of pastries on the coffee table with a jar of Nutella and two glasses of water. "Here's a starter for you two *piccioncini*."

I looked at Bradley. "That means 'lovebirds.'"

Or does he already know that since he's part Italian?

Questions flooded my mind as I bit into a croissant.

Bradley pulled me into his chest. "We need to talk about our wedding."

The questions vanished, because I couldn't wait to talk about marrying him.

His gorgeous blue eyes looked into mine. "I hope you've changed your mind about a Boston wedding, because I don't have the stomach to argue with you about the location." His gaze turned mischievous. "It must be my weak digestion."

"Oh, I can fix that." I grinned and reached for the Nutella. I rinsed the spoon in my glass of water and fed him a bite of the chocolate-hazelnut voodoo, the love-potion antidote to the cayenne pepper.

I ate a spoonful myself for good measure. "About the location, I want us to find a place we're both excited about."

He kissed me with lips that tasted like Nutella Nirvana. "I'll marry you anywhere, Francesca Lucia Amato." He paused. "It's just too bad there isn't a dowry."

I lunged for him, and he shielded his chest, laughing.

"Seriously, though," he said, "I'm looking forward to whatever you have in mind for the wedding, because it's sure to be interesting."

I leaned back. "Are you suggesting that it'll be wacky?"

His head recoiled in mock surprise. "I didn't say that."

I smacked his thigh. "No, but that's what you meant. Why would you even think such a thing?"

He gave me the side-eye. "Franki..."

Not even I could argue with that.

I put the spoon on the tray and noticed an invoice on the table. "What's this?"

My mother entered with two espresso cups. "The bill for the boaed pig bomboniere Rosalie ordered." She raised an eyebrow. "I told her no. You didn't."

My fingers flew to my lips. I'd hung up on Rosalie when she'd called about adding rose gold lipstick on the pigs.

Bradley slid his arm around me. "Told you it would be interesting."

And expensive. Because the wedding that my parents were now definitively paying for was going to cost me a fortune.

Lillian emerged from the kitchen with wine glasses and a bottle.

I was glad that it was Valpolicella, and not Marsala.

My mom, Nonna, and Cordelia lined up beside her with their wine. She handed goblets to me and Bradley that had our names on them. "We realize it's early, but this occasion calls for a toast."

I was the last person to disagree with her.

Lillian raised her glass and blew me a kiss. "To new family."

Nonna's black eyes twinkled. "Like-a *bambini*."

"Hear, hear," Cordelia cheered. "And to new traditions."

My mother smiled at me and then Bradley. "I second all of that, but especially the bambini part."

"*Mom*," I protested. Then I lifted my glass to my lips, and it overflowed like my heart. With our families united, Bradley and I were going to knock this wedding thing out of the piazza.

A COCKTAIL AND DESSERT

THE LOST SAILOR

Tradition is a major theme of *Marsala Maroon*, and I have a personal tradition of drinking the liqueur or wine in a Franki Amato title on the day that I finish writing the mystery. I chose to toast "The End" of *Marsala Maroon* with The Lost Sailor, because the drink is a variation on the Negroni, which is one of my faves, and because the name captures how I felt trying to write a book during the rough seas of 2020.

Ingredients
    1 and 1/2 ounces sweet Marsala
    1 and 1/2 ounces Campari
    1 and 1/2 ounces gin
    1 orange twist

Mix in a tall glass (no ice). Garnish with an orange twist or an orange wedge for extra sweetness.

RICOTTA-MASCARPONE CANNOLI

One of the best things to do with Marsala is to use it in cannoli, both the shells and the filling. Personally, I use pre-made shells from Italy because they're excellent and oh-so easy (you'll see what I mean when you read the instructions below for making the shells)! Also, I like this recipe because it uses both ricotta and mascarpone for the filling, both of which are used in Sicily. The mascarpone gives the filling a creamier, more decadent texture, which I'm all about! By the way, the name "cannoli" comes from river reeds that were originally used to roll and shape the shells.

The Shells
> 1 cup all-purpose flour
> 2 tablespoons granulated sugar
> 1/2 teaspoon unsweetened cocoa powder
> 1/2 teaspoon cinnamon
> 1/4 teaspoon salt
> 1/2 cup sweet Marsala
> 1 and 1/2 tablespoons vegetable oil
> 1 egg white, beaten
> Vegetable oil, for frying

The Filling
> 3/4 cup whole milk ricotta, drained and squeezed dry
> 3/4 cup mascarpone cheese
> 1/2 cup powdered sugar
> 1 teaspoon vanilla extract
> 1/2 teaspoon cinnamon
> a dash of sweet Marsala
> a pinch of salt
> 3/4 cup pistachios or mini chocolate chips, plus more for decorating the ends of the cannoli

To Make the Filling
> Beat ricotta, mascarpone, confectioners sugar, vanilla, cinnamon,

and salt together until smooth. Fold in pistachios or mini chocolate chips (or both!). Cover and refrigerate for 2 hours.

To Make and Fill the Shells

Using a mixer, combine the flour, sugar, cocoa powder, cinnamon, and salt. Add the Marsala and the oil and beat on medium speed just until dough comes together. Knead dough on a lightly floured surface until very smooth, about 15 minutes. Wrap in plastic and let rest for 30 minutes. (NOTE: The dough starts out very sticky. Continue kneading for the full 15 minutes, adding flour as needed. Near the end of the 15 minutes, the dough comes together and is silky smooth and no longer sticks to your hands.)

Divide dough in half, leaving one half wrapped in the plastic. Roll out dough on a lightly floured surface until it is very thin, about the thickness of a penny (poor Franki has none of these!). Using a round cutter, or the rim of a container about 3 1/2 inches in diameter, cut out circles. Repeat with remaining half of the dough.

Pour a few inches of oil in a large, heavy-bottomed saucepan or pot. Heat over medium heat until a thermometer registers 375 degrees, regulating heat to maintain temperature around 375-380 degrees F.

Wrap each circle of dough around a cannoli form, and seal with the egg white (just a dab will work like glue). Leave the dough on the form.

In batches of 2, fry cannoli shells until golden, about 1 minute. Carefully remove the shells from the oil using a skewer inserted through the metal tube, or using tongs.

Allow to drain and cool on paper towel for a few minutes before sliding the metal cannoli mold out from the shell. Repeat with remaining dough.

When the shells are ready, use a piping bag with an opening about the same diameter as your shells to add the filling. Roll each end of the filled cannoli in the remaining pistachios or mini chocolate chips.

Buon appetito!

CALL TO ACTION

Dear reader,

Thank you so much for reading *Marsala Maroon*! The writing business is tough and getting tougher, so I appreciate your support. We authors would simply not exist without you.

To that end, there are things that you can do to help besides buying and reading books:

1. Write a review of *Marsala Maroon* on Amazon, Barnes and Noble, Goodreads, and BookBub.

2. Sign up for my newsletter at traciandrighetti.com. I'll send you "Fragolino Fuchsia" for FREE!

3. Follow me on Facebook, Twitter, Instagram, BookBub, Amazon, and Goodreads. The links are provided in the About the Author section.

4. And email me at traci@traciandrighetti.com. Your comments often get me through the writing day. And like I said in the Book Backstory, some of your ideas make their way into my books!

A presto,
Traci

Cremoncello cream

A Franki Amato Mystery

DO NOT CROSS

CRIME SCEN

USA TODAY BESTSELLING AUTHOR

TRACI ANDRIGHETTI

FREE SHORT MYSTERY OFFER

Sign up for my newsletter at traciandrighetti.com to be the first to know about my new releases, deals, and giveaways. And I'll email you a link to download "Fragolino Fuchsia," a Franki-goes-to-Rome short mystery, for FREE!

MIRTO MAGENTA

by

TRACI ANDRIGHETTI

***

Copyright © 2020 by Traci Andrighetti

Cover design by Lyndsey Lewellyn

Limoncello Press www.limoncellopress.com

All rights reserved. Without limiting the rights under copyright reserved above, no part of this publication may be reproduced, stored in or introduced into a retrieval system, or transmitted, in any form, or by any means (electronic, mechanical, photocopying, recording, or otherwise) without the prior written permission of both the copyright owner and the above publisher of this book.

This is a work of fiction. Names, characters, places, brands, media, and incidents are either the product of the author's imagination or are used fictitiously. The author acknowledges the trademarked status and trademark owners of various products referenced in this work of fiction, which have been used without permission. The publication/use of these trademarks is not authorized, associated with, or sponsored by the trademark owners.

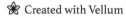 Created with Vellum

STORY BACKSTORY

Thank you in advance for reading Mirto Magenta! This short mystery was one of my favorites to write. I had the title in a file for a few years, but I didn't have a clue what to do with it until I stumbled across an article about Sardinia (*Sardegna* in Italian) that said Mirto, a myrtle berry liqueur, was the drink of the island. Once I had a location, the plot started to thicken, or maybe pour.

Another reason I loved writing Mirto Magenta is that Sardinia is truly considered an island of mystery (you'll find out the reasons along with Franki). And the lure of setting a story in Nora, a submerged ancient Roman city, was great. But honestly, the clincher was when I learned that Sardinia is home to the Gulf of Angels, which has a cove called the Devil's Saddle. I mean, what a perfect place to put Franki—with her sixty-something ex-stripper landlady, Glenda! Oh, and some goats.

Speaking of the marine Pompeii, as I will call it, thanks to my old college roommate, Stephanie Webber, I am a certified scuba diver. Franki, however, is not. And Mirto Magenta was my chance to write about that old skill and put Franki in over her head, literally.

Cin cin (Cheers)!
Traci

COCKTAIL

MIRTO MARTINI

Martha Stewart makes a mirto and tonic with a spring of rosemary, but as a fan of mixed drinks, I prefer a good martini—and so does Franki.

Ingredients
  1 ounce orange vodka
  3/4 ounce Mirto
  3/4 ounce fresh lime juice
  1/2 ounce Cointreau or other triple sec
  1/4 ounce simple syrup
  4 blueberries skewered on a pic
  ice

Fill a cocktail shaker with ice. Add the remaining ingredients and shake well. Strain into a chilled martini glass and garnish with the skewered blueberries. Sip while savoring Franki's adventure in Mirto Magenta!

1

"I don't know why New Orleanians call the summer humidity an 'oppressive soup.'" I let the door to Private Chicks, Inc., slam behind me and tied my brown hair into a top knot. "The air is as thick as gumbo."

My BFF and boss, Veronica Maggio, didn't look up from the papers on the lobby coffee table. "I've been hydrating with watermelon snoballs." She flicked her blonde ponytail from her neck and pointed to a Pandora's cup. "I got you tiger's blood."

I picked up the red shaved ice and stabbed at it with a spoon. "Everyone in the French Quarter is hydrating with something stronger, and I'm ready to join them. Did you get my prosecco from Vieux Carré Wine & Spirits? It would be delish in this."

"I refused."

"What? Why?"

"They raised their prices by two dollars, and I wasn't going to pay that."

The bad booze news forced my heat-exhausted limbs to surrender, and I slumped onto the couch beside her.

Veronica punched the keys of a calculator. "While I was there, a woman was outside the door with a life-sized Medusa head."

As a PI in The Big Easy, nothing surprised me. "When the heat spikes in this city, so does the crazy. Even the insects bug out. Termites swarm, caterpillars sting, and cockroaches fly—it just isn't natural." I dropped the back of my head onto the couch cushion. "And it's only the beginning of August."

"Why don't you go away for a few days? Business is slow, and I'm tied up with this tax audit."

"Nah, Bradley has to work."

She sat up, emitting a waft of floral perfume. "Francesca Amato, you're an independent woman. Go somewhere without him."

I lifted my head to make sure she could see my pointed look. "The only place my bank account will take me is out to eat."

She smoothed her white linen dress. "We'll get a big case soon, Franki. In the meantime, the restaurants have some great specials for COOLinary month, so you could treat Bradley to a fancy prix-fixe meal on the cheap."

"Dat Dog is more my price range." I took a sad slurp from my cup.

"There's always Houston."

I grimaced and pressed my fingers into my forehead. "Either the brain freeze distorted my hearing, or you just suggested that I vacation at my parents' house."

She shrugged. "It *is* a free trip."

"Except for the cost of my sanity. And anyway, Houston is almost as humid."

"Yes, but you can escape to Galveston and sip fruity drinks on the beach."

My look went from pointed to piercing. "As a fellow Italian-American, you know the fundamental principle of our ethnicity—you can't. escape. the family." I smacked the cup on my hand to underscore the burden of the words. "I can see me now, sweating on the hot sand with my nonna on one side calling me a *zitella*, and my mom on the other lamenting that I'm thirty-one and still haven't given her a grandkid." I shoved a bloody bite into my mouth. "The next thing you know, this childless old maid will be standing in front of a liquor store with a severed Medusa head."

She buried a smile in a spoonful of ice. "Too bad you couldn't go to Sardinia with Glenda."

I almost spat snoball at the mention of our landlady. "As if. You remember what happened when she tagged along on the Rome investigation."

"I know, I know, she didn't do as the Romans do."

"No, she did as sixty-something ex-strippers do, which is a problem in a country of Italian men. Besides, she's with her ex-boss and his Sardinian wife, and I don't want to stay in a beach house that belongs to strip club owners."

"The pictures Glenda texted might change your mind. Thanks to the money they make from Madame Moiselle's, that beach house is a beach mansion overlooking the *Costa Smeralda*."

I cold-stared into her cornflower blues. "Let me be clear, I'd rather visit Dante's nine circles of hell than go on another trip with Glenda —or see her stripper swimsuits."

Veronica's cell phone vibrated on the coffee table. "Well, speak of the she-devil. I'll put her on speaker."

Even though we were alone, I glanced around the lobby. Our landlady's mouth was a minefield of explosive statements.

"Ciao, bella!" Veronica slid the phone to the middle of the table. "I'm here with Franki, and we want details."

"It's filthy seductive, Miss Ronnie." Glenda's sultry voice sexed up the room. "I've definitely found my people."

Unless Sardinia was an island of aging ex-strippers, I didn't see how that was possible. "How so?"

"The Sardinians are as wild as the landscape, Miss Franki."

"That's a stereotype."

"It isn't. The island's known for its shepherds and bandits. It's a wildman paradise."

Veronica looked at me. "She's not wrong. I read that the banditry has to do with the island's history as an inland colony and its pastoral economy. Sheep outnumber people two to one."

It sounded more like a pasture than a paradise. "Is it hot?"

"Sizzling, sugar. Did you not hear what I said about the menfolk?"

Of course I'd meant the weather, but I didn't force the issue. Despite her age, Glenda was in perpetual heat and apparently unable to distinguish between sex and temperature.

Veronica leaned forward. "Where are you now?"

"Poetto Beach." Glenda paused, and the click of a lighter was followed by a sharp intake of breath. "It's in the Gulf of Angels, and it's got a cove called the Devil's Saddle. Lucifer lost it when he fell off his horse in a battle against the Archangel Michael for control of the gulf, and now I'm riding that thing like a hellion cowgirl."

I shot a *see-what-I-mean?* look at my BFF and boss, whose smile turned diabolical. "Franki was just telling me she'd like to visit a place like that."

My face contorted à la Medusa, and I waved my arms like frenzied snakes.

"Perfect, Miss Ronnie, because I've got a proposition for her."

Nervous, I shifted on the couch. "Save it for the shepherds and bandits."

"Save it?" Glenda exhaled. "Child, you know that's not my style."

Oh, I do.

"Anyhoo, sugar, Harry needs a PI to look into a theft at his father-in-law's business, so I told him about Private Chicks and how you girls met at the University of Texas studying Italian. Now he wants to contract your services, Miss Franki."

Veronica gasped.

I held up my hand to stop her from accepting. "Actually, Sardinian is the closest living language to Latin, so my Italian might not help. And you can tell Little Bo Peep that I don't do lost-sheep investigations."

"It's not sheep, sugar. His father-in-law, Efisio, makes a myrtle berry liqueur called *Mirto*. The brand name is Mirto d'Efisio, and his company's entire production was stolen from the warehouse down south in Pula."

Veronica's eyes glowed like the Mediterranean. "There's your 'something stronger,' Franki."

Not even a treasure trove of Italian liqueur—and a bonus chest of

Nutella—could convince me to take the case. "Honestly, Glenda, that's something the police in Pula should investigate."

"They did, and the carabinieri located a few of the bottles in a dumpster near some Roman ruins, but they still haven't figured out who stole it. That's where you come in. Not only will Harry pay your wages and expenses, he'll put you up in a bungalow at a spa resort."

Veronica's hand went to her mouth. "Oh, Franki. You've got to take this case."

"C'mon, sugar. You know what they say—all roads lead to Roman ruins."

The phrase *road to ruin* came to mind, as in mine. "Those roads lead to Rome, not Sardinia, so it's a no."

My text tone dinged.

I pulled my phone from the pocket of my khaki capris, and my veins chilled as though filled with tiger's blood snoball. "I can be on a plane first thing tomorrow."

Glenda gave a raucous cheer. "I'm glad you came around. I'll talk to Harry and text you the arrangements. *Arrivederci*, ladies!"

Veronica hung up. "What prompted *that* about-face?"

"You mean, my descent into the first circle of hell?" I leaned over and put my head between my knees. "Something more horrifying than a vacation with Glenda—my mom and Nonna are coming in the morning for a wedding and a baptism."

2

"*Intra.*" A thin woman in a brown headscarf and sack dress gestured for me to enter the dilapidated stucco structure.

I'd been traveling for twenty-three hours, and yet I didn't want to follow her. Maybe it was the sleep deprivation, but in the evening darkness the so-called spa looked like a farm for wayward animals.

"You enter," she said, as though I hadn't understood.

But I didn't move. I would have rather pitched a tent in the Devil's Saddle than stay in what looked like the second circle of hell.

The woman put hands to bony hips and gave me a once-over. Then she turned to my driver and fired off frustrated Sardinian, which, despite my knowledge of Italian and Sicilian, sounded Greek. And that wasn't good.

The driver, who had the face and demeanor of a Mafia hitman, grabbed my bags and made off around the side of the house.

The woman lowered her scarfed head, charged down the steps, and wrapped steely fingers around my wrist. "You come. I am Zena."

Like the warrior princess.

I let her pull me through the dimly lit house so that I could find my luggage. We exited onto to a back porch overlooking a grassy yard, and I spotted the driver depositing my things inside a cabin straight out of *Friday the 13th*.

Zena pointed to a long wooden table. "Sit. I bring food."

I was so tired that I did as she commanded. Plus, I wasn't one to turn down a meal even under the most suspect of circumstances.

She went inside, and I rummaged in my straw tote bag for my phone. I had to find Glenda and get off the farm. I came across a half-eaten bag of airplane peanuts and put it on the table.

Thumping ensued, like hooves.

Two white goats emerged from the darkness and charged with horns lowered.

This place is a farm for wayward animals. I leapt up as the goats arrived and nibbled on my tote. "Shoo! Back off!"

They persisted as stubborn as goats.

I swung my bag and gave a warning kick.

But they turned their teeth to the rope on my espadrilles.

"Uh-uh. No. Those cost me fifty bucks." I did a shuffle step to stop them.

The goats peeled back their lips, exposing long lower chompers and bare upper gums. Then they bleated, clearly yucking it up at my expense.

Glenda said Sardinia was wild, but this was the pits. I poured the peanuts on the ground to distract the biting beasts, and I pulled out my cell and punched her number.

"*Benvenuta*, Miss Franki." Glenda sing-songed the *welcome* greeting to the tune of dance music in the background. "Have you had your massage?"

"No, but I've been manhandled."

"I like the sound of that."

"I don't because I'm not at a spa." I ground out the words in a guttural tone, and one of the goats gaped. "This place is either an *agriturismo* or a serial killer's headquarters."

"It's that driver, Miss Franki. Harry said he was going to fire him because he's been screwing up."

Nevertheless, he let the guy pick me up from the airport and drive me to this dump. "I'll bet he took me to a family member's place. Can you come meet me so we can straighten this out?"

"No can do, sugar. When we heard you'd be arriving at nine, we figured you'd want to go straight to bed. So I'm still up north on the Emerald Coast at a yacht party."

Why? Why had I come on this trip? "Could you at least tell me the name of the spa I'm supposed to be at?"

Her laugh was as bubbly as the champagne she'd undoubtedly been drinking. "Child, I can't remember that, but it's on the beach and has swimming pools and a water park."

I could smell the sea, but the only pool I saw was a rusty tub where the goats were quenching their post-accessory-eating thirst.

"Oh, and Harry said the restaurant has a Michelin star, and Sting performed at their concert stage."

As if on cue, Zena plunked a basket of bread in front of me, and the driver plucked a mandolin.

I waited until the warrior princess went back into the house, and then I turned my back to the driver. "Get the spa name and call me back. If you don't, I could end up the star of a Sardinian slasher flick."

"It'll have to wait till tomorrow, sugar. Sabina is off mingling, and Harry goes to bed at eight."

"And he calls himself a strip-club owner?" I whisper-huffed.

"He says he needs his beauty sleep. You get some too, and I'll meet you for breakfast at a restaurant called Blu Moon at nine. It's near where Efisio's empty bottles of Mirto were found, and it's on the beach overlooking the Roman ruins."

Of course it was. The road to my ruin.

"As they say on the island, Miss Franki, *adiosu.*"

I tossed the phone onto the table and turned around.

And I jumped.

A balding man with a narrow face and a protruding mouth was beside me, holding a primitive knife.

3

The man followed my alarmed gaze to the tip of the blade and grinned, revealing long bottom teeth and toothless top gums—like the goats. "I yam-a Jaku. I sell *vinu*." He opened his hand to show me the knife, which had a curved goat horn for a handle. "This *pattada*." He retrieved a wine bottle from a crate on the ground. "For open *vinu*."

I relaxed and glared at the goats. "That horn will be yours if you keep eating my stuff."

They fixed their slanted eyes on me as if to say, "Bite me, lady."

Zena reappeared sans headscarf, revealing a bun of frizzy, gray-black hair, and wearing a necklace of red coral spikes. She placed a wheel of cheese with a hard rind and soft center on the table. "*Casu marzu*."

Jaku poured me a glass of wine, and I thought of the liqueur I'd come to investigate. "Do you have any Mirto?"

Zena twisted a coral spike. "No."

I interpreted her curt reply as a sign that she was upset about my earlier slight, and since I needed to spend the night, I had to make amends. "Your necklace is beautiful. Can I buy coral here in Pula?"

"The red. If it is magenta, it is fake." She went inside.

It was always nice when hospitality workers shared details of their culture.

Jaku took a seat and scooped casu marzu with his knife, offering me a bite.

I shook my head. It might have been the exhaustion, but I would've sworn the cheese was moving.

My phone rang.

I rose, glad to have an excuse to leave. "I'll take this call in my room."

With the goats in tow, I bounded across the yard, entered my cabin, and latched the rickety door behind me.

The ringing had stopped, so I took a moment to take in my surroundings—a dusty armoire, a crooked night table, and a brass bed with Medusa on the headboard, all against a backdrop of dirty, crumbling red walls. If the house was the second circle of hell, my room was definitely the third.

The ringing resumed, and I answered. "Hi, Mom."

"Francesca," her voice was as shrill as a three-a.m. alarm, "is that you?"

"You're calling me on my cell phone. Obviously it's me."

"That's a fine tone to take with your mother."

Five seconds into the call, and I already needed to lie down. I tossed myself onto the bed and heard the grating of metal. One end collapsed, and the footboard fell off. I rolled and landed face-down on the tile.

"What are you doing, Francesca?" My mother's pitch was not unlike the metal screech.

I shot a side-eye at the phone beside me. "The bed broke, and I fell on the floor."

"For heaven's sake, get up. I'm sure it's filthy."

I stayed down since calls from home usually laid me out. "So, what's up?"

"Well, your nonna and I enjoyed the wedding, even though your

father refused to come with us. I'm telling you, that man is the definition of an old goat."

She didn't have a clue.

I heard the click of another line joining the call—the sound of my
nonna on a meddling mission. The woman had been trying to get me
married for so long that I doubted she'd stop even after I'd tied the knot.

"Ciao, Franki," Nonna rasped in a thick Sicilian accent, "I saw my
old-a friend, Adele Gallo, at-a the reception, and she has a grand-a-
son that live-a near Pula."

I wasn't surprised she'd located a bachelor in the vicinity. Her
network of family and friends operated in more countries than
Amazon.com. "You can both give it up. I'm engaged to Bradley, and
even if we were broken up, this is a business trip."

"We're not suggesting a *date*, Francesca," my mother fibbed
through two full rows of teeth. "We just thought you'd like to have a
contact while you were there."

"*Sì*, and-a one who has a thousand-a sheep."

A sheepherder? It was a hard no. I couldn't even handle two goats.

A knock brought me to my feet.

"Someone's here. Gotta go!" I hung up and peered through a
crack in the door.

And I stepped back.

It was a stooped, elderly woman with the bulbous nose and
protruding chin of La Befana, the Italian Epiphany witch.

A tantalizing odor wafted in, so I took another look—and threw
open the door.

The La Befana lookalike had a plate of dumplings in red sauce.

She smiled and pointed to the food. "*Culurgiones cun patate,
pecorino e menta.*"

The name *culurgiones* meant nothing to me, but the potatoes,
pecorino cheese, and mint did. I took the plate. "*Grazie.*"

She looked over her shoulder. Then her smile slid away and her
brown eyes threatened to pop from their sockets. "*Attenta alla
Medusa!*"

Watch out for the Medusa? I glanced at the headboard. That bed was dangerous, all right. I turned to ask whether someone could come and fix it.

She ran a finger across her throat and shuffled into the night.

4

The sun was hot on my skin as I lay on the beach in the Devil's Saddle. An occasional wave washed ashore and licked at my feet. This was the trip I'd been promised, a luxury spa getaway with no Glenda and no goats.

Elated, I made a snow angel in the sand.

Someone grasped my big toe.

My masseuse.

A pinch sent pain surging from my foot to my hip.

No, a crab!

My eyes shot open as I shot up.

I wasn't on the beach. I was in bed in my cabin, and one of the goats stood where the broken footboard should have been—by my throbbing foot.

"Maybe that's why the old woman warned me about Medusa," I grumbled, "because this damn bed is clearly cursed."

I kicked off the covers and spotted a trail of my clothing that led to a hole in the door. Those godawful goats had chewed through the wood, probably to get to my dinner plate, and rifled through my luggage.

Rage coursed through my veins like caffeine from a triple

espresso, and I picked up the footboard and ushered them from the cabin. "You touch my stuff again, and you'll be horizontal like your pupils."

They bared their teeth and bleated, and one of their lips was unnaturally pink.

I squinted. *Was he freaking wearing my lipstick?*

I stormed inside. The greedy goats had not only grazed on my clothing, they'd gobbled some of my makeup.

An unsettling thought struck me. I hadn't read Dante since college, but I was pretty sure the third circle of hell was gluttony.

I gathered my things and stuffed them into the suitcase, certain that something was missing. But I didn't have time to figure out what it was. I had to get off the farm before Zena the warrior princess woke up.

I threw on a blue cotton dress and slipped on my espadrilles. I looked down, and the rage resurged. My shoes had been sheered of their rope like a sheep of its fleece. I took deep, calming breaths. I couldn't let goats get my goat.

After making sure the coast was clear, I grabbed a Sardinia travel guide I'd purchased and sped across the yard. From the road, an old tower and some columns were visible against a backdrop of blue.

The Roman ruins.

I set off for Nora on high alert, and not just for Zena and the driver. If the goats on the farm were any indication, no one was safe from the sheep on Sardinia.

It took fifteen minutes to reach the site. The ruins were immense, extending on both sides of the Capo di Pula peninsula, with shop stalls, baths, and a huge Roman theater. Poppies and dandelions grew among crumbling walls, columns, and earthenware jars, known as *dolia*, embedded in the ground for holding food. With the Tyrrhenian Sea in the background, the scene was postcard perfect. And I had it all to myself.

I opened my travel guide and browsed the history of the area. The indigenous inhabitants were an ancient sea people known as the Sherden. But because the peninsula was a convenient location for trade, Nora was founded by invading Phoenicians in the seventh century B.C. and subsequently ruled by Carthaginians and then Romans before the Vandals arrived in the fifth century A.D. and drove the population inland. The wealthy port city was named after the Greek God Norax, who was the son of Hermes and Erythia—the great-granddaughter of Medusa.

"Go figure."

The Medusa reference wasn't the only thing that caught my attention. Over the centuries, the sea level had risen, submerging roughly half of the ancient city. And its most famous feature was a Roman road made from volcanic bricks that went straight into the sea and continued two hundred yards underwater, where it abruptly dropped off because of a fracture along a geological fault line.

"Imagine that." My tone was bone dry as I gazed at the water. "Glenda brought me to an actual Roman road to ruin."

I had time to kill before meeting my landlady at the restaurant, so I decided to explore. Also, according to the travel guide, I was beside a row of communal toilets, and even though they hadn't been used since ancient Roman times, that was still too recent. I headed toward four columns belonging to a house with a tetrastyle atrium that was famous for its mosaic floor depicting Nero on a marine centaur. I walked up a dirt path, and a goat ran across it.

With a pair of my underwear.

My jaw tightened. Those goats were lucky that I was an animal lover. Otherwise, I would have led them to the nearest butcher like lambs to the slaughter.

"*Excuse, miss.*"

The male voice behind me was too close. I did a one-eighty.

A tanned, thirty-something man with black hair and a long mustache stood three feet away, which I didn't like. I stepped back and scanned the ruins. I was alone with the guy and far from help.

His full lips curled. "I know you."

I tensed. *Was he the sheepherder my nonna wanted to hook me up with?*

"You are woo-man who like-a beautiful tings."

I glanced at my sheered shoes. *He wasn't the sheepherder suitor—he was a slick salesman.* "Yes, this view."

"I 'ave someting you buy. Very nice." He pulled a coral bracelet from his pocket.

"I'm not interested."

His brow lowered, and his brown eyes went as black as the circles beneath them. He reached for his back waistband.

And he pulled out a jagged knife.

My gut tightened, steeling itself for the blade. The guy was no sheepherder or salesman. He was a bona fide Sardinian bandit from the fourth circle of hell.

5

The mustached man came toward me, knife extended.

I backed away and stumbled over a crumbling wall. The dang ruins belonged in a museum.

His dark eyes were devoid of compassion. "I cut fresh."

What? My throat?

He gestured toward the water. "Much coral. You wait-a."

I let out a strangled breath, relieved I'd misunderstood his intent but still on edge. Bandit or no, there was something off about a guy who brandished a knife without warning. "*Sì*, I wait."

He stripped off his shirt, revealing muscles so defined they could have been cut with his blade, and waded into the sea.

I made like one of the columns until his head went under, and then I dashed toward a commercial center. A sign for the Blu Moon, where I was supposed to meet Glenda for breakfast, was visible a few hundred yards up the beach.

I approached the restaurant, gasping from the sprint, and two elderly women sitting at a table on a covered terrace scrutinized me with interest. Their wise hazel eyes, small mouths, and turkey wattles made it apparent that they were sisters, but their contrasting outfits gave them the appearance of dueling Miss Marples.

The one in a white lace hat and ruffled dress waved. "Are you all right, dear?"

I swallowed a smile at her British accent. "Yes, but I just had a run-in at the ruins with a knife-wielding salesman."

The sisters' heads didn't move, but their eyes met in their respective corners.

The one with a black hat and tweed skirt suit leaned forward. Unlike her sister, who had prominent cheek bones, she had a fleshy, sagging face. "Did he try to sell you an ancient Roman amphora?"

"No, a coral bracelet. Why do you ask?"

She rested interlaced fingers at her plump waist. "Rumor has it there's a counterfeit ring on the island."

The one in the lace hat frowned. "Do come sit with us, as I'm afraid we've ordered more than we can eat." She pointed to two plates. "These delightful saffron-and-lemon ricotta dumplings are called *pardulas*, whilst these are *seadas*, citrus-scented cheese pastries fried and drizzled with warm honey."

Never mind the descriptions, the scent alone was enough to lure me to their table. I sat facing the water to keep an eye out for the businessman bandit and helped myself to one of each. "I'm Franki Amato."

The one with the black hat lifted her considerable chin. "Madge Maven, and this is my younger sister, Midge Maven."

Those names were as big a mouthful as the *pardula* I'd popped.

Midge raised a teacup. "Are you here on holiday?"

"Business. I'm a PI on a case for some friends of my landlady."

The Mavens' eyes again gravitated to their corners.

I wrote off the reaction to my profession. Plus, Agatha Christie had taught me that elderly British women were eccentric.

Midge's eyes sparkled. "Do you mind if I inquire about your case? Madge and I do love a mystery."

I supposed it wouldn't hurt. "I'm trying to find some Mirto thieves."

"Ah." Madge gave a smug smile. "The liqueur made from the myrtle bush. It was sacred to Aphrodite and Demeter, which is precisely the reason that magistrates and judges in ancient Athens were crowned with myrtle wreathes."

Midge nodded. "And the Sardinians say that Mirto has healing properties."

Didn't all alcohol?

Her eyes shifted to the beach. "I daresay it's Bo Derek from *Ten*, some forty years later."

"Who?" I followed her gaze. My landlady sashayed up the sand in platform flip flops, and her outfit did nothing to allay my Glenda-vacation reservations—two purple clamshells and a thong under a tight green fisherman's net. Her platinum hair was done in dozens of braids, but if it had been red and flowing she would've looked like The Little Mermaid after a few decades of ocean acidification. "That's Glenda O'Brien. My best friend and I rent apartments in her fourplex in New Orleans."

The Mavens exchanged another look, which I understood. The Big Easy probably confirmed their suspicion that I lived in a house of ill repute. And they were right, in a way, because my furnished apartment resembled an old French brothel.

Glenda arrived, gripped a chair back, and struck a pose with a Mae West-style cigarette holder. "What's shaking, ladies?"

The honest answer was the Mavens' turkey necks and Glenda's clamshells. "I was just telling Midge and Madge here about you and the case."

Madge patted the seat beside her. "Yes, do join us and tell us more."

Glenda stubbed out her cigarette and sunk into the chair. She pulled a magazine photo from a clamshell of a black bottle with a purple label. "Well, I had Miss Franki meet me here because a few of these were found in a dumpster out back."

Midge's chin disappeared into her throat. "Our breakfast location has suddenly become more interesting, hasn't it, Madge?"

"Oh, most."

I had to agree, although I wasn't sure whether she was talking about the bottle discovery or the clamshell reveal.

A young waitress with black coiled curls came over to me. "You order now?"

"Mirto, *per favore*. The d'Efisio brand, if you have it."

Her mouth opened and snapped shut.

I wondered why she seemed surprised, but it *was* early to be drinking.

Glenda tapped her cigarette holder. "Make that two. I'm a NOLA girl, so I'll keep the party going."

Midge touched a finger to her chin. "Bring a round for the table."

My mouth opened and shut like the waitress's. I'd taken the Mavens for tea-drinking teetotalers.

Madge wrinkled her nose. "We've got a touch of the rheumatism."

The waitress went inside, and Midge leaned toward her sister. "Her behavior was a bit odd."

Madge waved off the thought. "It's the local culture. Sardinia has always been an island of mystery."

Glenda's tongue touched her upper lip. "And men."

I cleared my throat. "How so, Madge?"

"Well, a catastrophic event of uncertain origin happened around 1175 B.C., which all but extinguished the Sardinian people, as well as Etruscans who'd settled on the island."

"Mm-mm-mm." Glenda shook her braids. "Sounds like a Stone Age STD."

Welcome to circle of hell number five.

Midge raised her teacup. "Actually, the prevailing theory is an enormous tidal wave. Whatever the cause, Sardinia has a number of ancient structures that scholars can't entirely decipher—sacred wells, prehistoric monuments similar to Stonehenge, and over twenty thousand megalithic structures with stone towers called *nuraghi*."

Madge nodded. "And curiously, each nuraghe has a hole above the entrance that reflects the image of a bull on an interior wall when the sun hits it just so."

I tilted my head. "You sure it's not a goat?"

"Quite. But the Sardinians do celebrate a pre-Christian ritual with men in goat skins, bells, and terrifying horned masks, called

Mamuthones. There is also a citrus festival, the *Sagra Degli Agrumi*, that features demon goat men."

Glenda crossed her legs and flipped a flip flop. "Devil goats on an island full of sheep makes no sense."

Based on my experience in Sardinia, it did.

The waitress returned and passed out cordial glasses filled with a magenta-colored liquid that smelled like rubbing alcohol.

Midge surveyed the table. "Shall we toast?"

Glenda raised her glass. "At Madame Moiselle's on Bourbon Street, we girls always say—"

"Uh," I interrupted, "how about something British?"

Madge's lower lip protruded. "Very well." She rose and raised her Mirto with the solemn resolve of one preparing to give the Loyal Toast on behalf of the Crown. "May your glass be ever full. May the roof over your head be always strong. And may you be in heaven half an hour before the devil knows you're dead."

I'd expected a customary *The Queen*, but the roof and devil reminded me that Glenda and I needed to talk about my farm accommodations.

Glenda shot her drink, and her braids writhed around her neck like tiny snakes.

Attenta alla Medusa! echoed in my head. I swallowed a sip of the sweet, herbal-berry liqueur and turned to the Mavens. "Have either of you heard any local legends about Medusa?"

Glenda grimaced. "All I know is that she turned men to stone, Miss Franki, which is such a waste. We women know that it's much more fun to turn them into molten lava."

The Mavens' cheeks turned as magenta as the Mirto, and Madge tugged at her jacket. "According to the myth, Medusa turned all onlookers to stone. And although I'm unaware of any local mythology, I do know that the most famous artifact at the Giovanni Patroni Archaeological Museum here in Pula is a Medusa from the Nora ruins."

I wasn't sure whether it was worth a visit or a dead end. But if the old woman at the farm was right, my life was at risk, and I had to know the reason. "I think I'll head over now and check it out."

I wanted to repay the Mavens' hospitality by picking up the tab, so I stood and looked for the waitress. I saw her through a restaurant window. Her back was to me, but the person's she was talking to wasn't.

Jaku from the farm.

He turned and disappeared through a kitchen door, leaving me to wonder whether he really was a wine seller—or a wolf in goat's clothing.

6

"That's the Nora Stone, the oldest document in the western world." The voice was American, and deep.

I looked up from the museum brochure, expecting a docent. Instead, I came face to face with a wannabe Indiana Jones, complete with fedora and leather jacket. But his nametag read *Clarence Scruggs, PhD*, which didn't have the same ring to it.

He raised the brim of his hat. "If you want to see it, you'll have to go to the archaeological museum in Cagliari, twenty miles from here."

"That's okay." I put the brochure back on the ticket counter. "No offense, but it looks like a slab of concrete that chickens walked across when it was wet."

He chuckled. "That's a fairly apt characterization of Phoenician writing. However, the stone recounts a battle from the eighth century B.C., and it contains the earliest known reference to Sardinia."

"Someone told me that Sardinians were killed by a tidal wave a few centuries before then."

He rubbed his stubbled jaw. "That's one of the possibilities, and it supports a theory that Sardinia is Plato's lost city of Atlantis. If you fly over this end of the island, you'll see a marine Pompeii."

The image was haunting. "I had no idea the ruins were that extensive."

"If you'd like to see some of the artifacts, the museum has a wing dedicated to underwater archeology."

"Actually, I came to see the Medusa."

He removed his hat. "I'll take you to her."

"But I don't have a ticket."

He put a finger to his lips. "I won't tell anyone if you won't."

I smiled and followed him through the exhibits. As we passed through rooms full of relics, I thanked the heavens that Glenda was back in the Devil's Saddle. The ancient Romans were fond of phallic symbols, and she would have gotten over-stimulated.

Dr. Scruggs stopped at a glass case. "Here she is, the Gorgon Medusa, from a tomb at Nora's Carthaginian necropolis."

The piece was striking. Not only was the screaming goddess on gold leaf, she looked an awful lot like Glenda. "What does she represent?"

"In ancient times, the natural cycle of birth, death, and rebirth. But in the modern era, feminists have reclaimed her image as a symbol of female rage."

That was probably why the woman at Vieux Carré Wine & Spirits had held a Medusa head—to express her rage about the wine price hike. What I still couldn't comprehend was why the old woman at the farm had warned me about Medusa—and run her finger across her throat. "Are there any myths about her that are specific to Nora or Sardinia?"

"Not that I'm aware of, but I'm a scholar of ancient amphorae. That's what brought me to Pula from the University of Florida."

I thought of the counterfeit ring the Mavens had mentioned. "Just out of curiosity, what were the amphorae used for?"

He shrugged. "It depends. Phoenician amphorae found in Nora contained bone fragments, suggesting that they contained meat, but the Roman amphorae held fish sauce and a condiment called *defrutum*."

"What's that? Fruit preserves?"

"A syrup made from grape must. When the amphorae were opened, the defrutum had maintained its purplish-black color thanks to the cold sea environment."

"I'm amazed that they had food in them after thousands of years."

He returned his hat to his head. "If you have time, you should see Nora underwater. There are still amphorae and other artifacts on the seabed."

"I don't know how to scuba dive."

"Not a problem. A company on the beach will teach you in an afternoon."

It was tempting, but I had to find a Mirto thief. "I'll think about it."

My phone began to ring.

"I'll leave you to your call." He tipped his hat and left.

I wished he hadn't. The caller was my mother, who was undoubtedly on a post-baptism mission to get herself a grandkid. Reluctantly, I answered and made my way back to the entrance. "Hi, Mom. It's your daughter, Francesca."

"Well, who else would be answering your phone?"

Yep. Circle of hell number six.

She let out a long-suffering sigh. "You're so lucky you're in Sardinia. I can't even get your father to take me to Galveston."

Proof that if I'd gone home to Houston for a vacation, she would have crashed my beach escape. "I've got a case to investigate. Can we make this quick?"

"Francesca Lucia Amato, if I remember correctly, I taught you manners."

She did, which was the only reason I hadn't hung up. "I'm being paid by the day, so I need to limit personal calls."

"This will only take minute, dear."

It already had. I shoved open the door and headed for the Blu Moon restaurant by way of the shoreline. "What did you want to tell me?"

"Your nonna and I went to the baptism, and that little boy thrashed when the priest poured the water on his forehead."

My nonna cackled. "He's-a gonna be a devil, that-a one."

I puckered. I hadn't realized she was on the line. "Give the kid a break. I'm sure he was terrified."

"Well, dear, he'll learn soon enough that there are things you have to do in life, whether you're ready or not."

I waited for the punchline, i.e., the one to my gut.

"Your *mamma* is-a right. And-a one of those-a things is-a getting married."

And there it was. "Bradley and I will get married when we're ready, Nonna, and not before."

"Sometimes, Francesca," my mother preach-sighed, "you just have to take the plunge."

I stopped and gazed at the sea. The only plunge I wanted to take was with my phone so they couldn't call it again.

"Are you there, dear?"

"Yes." *Unfortunately.* I resumed my stroll up the beach.

And I dropped my cell in the sand.

The knife-wielding bandit was walking toward the water—and Jaku was with him.

Frantic, I grabbed my phone and ran to a cave. I crouched and peered out.

"Are you listening to me, Francesca?" my mother shrilled.

I exhaled and moved to hang up.

A hand clamped over my mouth as an arm encircled my waist. I struggled to break free, but my assailant pulled me backwards, and my espadrilles slipped on the wet rock.

I went down. And dark.

7

The back of my head ached so badly that I couldn't open my eyes. But I had to. The bandit had me in his clutches, and he also had that knife.

"My dear girl, do wake up."

Wait. The bandit wasn't British. Or female.

"Francesca Lucia Amato, are you listening to me?"

Or my mother?

I wrenched open my eyelids.

And I blinked.

Madge Maven was stooped over me, and Midge hovered above her.

Madge scrunched her mouth. "You've taken a nasty spill, but it's time to get up." She handed me my phone. "And you must answer your poor mother."

"I hear British." My mom's high pitch hit my skull like an anchor. "Did you go to England, Francesca?"

"Mom, I'll call you back." I ended the call and sat up. "Who are you, and why did you pull me into this cave?"

The sisters exchanged their signature side-eye, and Madge clasped her hands behind her back. "I'm afraid we weren't entirely transparent in the restaurant. We're in Sardinia on assignment for a counterfeit artifact case."

I gasped. "You're Interpol?"

"Nothing of the sort. We're Maven Investigations, PIs like yourself."

So they were *Miss Marples.*

Midge raised a camera with a telephoto lens. "And at this moment, we're trying to separate the sheep from the goats."

I shot a panicked look around the cave. *Were they in here too?*

Madge positioned a sensibly shoed foot on a rock. "We've been watching some local hooligans who sold fake amphorae to a group of British collectors. Two days ago, we traced their headquarters to an agriturismo up the road."

The farm. "Is it a one-story stucco place?"

"That's it. A real hovel."

"Quite," I said in British. "I stayed there last night."

Midge lowered her camera. "That's why we invited you to share our breakfast, to find out whether you were part of the counterfeiting ring."

I should have suspected that they were sleuthing, especially given their outfits. "Well, I didn't stay there by choice. A driver took me there instead of a spa."

"Following orders, no doubt. Someone must have tipped off the counterfeiters that you're a PI."

Madge nodded. "Most assuredly one of the two hooligans on the beach. The mustached chap is Pedru Basili, a notorious bandit, and the one in need of dentures is Jaku Sanna, a wine salesman."

So I'd been right about both men. "What're they doing now?"

She extended a telescope with the pomp and circumstance of an admiral in the British Navy. "Preparing to deposit a new batch of fake amphorae below a buoy south of the Punta del Coltellazzo, where the sixteenth-century tower is located."

I smirked at the name. The tract of land where I'd had the run-in with the bandit was called Big Knife Point.

Madge lowered the telescope. "They leave them in the sea long enough to give them a weathered look, and then they sell them to unsuspecting buyers."

"How will you link the amphorae to these guys?"

Midge grinned like a schoolgirl who'd played a prank on her teacher. "Two days ago, we broke into their storage room, and I put a tracking device in one of them."

The Mavens weren't Miss Marples, they were Bond Girls—some sixty years later. "That's ingenious."

Madge's jaw went as jaunty as the angle of her hat. "Tis rather, isn't it?"

"Oh!" Midge grabbed her camera bag. "The boat has left shore. Advance to the next position."

Madge hoisted her telescope and a canvas tote. "Full speed ahead."

The Mavens scurried from the cave and, folding like collapsible chairs with rusted hinges, eased onto their bellies behind a patch of reeds.

I hated to waste time on a case that wasn't mine, but I needed to know why the hooligans had brought me to their headquarters. I darted from the cave and slid onto the sand beside Madge. "I can't believe they're going to dump the fake amphorae in the middle of the day when people can see them."

Midge snapped a picture. "There are so many fishing and tourist boats that no one will pay attention. They would arouse more suspicion on the water at night."

We watched as Pedru the bandit rowed Jaku toward the Punta del Coltellazzo. Thanks to his muscles and the calm sea, they neared their destination in under fifteen minutes.

A body sidled up to mine—with hair like snakes.

And I let out a scream worthy of the Gorgon goddess.

Madge waved a hand. "Quiet, girl. You'll torpedo the mission."

I glared at Glenda. If anyone was going to sink a mission, it was my landlady in her Little Medusa Mermaid costume. "How did you know I was here?"

She dragged from her cigarette holder. "Find My Friends, sugar."

That was it. My phone was taking the plunge to the marine Pompeii.

Glenda squinted through the reeds. "Are we on a stakeout?"

"Yes, so keep your eyes on the two men in that boat."

"How about if I just eye the one with the muscles?"

I shot her a Maven-style side-eye. "Fine. But put out that fire starter before you burn down our cover."

Glenda stubbed her cigarette in the sand, and after the smoke had cleared, I turned my attention to the boat. Pedru had shifted south, straight for the buoy.

As we waited for the deposit, Glenda knocked my foot to one side. Repeatedly. "Would you stop kicking?"

"I haven't moved, Miss Franki."

My head shot over my shoulder.

One of the goats was nibbling the last bits of my espadrille rope.

And I was willing to bet my bottom teeth that if I looked up the seventh circle of hell, the goats and Glenda would be in it.

"Crate overboard!" Midge crowed.

I spun and got a face full of Glenda's braids. "Would you stay in your spot?"

"He was dropping the crate, sugar, and I needed a better view of those muscles in action."

I clenched my jaw and pushed her back—but not too hard. I wanted her to keep her clamshells on.

Madge collapsed the telescope. "As I suspected, they unloaded their counterfeit cargo in the vicinity of the buoy. Now we shall wait for them to leave, photograph the amphorae *in situ*, and alert the authorities."

My eyes strained against their sockets. "You're not going to scuba dive?"

"I don't see why not. I was the first in my Girl Guides troop to earn the Scuba Diving badge."

Midge nodded. "And the first to earn her Dairymaid badge too."

Good to know. Maybe she could help me lose the goats. "But why would you dive when you can pinpoint the location of the amphorae with your tracking device?"

Madge puckered. "The coordinates won't be exact because the signal can't transmit from underwater. But even if it could, any PI worth her salt must verify her findings and provide photographic evidence to the clients, particularly when they've been swindled out of thousands of pounds."

Glenda shook her snakes. "What's in those jugs? Liquid gold?"

"Hardly," Midge scoffed. "An ancient Roman condiment as counterfeit as the amphorae."

Madge jutted out her chin. "Made from cooked wine, I should say."

I stared at the water. *Was my case connected to the counterfeiting ring, after all?* If so, there was only one way to find out—and to separate me from the goats. Ready or not, I had to take the plunge.

8

T he dive boat was within swimming distance of the buoy. "Could we stop here?"

"*Certo, signorina.*" The scuba instructor, Ànghelu, a short, stocky guy in his fifties, climbed the steps to the upper deck to alert the captain.

His name meant *angel*, but he wasn't judging from the way he ogled my rack. One of Dante's circles of hell involved lust, and since Glenda was on board too, I wondered whether I'd entered number eight.

Ànghelu came downstairs, pulling a mask and snorkel on his head. "When-a your friend come-a out, we start-a the scuba lesson."

I glanced at the restroom, hoping it wouldn't take Glenda much longer to get into her short wetsuit. But it had been a struggle for me to get the thing on, and unlike her I was used to wearing clothing.

I gazed over the side of the boat to check the visibility. The water was the bluest I'd seen, and clear, but all I could see were murky shapes.

Ànghelu moved beside me. "We call it *La Città Sommersa*, The Submerged City."

"Yes, I speak Italian."

A flame burned in his black eyes. "I thought-a you might."

To extinguish his fire, I grabbed my phone from my bag and did a Google search. Lust was the second circle of hell, and fraud was the eighth, which was fitting since I was about to hunt counterfeit amphorae. "Are there a lot of artifacts in this area?"

"Not-a many." He frowned. "It is a protected-a site, but-a this is-a Italy."

I shared his dismay. The entire country was a museum, which made it impossible to safeguard all of its treasures.

"There is much-a silt and-a Neptune grass, but-a you can see some-a buildings from-a the ancient port, and three Roman roads."

Foreboding fluttered in my stomach, but that was irrational. The road-to-ruin thing had been a joke, but then again, so had the circles of hell.

The restroom door opened, and Glenda sashayed out sans fishnet skirt—in a lone clamshell thong.

I glanced at Ànghelu, who stood at attention. "Uh, where's your wetsuit?"

"I can't swim in that fitted body bag, sugar, so Ànghelu said I could skin-dive."

What a gentleman. I just hoped she didn't take his recommendation any more literally. Knowing my landlady, once she got in the water she'd ditch all of her clamshells and go full mermaid.

"Ho-kay." Ànghelu rubbed his hands together. "I teach-a you to dive." He reached for a tube dangling from his oxygen tank. "Put-a the mouth-a-piece in-a your mouth, and-a kick-a your fins." He pulled down his mask. "*Andiamo.*"

I huff-snorted. "That's it? *That's* the lesson?"

He raised his chin, and his lower lip rose. "Eh, *sì*."

"What about the techniques and the safety regulations?"

His lips slid into a smile. "Rules are just-a suggestions."

I'd heard that from more than one Italian, starting with my nonna.

I pulled on my mask as Ànghelu helped Glenda onto the side of the boat with a liberal use of his hands.

She gave a girly giggle. "Oh, Ànghelu! You, devil!"

I shoved in my mouthpiece and threw myself overboard. The sea was the temperature of bathwater and smelled like a seaweed soak—probably as close as I was going to get to a spa experience.

Glenda jumped in, followed by Ànghelu. They surfaced, and he wiped water from his mouth. "*Signorine*, when-a we go down-a, be careful of-a the *medusa*!"

Stunned, I raised my mask. "What are you talking about?"

"In-a English, it mean-a the *jellyfish*."

I'd never heard that use of the term at home or in Italian class. *But why would the old woman warn me about jellyfish on the farm?* "Does *medusa* mean anything else, besides referring to the goddess?"

"No, but in Italy we say that-a the coral is-a the spilt-a blood of Medusa, when she lost-a her head." He ran his finger across his throat—like the old woman had.

I shivered. *Maybe I was on the road to ruin.*

Ànghelu and Glenda dipped underwater.

I checked my mouthpiece and dived after them. The fins made the descent deceptively easy. According to a gauge on my tank, I went fifteen feet in what seemed like five.

Ànghelu pointed to an anchor and a pile of rubble in front of four brown walls dotted with seaweed and barnacles, and I realized that we were above the ruins of a port building.

He descended to the sea bottom and ran a hand over the silt. A patterned marble floor appeared.

Glenda clapped and went to join him.

I looked up and located the bottom of the buoy. We'd moved closer to the amphorae dump. I swam to the edge of a wall to scan the sea bottom.

And a huge jellyfish rose up.

I understood why the Italians had named them after the goddess. It's tentacles writhed like Medusa's snakes—and Glenda's Bo Derek braids.

I kicked my feet to get out of its way, and my fins cleared a patch of silt, revealing oblong stone slabs that had been fitted together. I followed them a short distance, and they ended abruptly.

I was on the Roman road to nowhere.

My stomach fluttered like my fins, but I swam past the precipice to look for amphorae. The water was too cloudy, so I turned to head back and spotted a patch of red ten feet from the road.

The amphorae?

No, coral. The spilt blood of Medusa.

My hand went to my neck.

Zena's coral necklace. She was the Medusa the old woman had warned me about. The woman wouldn't have said Zena's name for fear of being overheard and suffering who knows what fate.

Bubbles rose from the deep, interrupting my revelation. Not wanting to meet their maker—or mine—I swam toward the road.

But Zena surged from the abyss and blocked my path. Her gray-brown curls writhed around her scuba mask like serpents, and her round mouthpiece simulated a permanent scream.

She looked like a marine Medusa.

And I turned to stone.

9

*Z*ena pulled a dive knife from a sheath strapped to her thigh, ready to defend the net bag of amphorae dangling from her waist and the entire counterfeiting operation.

My mind implored me to move, but my body didn't listen. The ninth circle of hell was treachery, where Satan resided, and I was suspended in it, quite literally between the devil and the deep blue sea.

She blew out a blast of air bubbles and charged like a warrior princess.

I raised my fins for protection, but she managed to slice my ankle.

Blood the color of Sardinian coral spilled into the sea.

Mine, not Medusa's.

Dr. Scruggs' words about feminists appropriating her image as a symbol of female rage powered my limbs like a generator. And I went off on her like an Italian-American Athena. I grabbed her wrist with my left hand and used my right to pull at her mouthpiece.

Eyes flashing behind her mask, she bit down and wrested from my grip. Then she struck at me with the speed of a snake, despite being underwater.

I propelled myself up, and she grabbed my fin.

I kicked and flailed, but she hung on. I bent to free my foot, and she grasped my oxygen tube—and sliced it in two.

My air was cut off, forty feet below the sea, but the fight wasn't over.

I yanked her by the snakes, pulled off her mask, and dug my nails into her wrist.

She loosened her grip enough for me to take the knife and cut the bag of amphorae from her hip.

Then I kicked off from her chest, sending her spiraling backwards.

Or upwards?

Panic sucked oxygen from my lungs. It wasn't the time to be disoriented. I couldn't hold my breath much longer, and my wound was a smoke signal for bloodthirsty sharks.

Go toward the light.

The cliché struck fear in my gut because the phrase implied the afterlife.

Were these my last moments?

Hell no.

Lungs aflame, I glanced around until I saw the light. I kicked with everything I had left, and my fins propelled me upward like the wings on Hermes' feet. And I erupted from the depths of inferno into the Gulf of Angels and took a lifesaving breath.

Heaven.

"Ahoy!" Midge waved a handkerchief from the deck of a red-and-white vessel with Madge at her side. And Glenda.

Was I hallucinating from oxygen deprivation?

I ripped off my mask.

The Mavens had brought in the Italian Coast Guard.

But I still wasn't safe. "Zena is in the water!"

Glenda pointed. "Behind you, Miss Franki."

I spun. Ànghelu was helping two Coast Guard officers load a kicking and scratching Zena onto a life raft.

Clutching the amphorae, I swam toward the boat. Two sailors

pulled me on board. One removed my scuba gear, and the other bandaged my ankle. Then I collapsed on deck.

Madge hovered over me, as she'd done in the cave. "We saw Zena rowing to the buoy and called for help."

Midge nodded. "Jaku and Pietro have been arrested, and so has your driver. Zena had him bring you to the farm to keep an eye on you. He was the one who told her about the Mirto warehouse."

I sat up. "Let me guess, they used Mirto in the amphorae instead of wine because Jaku is a wine seller, and that would have made him an obvious suspect if anyone ever reported their crime."

Midge side-eyed her sister. "She has keen instincts, Madge."

"As solid as steak and kidney pie. I'm tempted to offer her employment." She smiled and raised her nose. "At any rate, the Carabinieri have also seized the remaining amphorae from the agriturismo and issued a citation for possession of illegal cheese."

The one Jaku ate at the farm. "How can cheese ever be a crime?"

Her nose scrunched. "When it's teaming with the larvae of skipper flies that coil like springs and leap from the cheese as it's cut. They carry a number of diseases."

Apparently, I'd dodged a foe more deadly than Zena.

Glenda's phone rang, and she slipped inside the main cabin, reminding me that I still had a case to solve. "I need something to open one of the amphorae."

A sailor handed me a switch blade.

How many types of knives were on this island?

I cut a waxy plug from the opening and poured the alleged Roman condiment into my hand. It looked and smelled like Mirto.

"If it's magenta, it's fake." I quoted Zena, thinking how ironic it was that she'd warned me about imitation coral when she was behind the amphorae business.

"Land, ho!" Midge crowed.

For a reserved Brit, she was awfully fond of shouting.

I glanced at the beach. *Surely this was a hallucination?*

After a deep breath, I looked again.

Nope. The goats were still there, staring at me.

Madge extended her hand. "I fear we must bid one another farewell."

Midge dabbed her eyes with her handkerchief. "Smoke does get in one's eyes."

I smiled because Glenda had put out her cigarette before entering the cabin. "Maybe we'll see each other again."

Madge puffed her cheeks. "Should you come to Italy again, give us a ring." She pulled a card from her tote and handed it to me. "Midge and I own a food tourism company based in Rome, and we would be delighted to give you a free tour."

"If it involves a Nutella factory, I'll make a special trip back."

"That, my dear girl, can be arranged." Madge saluted the sailors and followed Midge off the vessel.

Glenda emerged from the cabin. "It was the spa, sugar. They told me you never checked in, but a sheepherder is there waiting for you."

The suitor my nonna had sent.

Glenda sidled up to a sailor. "The four of us should do a couples' massage. The spa's just up the road."

The plan could have been Dante's tenth circle of hell, if he'd created one, not to mention the ruin of my relationship with Bradley. "The only road I'm taking is the one to the airport."

ABOUT THE AUTHOR

Traci Andrighetti is the *USA TODAY* bestselling author of the Franki Amato Mysteries and the Danger Cove Hair Salon Mysteries. In her previous life, she was an award-winning literary translator and a Lecturer of Italian at the University of Texas at Austin, where she earned a PhD in Applied Linguistics. But then she got wise and ditched that academic stuff for a life of crime—writing, that is. Her latest capers are teaching mystery for Savvy Authors and taking authors on writing retreats to Italy with LemonLit.

To learn more about Traci, check out her websites: www. traciandrighetti.com
www.lemonlit.com

ALSO BY TRACI ANDRIGHETTI

Also by Traci Andrighetti

DANGER COVE HAIR SALON MYSTERIES

Deadly Dye and a Soy Chai
A Poison Manicure and Peach Liqueur
Killer Eyeshadow and a Cold Espresso